NORTH SEA

Calais

Flanders

Artois

Crécy

Somme R.

Amiens

Coucy

Normandy

Evreux

Paris

Champagne

Chartres

Seine R.

Reims

Meuse R.

Orléans

Loire R.

Dijon

Lorraine

Berry

DOM of FRANCE

Burgundy

ers

Bourbon

Limoges

Lyon

Dauphiny

enne

Avignon

Toulouse

Languedoc

Foux

MEDITERRANEAN SEA

The Accursed Kings

The Iron King
The Strangled Queen
The Poisoned Crown
The Royal Succession
The She-Wolf
The Lily and the Lion
The King Without a Kingdom

THE IRON KING

Book One of the Accursed Kings

M A U R I C E   D R U O N

Translated from French by
Humphrey Hare

HarperCollins*Publishers*

HarperCollins*Publishers*
77–85 Fulham Palace Road,
Hammersmith, London w6 8jb

www.harpercollins.co.uk

First published in Great Britain by Rupert Hart-Davis 1956
Century edition 1985
Arrow edition 1987

Published by HarperCollins*Publishers* 2013

1

A catalogue record for this book is
available from the British Library

ISBN: 978-00-0-749125-4

Printed and bound in Great Britain by
Clays Ltd, St Ives plc

MIX
Paper from
responsible sources
FSC
www.fsc.org   **FSC™ C007454**

FSC is a non-profit international organization established
to promote the responsible management of the world's forests.
Products carrying the FSC label are independently certified
to assure consumers that they come from forests that are managed
to meet the social, economic and ecological needs
of present and future generations.

Find out more about HarperCollins and the environment at
www.harpercollins.co.uk/green

'History is a novel that has been lived'
E. & J. DE GONCOURT

Foreword

GEORGE R.R. MARTIN

Over the years, more than one reviewer has described my fantasy series, *A Song of Ice and Fire*, as historical fiction about history that never happened, flavoured with a dash of sorcery and spiced with dragons. I take that as a compliment. I have always regarded historical fiction and fantasy as sisters under the skin, two genres separated at birth. My own series draws on both traditions . . . and while I undoubtedly drew much of my inspiration from Tolkien, Vance, Howard, and the other fantasists who came before me, *A Game of Thrones* and its sequels were also influenced by the works of great historical novelists like Thomas B. Costain, Mika Waltari, Howard Pyle . . . and Maurice Druon, the amazing French writer who gave us the *The Accursed Kings*, seven splendid novels that chronicle the downfall of the Capetian kings and the beginnings of the Hundred Years War.

Druon's novels have not been easy to find, especially in English translation (and the seventh and final volume was never translated into English at all). The series has *twice* been made into a television series in France, and both versions are available on DVD . . . but only in French, undubbed, and without English subtitles. Very frustrating for English-speaking Druon fans like me.

The Accursed Kings has it all. Iron kings and strangled queens, battles and betrayals, lies and lust, deception, family rivalries, the curse of the Templars, babies switched at birth, she-wolves, sin, and swords, the doom of a great dynasty . . . and all of it (well, most of it) straight from the pages of history. And believe me, the Starks and the Lannisters have nothing on the Capets and Plantagenets.

Whether you're a history buff or a fantasy fan, Druon's epic will keep you turning pages. This was the original game of thrones. If you like *A Song of Ice and Fire*, you will love *The Accursed Kings*.

George R.R. Martin

Author's Acknowledgements

I AM most grateful to Georges Kessel, José-André Lacour, Gilbert Sigaux and Pierre de Lacretelle for the assistance they have given me with the material of this book; to Colette Mantout, Christiane Souillard and Christiane Templier for their help in compiling it; and to the *Bibliothèque Nationale* for indispensable aid in research.

Contents

1111111

Part Two: The Adulterous Princesses

Part Three: The Hand of God

The Characters in this Book

THE KING OF FRANCE:
PHILIP IV, called Philip the Fair, aged 46, grandson of
Saint Louis.

HIS BROTHERS:
MONSEIGNEUR CHARLES, Count of Valois, Titular Emperor
of Constantinople, Count of Romagna, aged 44.
MONSEIGNEUR LOUIS, Count of Evreux, about 40 years old.

HIS SONS:
LOUIS, King of Navarre, aged 25.
PHILIPPE, COUNT of Poitiers, aged 21.
CHARLES, aged 20.

HIS DAUGHTER:
ISABELLA, Queen of England, aged 22, wife of King
Edward II.

HIS DAUGHTERS-IN-LAW:
MARGUERITE OF BURGUNDY, aged about 21, wife of Louis,
daughter of the Duke of Burgundy, granddaughter of
Saint Louis.

JEANNE OF BURGUNDY, aged about 21, daughter of the Count Palatine of Burgundy, wife to Philippe.

BLANCHE OF BURGUNDY, her sister, aged about 18, wife to Charles.

HIS MINISTERS AND JUSTICIARS:

ENGUERRAND LE PORTIER DE MARIGNY, aged 52, Coadjutor and Rector of the Kingdom.

GUILLAUME DE NOGARET, aged 54, Keeper of the Seals and Secretary-General of the Kingdom.

HUGUES DE BOUVILLE, Grand Chamberlain.

THE ARTOIS BRANCH, DESCENDED FROM A BROTHER OF SAINT LOUIS:

ROBERT III OF ARTOIS, Lord of Conches, Count of Beaumont-le-Roger, aged 27.

MAHAUT, his aunt, aged about 40, widow of the Count Palatine of Burgundy, Countess of Artois, a peer of France, mother of Jeanne and Blanche of Burgundy and cousin of Marguerite of Burgundy.

THE TEMPLARS:

JACQUES DE MOLAY, aged 71, Grand Master of the Order of Knights Templar.

GEOFFROY DE CHARNEY, Preceptor of Normandy.

EVERARD, one-time Knight of the Order of Templars.

THE LOMBARDS:

SPINELLO TOLOMEI, a Siennese banker living in Paris.

GUCCIO BAGLIONI, his nephew, aged about 18.

THE BROTHERS AUNAY:

GAUTIER, son of the Chevalier d'Aunay, aged about 23, Equerry to the Count of Poitiers.

PHILIPPE, his brother, aged about 21, Equerry to the Count of Valois.

THE CRESSAY FAMILY:

DAME ELIABEL, widow of the Squire of Cressay, aged about 40.

PIERRE AND JEAN, her sons, aged 20 and 22.

MARIE, her daughter, aged 16.

AND THESE:

JEAN DE MARIGNY, Archbishop of Sens, younger brother of Enguerrand de Marigny.

BEATRICE D'HIRSON, first lady-in-waiting to the Countess Mahaut, aged about 20.

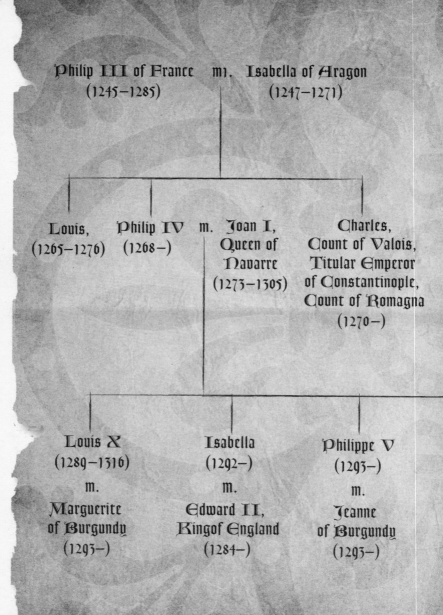

Philip III of France   m).   Isabella of Aragon
(1245–1285)   (1247–1271)

Louis,   Philip IV   m.   Joan I,   Charles,
(1265–1276)   (1268–)   Queen of   Count of Valois,
                                   Navarre   Titular Emperor
                                   (1273–1305)   of Constantinople,
                                                       Count of Romagna
                                                       (1270–)

Louis X   Isabella   Philippe V
(1289–1316)   (1292–)   (1293–)

m.   m.   m.

Marguerite   Edward II,   Jeanne
of Burgundy   King of England   of Burgundy
(1293–)   (1284–)   (1293–)

m2.   Marie of Brabant
(1254–1321)

Louis Capet,
Count of Evereux
(1276–)

Blanche
(1278–1305)

Margaret
of France
(1282–)

Charles IV
(1294–)
m.
Blanche
of Burgundy
(1296–)

The
House of
Capet 1314

The Iron King

The Grand Master felt surging within him one of those half-crazy rages which had so often come upon him in his prison, making him shout aloud and beat the walls. He felt that he was upon the point of committing some violent and terrible act – he did not know exactly what – but he felt the impulse to do something.

He accepted death almost as a deliverance, but he could not accept an unjust death, nor dying dishonoured. Accustomed through long years to war, he felt it stir for the last time in his old veins. He longed to die fighting.

He sought the hand of Geoffroy de Charnay, his old companion in arms, the last strong man still standing at his side, and clasped it tightly.

Raising his eyes, the Preceptor saw the arteries beating upon the sunken temples of the Grand Master. They quivered like blue snakes.

The procession reached the Bridge of Notre-Dame.

Prologue

At the beginning of the fourteenth century, Philip IV, a king of legendary personal beauty, reigned over France as absolute master. He had defeated the warrior pride of the great barons, the rebellious Flemings, the English in Aquitaine, and even the Papacy which he had proceeded to install at Avignon. Parliaments obeyed his orders and councils were in his pay.

He had three adult sons to ensure his line. His daughter was married to King Edward II of England. He numbered six other kings among his vassals, and the web of his alliances extended as far as Russia.

He left no source of wealth untapped. He had in turn taxed the riches of the Church, despoiled the Jews, and made extortionate demands from the community of Lombard bankers. To meet the needs of the Treasury he debased the coinage. From day to day the gold piece weighed less and was worth more. Taxes were crushing: the police multiplied. Economic crises led to ruin and famine which, in turn, caused uprisings which were bloodily put down. Rioting ended upon the forks of the gibbet. Everyone must accept the royal authority and obey it or be broken by it.

This cruel and dispassionate prince was concerned with the ideal of the nation. Under his reign France was great and the French wretched.

One power alone had dared stand up to him: the Sovereign Order of the Knights Templar. This huge organisation, at once military, religious and commercial, had acquired its fame and its wealth from the Crusades.

Philip the Fair was concerned at the Templars' independence, while their immense wealth excited his greed. He brought against them the greatest prosecution in recorded history, since there were nearly fifteen thousand accused. It lasted seven years, and during its course every possible infamy was committed.

This story begins at the end of the seventh year.

PART ONE
A CURSE

I

The Loveless Queen

A HUGE LOG, LYING UPON a bed of red-hot embers, flamed in the fireplace. The green, leaded panes of the windows permitted the pale light of a March day to filter into the room.

Sitting upon a high oaken chair, its back surmounted by the three lions of England, her chin cupped in her hand, her feet resting upon a red cushion, Queen Isabella, wife of Edward II, gazed vaguely, unseeingly, at the glow in the hearth.

She was twenty-two years old, her complexion clear, pretty and without blemish. She wore her golden hair coiled in two long tresses upon each side of her face like the handles of an amphora.

She was listening to one of her French Ladies reading a poem of Duke William of Aquitaine.

> *D'amour ne dois-je plus dire de bien*
> *Car je n'en ai ni peu ni rien,*
> *Car je n'en ai qui me convient . . .*

The sing-song voice of the reader was lost in this room which was too large for women to be able to live in happily.

> *Bientôt m'en irai en exil,*
> *En grande peur, en grand péril . . .*

The loveless Queen sighed.

'How beautiful those words are,' she said. 'One might think that they had been written for me. Ah! the time has gone when great lords were as practised in poetry as in war. When did you say he lived? Two hundred years ago! One could swear that it had been written yesterday.'

And she repeated to herself:

> *D'amour ne dois-je plus dire de bien*
> *Car je n'en ai ni peu ni rien . . .*

For a moment she was lost in thought.

'Shall I go on, Madam?' asked the reader, her finger poised on the illuminated page.

'No, my dear,' replied the Queen. 'My heart has wept enough for today.'

She sat up straight in her chair, and in an altered voice said, 'My cousin, Robert of Artois, has announced his coming. See that he is shewn in to me as soon as he arrives.'

'Is he coming from France? Then you'll be happy to see him, Madam.'

'I hope to be . . . if the news he brings is good.'

The door opened and another French lady entered, breathless, her skirts raised the better to run. She had been born Jeanne de Joinville and was the wife of Sir Roger Mortimer.

'Madam, Madam,' she cried, 'he has talked.'

4

'Really?' the Queen replied. 'And what did he say?'

'He banged the table, Madam, and said: "Want!"'

A look of pride crossed Isabella's beautiful face.

'Bring him to me,' she said.

Lady Mortimer ran out and came back an instant later carrying a plump, round, rosy infant of fifteen months whom she deposited at the Queen's feet. He was clothed in a red robe embroidered with gold, which weighed more than he did.

'Well, Messire my son, so you have said: "Want",' said Isabella, leaning down to stroke his cheek. 'I'm pleased that it should have been the first word you uttered: it's the speech of a king.'

The infant smiled at her, nodding his head.

'And why did he say it?' the Queen went on.

'Because I refused him a piece of the cake we were eating,' Lady Mortimer replied.

Isabella gave a brief smile, quickly gone.

'Since he has begun to talk,' she said, 'I insist that he be not encouraged to lisp nonsense, as children so often are. I'm not concerned that he should be able to say "Papa" and "Mamma". I should prefer him to know the words "King" and "Queen".'

There was great natural authority in her voice.

'You know, my dear,' she said, 'the reasons that induced me to select you as my son's governess. You are the great-niece of the great Joinville who went to the crusades with my great-grandfather, Monsieur Saint Louis. You will know how to teach the child that he belongs to France as much as to England.'[1]*

* The numerals in the text refer the reader, if he so desires, to a few notes containing additional information placed at the end of the book.

Lady Mortimer bowed. At this moment the first French lady returned, announcing Monseigneur Count Robert of Artois.

The Queen sat up very straight in her chair, crossing her white hands upon her breast in the attitude of an idol. Though her perpetual concern was to appear royal, it did not age her.

A sixteen-stone step shook the floor-boards.

The man who entered was six feet tall, had thighs like the trunks of oak-trees, and hands like maces. His red boots of Cordoba leather were ill-brushed, still stained with mud; the cloak hanging from his shoulders was large enough to cover a bed. With the dagger at his side, he looked as if he were going to the wars. Wherever he might be, everything about him seemed fragile, feeble, and weak. His chin was round, his nose short, his jaw powerful and his stomach strong. He needed more air to breathe than the common run of men. This giant of a man was twenty-seven years old, but his age was difficult to determine beneath the muscle, and he might well have been thirty-five.

He took his gloves off as he approached the Queen, went down on one knee with surprising nimbleness in one so large, then stood erect again without even allowing time to be invited to do so.

'Well, Messire, my Cousin,' said Isabella, 'did you have a good crossing?'

'Horrible, Madam, quite appalling,' replied Robert of Artois. 'There was a storm to make you bring up your guts and your soul. I thought my last hour had come and began to confess my sins to God. Fortunately, there were so many that we'd arrived before I'd had time to recite the half of them. I've still got sufficient for the return journey.'

He burst out laughing and the windows shook.

'And, by God,' he went on, 'I'm more suited to travelling upon dry land than crossing salt water. And if it weren't for the love of you, Madam, my Cousin, and for the urgent tidings I have for you . . .'

'Do you mind if I finish with him, cousin,' said Isabella, interrupting him.

She pointed to the child.

'My son has begun to talk today.'

Then to Lady Mortimer: 'I want him to get accustomed to the names of his relatives and he should know, as soon as possible, that his grandfather, Philip the Fair, is King of France. Start repeating to him the *Pater* and the *Ave*, and also the prayer to Monsieur Saint Louis. These are things that must be instilled into his heart even before he can understand them with his reason.'

She was not displeased to be able to show one of her French relations, himself a descendant of a brother of Saint Louis, how she watched over her son's education.

'That's sound teaching you're giving the young man,' said Robert of Artois.

'One can never learn to reign too soon,' replied Isabella.

Unaware that they were talking of him, the child was amusing himself by walking with that careful, uncertain step peculiar to infants.

'To think that we were once like that!' said Artois.

'It is certainly difficult to believe it when looking at you, Cousin,' said the Queen smiling.

For a moment she thought of what the woman must feel who had given birth to this human fortress and of what she herself would feel when her son became a man.

The child went over to the hearth as if he wished to seize a flame in his tiny fist. Extending a red boot, Robert of Artois barred the road. Quite unafraid, the little Prince seized the leg in arms which could barely encircle it and, sitting astride the giant's foot, he was lifted three or four times into the air. Delighted with the game, the little Prince laughed aloud.

'Ah! Messire Edward,' said Robert of Artois, 'later on, when you're a powerful prince, shall I dare remind you that I gave you a ride on my boot?'

'Yes, Cousin,' replied Isabella, 'if you always show yourself to be our loyal friend. You may leave us now,' she added.

The French ladies went, taking with them the infant, who, if fate pursued its normal course, would one day become Edward III of England.

Robert of Artois waited till the door was closed.

'Well, Madam,' he said, 'to complete the admirable lessons you have given your son, you will soon be able to inform him that Marguerite of Burgundy, Queen of Navarre, future Queen of France, granddaughter of Saint Louis, is qualifying to be called by her people Marguerite the Whore.'

'Really?' asked Isabella. 'Is what we suspected true then?'

'Yes, Cousin. And not only in respect of Marguerite. It's true for your two sisters-in-law as well.'

'What? Both Jeanne and Blanche?'

'As regards Blanche, I'm sure of it. Jeanne . . .'

Robert of Artois sketched a gesture of uncertainty with his hand.

'She's cleverer than the others,' he added; 'but I've every reason to believe that she's as much of a whore.'

He paced up and down the room and then sat down again saying, 'Your three brothers are cuckolds, Madam, as cuckold as any clodhopper!'

The Queen rose to her feet. Her cheeks showed signs of blushing.

'If what you're saying is sure, I won't stand it,' she said. 'I won't tolerate the shame, and that my family should become an object of derision.'

'The barons of France won't tolerate it either,' said Artois.

'Have you their names, the proof?'

Artois sighed heavily.

'When you came to France last summer with your husband, to attend the festivities at which I had the honour to be dubbed knight with your brothers – for you know,' he said, laughing, 'they don't stint me of honours that cost nothing – I told you of my suspicions and you told me yours. You asked me to watch and keep you informed. I'm your ally; I've done the one and I've come here to accomplish the other.'

'Well, what have you discovered?' Isabella asked impatiently.

'In the first place that certain jewels have disappeared from the casket of your sweet, worthy and virtuous sister-in-law, Marguerite. Now, when a woman secretly parts with her jewels, it's either to make presents to her lover or to bribe accomplices. That's clear enough, don't you agree?'

'She can pretend to have given alms to the Church.'

'Not always. Not, for instance, if a certain brooch has been exchanged with a Lombard merchant for a Damascus dagger.'

'And have you discovered at whose belt that dagger hangs?'

'Alas, no,' Artois replied. 'I've searched, but I've lost the scent. They're clever bitches, as I've told you. I've never hunted stags in my forest of Conches that knew better how to conceal their line and take evasive action.'

Isabella looked disappointed. Stretching wide his arms Robert of Artois anticipated what she was going to say.

'Wait, wait,' he cried. 'That is not all. The true, pure, chaste Marguerite has had an apartment furnished in the old tower of the Hôtel-de-Nesle, in order, so she says, to retire there to say her prayers. Curiously enough, however, she prays there on precisely those nights your brother Louis is away. The lights shine there pretty late. Her cousin Blanche, sometimes her cousin Jeanne, joins her there. Clever wenches! If either of them were questioned, she's merely to reply, "What's that? Of what are you accusing me? But I was with the other." One woman at fault finds it difficult to defend herself. Three wicked harlots are a fortress. But listen; on those very nights Louis is away, on the nights the Tower of Nesle is lit up, there has been movement seen on that usually deserted stretch of river bank at the tower's foot. Men have been seen coming from it, men who were certainly not dressed as monks and who, if they had been saying evensong, would have left by another door. The Court is silent, but the populace is beginning to chatter, since servants always start gossiping before their masters do.'

He spoke excitedly, gesticulating, walking up and down, shaking the floor, beating the air with great swirls of his cloak. Robert of Artois paraded his superabundant strength as a means of persuasion. He sought to convince with his muscles as well as with his words; he enclosed his interlocutor in a whirlwind; and the coarseness of his language, so much in keeping with his appearance, seemed proof of a rude good faith. Nevertheless, upon looking closer, one might well wonder whether all this commotion was not perhaps the showing-off of a mountebank, the playing of a part. A calculated, unremitting hatred glowed in the giant's grey eyes; and the young Queen concentrated upon remaining mistress of herself.

'Have you spoken of this to my father?' she asked.

'My good Cousin, you know King Philip better than I. He believes so firmly in the virtue of women that one would have to show him your sisters-in-law in bed with their lovers before he'd be willing to listen. Besides, I'm not in such good favour at Court since I lost my lawsuit.'

'I know that you've been wronged, Cousin, and if it were in my power that wrong would be righted.'

Robert of Artois seized the Queen's hand and placed his lips upon it in a surge of gratitude.

'But precisely because of this lawsuit,' Isabella said gently, 'might one not think that your present actions are due to a desire for revenge?'

The giant bounded to his feet.

'But of course I'm acting out of revenge, Madam!'

How disarming this big Robert was! You thought to lay a trap for him, to take him at a disadvantage, and he was as wide open with you as a window.

'My inheritance of my County of Artois has been stolen from me,' he cried, 'that it might be given to my aunt, Mahaut of Burgundy – the bitch, the sow, may she die! May leprosy rot her mouth, and her breasts turn to carrion! And why did they do it? Because through trickery and intrigue, through oiling the palms of your father's counsellors with hard cash, she succeeded in marrying off to your brothers her two sluts of daughters and that other slut, her cousin.'

He began mimicking an imaginary conversation between his aunt Mahaut, Countess of Burgundy and Artois, and King Philip the Fair.

'My dear lord, my cousin, my gossip, supposing you married my dear little Jeanne to your son Louis? What, he doesn't want her? He finds her rather sickly-looking? Well then, give him Margot, and Philip, he can have Jeanne, and my sweet Blanchette can marry your fine Charles. How delightful that they should all love each other! And then, if I'm given Artois which belonged to my late brother, my Franche-Comté of Burgundy will go to those girls. My nephew Robert? Give that dog some bone or other! The Castle of Conches and the County of Beaumont will do well enough for that boor! And I whisper malice in Nogaret's ear, and send a thousand presents to Marigny . . . and then I marry one off, and then two, and then three. And no sooner are they married than the little bitches start plotting, sending each other notes, taking lovers, and set about betraying the throne of France. . . . Oh! if they were irreproachable, Madam, I'd hold my peace. But to behave so basely after having injured me so much, those Burgundy girls are going to learn what it costs, and I shall avenge myself on them for what their mother did to me.'²

Isabella remained thoughtful during this outpouring. Artois went close to her and, lowering his voice, said, 'They hate you.'

'Though I don't know why, it is true that as far as I am concerned, I never liked them from the start,' Isabella replied.

'You didn't like them because they're false, because they think of nothing but pleasure and have no sense of duty. But they hate you because they're jealous of you.'

'And yet my position is not a very enviable one,' said Isabella sighing; 'their lot seems to me far pleasanter than my own.'

'You are a Queen, Madam; you are a Queen in heart and soul; your sisters-in-law may well wear crowns but they will never be queens. That is why they will always be your enemies.'

Isabella raised her beautiful blue eyes to her cousin and Artois sensed that this time he had struck the right note. Isabella was on his side once and for all.

'Have you the names of the men with whom my sisters-in-law . . . ?' she asked.

She lacked the crudeness of her cousin and could not bring herself to utter certain words.

'Do you not know them?' she said. 'Without their names I can do nothing. Get them, and I promise you that I shall come to Paris at once upon some pretext or other, and put an end to this disorder. How can I help you? Have you told my uncle Valois?'

She was once more decisive, precise and authoritative.

'I took care not to,' answered Artois. 'Monseigneur of Valois is my most loyal patron and my greatest friend; but he is the exact opposite of your father. He'd go gossiping all over the place about what we want to keep quiet, he'd put them on their guard, and when the moment came when we were ready to catch the bawds out, we should find them as pure as nuns.'

'Well, what do you suggest?'

'Two courses of action,' said Artois. 'The first is to appoint to Madam Marguerite's household a new lady-in-waiting who will be in our confidence and who will report to us. I have thought of Mme de Comminges for the post. She has recently been widowed and deserves some consideration. And in that your uncle Valois can help us. Write him a letter expressing your wish, and pretending to interest on the widow's behalf. Monseigneur has great influence over your brother Louis and, merely in order to exercise it, will at once place Mme de Comminges in the Hôtel-de-Nesle. Thus we shall have a creature of ours on the spot, and as we say in military parlance, a spy within the walls is worth an army outside.'

'I'll write the letter and you shall take it back with you,' said Isabella. 'And what more?'

'You must allay your sisters-in-law's distrust of you; you must make yourself amiable by sending them nice presents,' Artois went on. 'Presents that would do as well for men as women. You can send them secretly, a little private friendly transaction between you, which neither father nor husbands need know anything about. Marguerite despoils her casket for a good-looking unknown; it would really be bad luck if, having a present she need not account for, we don't find it upon the gallant in question. Let's give them opportunities for imprudence.'

Isabella thought for a moment, then went to the door and clapped her hands.

The first French lady entered.

'My dear,' said the Queen, 'please bring me the golden almspurse that the Merchant Albizzi brought me this morning on approval.'

During the short wait Robert of Artois for the first time ceased to be concerned with his plots and preoccupations and looked round the room, at the religious frescoes painted on the walls, at the huge, beamed roof that looked like the hull of a ship. It was all rather new, gloomy and cold. The furniture was fine but sparse.

'Your home is not very gay, Cousin,' he said. 'One might think one was in a cathedral rather than a palace.'

'I hope to God,' Isabella said in a low voice, 'that it does not become my prison. How much I miss France!'

He was struck by her tone of voice as much as by her words. He realised that there were two Isabellas: on the one hand the young sovereign, conscious of her role and trying to live up to the majesty of her part; and on the other, behind this outward mask, an unhappy woman.

The French lady-in-waiting returned, bringing a purse of interwoven gold thread, lined with silk and fastened with three precious stones as large as thumbnails.

'Splendid!' Artois cried. 'This is exactly what we want. A little heavy for a woman to wear; but exactly what a young man at Court dreams of fastening to his belt in order to show off.'

'You'll order two similar purses from the merchant Albizzi,' said Isabella to her lady-in-waiting, 'and tell him to make them at once.'

Then, when the Frenchwoman had gone out, she added for Robert's ear, 'You'll be able to take them back to France with you.'

'No one will know that they passed through my hands,' he said.

There was a noise outside, shouts and laughter. Robert of Artois went over to the window. In the courtyard a company of masons were hoisting to the summit of an arch an ornamental stone engraved in relief with the lions of England. Some were hauling on pulley-ropes; others, perched on a scaffolding, were making ready to seize hold of the block of stone, and the whole business seemed to be carried out amid extraordinary good humour.

'Well!' said Robert of Artois. 'It appears that King Edward still likes masonry.'

Among the workmen he had just recognised Edward II, Isabella's husband, a good-looking man of thirty, with curly hair, wide shoulders and strong thighs. His velvet clothes were dusty with plaster.[3]

'They've been rebuilding Westminster for more than fifteen

years!' said Isabella angrily. (She pronounced it Vestmoustiers, in the French manner.) 'For the whole six years I've been married I've lived among trowels and mortar. They're always pulling down what they built the month before. It's not masonry he likes, it's his masons! Do you imagine they even bother to say "Sire" to him? They call him Edward, and laugh at him, and he loves it. Just look at him.'

In the courtyard, Edward II was giving orders, leaning on a young workman, his arm round the boy's neck. About him was an air of suspect familiarity. The lions of England had been lowered back to earth, doubtless because it was thought that their proposed site was unsuitable.

'I thought,' Isabella went on, 'that I had known the worst with Sir Piers Gaveston. That insolent, boastful Béarnais ruled my husband so successfully that he ruled the country too. Edward gave him all the jewels in my marriage casket. In one way or another it seems to be a family custom for the women's jewels to end up on men!'

Having beside her a relation and a friend, Isabella at last allowed herself to express her sorrows and humiliations. The morals of Edward II were known throughout Europe.

'A year or so ago the barons and I succeeded in bringing Gaveston down; his head was cut off, and now his body lies rotting in the ground at Oxford,' the young Queen said with satisfaction.

Robert of Artois did not appear surprised to hear these cruel words uttered by a beautiful woman. It must be admitted that such things were the common coin of the period. Kingdoms were often handed over to adolescents, whose absolute power fascinated them as might a game. Hardly grown out of the age in which it is fun to tear the wings from flies, they might now amuse themselves by tearing the heads from men. Too young to fear or even imagine death, they would not hesitate to distribute it around them.

Isabella had ascended the throne at sixteen; she had come a long way in six years.

'Well! I've reached the point, Cousin, when I regret Gaveston,' she went on. 'Since then, as if to avenge himself upon me, Edward brings the lowest and most infamous men to the palace. He visits the low dens of the Port of London, sits with tramps, wrestles with lightermen, races against grooms. Fine tournaments, these, for our delectation! He has no care who runs the kingdom, provided his pleasures are organised and shared. At the moment it's the Barons Despenser; the father's worth no more than the son, who serves my husband for a wife. As for myself, Edward no longer approaches me, and if by chance he does, I am so ashamed that I remain cold to his advances.'

She lowered her head.

'If her husband does not love her, a queen is the most miserable of the subjects of a kingdom. It is enough that she should have assured the succession; after that her life is of no account. What baron's wife, what merchant's or serf's would tolerate what I have to bear ... because I am Queen? The least washerwoman in the kingdom has greater rights than I: she can come and ask my protection.'

Robert of Artois knew – as indeed who did not? – that Isabella's marriage was unhappy; but he had had no idea of the seriousness of the situation, nor how profoundly she was affected by it.

'Cousin, sweet Cousin, I will protect you!' he said warmly.

She sadly shrugged her shoulders as if to say: 'What can you do for me?' They were face to face. He put out his hands and took her by the elbows as gently as he could, murmuring at the same time, 'Isabella . . .'

She placed her hands on the giant's arms and said, 'Robert . . .'

They gazed at each other with an emotional disturbance they had not foreseen. Artois had the impression that Isabella was making him some mute appeal. He suddenly found that he was curiously moved, oppressed, a prey to a force he feared to use ill.

Seen close to, Isabella's blue eyes, under the fair arches of her eyebrows, were more beautiful still, her cheeks of a yet softer bloom. Her mouth was half open and the tips of her white teeth showed between her lips.

Artois suddenly longed to devote his days, his life, his body and soul to that mouth, to those eyes, to this delicate Queen who, at this moment, became once more the young girl which indeed she still was; quite simply, he desired her with a sort of robust immediacy he did not know how to express. In the ordinary way his tastes were not for women of rank and his nature was unsuited to the graces of gallantry.

'Why have I confided all this to you?' said Isabella.

They were still looking into each other's eyes.

'What a king disdains, because he is unable to recognise its perfection,' said Robert, 'many other men would thank heaven for upon their bended knees. Can it be true that at your age, fresh and beautiful as you are, you are deprived of natural joys? Can it be true that your lips are never kissed? That your arms . . . your body . . . Oh! take a man, Isabella, and let that man be me.'

Certainly he said what he wanted to say roughly enough. His eloquence bore little resemblance to the poems of Duke William of Aquitaine. But Isabella hardly heard him. He dominated her, crushed her with his mere size; he smelt of the forest, of leather, of horses and armour; he had neither the voice nor the appearance of a seducer, yet she was charmed. He was a man, a real man, a rugged and violent male, who breathed deep. Isabella felt her will-power dissolve, and had but one desire: to rest her head upon that leathern breast and abandon herself to him . . . slake her great thirst . . . She was trembling a little.

Suddenly she broke away from him.

'No, Robert,' she cried, 'I am not going to do that for which I so much blame my sisters-in-law. I cannot, I must not. But when I think of what I am denying myself, what I am giving up, then I know how lucky they are to have husbands who love them. Oh, no! They must be punished, properly punished!'

In default of allowing herself to sin, her thoughts were obstinately bent upon the sinners. She sat down once more in the great oak chair. Robert came and stood by her.

'No, Robert,' she said again, spreading out her hands. 'Don't take advantage of my weakness; you will anger me.'

Extreme beauty inspires as much respect as majesty, and the giant obeyed.

But what had happened would never be effaced from their memories. For an instant the barriers between them had been lowered. They found it difficult not to gaze into each other's eyes. 'So I can be loved after all,' thought Isabella, and she was almost grateful to the man who had given her this certainty.

'Is that all you have to tell me, Cousin? Have you brought me no other news?' she said, trying hard to regain control of herself.

Robert of Artois, who was wondering whether he was

right not to pursue his advantage, took some time to answer.

He breathed deeply and his thoughts seemed to return from a long way off.

'Yes, Madam,' he said, 'I have also a message from your uncle Valois.'

There was now a new link between them, and each word that they uttered seemed to have strange reverberations.

'The dignitaries of the Temple are soon to come up for judgment,' went on Artois, 'and there is a fear that your god-father, the Grand Master Jacques de Molay, will be condemned to death. Your uncle Valois asks you to write to the King to ask his clemency.'

Isabella did not reply. Once more her chin was resting in the palm of her hand.

'How like him you are, when you sit like that!' said Artois.

'Like whom?'

'King Philip, your father.'

'What the King, my father, decides, is rightly decided,' Isabella replied slowly. 'I can intervene upon matters that touch the family honour; I have nothing to do with the government of the Kingdom of France.'

'Jacques de Molay is an old man. He was noble and great. If he committed faults, he has sufficiently expiated them. Remember that he held you at the baptismal font. Believe me, a great wrong is about to be done, and we owe it once more to Nogaret and Marigny! In attacking the Templars, these men, risen from nothing, are attacking the great barons and the Chivalry of France.'

The Queen was perplexed; the whole business was beyond her.

'I cannot judge,' she said, 'I cannot judge.'

'You know I owe a great debt to your uncle Valois, and

he would be very grateful if I could get a letter from you. Moreover, compassion never ill-becomes a queen; it's a feminine trait for which you can but be praised. There are some who reproach you with hardness of heart: this will be your answer to them. Do it for yourself, Isabella, and do it for me.'

He said 'Isabella' in the same tone of voice that he had used earlier by the window.

She smiled at him.

'You're clever, Robert, beneath your boorish air. All right, I'll write the letter you want and you can take everything away together. I'll try to get the King of England to write to the King of France, too. When are you leaving?'

'When you command me, Cousin.'

'The purses will be ready tomorrow, I think; it's very soon.'

There was regret in the Queen's voice. He gazed into her eyes and she was troubled once more.

'I'll await a messenger from you to know when I must leave for France. Good-bye, Cousin. We shall meet again at supper.'

He took his leave and, when he had gone out, the room seemed to the Queen to have become strangely quiet, like a valley after a storm. Isabella closed her eyes and for a long moment remained still.

'He is a man who has grown wicked because he has been wronged,' she thought. 'But, if one loves him, he must be capable of love.'

Those called upon to play a decisive part in the history of nations are more often than not unaware of the destinies they embody. These two people who had had this long interview upon a March afternoon of 1314, in the Palace of Westminster, could not know that, as a result of their actions, they would, almost alone, become the artisans of a war between the kingdoms of France and England which would last more than a hundred years.

2

The Prisoners in the Temple

THE WALL WAS COVERED with a damp mould. A smoky, yellow light began to filter down into the vaulted, underground room.

The prisoner was dozing, his arms crossed beneath his beard. Suddenly he shivered and sat up, haggard, his heart beating. For a moment he remained still, gazing at the morning mist which was blowing in through the little window. He was listening. Quite distinctly, though the sound was necessarily somewhat softened by the thickness of the walls, he could hear the pealing of the bells of Paris announcing the first Mass: the bells of Saint-Martin, of Saint-Merry, of Saint-Germain-l'Auxerrois, of Saint-Eustache and of Notre-Dame; the country bells of the nearby villages of La Courtille, of Clignancourt and of Mont-Martre.

The prisoner heard no particularly arresting sound. It was distress alone that made him start awake, the distress he suffered at each awakening, as he suffered nightmares whenever he slept.

He pulled a big wooden bowl of water to him and drank

largely to allay the fever from which he had now suffered for days and days. Having drunk, he allowed the water in the bowl to subside into stillness and leaned over it as if it were a mirror or the depths of a well. The reflection he saw, though shadowy and indistinct, was that of a centenarian. He remained thus for some moments, searching for some likeness to his old appearance in the floating face with its ancestral beard, the lips sunken in a toothless mouth, the long, thin nose, the shadowed, deep-set eyes.

He put the bowl on one side, got up, then took a few steps till he felt the tautening of the chain that bound him to the wall. Suddenly, he began to scream: 'Jacques de Molay! Jacques de Molay! I am Jacques de Molay!'

There was no answer; he knew there was no one to answer him, not even an echo.

But he needed to scream his own name, to hurl it at the stone columns, at the vaults, at the oak door, to prevent his mind dissolving into madness, to remind himself that he was sixty-two years old, that he had commanded armies, governed provinces, that he had possessed power equal to sovereigns, and that as long as he still drew breath he would continue to be, even in this dungeon, the Grand Master of the Order of Knights Templar.

From a refinement of cruelty, or perhaps contempt, he and the principal dignitaries of the Order had been imprisoned in the cellars, now transformed into dungeons, of the great tower of the Hôtel-du-Temple, their own building, their Mother House.

'To think that it was I who had this tower repaired!' the Grand Master murmured angrily, hitting the wall with his fist.

The blow made him cry out, it renewed an appalling pain in his hand, whose crushed thumb was no more than a stump of half-healed flesh. But indeed, what part of his body was neither an open sore nor the seat of some internal agony? Since he had suffered the torture of the boot, he had been a victim to bad circulation in the legs and abominable cramps. His legs strapped between boards, he had undergone the sharp anguish of oaken wedges tapped into place by the executioners' mallets, while Guillaume de Nogaret, Keeper of the Seals of the Kingdom, asked him questions, trying to persuade him to confess. To confess what? He had fainted.

Dirt, damp and lack of food had had their effect upon his torn and lacerated body.

And more recently he had undergone the torture by stretching, the most appalling perhaps of all those to which he had been subjected. A weight of two hundred pounds had been tied to his right foot while he, old as he was, had been hoisted to the ceiling by a rope and pulley. And all the time Guillaume de Nogaret's sinister voice kept repeating, 'Confess, Messire, why don't you confess?' And since he still obstinately refused, they had hauled him from floor to ceiling more hurriedly, more jerkily. He had felt his limbs becoming disjointed, the articulations parting, his whole body seemed to be bursting, and he had begun to scream that he would confess everything, admit every crime, all the crimes of the world. Yes, the Templars practised sodomy among themselves; yes, to gain entrance to the Order, it was necessary to spit upon the Cross; yes, they worshipped an idol with the head of a cat; yes, they practised magic, and sorcery, and had a cult for the Devil; yes, they embezzled the funds confided to their care; yes, they had fomented a plot against the Pope and the King . . . And what more besides?

Jacques de Molay wondered how he had managed to survive it all. Doubtless because the tortures had been exactly calculated, never pushed to the point where there was a risk of his dying, and because, too, the constitution of an old knight, trained to arms and war, had greater resistance than he himself could have believed.

He knelt down, his eyes turned towards the beam of light that entered by the little window.

'Oh, Lord my God,' he cried, 'why hast Thou given me greater strength of body than of mind? Was I worthy to command the Order? Thou hast not prevented my falling into cowardice; spare me, Lord God, from falling into folly. I cannot hold out much longer, no, not for much longer.'

He had been in chains for seven years, only leaving his dungeon to be dragged before the commission of inquiry, and to be submitted to all the pressures and threats that the theologians and lawyers could devise.

In the circumstances one might well fear madness. Often the Grand Master lost all sense of time. As a distraction, he had attempted to tame a couple of rats that came every night to eat the remains of his bread. He passed quickly from anger to tears, from crises of religious devotion to a longing for violence, from idiocy to fury.

'They'll die of it, they'll die of it,' he kept repeating to himself.

Who would? Clement, Guillaume, Philip. . . . The Pope, the Keeper of the Seals and the King. They would die. Molay did not know how, but it would certainly be amid appalling suffering and in expiation of their crimes. He unceasingly chewed over these three hated names.

Still upon his knees, his beard raised towards the narrow window, the Grand Master murmured, 'I thank thee, Lord God, for leaving me hatred. It is the sole force that sustains me now.'

He got painfully to his feet and went back to the stone bench which, cemented to the wall, served both for seat and bed.

Who could ever have thought that he would come to this? His mind constantly returned to his youth, to the boy he had been fifty years before, as he came down the slopes of his native Jura in search of adventure.

Like all the younger sons of the nobility of the time, he had dreamed of wearing the long white mantle with the black cross, the uniform of the Order of the Knights Templar. In those days, the mere name of Templar evoked the epic and the exotic, ships with bellying sails scudding towards the Orient, lands where the skies were always blue, charges at the gallop across the desert sands, treasures of Arabia, ransomed prisoners, captured and pillaged cities, fortresses with huge staircases, built beside the sea. It was even said that the Templars had secret ports from which they embarked for unknown continents.[4]

And Jacques de Molay had achieved his dream; he had marched proudly through distant cities, clothed in the superb mantle whose folds hung down to his golden spurs.

He had risen in the Order's hierarchy, higher than he had ever dared hope, achieving every dignity in turn, at last to be elected by the brothers to the supreme function of Grand Master of France and Overseas, and to the command of fifteen thousand knights.

And all this had but led to a dungeon, horror and destitution. Surely few people's lives could show such prodigious success followed by so great a fall.

Jacques de Molay was idly tracing lines with one of the links in his chain upon the damp mould on the wall, lines which reminded him of the plan of some fortress, when he heard heavy footsteps and the noise of arms upon the staircase that led down to his cell.

Once more he was seized with a feeling of pain, but this time it was precise and definite.

The heavy door creaked open and, behind the gaoler, Molay saw four archers dressed in leather tunics and carrying pikes. Their breath spread out in a thin cloud before their faces.

Their chief said, 'We have come to fetch you, Messire.'

Molay rose silently to his feet.

The gaoler came forward and with cold chisel and heavy blows of a hammer broke the rivet that fastened the chain to the heavy iron anklets. Each weighed four pounds.

He clasped his great, illustrious mantle, now no more than a grey rag, its black cross in tatters at the breast, about his emaciated shoulders.

They left the dungeon. And in that reeling exhausted old man, his feet weighed down with fetters as he mounted the tower's steps, there could still be seen something of the commander who had recaptured Jerusalem from the Saracens for the last time.

'Oh, Lord my God,' he murmured to himself, 'give me strength, give me a little strength.' And to help himself find it, he repeated the names of his three enemies: Clement, Guillaume, Philip.

Fog lay thick upon the huge court of the Temple, cloaked the turrets of the enclosing wall, flowed through the crenellations, and obscured the spire of the great church on the right of the tower.

A hundred soldiers were standing at ease, talking quietly among themselves, as they stood round a big, square, uncovered wagon.

From beyond the walls he could hear the murmur of Paris and the occasional neigh of a horse, sounds that moved him with an ineffable sadness.

Messire Alain de Pareilles, Captain of the King's Archers, the man who attended every execution, who accompanied the condemned to sentence and torture, was walking up and down the centre of the yard, his face impassive, his expression bored. He was forty years old and his steel-coloured hair fell in a short fringe across his square forehead. He wore a coat of mail, had a sword at his side, and carried his helmet in the crook of his arm.

He turned as he heard the Grand Master's approach, and the latter, seeing him, turned pale, if it were possible for his pallor to increase.

Merely for interrogations there was not, as a rule, so much display; there were neither wagon nor men-at-arms. A few royal agents came to escort the accused, generally at nightfall, by boat across the Seine.

The presence of Alain de Pareilles was alone significant enough.

'Has judgment been pronounced?' Molay asked the Captain of the Archers.

'It has, Messire,' he replied.

'And do you know, my son,' Molay asked after a moment's hesitation, 'what that judgment contains.'

'I do not, Messire. My orders are to conduct you to Notre-Dame to hear it read.'

There was a silence, then Jacques de Molay asked, 'What day is it?'

'The Monday after the feast of Saint Gregory.'

This corresponded to the 18th March, the 18th March 1314.[5]

'Am I being taken out to die?' Molay wondered.

The door of the tower opened again, and three other dignitaries appeared in their turn, escorted by guards, the Visitor General, the Preceptor of Normandy and the Commander of Aquitaine.

They had white hair, and white unkempt beards, their deep-sunken eyes blinked in the light, their bodies seemed to float in their ragged mantles; for a moment they stood still, like great night-birds unable to see in the light. Moreover, the Commander of Aquitaine had a white film over his left eye which gave him something of the appearance of an owl. He seemed completely stupefied. The semi-bald Visitor General had horribly swollen hands and feet.

It was Geoffroy de Charnay, the Preceptor of Normandy, who first, though hampered by his irons, rushed up to the Grand Master and embraced him. There was a long friendship between the two men. Indeed, it was Jacques de Molay who had helped Charnay in his career. Ten years younger than himself, he had looked upon Charnay as his successor.

Charnay's forehead was furrowed by a deep scar, the legacy of an old battle in which a sword-cut had also given him a crooked nose. This rugged man, his face marked by war, leant his forehead against the Grand Master's shoulder to hide his tears.

'Have courage, Brother, have courage,' said the Grand Master, clasping him in his arms. 'And you, too, my Brothers, have courage,' he went on, embracing the other dignitaries in turn.

Seeing each other, they were able to judge of their own appearance.

A gaoler came up.

'You have the right to have your irons removed, Messires,' he said.

The Grand Master spread wide his arms in a bitter, hope-less gesture.

'I have not the money,' he replied.

For each time they left their prison, in order to have their irons removed and replaced, the Templars had to pay a denier out of the dozen they were allowed for their wretched food, the straw in their dungeons and the laundering of their single shirt. Another of Nogaret's subtle cruelties! They were accused, but not condemned. They had the right to a main-tenance allowance. What was the use of twelve deniers, when a small joint of meat cost forty? It meant starving four days in eight, sleeping on the hard stone, rotting in squalor.

The Preceptor of Normandy took the last two deniers from the old leather purse attached to his belt and threw them on the ground, one for his own irons and one for those of the Grand Master.

'My Brother!' said Jacques de Molay with a gesture of refusal.

'For all the use they are likely to be to me now,' replied Charnay. 'Accept them, Brother; there is not even merit in the giving.'

As the iron pins were removed, they felt the hammer-blows resounding in their bones. But they felt the blood pounding in their chests more strongly still.

'This time, we've come to the end,' Molay murmured.

They wondered what kind of death had been reserved for them, whether they would be subjected to ultimate tortures.

'It is perhaps a good sign that our irons are being removed,' said the Visitor General, shaking his swollen hands. 'Perhaps the Pope has decided upon clemency.'

There were still a few broken teeth in the front of his

mouth and these made him lisp, while the dungeon had turned his mind childish.

The Grand Master shrugged his shoulders and pointed to the phalanx of a hundred archers.

'We must prepare to die, Brother,' he said.

'Look, look what they have done to me,' cried the Visitor, pulling up his sleeve to show his swollen arm.

'We have all been tortured,' said the Grand Master.

He looked away, as he always did when someone spoke of torture. He had yielded, he had signed false confessions and could not forgive himself.

He looked round upon the huge group of buildings which had been the seat and symbol of their power.

'For the last time,' he thought.

For the last time he gazed upon the vast assembly of tower and church, palace and houses, courts and gardens, a fortified town within Paris itself.[6]

Here it was that for two centuries the Templars had lived, prayed, slept, given judgment, transacted business, and decided upon their expeditions to distant lands. In this very tower the treasure of the Kingdom of France had been deposited, confided to their care and guardianship.

It was here, after the disastrous expeditions of Saint Louis, in which Palestine and Cyprus had been lost, that they had come, bringing with them in their train their esquires, their mules laden with gold, their stud of Arabian horses and their negro slaves.

Jacques de Molay saw in his mind's eye this return of the vanquished. Even so, it had something of an epic quality.

'We had become useless, and we did not know it,' thought the Grand Master. 'We were always talking of reconquest and new crusades. Perhaps we showed too much arrogance, and enjoyed too many privileges while no longer doing anything to justify them.'

From being the permanent militia of the Christian world, they had become the permanent bankers of Church and King. To have many debtors is to have many enemies.

Oh, the plot had been well conceived! The drama had begun upon the day when Philip the Fair had asked to join the Order that he might become its Grand Master. The Chapter had replied with a curt and definite refusal.

'Was I wrong?' Jacques de Molay asked himself for the hundredth time. 'Was I too jealous of my authority? But no; I could not have acted otherwise; our rule is binding: no sovereign princes in our ranks.'

King Philip had never forgotten the repulse and the insult. He had begun by dissimulating, lavishing favours and kindnesses upon Jacques de Molay. Was not the Grand Master godfather to his daughter, Isabella? Was not the Grand Master the prop and stay of the kingdom?

Yet the royal treasure had been transferred from the Temple to the Louvre. At the same time a low, venomous campaign of obloquy had begun against the Templars. It was said that they speculated in corn and were responsible for famines, that they thought more of increasing their fortune than of capturing the Holy Sepulchre from the heathen. They were accused of blasphemy merely because they spoke the rough language of the camp. 'To swear like a Templar' became the current saying. From blasphemy to heresy was but a step. It was said that they practised unnatural vice and that their black slaves were sorcerers.

'True it is that all our Brothers were not saints and that inaction was bad for many of them.'

Above all, it was said that during the ceremonies of

initiation the neophytes were compelled to deny Christ and spit upon the Cross, that they were subjected to obscene practices.

Under the pretext of putting an end to these rumours, Philip had suggested to the Grand Master, for the sake of the honour and interest of the Order, that an inquiry should be opened.

'And I accepted,' thought Molay; 'I was abominably duped and deceived.'

For, upon a certain day in October 1307 . . . oh, how well Molay remembered that day! 'Upon its eve, he was still embracing me, and calling me brother, indeed giving me the place of honour at the funeral of his sister-in-law, the Countess of Valois.'

To be precise it was upon a Friday the thirteenth, an unlucky day if ever there was one, that King Philip, by means of a widespread police net, prepared long before, had arrested all the Templars of France at dawn upon a charge of heresy in the name of the Inquisition.

And Nogaret himself had come to seize Jacques de Molay and the hundred and forty knights of the Mother House.

Suddenly an order rang out. It startled the Grand Master and interrupted the flow of his thoughts, those thoughts in which he sifted yet once more the cause of the disaster. Messire Alain de Pareilles was drawing up his archers. He had put on his helmet. A soldier had his horse by the head and was holding his stirrup.

'Let us go,' said the Grand Master.

The prisoners were hustled towards the wagon. Molay climbed into it first. The Commander of Aquitaine, the man with the white film over his eye, who had defeated the Turks at Acre, still appeared utterly stupefied. He had to be hoisted up. The Brother Visitor was moving his lips in ceaseless, silent muttering. When Geoffroy de Charnay's turn came to climb onto the wagon, an unseen dog began howling from somewhere in the neighbourhood of the stables, and the scar upon the Preceptor of Normandy's forehead puckered deeply.

Drawn by four horses in tandem, the heavy wagon began to move forward.

As the huge gates opened, the crowd set up a great clamouring. Several thousand people, all the inhabitants of that district and the neighbouring ones, were crowding against the walls. The leading archers had to force a passage through the howling mob with blows of their pike-shafts.

'Make way for the King's men!' cried the archers.

Erect upon his horse, his expression still impassively bored, Alain de Pareilles dominated the tumult.

But when the Templars appeared, the clamour was suddenly stilled. At the spectacle of these four emaciated old men, whom the jolting of the unsprung wheels jostled against each other, the people of Paris suffered a moment of dumb stupefaction, of spontaneous compassion.

But then cries arose of 'Death! Death to the heretics!' from royal agents mingling with the crowd. And then the people, always prepared to shout on the side of power and to make a noise when it costs them nothing, began to yell in concert, 'Death to them!'

'Thieves!'

'Heretics!'

'Look at them! They're no longer so proud today, heathens that they are! Death to them!'

Insults, gibes, threats rose along the whole length of the grim procession. But the frenzy was sporadic. A whole section of the crowd remained silent, and its silence, though prudent, was none the less significant.

For things had changed in the seven years that had elapsed. The way the case had been conducted was known. People had seen Templars at the church doors showing the public the bones fallen from their feet as the result of the tortures they had suffered. It was known that in many of the towns of France the Knights had been burned by hundreds at the stake. It was known, too, that certain Ecclesiastical Commissions had refused to condemn them, and that new bishops had had to be appointed to undertake the task, and that one of them was the brother of the First Minister, Enguerrand de Marigny. It was said that Pope Clement V himself had only yielded against his will because he was in the power of the King and feared to suffer the same fate as Pope Boniface, his predecessor. And, moreover, during these seven years, corn had become no more abundant, while the price of bread had risen still further, proof that it could no longer be the fault of the Templars.

Twenty-five archers, their bows slung, their pikes upon their shoulders, marched in front of the wagon, twenty-five on each flank, and as many more brought up the rear of the procession.

'Oh, if we only still had a little bodily strength!' thought the Grand Master. At twenty, he would have leapt upon an archer, seized his pike and tried to escape, or fought there to the death. And now he could hardly have climbed over the wagon's side.

Behind him, the Brother Visitor was muttering through his broken teeth, 'They won't condemn us. I cannot believe that they'll condemn us. We're no longer dangerous.'

And the old Templar with the film across his eye had at last emerged sufficiently from his prostration to murmur, 'It's good to be out of doors! It's good to breathe the fresh air again. Isn't that so, Brother?'

'They're not even conscious of where we're being taken,' thought the Grand Master.

The Preceptor of Normandy placed a hand upon his arm.

'Messire, my Brother,' he said in a low voice, 'I can see two people among the crowd weeping and others making the sign of the Cross. We are not alone upon our Calvary.'

'Those people may be sorry for us, but they can do nothing to save us,' replied Jacques de Molay. 'I am looking for other faces.'

The Preceptor understood to whose faces the Grand Master referred, and to what supreme, incredible hope he clung. In spite of himself, he also began searching the crowd. For, among the Knights Templars, a certain number had escaped the net drawn about them in 1307. Some had taken refuge in monasteries, others had renounced their order and lived secretly in town or countryside; others again had reached Spain where the King of Aragon, refusing to obey the injunctions of the King of France and the Pope, had left the Templars their commanderies and founded a new Order for them. And then, still others, having appeared before more merciful tribunals, had been handed over to the guardianship of the Knights Hospitaler. All these veteran knights had kept in as close touch as they were able, forming a sort of secret society among themselves.

And Jacques de Molay told himself that perhaps . . .

Perhaps a plot had been made. Perhaps, from the corner of a street, from the corner of the rue des Blancs-Manteau, or the corner of the rue de la Bretonnerie, or from the cloister of Saint-Merry, would surge a group of men who, drawing their swords from beneath their cloaks, would fall upon the archers while others, posted at windows, would let fly their bolts. A cart moved into place at the gallop would block the street and complete the panic.

'And yet, why should our late brothers do this?' thought Molay. 'Merely to rescue their Grand Master who has betrayed them, forsworn the Order, yielded to torture.'

Nevertheless, his eyes searched the crowd, but he saw nothing but fathers of families who had hoisted their young children upon their shoulders, that they might miss nothing of the spectacle, children who, in later years, when they heard mention of the Templars, would remember nothing but the sight of four bearded, shivering old men surrounded, like common criminals, by men-at-arms.

In the meantime, the Visitor General went on spitting through his teeth, and the hero of Acre merely kept repeating that it was nice to be out of doors this fine morning.

The Grand Master felt surging within him one of those half-crazy rages which had so often come upon him in his prison, making him shout aloud and beat the walls. He felt that he was upon the point of committing some violent and terrible act – he did not know exactly what – but he felt the impulse to do something.

He accepted death almost as a deliverance, but he could not accept an unjust death, nor dying dishonoured. Accustomed through long years to war, he felt it stir for the last time in his old veins. He longed to die fighting.

He sought the hand of Geoffroy de Charnay, his old companion in arms, the last strong man still standing at his side, and clasped it tightly.

Raising his eyes, the Preceptor saw the arteries beating

upon the sunken temples of the Grand Master. They quivered like blue snakes.

The procession reached the Bridge of Notre-Dame.

3

The Royal Daughters-in-law

THE BASKET PERFUMED the air about it with a delicious odour of hot flour, butter and honey.

'Hot, hot pancakes! There won't be enough to go round! Come on, citizens, eat up! Hot pancakes!' cried the merchant, busy behind his open-air stove.

He seemed to be doing a great many things at the same time, rolling out his paste, removing the cooked pancakes from the fire, giving change, and keeping an eye on the street urchins to see they did not rob his stove.

'Hot pancakes!'

He was so busy that he paid no particular attention to the customer who, extending a white hand, placed a denier on the board in payment for a small pancake. He only saw the left hand put the wafer, from which but a single bite had been taken, down again.

'Well, he's a fussy one,' he said, poking his fire. 'To hell with him; it's pure wheaten flower and butter from Vaugirard ...'

At that moment he looked up and was startled out of his

wits. On seeing who the customer was, his words were stifled in his throat. He saw a very tall man with huge unblinking eyes, wearing a white hood and a half-length tunic.

Before even the merchant could manage a bow or stammer out an excuse, the man in the white hood had already moved away. The confectioner, with hanging arms, watched him disappear into the crowd, while his latest batch of pancakes began to burn.

The business streets of the city, according to travellers in Africa and the Orient, were at that time very similar to the *souks* of an Arab town. The same incessant din, little stalls touching one another, odours of frying-fat, spices and leather, the same slow promenading of shoppers and loungers, the same difficulty in forcing a way through the crowd. Each street, each alley, had its own special brand of goods, its own particular trade; here, in back shops, weavers' shuttles went to and fro upon the looms; there, cobblers sat at their lasts; farther on, saddlers tugged at their awls; and beyond again, carpenters turned the legs of stools.

There was a street of birds, a street of herbs and vegetables, a street of smiths whose hammers resounded upon their anvils while their braziers glowed at the back of their workshops. The goldsmiths, working at their crucibles, were gathered along the quay that bore their name.

There were thin ribbons of sky between the houses which were built of wood or mud, their gables so close together that one could shake hands from window to window across the street. Almost everywhere the ground was covered with a stinking film of mud in which people walked, either barefoot, in wooden clogs, or in leather shoes, according to their condition.

The man with the tall shoulders and the white hood walked

slowly on through the mob, his hands clasped behind his back, apparently careless of being jostled. Many, indeed, made way for him and saluted him. He responded with a curt nod. He had the appearance of an athlete; fair silky hair, almost auburn in colour and curling at the ends, fell nearly to his collar, framing regular features which were at once impassive and singularly beautiful.

Three royal sergeants-at-arms, in blue coats and carrying in the crooks of their arms the staves surmounted with lilies that were the insignia of their office,[7] followed the stroller at a distance, but without ever losing sight of him, stopping when he stopped, moving on again as soon as he did.

Suddenly a young man in a tight-fitting tunic, dragged along by three fine greyhounds on a leash, debouched from an alley, jostling the stroller and very nearly knocking him over. The hounds became entangled about his feet and began barking.

'You scoundrel!' the young man cried in a noticeably Italian accent. 'You nearly trod on my hounds. I wouldn't have cared a damn if they'd bitten you.'

No more than eighteen, short and good-looking, with dark eyes and finely chiselled features, the young man stood his ground in the middle of the street, raising his voice in simulated manliness. Someone took him by the arm and whispered a word in his ear. At once the young man removed his cap, bowing respectfully though without servility.

'Those are fine hounds; whose are they?' asked the stroller, gazing at the boy out of huge, cold eyes.

'They belong to my uncle, Tolomei, the banker, at your service,' replied the young man.

Without another word, the man in the white hood went on his way. As soon as he and the sergeants-at-arms who followed him were out of sight, the people standing round the young Italian guffawed. The latter stood still, apparently having some difficulty in recovering himself after his mistake; even the hounds were still.

'Well, well! He's not so proud now!' they said, laughing.

'Look at him! He nearly knocks the King down and then adds insult to injury.'

'You can count on spending the night in prison, my boy, with thirty strokes of the whip into the bargain.'

The Italian turned upon the bystanders.

'Damn it! I'd never seen him before; how could I be expected to recognise him? And what's more, citizens, I come from a country where there's no king for whom one has to make way. In my city of Sienna every citizen can be king in turn. And if anyone feels like mocking Guccio Baglioni, he need only say the word.'

He uttered his name like a challenge. The quick pride of Tuscany shone in his eyes. A carved dagger hung at his side. No one persisted; and the young man flicked his fingers to put the hounds in motion again. He went on his way with more apparent assurance than he felt, wondering whether his stupidity would have unpleasant consequences.

For it was indeed King Philip the Fair whom he had jostled. This sovereign, whom none other equalled in power, liked to stroll through his city like a simple citizen, informing himself upon prices, tasting foodstuffs, examining cloth, listening to people talking. He was taking the pulse of his people. Strangers, ignorant of who he was, asked him the way. One day a soldier had stopped him to ask for his pay. As mean with words as he was with money, it was rare that in a whole outing he said more than three sentences or spent more than three pence.

The King was passing through the meat-market when the great bell of Notre-Dame began ringing and a loud clamour arose.

'There they are! There they are!' people were shouting.

The clamour drew nearer; the crowd became excited, people began to run.

A fat butcher came out from behind his stall, knife in hand, and yelled, 'Death to the heretics!'

His wife caught him by the sleeve.

'Heretics? They're no more heretics than you are,' she said. 'You'd do better to stay here and serve the shop, you idler, you.'

They began quarrelling. A crowd gathered at once.

'They've confessed before the judges!' the butcher went on.

'The judges?' someone replied. 'They've always been the same ones. They judge as they're told to by those who pay them, and they're afraid of a kick up the arse.'

Then everyone began to talk at once.

'The Templars are saintly men. They've always given a lot to charity.'

'It was a good thing to take their money away, but not to torture them.'

'It was the King who owed them most, that's why it was.'

'The King did the right thing.'

'The King or the Templars,' said an apprentice, 'they're one and the same thing. Let the wolves eat each other and then they won't eat us.'

At that moment a woman happened to turn round, grew suddenly pale, and made a sign to the others to be quiet. Philip the Fair was standing behind them, gazing at them with his unwinking, icy stare. The sergeants-at-arms had drawn a little closer to him, ready to intervene. In an instant the crowd had dispersed; those who had composed it ran off shouting at the tops of their voices, 'Long live the King! Death to the heretics!'

The King's expression remained perfectly impassive. One might have thought that he had heard nothing. If he took pleasure in taking people by surprise, it was a secret pleasure.

The clamour was growing louder. The procession of the Templars was passing the end of the street. Through a gap between the houses, the King saw for an instant the Grand Master standing in the wagon surrounded by his three companions. The Grand Master stood upright; in the King's eyes this was an irritation; he looked like a martyr, but undefeated.

Leaving the crowd to rush towards the spectacle, Philip the Fair passed through the suddenly empty streets at his usual slow pace, and returned to his palace.

The people might well grumble a bit, and the Grand Master hold his old and broken body upright. In an hour the whole thing would be over, and the sentence, so the King believed, would be generally well received. In an hour's time the work of seven years would be finished and completed. The Episcopal Tribunal had issued their decree; the archers were numerous; the sergeants-at-arms patrolled the streets. In an hour the case of the Templars would be erased from the list of public cares, and from every point of view the royal power would come out of the affair enhanced and reinforced.

'Even my daughter Isabella will be satisfied. I shall have acceded to her plea, and so contented everyone. But it was time to put an end to it,' Philip the Fair told himself as he thought of the words he had just heard.

He went home by the Mercers' Hall.

Philip the Fair had entirely renovated and rebuilt the Palace, preserving only such ancient structures as the Sainte-Chapelle, which dated from the time of his grandfather, Saint Louis. It was a period of building and embellishment. Princes rivalled each other; what had been done in Westminster had been done in Paris too. The mass of the Cité with its great white towers dominating the Seine was brand-new, imposing and, perhaps, a little ostentatious.

Philip, if he watched the pennies, never hesitated to spend largely when it was a question of demonstrating his power. But, since he never neglected an opportunity of profit, he had conceded to the mercers, in consideration of an enormous rent, the privilege of transacting business in the great gallery which ran the length of the palace, and which from this fact was known as the Mercers' Hall, before it became known as the Merchants' Hall.[8]

It was a huge place with something of the appearance of a cathedral with two naves. Its size was the admiration of travellers. At the summits of the pillars were the forty statues of the kings who, from Pharamond and Mérovée, had succeeded each other at the head of the Frankish kingdom. Opposite the statue of Philip the Fair was that of Enguerrand de Marigny, Coadjutor and Rector of the Kingdom, who had inspired and directed the building.

Round the pillars were stalls containing articles of dress, there were baskets of trinkets, and sellers of ornaments, embroidery and lace. About them were gathered the pretty Parisian women and the ladies of the Court. Open to all comers, the hall had became a place for a stroll, a meeting-place for transacting business and exchanging gallantries. It resounded with laughter, conversation and gossip, with the claptrap of the salesmen over all. There were many foreign accents, particularly those of Italy and Flanders.

A raw-boned fellow, who had determined to make his fortune out of spreading the use of handkerchiefs, was demonstrating the articles to a group of fat women, shaking out his squares of ornamented linen.

'Ah, my dear ladies,' he cried, 'what a pity to blow one's nose in one's fingers or upon one's sleeve, when such pretty handkerchiefs as these have been invented for the purpose? Are not such elegant things precisely made for your ladyships' noses?'

A little farther on, an old gentleman was being pressed to buy a wench some English lace.

Philip the Fair crossed the Hall. The courtiers bowed to the ground. The women curtsied as he passed. Without seeming to do so, the King liked the liveliness of the scene, the laughter, as well as the marks of respect which gave him assurance of his power. Here, because of the tumult of voices, the great bell of Notre-Dame seemed distant, lighter in tone, more benign.

The King caught sight of a group whose youth and magnificence were the cynosure of every eye: it consisted of two quite young women and a tall, fair, good-looking young man. The young women were two of the King's daughters-in-law, those known as the 'sisters of Burgundy', Jeanne, the Countess of Poitiers, married to the King's second son, and Blanche, her younger sister, married to the youngest son. The young man with them was dressed like an officer of a princely household.

They were whispering together with restrained excitement. Philip the Fair slowed his pace the better to observe his daughters-in-law.

'My sons have no reason to complain of me,' thought Philip the Fair. 'As well as making alliances useful to the Crown, I gave them very pretty wives.'

The two sisters were very little alike. Jeanne, the elder, the wife of Philippe of Poitiers, was twenty-one years old. She was tall and slender, her hair somewhere between blond and chestnut, and something in the way she held herself, something formal about the line of the neck and the slant of the eye, reminded the King of the fine greyhounds in his kennels. She dressed with a simplicity and sobriety that was almost an affectation. This particular day she was wearing a long dress of grey velvet with tight sleeves; over it she wore a surcoat edged with ermine, reaching to the waist.

Her sister Blanche was smaller, rounder, rosier, with greater spontaneity. Though she was only three years younger than Jeanne, she still had childish dimples in her cheeks and, doubtless, they would remain there for some time yet. Her hair was of a bright blond and her eyes, and this is rare, were of a clear and brilliant brown; she had small transluscent teeth. Dress was more to her than a game, it was a passion. She devoted herself to it with an extravagance that was not always in the best of taste. She wore enormous pleated coifs and hung as many jewels as she could upon her collar, sleeves and belt. Her dresses were embroidered with pearls and gold thread. But she was so graceful that everything could be forgiven her, and appeared so pleased with herself that it was a pleasure to see.

The little group was talking of a matter of five days. 'Is it reasonable to be so concerned about a mere five days?' said the Countess of Poitiers, at the moment the King emerged from behind a pillar masking his approach.

'Good morning, my daughters,' he said.

The three young people fell suddenly silent. The good-looking boy bowed low and moved a pace or two aside with his eyes upon the ground as befitted his rank. The two young women, having made their curtsies, became tongue-tied, blushing and a little embarrassed. They looked as if they had been caught out.

'Well, my daughters,' the King went on, 'one might well think that I had arrived at an inappropriate moment? What were you saying to each other?'

He was not surprised at his reception. He was accustomed to the fact that everyone, even his greatest friends, even his closest relations, were intimidated by his presence. He was often surprised by the wall of ice that fell between him and everyone who came near him – all, that is, except Marigny and Nogaret – and he found it difficult to explain away the terror that seized strangers whom he happened to meet. Indeed, he believed he did everything possible to appear pleasant and amiable. He wanted to be loved and feared at the same time. And it was asking too much.

Blanche was the first to recover her assurance.

'You must forgive us, Sire,' she said, 'but it is not an easy thing to repeat!'

'Why not?' asked Philip the Fair.

'Because . . . we were saying unkind things about you,' Blanche replied.

'Really?' said Philip, uncertain whether she was teasing, astonished that anyone should dare tease him.

He glanced at the young man, standing a little apart, who seemed very ill at ease. Jerking his chin towards him, he said, 'Who is he?'

'Messire Philippe d'Aunay, equerry to our uncle Valois who

has lent him to me as escort,' replied the Countess of Poitiers.

The young man bowed once again.

For an instant the idea crossed the King's mind that his sons were wrong to permit their wives to go abroad accompanied by such good-looking equerries, and that the old-fashioned custom, which insisted that princesses should be accompanied by ladies-in-waiting, had undoubtedly a good deal of sense to it.

'Haven't you a brother?' he asked the equerry.

'Yes, Sire, my brother is in the service of Monseigneur of Poitiers,' answered young Aunay, bearing the King's gaze with some discomfort.

'That's it; I always confuse you,' said the King.

Then, turning back to Blanche, he said, 'Well, then, what unkind things were you saying of me, my girl?'

'Jeanne and I are in complete agreement that we owe you a grudge, Father. For five consecutive nights we have not had our husbands at our service because you keep them in council or send them far away on affairs of state.'

'My dear daughters, these are not matters to be spoken of out loud,' said the King.

He was a prude by nature, and it was said had remained chaste for all the nine years that he had been a widower. But he could not be severe with Blanche. Her liveliness, her gaiety, her daring, to say the least, disarmed him. He was at once amused and shocked. He smiled, which was a thing that hardly happened to him once a month.

'And what does the third one say?' he added.

By the third one, he meant Marguerite of Burgundy, the cousin of Jeanne and Blanche, who was married to his eldest son, Louis, King of Navarre.

'Marguerite?' cried Blanche. 'She's shut herself up, she's

sulking, and she says that you're as wicked as you're good-looking.'

Once more the King found himself in uncertainty; wondering how he should interpret the last phrase. But Blanche's expression was so limpid, so candid! She was the only person who dared tease him, the only person who did not tremble in his presence.

'Well, you can reassure her, and reassure yourself, Blanche; Louis and Charles can keep you company tonight. Today is a good day for the kingdom,' said Philip the Fair. 'There will be no Council tonight. As for your husband, Jeanne, I can tell you that he'll be home tomorrow and that he has forwarded our affairs in Flanders. I am pleased with him.'

'Then I shall make him doubly welcome,' said Jeanne, inclining her beautiful neck.

This conversation was a peculiarly long one for King Philip. He turned quickly away without saying good-bye, and went towards the grand staircase which led to his apartments.

'Ouf!' said Blanche, her hand on her heart as she watched him disappear. 'We were lucky to get away with it that time.'

'I thought I should faint with terror,' said Jeanne.

Philippe d'Aunay was blushing to the roots of his hair, not from embarrassment as a moment ago, but from anger.

'Thank you,' he said drily to Blanche. 'What you've just said made nice hearing.'

'What did you expect me to do?' Blanche cried. 'Did you think of anything better yourself? You stood there like a stuck pig. He came upon us without warning. He's got the sharpest pair of ears in the kingdom. If by any chance he heard our last words, it was the only way to put him off the scent. And instead of blaming me, Philippe, you'd do better to congratulate me.'

'Don't begin again,' said Jeanne. 'Let's walk towards the stalls and stop looking as if we were plotting.'

They moved forward, looking unconcerned, and acknowledging the bows in their honour.

'Messire,' said Jeanne in a low voice, 'I must tell you that it's you and your ridiculous jealousy that cause all the trouble. If you hadn't started groaning here about what you suffer at the Queen of Navarre's hands, we wouldn't have run the risk of the King hearing too much.'

Philippe went on looking gloomy.

'Really,' Blanche said, 'your brother is much more agreeable than you are.'

'Doubtless he's better treated, and I'm glad of it for his sake,' answered Philippe. 'No doubt I'm a fool, a fool to allow myself to be humiliated by a woman who treats me as a servant, who summons me to her bed when she feels inclined, who sends me about my business when the inclination has passed, who leaves me whole days without a sign, and pretends not to recognise me when we meet. After all, what game is she playing?'

Philippe d'Aunay, equerry to Monseigneur the Count of Valois, the King's brother, had been for three years the lover of Marguerite, the eldest of Philip the Fair's daughters-in-law. And he dared to speak thus to Blanche of Burgundy, the wife of Charles, Philip the Fair's third son, because Blanche was the mistress of his brother, Gautier d'Aunay, equerry to the Count of Poitiers. And if he dared to speak thus to Jeanne, Countess of Poitiers, it was because Jeanne, no one's mistress as yet, nevertheless was a party, partly from weakness, partly because it amused her, to the intrigues of the other two royal daughters-in-law. She arranged meetings and interviews.

Thus it was that in the early spring of 1314, upon the very day that the Templars came up for judgment, the very day this serious matter was the Crown's main concern, of the three royal sons of France, the eldest, Louis, and the youngest, Charles, were cuckolded by two equerries, one of whom was in their uncle's household and the other in their brother's, and all this was taking place under the auspices of their sister-in-law, Jeanne, who, though faithful as a wife, was a benevolent go-between, finding a pleasurable excitement in living the loves of others.

The report that had been given the Queen of England a few days earlier was thus very far from false.

'In any case, there'll be no Tower of Nesle tonight,' said Blanche.

'As far as I'm concerned, it won't be any different from previous nights,' replied Philippe d'Aunay. 'But what makes me absolutely furious is the thought that tonight, in the arms of Louis of Navarre, Marguerite will say the very same words that she has so often said to me.'

'That's going too far, my friend,' said Jeanne with considerable haughtiness. 'A little while ago you were accusing Marguerite, quite unreasonably, of having other lovers. Now you wish to prevent her having a husband. The favours she gives you have made you forget your place. Tomorrow I think I shall advise our uncle to send you into his county of Valois for several months. Your estates lie there and it will be good for your nerves.'

At once, good-looking young Philippe calmed down.

'Oh, Madam!' he murmured. 'I think I should die of it.'

He was much more attractive in this mood than when angry. It was a pleasure to frighten him, merely to see him lower his long silken eyelashes and watch the slight trembling of his white chin. He was suddenly so unhappy, so pathetic, that the two young women, forgetting their alarm, could do no other than smile.

'You must tell your brother, Gautier, that I shall sigh for him tonight,' said Blanche in the kindest possible way.

Once again, it was impossible to tell whether she was lying or telling the truth.

'Oughtn't Marguerite to be warned of what we've just learnt?' said Aunay hesitatingly. 'In case she intended to-night . . .'

'Blanche can do what she likes; I won't undertake anything more,' said Jeanne. 'I was too frightened. I don't want to have anything more to do with your affairs. It'll all end badly one day, and I'm really compromising myself for nothing at all.'

'It's quite true,' said Blanche; 'you get nothing out of our good fortune. And of us all, it's your husband who's away most often. If only Marguerite and I had your luck.'

'But I've no taste for it,' Jeanne answered.

'Or no courage,' said Blanche gently.

'It's quite true that even if I did want it, I haven't your facility for lying, Sister, and I'm sure that I should betray myself at once.'

Having said so much, Jeanne was pensive for a moment or two. No, certainly, she had no wish to deceive Philippe of Poitiers; but she was tired of appearing to be a prude.

'Madam,' said Aunay, 'couldn't you give me a message for your cousin?'

Jeanne looked covertly at the young man with a sort of tender indulgence.

'Can't you survive another day without seeing the beautiful Marguerite?' she said. 'Well then, I'll be kind. I'll buy a jewel for Marguerite and you shall go and give it to her on my behalf. But it's the last time.'

They went to one of the baskets. While the two young women were making their choice, Blanche at once selecting the most expensive trinkets, Philippe d'Aunay was thinking again of the meeting with the King.

'Each time he sees me, he asks me my name over again,' he thought. 'This must be the tenth time. And every time he makes some allusion to my brother.'

He felt a sort of dull apprehension and wondered why the King frightened him so much. No doubt it was because of the way he looked at you out of those over-large, unwinking eyes with their strange, indefinite colour which lay somewhere between grey and pale blue, like the ice on ponds on winter mornings, eyes that remained in the memory for hours after you had looked into them.

None of the three young people had noticed a tall man, dressed in hunting-clothes, who, from some distance off, while pretending to buy a buckle, had been watching them for some little time. This man was Count Robert of Artois.

'Philippe, I haven't enough money on me, do you mind paying?'

It was Jeanne who spoke, drawing Philippe out of his reflections. And Philippe responded with alacrity. Jeanne had chosen for Marguerite a girdle woven of gold thread.

'Oh, I should like one like it!' said Blanche.

But she had not the money either, and it was Philippe who paid.

It was always thus when he was in company with these ladies. They promised to pay him back later on, but they always forgot, and he was too much the gallant gentleman ever to remind them.

'Take care, my son,' Messire Gautier d'Aunay, his father, had said to him one day, 'the richest women are always the most expensive.'

He realised it when he went over his accounts. But he did not care. The Aunays were rich and their fiefs of Vémars and of d'Aulnay-les-Bondy, between Pontoise and Luzarches, brought them in a handsome income. Philippe told himself that, later on, his brilliant friendships would put him in the way of a large fortune. And for the moment nothing cost too much for the satisfaction of his passion.

He had the pretext, an expensive pretext, to rush off to the Hôtel-de-Nesle, where lived the King and Queen of Navarre, beyond the Seine. Going by the Pont Saint-Michel, it would take him but a few minutes.

He left the two princesses and quitted the Mercers' Hall.

Outside, the great bell of Notre-Dame had fallen silent and over all the island of the Cité lay a menacing and un-accustomed quiet. What was happening at Notre-Dame?

4

At the Great Door of Notre-Dame

THE ARCHERS HAD FORMED a cordon to keep the crowd out of the space in front of the cathedral. Heads appeared in curiosity at every window.

The mist had dissolved and a pale sunlight illumined the white stone of Notre-Dame of Paris. For the cathedral was only seventy years old, and work was still continuously in progress upon the decorations. It still had the brilliance of the new, and the light emphasised the curve of its ogival windows, pierced the lacework of its central rose and accentuated the teeming statues of its porches with rose-coloured shadows.

Already, for an hour, the sellers of chickens who, every morning, did business in front of the cathedral, had been driven back against the houses.

The crowing of a cock, stifling in its cage, split the silence, that weighty silence which had so surprised Philippe d'Aunay as he came out of the Mercers' Hall; while feathers floated head-high in the air.

Captain Alain de Pareilles stood stiffly to attention in front of his archers.

At the top of the steps leading up from the open space, the four Templars stood, their backs to the crowd, face to face with the Ecclesiastical Tribunal which sat between the open doors of the great portico. Bishops, canons, and clerics sat in rows upon benches specially placed for them.

People looked with curiosity at the three Cardinal Legates, sent especially by the Pope to signify that the sentence was without appeal and had the final approval of the Holy See. The attention of the spectators was also particularly held by Jean de Marigny, the young Archbishop of Sens, brother of the First Minister, who had conducted the whole prosecution, and by Brother Renaud, the King's confessor and Grand Inquisitor of France.

Some thirty monks, some in brown habits, some in white, stood behind the members of the Tribunal. The only civilian in the assembly, Jean Ployebouche, Provost of Paris, a man of some fifty years, thick-set and frowning, seemed not altogether happy in the company in which he found himself. He represented the royal power and was responsible for the maintenance of order. His eyes moved continuously from the crowd to the Captain of the Archers, from the Captain to the young Archbishop of Sens; one could imagine that he was thinking, 'Provided everything goes off quietly.'

The sun played upon the mitres, the crosses, the purple of the cardinalatial robes, the amaranth of the bishops, the cloaks of ermine and velvet, the gold of pectoral crosses, the steel of coats of mail and of the weapons of the guard. These brilliant, scintillating colours rendered more violent yet the contrast with the accused on whose account all this pomp was gathered together. The four ragged Templars, standing shoulder to shoulder, looked as if they had been sculptured out of cinders.

The Cardinal-Archbishop of Albano rose to his feet and read the heads of the judgment. He did it slowly and with emphasis, savouring the sound of his own voice, pleased both with himself and with the opportunity of appearing before a foreign audience. Every now and then he pretended to be horrified at having even to mention the crimes he was enumerating, and at these moments his reading assumed an unctuous majesty of diction in order to relate some new transgression, some as yet unmentioned crime, and to announce yet further evidence, of an appalling nature.

'We have heard the Brothers Géraud du Passage and Jean de Cugny, who assert with many others that they were compelled by force, upon being received into the Order, to spit upon the Cross, since, as they were told, it was only a piece of wood while the true God was in Heaven . . . We have heard Brother Guy Dauphin upon whom it was enjoined that, if one of his superiors were tormented by the flesh and desired to find satisfaction upon his body, he must consent to everything that was asked of him . . . We have heard upon this point the Sire de Molay who, under interrogation, has admitted and avowed that . . .'

The crowd had to listen hard to grasp the meaning of the words which were disfigured both by the Italian accent and the emphasis of their utterance. The Legate made too much of them and went on too long. The crowd began to grow impatient.

During this recital of accusation, false witness, and extorted confession, Jacques de Molay murmured to himself 'Lies . . . lies . . . lies.'

The hoarse repetition of this word uttered in an undertone, reached his companions.

The anger the Grand Master had felt rising in him during the ride in the wagon, far from diminishing, was increasing. The blood began to beat more strongly yet behind his sunken temples.

Nothing had happened to interrupt the progress of the nightmare. No band of ex-Templars had burst out of the crowd. Fate appeared inexorable.

'We have heard the Brother Hugues de Payraud, who admits that he obliged novices to deny Christ three times.'

Hugues de Payraud was the Brother Visitor. He turned to Jacques de Molay with an expression of horror and said in a low voice, 'Brother, Brother, could I really have said that?'

The four dignitaries were alone, abandoned by God and man, held as in a giant vice between the soldiers and the Tribunal, between the royal power and the power of the Church. Each word pronounced by the Cardinal-Legate but screwed the vice tighter, till it was clear that the nightmare could end only in death.

How could the Commissions of Inquiry have failed to understand, for it had been explained to them a hundred times, that this test of denial had been imposed upon the novices for the sole purpose of discovering their attitude in the event of their being taken a prisoner by the Saracens and called upon to deny their religion?

The Grand Master had a wild longing to throw himself at the Prelate's throat, beat him, throw his mitre to the ground, and strangle him; all that prevented him was the certainty of being stopped before he could ever reach him. Besides, it was not only the Legate whom he longed to attack, but the young Marigny too, the fop with the golden hair who adopted such a negligent air. But, above all, he longed to attack his three real absent enemies: the King, the Keeper of the Seals, and the Pope.

Powerless rage, heavier to bear than all his chains, impaired his vision, forming a red film before his eyes, and yet, something had to happen. . . . He was seized by so violent an attack of giddiness that he was afraid of falling to the ground. He did not even notice that Charnay had been seized by a similar fury and that the Preceptor of Normandy's scar had turned white across his crimson forehead.

The Legate was taking his time about the reading, lowering the parchment in his hand, only to raise it once again to the level of his eyes. He was making the performance last as long as possible. The depositions were over; the time had come to announce the sentence. The Legate continued, 'In consideration that the accused have avowed and recognised the above, they are condemned to solitary confinement for the term of their natural lives, that they may obtain the remission of their sins by means of their repentance. *In nomine patris. . . .*'

The Legate had finished. There was nothing left for him to do but sit down, roll up the parchment, and hand it to a priest.

At first there was no reaction from the crowd. After such a recital of crime, sentence of death had been so much expected that mere solitary confinement – that is to say, imprisonment for life, a dungeon, chains, and bread and water – appeared almost as an act of clemency.

Philip the Fair had perfectly gauged the situation. Popular opinion, taken aback, would accept without difficulty, almost disinterestedly, this ultimate resolution of a tragedy that had preoccupied it for seven years. The senior Legate and the young Archbishop of Sens exchanged an almost imperceptible smile of connivance.

'Brothers, Brothers,' stuttered the Brother Visitor, 'did I hear that correctly? They aren't going to kill us! They're going to spare us!'

His eyes filled with tears; his swollen hands trembled and his broken teeth parted as if he were about to laugh.

It was the sight of this hideous joy that let loose the flood-gates. For one instant Jacques de Molay looked at the half-witted face of a man who had once been brave and strong.

And suddenly from the top of the steps they heard a voice shout, 'I protest!'

And so powerful was the voice that at first they could not believe that it came from the Grand Master.

'I protest against an iniquitous sentence and I declare that the crimes of which we are accused are wholly invented!' cried Jacques de Molay.

A huge sigh came from the crowd. The Tribunal was thrown into confusion. The Cardinals looked at each other in stupefaction. No one had expected anything of the kind. Jean de Marigny leapt to his feet. The time for negligent airs had passed; he was pale and strained and trembling with rage.

'You are lying!' he shouted. 'You confessed before the Commission.'

From instinct, the archers had closed their ranks, awaiting an order.

'I am guilty,' went on Jacques de Molay, 'only of having yielded to your promises, your threats and your tortures. I protest, in the name of God who hears us, that the Order of which I am the Grand Master is innocent.'

And God indeed seemed to hear him, for the Grand Master's voice, caught up in the interior of the cathedral, reverberating in the vaults, returned as an echo, as if another, deeper voice, were repeating his words from the far end of the nave.

'You have confessed to sodomy!' cried Jean de Marigny.

'Under torture,' replied Molay.

'. . . under torture . . .' came the voice which seemed to resound from the tabernacle.

'You have admitted to heresy!'

'Under torture!'

'. . . under torture . . .' came the voice.

'I retract everything!' cried the Grand Master.

'. . . everything . . .' the whole cathedral seemed loudly to respond.

A new voice was raised. It was Geoffroy de Charnay, the Preceptor of Normandy, who, in his turn, was crossing swords with the Archbishop of Sens.

'Our weakness has been taken advantage of,' he said. 'We are the victims of your plotting and of your false promises. It is your hate and your vindictiveness that have brought us to this pass! But I, too, protest before God that we are innocent, and those who say otherwise are telling a damned lie.'

Then uproar broke loose. The monks, packed behind the Tribunal, began shouting, 'Heretics! To the stake with them, to the stake with the heretics!'

But their voices were soon drowned. With that feeling of generosity the populace always has for the weak and for courage in adversity, the majority of the crowd took the part of the Templars.

Fists were shaken at the judges. Disturbances began all over the square. There were shouts from the windows.

On the order of Alain de Pareilles, half the archers had formed up with linked arms to prevent the crowd swarming on to the staircase. The rest lined up with their pikes levelled at the populace.

The royal sergeants-at-arms were blindly raining down blows upon the crowd with their be-lilied staves. The merchants' baskets had been upset and the chickens screeched among the people's feet.

The Tribunal had risen to its feet in consternation. Jean de Marigny was conferring with the Provost of Paris.

'Decide anything you like, Monseigneur, anything you like,' the Provost was saying. 'But you can't leave them there. We shall all be overrun. You don't know what the people of Paris are capable of when they get out of hand.'

Jean de Marigny stretched out his hand and raised his episcopal crozier to indicate that he was about to speak. But no one wanted to listen to him any more. Insults were hurled at him.

'Torturer! False Bishop! God will punish you!'

'Speak, Monseigneur, speak!' The Provost was saying to him.

He was afraid for his job and his skin; he remembered the riots of 1306 when his predecessor, Provost Barbet, had had his house pillaged.

'I declare two of the condemned relapsed into heresy,' cried the Archbishop, shouting vainly. 'They have rejected the justice of the Church; the Church rejects them and remits them to the justice of the King.'

His words were lost in the hubbub. Then the whole Tribunal, like a flock of terrified guinea-fowl hurried into Notre-Dame and had the door quickly shut behind them.

Upon a sign from the Provost to Alain de Pareilles, a band

of archers rushed to the steps; the wagon was brought up and the prisoners were bundled into it with blows from pike-staves. They submitted with absolute docility. The Grand Master and the Preceptor of Normandy felt at once exhausted and relaxed. At last they were at peace with themselves. The other two were no longer capable of understanding anything.

The archers opened up a passage for the wagon, while Provost Ployebouche gave instructions to his sergeant-at-arms to clear the square as soon as possible. He was in a highly nervous condition, utterly beside himself.

'Take the prisoners back to the Temple,' he shouted to Alain de Pareilles. 'I shall go at once to inform the King.'

He took four sergeants-at-arms with him by way of escort.

5

Marguerite of Burgundy, Queen of Navarre

WHILE ALL THIS HAD been going on, Philippe d'Aunay had reached the Hôtel-de-Nesle. He had been asked to wait in the ante-room of the Queen of Navarre's private apartments. Time lagged. Philippe wondered whether Marguerite was detained by visitors or whether, quite simply, she was taking pleasure in keeping him waiting. It would be in character. And, quite possibly, after an hour or so, she would send to say that she could not see him. It made him furious.

Three years ago, when their liaison had begun, she would not have behaved like this. Or would she? He could no longer remember. He had succumbed to the delights of a new relationship in which vanity played as important a part as love. At that time he would have danced attendance for five hours at a stretch merely to catch sight of his mistress, to kiss her hand, and hear a whispered word promising a meeting.

But times had changed. The difficulties, which are the savour of a nascent love-affair, become intolerable after three years, and sometimes passion dies by the very thing that has brought it to birth. The continued uncertainty of meeting, appointments cancelled, the obligations of the Court, to which had to be added the eccentricities of Marguerite's own character, had aroused in Philippe a sense of exasperation, which could find expression only in anger and in making new demands upon her.

Marguerite seemed to take things much more easily. She enjoyed the double pleasure of deceiving her husband and torturing her lover. She was one of those women who can find satisfaction in love only through the spectacle of the suffering they inflict, till even that becomes a bore.

Not a day passed but Philippe told himself that a great love could find no satisfaction in adultery, and that he did not swear to break it off.

But he was weak, cowardly, and enmeshed. Like a gambler who doubles his stake, he followed up his fantasies of the past, his vain present, all the time he had wasted, and his former happiness. He lacked the courage to rise from the table and say, 'I've lost enough.'

And there he was, leaning against a window-frame, waiting to be told to come in.

To alleviate his impatience, he was watching the coming and going of the grooms in the courtyard of the house. They were leading out the horses to exercise on the little Pré-aux-Clercs near by. He watched the porters delivering sides of meat and baskets of vegetables.

The Hôtel-de-Nesle consisted of two distinct buildings: the Hôtel proper, which was of recent construction, and the tower erected under Philippe-Auguste, at the period when the town wall passed that way, in order to make a counterpart to the Tower of the Louvre on the left bank of the Seine. Six years earlier, Philip the Fair had bought the whole site from the Count Aumary de Nesle, and had granted it as a residence to his eldest son, the King of Navarre.[9]

Until then the tower had been used as a guardroom or garrison. It was Marguerite who had had it furnished as a retreat in which to meditate, or so she said, upon her Books of Hours above the flowing river. She declared that she needed solitude, and since she was known to be eccentric, Louis of Navarre had not been unduly surprised. In reality, she had desired this amenity merely for the purpose of receiving the good-looking Aunay the more easily.

For the latter, this had been a source of unparalleled pride. For him alone a Queen had turned a fortress into a love-nest.

And then, when his elder brother Gautier d'Aunay had become the lover of Blanche, the tower had also become the secret meeting-place of the new couple. The pretext had been easily conceived: Blanche merely came to visit her cousin and sister-in-law; and Marguerite had no wish but to be obliging.

But now, at this actual moment, as Philippe looked out upon the huge sombre tower, with its conical roof and high, narrow windows, overlooking the river, he could not help wondering whether other men had not shared those furtive embraces and tumultuous nights. Even to those who thought they knew her best, Marguerite was so unaccountable! And these last five days without a sign from her, when every circumstance lent itself to a meeting, were they not proof?

A door opened and a lady-in-waiting asked Philippe to follow her. His lips were dry and he felt a constriction about the heart, but he was determined not to let himself be put off this time. He walked down a long corridor and then the lady-in-waiting disappeared, while Philippe entered a low-ceilinged room, crowded with furniture, impregnated with that heady scent he knew so well, essence of jasmin brought by merchants from the Orient.

It took Philippe a moment to accustom himself to the twilight and heat of the room. A tree-trunk was smouldering above a heap of tinder-wood upon the great hearth.

'Madam . . .' he said.

A voice came from the end of the room, a rather hoarse and sleepy voice.

'Come over here, Messire.'

Was Marguerite alone? Was she daring to receive him in her room, without witnesses, when the King of Navarre might be in the vicinity?

He felt at once relieved and disappointed: the Queen of Navarre was not alone. She was reclining upon her bed, while an elderly woman-of-the-bedchamber, half-hidden by the curtain, was engaged in polishing her toe-nails.

Philippe went forward and in a courtly tone, which was at variance with his expression, announced that the Countess of Poitiers had sent him to ask after the Queen of Navarre, remit her compliments and deliver a present.

Marguerite listened without moving. Her beautiful naked arms were folded beneath her head and her eyes were half closed.

She was small, black-haired and olive-skinned. It was said that she had the most beautiful body in the world, and she was well aware of it.

Philippe looked at her round, sensual mouth, her short chin, her half-naked throat, and her plump, elegant legs revealed by the woman-of-the-bedchamber.

'Put the present on the table, I'll look at it in a moment,' said Marguerite.

She stretched and yawned. Philippe saw her pink tongue,

the roof of her mouth and her little white teeth. She yawned like a cat.

As yet, she had not once turned her eyes in his direction. He made an effort to keep himself under control. The woman-of-the-bedchamber looked covertly at Philippe in curiosity. He thought that his anger must be too apparent. He had never seen this particular duenna before. Was she newly in Marguerite's service?

'Am I to take back a reply to the Countess?' he asked.

'Oh!' cried Marguerite, sitting up, 'you're hurting me, woman.'

The woman murmured an excuse. Marguerite at last consented to look in Philippe's direction. She had beautiful dark, velvety eyes, which seemed to caress everyone and everything they looked upon.

'Tell my sister-in-law of Poitiers . . .' she said.

Philippe had moved to escape being observed by the woman-of-the-bedchamber. With a quick gesture of his hand he signed to Marguerite to send the old lady away. But Marguerite appeared not to understand; she smiled, but not in Philippe's direction; she seemed to be smiling into the void.

'On the other hand, perhaps not,' she went on. 'I'll write her a letter for you to give her.'

Then, to the woman-of-the-bedchamber, she said, 'That will do for the present. I must dress. Go and prepare my clothes.'

The old woman went into the next room but left the door open. Philippe realised that she was watching him.

Marguerite got up and, as she passed him, whispered almost without opening her lips, 'I love you.'

'Why haven't I seen you for five days?' he asked as quietly.

'Oh, how pretty it is,' she cried, unpacking the girdle.

'What good taste Jeanne has, and how I love her present!'

'Why haven't I seen you?' Philippe repeated in a low voice.

'It's the very thing to go with my new purse,' Marguerite went on. 'Messire d'Aunay, can you spare the time to wait while I write a word of thanks?'

She sat down at the table, took a goose's quill and a piece of paper[10] and signalled Philippe to draw near.

She wrote so that he could read the word over her shoulder: 'Prudence.'

Then to the woman in attendance, who could be heard in the neighbouring room, she cried: 'Madame de Comminges, will you fetch my daughter? I haven't given her a kiss all morning.'

The woman went out.

'You're lying,' said Philippe. 'Prudence is a good pretext for getting rid of one lover in order to receive others.'

She was not altogether lying. It is always towards the end of an affair, when lovers either begin to quarrel or get bored with each other, that they betray themselves to those about them, and that the world takes for something new what is in fact upon the point of coming to an end. Had Marguerite said something careless? Had Philippe's ill-temper been noted beyond the narrow world of Blanche and Jeanne? She felt absolutely certain of the porter and the chambermaid of the tower. They were two servants she had brought from Burgundy and whom she terrified with threats upon the one hand, and rewarded handsomely upon the other. But could one ever be certain? She felt that she was vaguely suspected. The King of Navarre had made several allusions to her success, husband's jokes which did not quite ring true. And then there was this new woman-of-the-bedchamber, Madame de Comminges, who had been forced upon her a few days ago in response to a recommendation from Monseigneur Charles of Valois. She was always trailing about in her widow's weeds. Marguerite felt herself less ready to take risks than in the past.

'You know, you're a bore,' she said. 'I love you and you never stop scolding me.'

'Well, I shall have no opportunity to be a bore tonight,' Philippe replied. 'The King told us himself that there was to be no Council, so you'll have all the time in the world to reassure your husband.'

From her expression Philippe could have guessed, had he not been so angry, that from that quarter at any rate he had nothing to fear.

'And I shall go and visit the whores!' he said.

'All right,' said Marguerite. 'I shall be delighted to know how they set about things.'

'Bitch! Bitch! Bitch!' thought Philippe. You never knew how to take her; she was as slippery as an eel.

She went to an open coffer, and took out a new purse of gold thread with three catches made of large precious stones. Philippe had never seen it before.

Two days earlier Marguerite had received it as a present from her sister-in-law, the Queen of England, by the hand of a discreet messenger who had brought two similar purses for Jeanne and Blanche. A note from Isabella asked them not to talk of them, for 'my husband watches carefully over my expenditure, and it might anger him.'

The three princesses had been somewhat surprised by their sister-in-law's unaccustomed kindness. 'She's having trouble at home,' they said to each other, 'and wants to be in our good books.'

'They go splendidly together,' said Marguerite, passing the girdle through the golden loops, holding it against her waist, and going to look at herself in a huge pewter mirror.

'Who gave you that purse?' asked Philippe.

'It was . . .'

She was quite simply going to tell him the truth. But she saw him stiffen with suspicion and was unable to resist teasing him.

'It was . . . someone,' she said.

'Who?'

'Guess.'

'Louis?'

'My husband isn't as generous as that!'

'Then, who?'

'Can't you guess?'

'I want to know. I have the right to know,' Philippe said, losing his temper. 'It's a present from a man, a rich man, a man in love . . . and because you've given him reason to be so, I should think.'

Marguerite went on looking at herself in the mirror, first trying the belt on one side, then on the other, then in the middle of her waist.

'It was Robert of Artois,' said Philippe.

'Oh, what bad taste you credit me with, Messire!' she said. 'That great lout, always smelling of game.'

Neither of them imagined how near they were to the truth, and what part Robert of Artois had played in the sending of the purse.

'Gaucher de Châtillon, then,' said Philippe. 'He's always hovering round you as he does round every woman he sees.'

Marguerite put her head on one side as if lost in thought.

'The High Constable?' she said. 'I hadn't noticed that he was interested in me, but since you tell me that he is . . . Thank you for drawing my attention to it.'

'I shall find out in the end.'

'When you've named everyone at the Court of France . . .'

She was going to add, 'Then perhaps you'll think of the Court of England.' But she was interrupted by the return of Madame de Comminges, who entered, pushing before her the Princess Jeanne, still almost an infant. The little girl walked slowly, made awkward by a long velvet dress embroidered with pearls. She bore no resemblance to her mother except for her round, swelling, almost convex brow. She was fair, had a thin nose and long eyelashes which fluttered over clear eyes. She might equally have been the daughter of the King of Navarre or of Philippe d'Aunay. But on that point, too, Philippe had never been able to discover the truth, and Marguerite was much too clever ever to give herself away on so important a matter. Every time Philippe saw the little Jeanne, he asked himself, 'Is she mine?' And he thought that one day he would have to bow as he received the orders of a princess who was perhaps his daughter and might well succeed to two thrones. For Louis of Navarre, the heir of France, and Marguerite his wife, had so far no other children.

Marguerite picked up the little Jeanne, kissed her forehead, and commenting that she looked well, handed her back to the woman-of-the-bedchamber.

'There, I've kissed her,' she said. 'You can take her away again.'

She became aware from Madame de Comminges's expression that the latter perfectly understood that she had only been sent to fetch the child in order to get rid of her for a moment. 'I must be relieved of this old woman,' thought Marguerite.

A lady-in-waiting entered hurriedly, asking if the King of Navarre were there.

'He's not usually to be found with me at this time of day,' said Marguerite.

'He's being searched for everywhere,' said the lady. 'The King wants him at once. There's an urgent Council at the palace.'

'Is it known what it's about?' Marguerite asked.

'If I understood aright, Madam, the Templars have rejected their sentence. The populace are rioting about Notre-Dame and the guards have been doubled everywhere.'

Marguerite and Philippe looked at each other. The same idea had struck them both and it had nothing to do with affairs of state. These events might compel Louis of Navarre to spend at least part of the night at the palace.

'Perhaps the day will not end as we thought,' said Philippe.

Marguerite looked at him for a moment and thought that she had made him suffer enough. He had resumed a respect-ful and distant mien; but his expression begged for happiness. She was moved by it and felt her love revive as in the early days.

'Perhaps, Messire,' she said.

At the same time, she was thinking that no one would ever love her more than he did.

She went over and picked up the piece of paper upon which she had written 'Prudence' and threw it into the fire, saying as she did so, 'I don't care for the letter I've written. I'll send another to the Countess of Poitiers later on; I shall hope for better news to give her. Good-bye, Messire.'

The Philippe who quitted the Hôtel-de-Nesle was not the same man who had entered it. On the strength of a single word of hope he had a new-found confidence in his mistress, in himself, in life in general, and this particular noon seemed radiant.

'She loves me as much as ever; I've been unjust to her,' he thought.

As he passed the guard, he ran into the Count of Artois who was coming in. One might have thought that the giant was following up Philippe's tracks. But it was not so. For the moment Artois was busy with other matters.

'Is Monseigneur the King of Navarre at home?' he asked Philippe.

'I know that they've been looking for him for the King's Council,' said Philippe.

'Were you sent to warn him?'

'Yes,' said Philippe instinctively.

And as soon as he had said it, he realised that the lie was foolish and too easy to check.

'I'm seeking him for the same reason,' said Artois. 'Monseigneur of Valois wishes to talk with him before the Council.'

They separated. But this chance meeting gave the giant a lead.

'Can it be he?' he suddenly thought as he crossed the courtyard. An hour earlier he had seen Philippe in the Mercers' Hall with Jeanne and Blanche. And now he had met him again at Marguerite's door.

'Is that young man their messenger, or is he the lover of one of them? If he is, I shall very soon know it.'

For he had lost no time since his return from England. Since entering Marguerite's service, Madame de Comminges sent him a report every day. He had a man of his own watching the surroundings of the Tower of Nesle at night. The net was spread. Bad luck to that gaily feathered bird should he be caught in it!

6

What Happened at the
King's Council

THE PROVOST OF PARIS, who had dashed off to see the King, found him in good humour. Philip the Fair was engaged in admiring three tall greyhounds which had been sent to him with the following letter:

Sire,

My nephew, abashed by his offence, has confessed to me that these three greyhounds, while held by him on a leash, have run against you. Humble though they are as an offering, I do not feel that I am worthy to keep them now that they have touched so high and mighty a Prince. They arrived the day before yesterday from England. I ask you to accept them that they may bear towards you the same devotion and humility as your servant,

SPINELLO TOLOMEI

'A clever man, this Tolomei,' said Philip the Fair.

Though he refused all other presents he was prepared to accept hounds. He had the best packs in the world, and to give him animals as beautiful as these was to humour his only passion.

While the Provost was explaining what had happened at Notre-Dame, Philip the Fair continued fondling the three greyhounds, raising their pendulous lips to examine their white teeth and black jaws, patting their deep chests.

Between the King and all animals, particularly dogs, there was an immediate, secret, silent understanding. Unlike men, dogs were never afraid of him. And, already, the largest of the three greyhounds had come of his own accord to place his head upon the King's knee and gaze up at his new master.

'Bouville!' called Philip the Fair.

Hugues de Bouville, first Chamberlain to the King, whose hair alternated curiously between white and black locks, making him look like a piebald horse, entered.

'Bouville, assemble the Inner Council within the hour,' said the King.

Then, dismissing the Provost, while giving him to understand that it was as much as his life was worth to allow the least disturbance to take place in Paris, Philip the Fair remained meditating in company with his hounds.

He decided that the largest greyhound, which seemed already to be attached to him, should be called Lombard, because he came from an Italian banker.

Soon the Inner Council was assembled. It did not meet in the vast Hall of Justice, which could hold a hundred people, and was used for the Grand Council, but in a small neighbouring room where a fire burned on the hearth.

The members of this smaller Council took their places round a long table to decide the fate of the Templars. The King sat at one end, his elbow on the arm of his great chair, his chin cupped in his hand. To his right sat Enguerrand de

Marigny, Coadjutor and Rector of the kingdom, Nogaret, the
Keeper of the Seals, Raoul de Presles, Lord Chief Justice, and
two other lawyers as secretaries; to his left sat his eldest
son, King Louis of Navarre, who had at last been found, and
Hugues de Bouville, the Grand Chamberlain. Two places
remained vacant, those of the Count of Poitiers, who had
been sent on a mission, and of Prince Charles, the King's
youngest son, who had gone hunting that morning and had
not been found in time. There was only Monseigneur of
Valois still to come. He had been sent for to his house, where,
doubtless, he was conspiring as he did before every Council.
The King had decided to begin without him.

Enguerrand de Marigny spoke first. Six years older than
Philip the Fair, less tall but of as imposing an aspect, this
great lord had not been born noble. He came of middle
class Norman stock, and had been called Enguerrand Le
Portier before becoming the Lord of Marigny. He had had a
fabulous career, which had aroused as much jealousy as
respect, and the title of Coadjutor, created especially for him,
had made him the King's *alter ego*. He was fifty-two years
old, of solid aspect, large-chinned, rugged-skinned, and lived
magnificently upon the huge fortune he had acquired. He
was considered to have the greatest gift for speaking in the
kingdom and his political intellect dominated his period from
a lofty eminence.

It took him only a few minutes to furnish a complete picture of the situation based upon the report that his brother,
the Archbishop of Sens, had given him.

'The Grand Master and the Preceptor of Normandy have
been remitted into your hands, Sire, by the Ecclesiastical
Commission,' he said. 'You have absolute power to dispose of
them as you will. Could we hope for anything better?'

He was interrupted by the door bursting open. Monseigneur of Valois, the King's brother and Emperor of Constantinople, entered. Without bothering to find out what had already been said, he cried, 'What's this I hear, Brother? Messire Le Portier de Marigny (he always inisted on saying "Le Portier") thinks that nothing could be better? Well, Brother, your counsellors are content with very little! I wonder when they'll think things are going badly!'

In Charles of Valois's presence, everything seemed suddenly to quicken in tempo. He seemed to move in a hurricane. He was two years younger than Philip the Fair, whom he resembled little. He was as excitable as the other was calm.

Semi-bald, with a large nose, his face blotched from a life of campaigning and from the excesses of the table, carrying a paunch before him, he was dressed with an almost oriental sumptuousness which, upon anyone but him, would have looked absurd. Born close to the throne of France, inconsolable at not having succeeded to it, this mischief-making prince had never ceased travelling the world in search of another throne upon which to take his seat. For a short time he had been King of Aragon, had then renounced that kingdom in order to intrigue for the crown of Emperor of Germany; but he had been defeated in the election. By his second marriage, to Catherine of Courtenay, he was Emperor-Pretender to Constantinople, though a real Emperor, Andronic II Paleologos, was at this moment ruling in Byzantium. Everything else about him was in keeping. His greatest claims to fame were his lightning campaign in Guyenne in 1297, for he was a good general, and his campaign in Tuscany where, supporting the Guelfs against the Ghibellines, he had ravaged Florence and sent a certain political rhymer, named Dante, into exile. It was upon this account that the late Pope had created him Count of Romagna. Valois kept royal state, had his court and his own chancellor; and he loathed Enguerrand de Marigny for many reasons, for his plebeian birth, for his title of Coadjutor, because his statue had been placed among those of kings in the Mercers' Hall, because his policy was hostile to the great feudal barons, indeed on every possible count. Valois could not stomach the fact, grandson of Saint Louis as he was, that the kingdom should be governed by a man of the people. On this particular day he was dressed in blue and gold from hat to shoes.

'What!' he cried. 'Four senile old men whose fate, so we were told, was all fixed – and how successfully, alas – can hold the royal power in check, and you say that all is for the best! The populace are spitting upon the verdict of the Ecclesiastical Commission – and what a Commission it is! – though it does represent the Church! And everything is for the best! The crowd is shouting – and do you know what, Brother? – *death* to you; and everything is for the best! Very well, Brother, everything is undoubtedly for the best!'

He raised his hands, which were fine and laden with rings, and sat down in the nearest chair at the bottom end of the table, as if to show that, if he could not sit at the King's right hand, he would sit opposite him.

Enguerrand de Marigny stood up, a flicker of irony showing at the corners of his mouth.

'Monseigneur of Valois must be misinformed,' he said calmly. 'Of the four old men of whom he speaks only two protested against their sentence. As for the populace, every report I have assures me that they are much divided in opinion.'

'Divided!' cried Charles of Valois. 'By what right are they

divided? Who asks the people their opinion? You do, Messire de Marigny, and one may well guess why. This is the result of your charming policy of assembling the middle class, the serfs and the peasants to approve the King's decisions. Now the populace think they can do as they please!'

In every period and in every country there have always been two parties: the reactionary and the progressive. These two tendencies came face to face at the King's Council. Charles of Valois considered himself the natural head of the great barons. He was the incarnation of the permanence of the past, and his political gospel derived from certain principles which he was prepared to defend to the last: the right of private war between the great barons, the right of the great feudal overlords to coin money within their own territories, a return to the morality of chivalry, submission to the Holy See as the supreme arbitrating power, and the maintenance of the feudal organisation of society in its integrity. All those things which had become established owing to the circumstances of society in previous centuries and which now Philip the Fair, inspired by Marigny, had abolished or still sought to overthrow.

Enguerrand de Marigny stood for progress. His main ideas concerned the centralisation of power, the unification of finance and administration, the independence of the civil power from religious authority, external peace by fortifying strategic towns and permanently garrisoning them, internal peace by enforcing submission to the royal authority, the augmentation of production and commerce, and the security of communications. But there was another side to the medal: police proliferated, and they were as expensive to maintain as fortresses were to build.

Vehemently opposed by the feudal party, Enguerrand succeeded in rallying to the King a new and growing class which was gradually becoming aware of its own importance: the middle class. On many occasions, for instance, when it was a question of raising taxes or over the affair of the Templars, he had called upon the middle class of Paris to gather before the Palace of the Cité. He had done the same thing in various provincial towns. He had in his mind the example of England, where the House of Commons was already functioning.

As yet, these small French assemblies had no right to discuss, they were merely to listen to the measures the King proposed and approve them.[11]

Blundering though he was in some ways, Valois was far from being a fool. He never missed an opportunity of trying to discredit Marigny. Their opposition, for long secret, had become an open struggle some months since, of which this particular Council of the 18th March was but a phase.

The controversy had taken a violent turn and argument grew heated.

'If the great barons, of which you, Monseigneur, are the greatest,' said Marigny, 'had submitted more willingly to the royal edicts, we should not have had to rely upon the support of the people.'

'A fine support indeed!' cried Valois. 'It's clear that you learnt no lesson from the riots of 1306, when the King and yourself had to take refuge in the Temple from a Paris in uproar! I tell you that if you go on like this, it won't be long before the middle class will govern without the King, and your assemblies will make the laws.'

The King remained silent, his chin cupped in his hand, and his wide-open eyes staring straight before him. He never blinked, and it was this peculiarity that gave his gaze a strangeness which frightened everyone.

Marigny turned towards him as if to ask him to use his authority to stop an argument which was getting away from the point at issue.

Philip the Fair raised his chin a little and said, 'Brother, our concern today is with the Templars.'

'Very well,' said Valois rapping the table, 'let's concern ourselves with the Templars.'

'Nogaret!' murmured the King.

The Keeper of the Seals rose to his feet. Since the beginning of the Council he had been burning with anger and was only waiting an opportunity to show it. A fanatic for the public weal and for the policy of the State, the affair of the Templars was *his* affair, and he brought to it an energy which was both tireless and limitless. Moreover, he owed his high position to this prosecution, for, at the dramatic Council of 1307, when the Archbishop of Narbonne, who at that time held the Seals, refused to apply them to the order for the Templars' arrest, Philip the Fair had taken the Seals from the Archbishop's hand and had placed them in Nogaret's. Dark, lanky, with a long face and narrow eyes, he was constantly fidgeting with some part of his clothing or biting the nail of one of his flat fingers. He was ardent, austere, and as hard as the scythe of death.

'Sire, the event that has just occurred, monstrous and terrible though it is to think on and horrible to hear,' he began in a rapid, emphatic voice, 'proves that every indulgence, every clemency you accord these devil's disciples is a weakness that turns back upon yourself.'

'It is quite true,' said Philip the Fair, turning towards Valois, 'that the clemency you advised, Brother, and that my daughter of England sent to ask of me, has not borne good fruit. Go on, Nogaret.'

'These vile dogs do not deserve to be left alive; instead of blessing the clemency of their judges, they took advantage of it to insult both the Church and the King. The Templars are heretics . . .'

'Were,' interrupted Charles of Valois.

'You were saying, Monseigneur?' asked Nogaret impatiently.

'I said *were*, Messire, because if my memory serves me right, of the fifteen thousand Templars that existed in France, you've only got four in your hands at the present moment; and it's embarrassing, I agree, that after seven years of trial, they should still insist upon their innocence! It seems to me that in the old days, Messire de Nogaret, you moved more swiftly, when at a single blow you eliminated a pope.'

Nogaret trembled with rage and his complexion grew darker yet under the blue shadow of his beard. He it was who had gone to depose old Pope Boniface VIII, who was eighty-six years of age, by hitting him in the face and pulling him off his pontifical throne by the beard. The Chancellor's adversaries never failed to remind him of this incident. Nogaret had been excommunicated for excess of zeal. And it had required all the authority that Philip the Fair had over Clement V to get the excommunication cancelled.

'We know, Monseigneur,' he replied, 'that you have always supported the Templars. Doubtless you were counting upon their armies to reconquer, even to the utter ruin of France, the phantom throne of Constantinople upon which you have never as yet been able to sit.'

He had returned insult for insult, and his complexion returned almost to normal.

'By thunder!' cried Valois, leaping to his feet and upsetting his chair behind him.

There was a barking from beneath the table at which

everyone jumped except Philip the Fair, while the King of
Navarre burst out laughing. The barking came from the
largest greyhound. Philip the Fair had kept him close and he
was not yet accustomed to these outbursts.

'Louis, be quiet,' said Philip the Fair, glancing coldly at his
son.

Then he clicked his fingers, saying, 'Lombard, stop it!'
Pulling the dog's head against his leg, he stroked it for a
moment.

Louis of Navarre, who was already nicknamed 'le Hutin',
that is to say the wayward fool, lowered his head to conceal
his inability to control his silly laughter. He was twenty-eight
years old, but his mental development was no greater than at
seventeen. He had his father's eyes, but with the difference
that his gaze was weak and lacked directness, and his father's
hair but without its lustre.

'Sire,' said Charles of Valois when Bouville, the Chamberlain, had picked up his chair for him, 'Sire, my Brother, God
is my witness that I have never desired anything but your
interest and your glory.'

Philip the Fair turned his eyes upon him, and Charles
of Valois felt his assurance ebbing. Nevertheless he went on,
'It is only of you I think, Brother, when I see all that has made
the strength of the kingdom being wantonly destroyed.
Without the Templars and without the Chivalry of France,
how can you undertake a crusade should the necessity arise?'

It was Marigny who replied.

'Under our King's wise reign,' he said, 'we have had no need
of a crusade, precisely because the Chivalry has remained
quiet, Monseigneur, and there has been no necessity to lead it
overseas to expend its ardour.'

'And the question of the Faith, Messire?'

'The gold taken from the Templars has swollen the Treasury, Monseigneur, as has the enormous trade and commerce that used to be carried on behind the banners of the Faith; goods are diffused just as well without crusades.'

'Messire, you talk like an infidel!'

'I talk like a servant of the kingdom, Monseigneur!'

The King lightly tapped the table.

'Brother,' he said once more, 'we have met to discuss the Templars. I ask you for your counsel.'

'My counsel . . . my counsel?' Valois repeated, taken aback.

He was always ready to reform the universe, but never to furnish any precise opinion.

'Well, Brother, let those who have conducted the business so well' – he indicated Nogaret and Marigny – 'inspire you with suggestions as to how it should be brought to an end. As far as I am concerned . . .'

He made the gesture of Pilate.

The Keeper of the Seals and the Coadjutor exchanged a glance.

'Louis, your counsel,' said the King.

Louis of Navarre gave a start, and took a moment to reply, in the first place because he had not the remotest idea what to say and in the second because he was sucking a sweet made of honey and it had stuck in his teeth.

'Supposing we handed over the Templars to the Pope,' he said at last.

'Be quiet, Louis,' said the King, shrugging his shoulders.

And Marigny raised his eyebrows in commiseration.

To send the Grand Master back to the jurisdiction of the Pope was to begin again at the beginning, to put everything in question once more, the whole basis and form of procedure, to give up the legal powers extracted with such difficulty from the Councils, to annul the whole effort of seven years and open the way once again to every ruse of the defence.

'And to think that this idiot is going to succeed me,' thought Philip the Fair, looking at his son. 'One can only hope that he will mature between now and then.'

A March shower rustled against the leaded windows.

'Bouville?' said the King.

Hugues de Bouville thought that the King was asking him his opinion. No one could have had greater devotion than the Grand Chamberlain, or greater obedience, fidelity, and desire to please, but he had no mental initiative. As always, he wondered what Philip the Fair wished to hear.

'I'm thinking, Sire, I'm thinking,' he replied.

'Send for candles, one can't see,' said the King. 'Nogaret, what are your views?'

'That those who have fallen into heresy should suffer the punishment for heresy, and without delay,' replied the Keeper of the Seals.

'What about the populace?' asked Philip the Fair, turning to Marigny.

'Their excitement will subside as soon as those who are its cause no longer exist,' said the Coadjutor.

Charles of Valois made a last effort.

'Brother,' he said, 'you must take into consideration the fact that the Grand Master ranked as a sovereign prince. To put him to death is contrary to the principle by which crowned heads are protected . . .'

The King's glance cut him short.

For a short while there was an oppressive silence, then Philip the Fair said, 'Jacques de Molay and Geoffroy de Charnay will be burned to death tonight on the Island of

Jews[12] opposite the Palace. Their rebellion was public; their punishment shall be public. I have spoken.'

He got up and everyone present followed his example.

'You will make out the order, Messire de Presles. I wish you all to be present at the execution, Messires, and that our son Charles should be present also. You will inform him, my son,' he said, looking at Louis of Navarre.

Then he called, 'Lombard!'

He went out with his hound at his heels.

At this Council, in which two kings, an emperor and a viceroy had taken part, two men had been condemned to death. But not for an instant had anyone felt that they were dealing with two human lives; it was a matter of politics.

'Nephew,' said Charles of Valois to Louis le Hutin, 'we have been present today at the demise of Chivalry.'

7

The Tower of Love

Night had fallen. Upon the gentle breeze were borne the odours of wet earth, mud and springing sap. Black clouds were flowing across a starless sky.

A boat, putting off from the river bank by the Tower of the Louvre, drifted across the Seine, whose waters gleamed like the oily surface of an old breastplate.

There were two passengers seated in the boat's stern, their faces hidden by the high collars of their cloaks.

'Funny weather today,' said the ferryman, bending slowly to his oars. 'In the morning you wake up to such a mist that you can't see two fathoms distance. And then about ten o'clock out comes the sun. One says to oneself "Here's spring on the way". And no sooner said than hailstorms set in for the afternoon. And now the wind's getting up, and there's going to be quite a blow, that's certain. Funny weather.'

'Get a move on,' said one of the passengers.

'I'm doing the best I can. Getting old, that's what it is. I'll be fifty-three at the feast of Saint Michael. I'm no longer as strong as you are, young sirs,' said the ferryman.

He was dressed in rags and seemed to take pleasure in his own querulous speech.

'You really want to go to the Tower of Nesle?' he asked. 'Is there anywhere to land there?'

'Of course,' replied the same passenger.

'We don't go there much, you know. It's little frequented.'

Some little distance away, on the left, the lights of the Island of Jews twinkled, and, still farther off, shone the lighted windows of the palace. Over there many boats were going to and fro.

'Well, gentlemen, aren't you going to watch the Templars grilled?' went on the ferryman. 'I'm told that the King is going to be there with his sons. Is that true?'

'So it seems,' said the passenger.

'And will the Princesses be there too?'

'I don't know. I expect so,' said the passenger, turning his head away to indicate that he had no wish to pursue the conversation.

Then he said in a low voice to his companion, between his teeth, 'I don't like this fellow, he talks too much.'

The other passenger carelessly shrugged his shoulders. Then, after a silence, he whispered, 'Who let you know?'

'It was through Jeanne, as always,' the first replied.

'Dear Countess Jeanne, how much we owe her!'

With every stroke of the oars, the Tower of Nesle drew nearer, a high black silhouette against the dark sky.

The taller of the passengers, he who had spoken second, placed a hand on his companion's arm.

'Gautier,' he murmured, 'I'm happy tonight. Are you?'

'I'm well content, Philippe.'

Thus spoke the two brothers Aunay, Gautier and Philippe, as they went to the meeting Blanche and Marguerite had arranged as soon as they knew their husbands would be detained by the King. And it was the Countess of Poitiers who, once more a go-between, had delivered the message.

Philippe d'Aunay found it difficult to keep his happiness and impatience under control. His distress of the morning had disappeared, all his suspicions seemed unjust and vain. Marguerite had sent for him; for him Marguerite was running every risk; in a few moments he would be holding her in his arms and he swore that he would be the most tender, gay and ardent lover in the world.

The boat grounded on the bank over which rose the high wall of the tower. The last spate had left a shoal of mud.

The ferryman lent his arm to assist the two young men ashore.

'You understand what you've got to do, fellow?' said Gautier. 'You'll wait for us close by and don't be seen.'

'I'll wait for the rest of my life, young sir, if you'll pay me for it,' said the ferryman.

'Half the night will be enough,' said Gautier.

He gave him a silver groat, twelve times what the journey was worth, and promised him another upon their return. The ferryman bowed low.

Taking care not to slip or get too muddy, the two brothers crossed the short distance to a postern and knocked a pre-arranged signal. The door was silently opened.

'Good evening, Sirs,' said the maid whom Marguerite had brought from Burgundy.

She carried a lantern and, having barricaded the door behind them, led the way into a turret staircase.

She showed them into the big room of the tower on the first floor. Its only light was a huge fire of logs on an open hearth. The glow rose and was lost among the tops of the twelve arches supporting the barrel roof.

Like Marguerite's, this room too was scented with jasmin; the furnishings seemed impregnated with it, the gold-embroidered hangings on the walls, the carpets, the furs of wild beasts spread about on low beds in the oriental manner.

The princesses were not there. The maid went out, saying that she would inform them of their arrival.

The two young men, having taken off their cloaks, went over to the fire and automatically held out their hands to the warmth.

Gautier d'Aunay was two years older than his brother, whom he very much resembled, though he was shorter, more solidly built and fairer. He had a thick neck, pink cheeks and laughed at life. He was not, as was his brother, a prey to passion. He was married – and well married – to a Montmorency by whom he already had three children.

'I always wonder,' he said, as he warmed his hands, 'why Blanche took me for a lover and, indeed, why she has a lover at all. As for Marguerite, it's obvious. One's only got to look at Louis of Navarre, with his downcast eyes, his gawky walk and hollow chest, and then compare him with you, to understand. And then, of course, there are other reasons of which we know.'

He was alluding to certain secrets of the alcove, to the King of Navarre's lack of sexual vigour and to the disharmony existing between husband and wife.

'But I don't understand Blanche,' Gautier d'Aunay went on. 'She's got a good-looking husband, much better-looking than I am. Of course he is, Philippe, don't protest. He looks exactly like his father the King. He loves her and, I believe, whatever she may say, that she loves him. Then why does she do it? Every time I see her I wonder why such a piece of luck should have come my way.'

'Because she wants to do the same as her cousin,' Philippe replied.

There were light steps and whisperings in the passage that led from the tower to the house, and the two princesses came in.

Philippe moved quickly towards Marguerite but suddenly stopped short. He had caught sight, at his mistress's belt, of the gold purse with the precious stones that had so much angered him in the morning.

'What's the matter with you, Philippe darling?' Marguerite asked, her arms extended towards him, her face raised to receive a kiss. 'Aren't you happy this evening?'

'Perfectly,' he answered coldly.

'What's happened? What are you angry about now?'

'Have you put that on merely to annoy me?' asked Philippe, pointing to the purse.

She laughed loudly and happily.

'How silly you are, how jealous and how sweet! Didn't you realise that I was teasing you? Just to calm you down, I'll give you the purse. You'll know then that it was no present from a lover.'

She took the purse from her waist and attached it to Philippe's belt. He was bewildered and made a gesture of protest.

'Yes, yes, I want you to have it,' she said. 'Now it really is a love-gauge for you. No, don't refuse. Nothing is too fine for my beautiful Philippe. But don't ask me again where the purse came from, or I shall have to take it back. I can only swear to you that it was not given me by a man. Besides, Blanche has got one too. Blanche,' she said, turning to her cousin, 'show your purse to Philippe. I have given him mine.'

Blanche was lying on one of the beds in the darkest part of the room. Gautier was beside her, kneeling on one knee and covering her throat and hands with kisses.

'I'll wager,' Marguerite murmured in Philippe's ear, 'that within a minute your brother will have received a similar present.'

Blanche raised herself on an elbow and said, 'Isn't it very rash, Marguerite, and have we the right to do it?'

'Of course,' Marguerite answered. 'No one but Jeanne has seen them or even knows that we have received them.'

'All right,' cried Blanche; 'I don't want my beautiful lover to be less loved and less adorned than yours.'

And she took off her purse which Gautier accepted with an easy grace since his brother had already done so.

Marguerite gave Philippe a look which said, 'Didn't I tell you so?'

Philippe smiled at her. 'How astonishing Marguerite is,' he thought.

He could never make her out or understand her. Was she the same woman who that morning had been cruel, teasing, perfidious, who had played with him as she might have turned a pheasant on a spit, and who now, having given him a present worth a hundred and fifty pounds, lay in his arms, submissive, tender, almost quivering?

'I believe the reason I love you so much,' he murmured, 'is because I don't understand you.'

No compliment could have given Marguerite greater pleasure. She thanked Philippe by burying her lips in his neck. Suddenly she disengaged herself and stood listening. Then she cried, 'Do you hear them? The Templars. They're being led out to the stake.'

Bright-eyed, her face alive with a sinister curiosity, she dragged Philippe to the window, a high funnel-shaped loop-hole built in the thickness of the wall, and opened the casement.

The loud murmuring of the crowd flowed into the room.

'Blanche, Gautier, come and look!' said Marguerite.

But Blanche replied in a happy, quavering voice, 'Oh! no, I'm much too happy where I am.'

Between the two princesses and their lovers all shame had long since vanished. It was their custom to enjoy all the pleasures of love in each other's presence. If Blanche on occasion turned her eyes away, and hid her nakedness in the shadowy corners of the room, Marguerite derived an added pleasure from watching others making love, as she did from being watched herself.

But at the moment, glued to the window, she was spell-bound by the spectacle of what was taking place in the middle of the Seine. There, on the Island of the Jews, a hundred archers, drawn up in a circle, held lighted torches in their hands; and the flames of the torches, flaring in the wind, formed a central pool of light in which could clearly be seen the huge pile of faggots and the assistant-executioners clambering over it and stacking heaps of logs. On the near side of the archers, the island, which normally was nothing but a field where cows and goats grazed, was covered with people; while a fleet of boats upon the river carried others who wished to watch the execution.

Coming from the right bank, a larger boat than the rest, carrying standing men-at-arms, had just come alongside the island. Two tall grey figures disembarked from it. They wore curious hats and were preceded by a monk bearing a cross. The murmuring of the crowd became a clamour. Almost at the same instant lights went on in the great loggia in the water-tower which stood on the point of the palace garden. Shadows emerged from the darkness of the loggia, and suddenly the clamouring of the crowd ceased. The King and his Council had taken their places.

Marguerite burst out laughing, a long, piercing, endless laugh.

'Why are you laughing?' Philippe asked.

'Because Louis is over there,' she said. 'And if it were daylight, he would be able to see me.'

Her eyes were bright; her black curls danced above the curve of her brow. With a rapid movement she pulled her dress from her beautiful amber shoulders, and let her clothes fall to the ground, standing quite naked, as if she wished to set at defiance the husband she detested across the intervening distance of the night. She took Philippe's hands and drew them to her hips.

At the far end of the room Blanche and Gautier were lying close in a confused embrace. Blanche's body had a pearly lustre.

Away in the centre of the river the clamour had begun again. The Templars were being bound to the pyre which was soon to be set alight.

Marguerite shivered in the night air and drew nearer the fire. For a moment she gazed into the hearth, exposing herself to the heat of the burning wood till its caress became intolerable. The flames threw dancing lights upon her skin.

'They're going to burn, they're going to be grilled,' she said in a hoarse, breathless voice, 'while we . . .'

Her eye sought in the heart of the fire infernal visions to excite her pleasure.

Abruptly she turned to face Philippe and gave herself to

him, standing, as the nymphs in the legend gave themselves to the fauns.

The fire cast their huge shadow across the wall and up to the beams in the roof.

8

'I Summon to the Tribunal of Heaven . . .'

ONLY A NARROW CHANNEL separated the palace garden from the Island of Jews. The pyre had been arranged so as to face the royal loggia; from his place Philip the Fair had a perfect view.

Spectators were still arriving in great numbers upon both banks of the river, and the island itself had almost disappeared beneath the crowd. The ferrymen had made a fortune tonight.

But the archers had been well disposed, and police agents mingled with the crowd. Pickets of men-at-arms had been posted on the bridges and upon all the roads leading to the Seine. There was nothing to fear.

'Marigny, you may compliment the Provost,' said the King to the Coadjutor who was standing by him.

The excitement, which in the morning had given rise to fears of revolution, had turned to holiday mood, a sort of outlandish gaiety, a tragic show offered by the King to his capital. There was an atmosphere of the fair-ground over all. Tramps mingled with townsfolk who had brought their families with them, painted and powdered prostitutes had come from the alleys behind Notre-Dame where they exercised their profession. Guttersnipes wove their way between people's legs to the front rows. A few Jews, standing in close, fearful groups, yellow badges upon their coats, had come to watch the execution which, for once, was not of one of their number.

Beautiful ladies in furred surcoats, in search of violent emotion, clung to their gallants, uttering little nervous cries.

It was turning chilly, and the wind blew in short gusts. The glow of the torches threw red lights upon the rippling surface of the river.

Messire Alain de Pareilles, the visor of his helmet raised, sat his horse in front of his archers, looking as bored as ever.

The pyre stood higher than a man's head; the chief executioner and his assistants, clothed in red and wearing hoods, were busying themselves about the pyre, aligning logs, preparing reserve faggots, with the precision of careful professionals.

Upon the summit of the pyre the Grand Master of the Templars and the Preceptor of Normandy were bound to stakes, side by side, facing the royal loggia. Upon their heads had been placed the infamous paper mitres which marked them as heretics. The wind played in their beards.

A monk, the same that Marguerite had seen from the Tower of Nesle, held up to them a great Cross while making the last exhortations. The crowd about him fell silent to hear what he said.

'In a moment you will appear before God,' cried the monk. 'There is still time to confess your faults and to repent. I adjure you to do so for the last time.'

Above him, the condemned men, motionless between

earth and sky, as if already detached from life, answered nothing. Their eyes, gazing down upon him, reflected utter contempt.

'They refuse to confess; they have not repented,' the crowd could be heard muttering.

The silence grew more profound, more dense. The monk had fallen to his knees and was murmuring prayers. The chief executioner took a glowing brand of tow from the hand of one of his assistants and waved it several times in a circle to encourage the flame.

A child sneezed and there was the sound of a slap.

Captain Alain de Pareilles turned towards the royal loggia as if awaiting an order, and all eyes, all heads were turned in the same direction. It was as if the whole crowd were holding its breath.

Philip the Fair was standing at the balustrade, the members of his Council motionless about him. The line of their faces was detached from the background by the light of the torches. They were like a bas-relief in rose-coloured marble sculptured across the flank of the tower.

Even the condemned raised their eyes to the loggia. The King's gaze met that of the Grand Master. They seemed to be taking each other's measure, their glances interlocked. Who could tell what thoughts were theirs, what emotions, what memories surged within these two enemies? Instinctively the crowd felt that something grand, something terrible and superhuman had become implicit in this mute confrontation between the all-powerful prince, surrounded by the servants of his will, and the Grand Master of Chivalry bound to the stake of infamy, between these two men whom birth and the accident of history had raised above all other men.

Would Philip the Fair, with a gesture of ultimate clemency,

reprieve the condemned? Would Jacques de Molay at this final moment humiliate himself and plead for mercy?

The King made a sign with his hand and an emerald shone upon his finger. Alain de Pareilles repeated the gesture to the executioner, who placed the lighted brand of tow under the faggots and brushwood of the pyre. A huge sigh rose from thousands of breasts, a sigh of relief and horror, excitement and dismay, a sigh made up of anguish and of revulsion and of pleasure.

Several women screamed. Children hid their heads in their parents' clothes. A man's voice was heard shouting, 'I told you not to come!'

Smoke was rising in dense spirals which a gust of wind blew towards the loggia.

Monseigneur of Valois began coughing with the maximum of ostentation. He took a step backwards between Nogaret and Marigny and said, 'If this goes on, we shall all be suffocated before your Templars are burned. You might at least have seen that they used dry wood.'

No one replied to his remark. Nogaret, with taut muscles and fiery eye, was greedily savouring his triumph. This pyre was the crown to seven years of struggle and of exhausting journeys, the result of thousands of words intended to convince, thousands of pages written to prove. 'Go on, flame and burn,' he thought. 'You've held me at bay long enough. But I was in the right, and you're defeated.'

Enguerrand de Marigny, taking his attitude from the King's, forced himself to remain impassive and to look upon the execution as one of the necessities of power. 'It had to be, it had to be,' he kept repeating to himself. But watching men die, he could not but help thinking of death. The two condemned men before him ceased to be mere political abstractions. That they should have been declared prejudicial to public order in no way prevented their being creatures of flesh and blood, capable of thought, desire and suffering, like any one else, indeed like himself. 'In their place, would I have been capable of such courage?' Marigny asked himself, making no effort to restrain his admiration. The words 'in their place' gave him a cold shiver down the spine. He recovered himself. 'Where the deuce do these thoughts come from?' he thought. 'I am as prone to illness and accident as anyone else, but nothing more. There is never a moment when my person is not guarded. I am as untouchable as the King.'

But seven years earlier the Grand Master had been in no danger, no one had been more powerful.

Hugues de Bouville, the good Chamberlain with the white and black hair, was secretly praying.

The wind veered, and the smoke, growing denser and rising higher every second, enveloped the condemned, almost hiding them from the crowd.

The two old men could be heard coughing and choking at their stakes.

Louis of Navarre, rubbing his red eyes, laughed inanely.

His brother Charles, the youngest of Philip the Fair's sons, turned his face away. It was obvious that he found the spectacle painful. He was twenty years old; he was slender and had a pink and white complexion. Those who had known his father at the same age said that the resemblance was startling but that Charles had less vitality, and less authority too, a weak copy of a great original. The appearance was there, but the temper was lacking.

'I've just seen a light in your house, in the tower,' he said to Louis in a low voice.

'It must be the guards wanting to have a look too.'

'They could have my place with pleasure,' murmured Charles.

'What? Doesn't it amuse you to see Isabella's godfather roast?' said Louis of Navarre.

'Yes, it's a fact that Molay was the godfather of our sister,' murmured Charles.

'I think that's funny,' said Louis of Navarre.

'Be quiet, Louis,' said the King, annoyed by their whispering.

To get rid of the uneasiness that was growing upon him, young Prince Charles compelled himself to think of something pleasant. He began to think of his wife Blanche, of Blanche's wonderful smile, of Blanche's body, of her tender arms soon to be stretched out to him, making him forget this horrible spectacle. How well she knew how to love him and spread happiness about her! If only their two children had not died when a few months old ... But they would have others and then life would contain no single shadow. Enchantment and plenitude. Blanche had told him that tonight she was going to keep her cousin Marguerite company. But she would be home by now. Had she covered herself up well? Had she taken a sufficient escort?

The roaring of the crowd made him start. Flames were now leaping from the pyre. On an order from Alain de Pareilles, the archers extinguished their torches in the grass, and the night was now lit by the great brazier alone.

The flames reached the Preceptor of Normandy first. He made a pathetic movement of withdrawal as the tongues of fire licked at him, and his mouth opened wide as if he were trying vainly to breathe. In spite of the rope that bound him, his body bent almost double; his paper mitre fell off and the great white scar across his purple face became visible. The fire was all about him. Suddenly a pall of grey smoke engulfed him. When it had dissipated, Geoffroy de Charnay was in flames, screaming and gasping and trying to tear himself from the fatal stake which was shaken to its base. The Grand Master could be seen shouting something to him, but the crowd was growling so loudly in an attempt to drown its own horror, that it was impossible to hear what he said, except for the word 'Brother' twice repeated.

The assistant executioners were falling over each other in their haste to bring up reserves of wood and poke the fire with long iron prongs.

Louis of Navarre, whose mind always worked slowly, asked his brother, 'Did you say that there was a light in the Tower of Nesle?'

For one moment he seemed disquieted.

Enguerrand de Marigny had placed a hand before his eyes as if to protect them from the light of the flames.

'A fine vision of hell you've given us here, Nogaret!' said Monseigneur of Valois. 'Were you thinking of your future life?'

Guillaume de Nogaret did not reply.

The pyre had become a furnace and Geoffroy de Charnay was now no more than a blackened, sizzling object, swollen and blistered, slowly collapsing into the cinders, becoming cinder itself.

Women were fainting. Others were going quickly to the river bank to vomit into the channel, almost beneath the King's nose. The crowd, after so much shouting, had grown calmer, and was beginning to talk about miracles because the wind obstinately continued blowing in the same direction and the flames had not yet reached the Grand Master.

How could he last so long? On his side the pyre seemed intact. Then, suddenly, the pyre caved in and the flames, reviving, leapt all about him.

'That's done for him too!' cried Louis of Navarre.

With his long face and neck thrust forward, he was suddenly shaken by one of those incomprehensible gusts of laughter that always seized him at the most tragic moments.

Even at this spectacle Philip the Fair's huge cold eyes were unblinking.

And suddenly the Grand Master's voice sounded out of the curtain of fire. As if addressed to each one present, it affected everyone individually. With great power, his voice sounding as if it were already coming from on high, Jacques de Molay spoke again as he had done at Notre-Dame.

'Shame! Shame! You are watching innocents die. Shame upon you! God will be your Judge.'

Flames whipped him, burning his beard, turning the paper hat in one second to ashes, setting his white hair alight.

The appalled crowd had fallen silent. It might have been a mad prophet who was being burned.

The Grand Master's burning face was turned towards the royal loggia. And the terrible voice cried, 'Pope Clement, Chevalier Guillaume de Nogaret, King Philip, I summon you to the Tribunal of Heaven before the year is out, to receive your just punishment! Accursed! Accursed! You shall be accursed to the thirteenth generation of your lines!'

The flames seemed to enter his mouth and stifle his last cry. And then, for what seemed an age, he fought against death.

At last he bent double. The cord broke. He fell forward into the furnace and only his hand remained raised among the flames. It stayed thus till it had turned entirely black.

Terrified by the curse, the crowd remained rooted to the spot. Nothing could be heard but sighs, murmurs of foreboding, consternation and anguish. The weight of the night and its horror seemed to lie over it; the shadows gradually gained ground against the dying light of the pyre.

The archers were trying to drive the crowd before them, but the people could not make up their minds to leave.

'It wasn't us whom he cursed; it was the King, wasn't it?' people were whispering.

People looked towards the loggia. The King was still standing by the balustrade. He was gazing at the Grand Master's black hand sticking up out of the red embers. A burnt hand; all that remained of so much power and glory, all that remained of the illustrious Order of the Knights Templar. But the hand was motionless, raised in a gesture of imprecation.

'Well, Brother,' said Monseigneur of Valois with a nasty smile, 'I suppose you're happy now?'

Philip the Fair turned round.

'No, Brother,' he said. 'I am not happy. I have committed an error.'

Valois was already preening himself, ready to enjoy his triumph.

'Yes, I have committed an error,' Philip repeated. 'I ought to have had their tongues torn out before burning them.'

Still impassive, he left to return to his apartments, followed by Nogaret, Marigny and his Chamberlain.

The pyre had now turned grey, with here and there a spark of fire suddenly glowing only to die as quickly again. The loggia was full of smoke and a bitter stench of burning flesh.

'It stinks,' said Louis of Navarre. 'I really think it stinks. Let's go.'

Young Prince Charles was wondering whether even in Blanche's arms he would manage to forget what he had seen.

9

The Cut-throats

ON LEAVING THE TOWER OF NESLE, the brothers Aunay, walking to and fro in the mud, gazed into the darkness with some indecision.

Their ferryman had disappeared.

'I told you I didn't like the look of the fellow,' said Gautier. 'I ought to have acted on my suspicions.'

'You gave him too much money,' Philippe replied. 'The scoundrel obviously thought he'd made enough for the day and went off to the execution.'

'Let's hope that's all there is to it.'

'What more could there be?'

'I don't know. But I don't like the look of it. The fellow came and offered to take us over, pleading that he hadn't earned a penny all day. We told him to wait; instead of doing so, he goes off.'

'But what else could we have done? We had no choice; he was the only one there.'

'Exactly,' said Gautier. 'And he asked rather too many questions.'

He stopped, listening for the sound of oars; but there was nothing but the rustling of the river and the widespread rumour from the crowd going back to their homes in Paris. Over there, upon the Island of Jews, which people from tomorrow would begin to call the Island of the Templars, the fire had gone out. A smell of smoke mingled with the dank stench of the Seine.

'There's nothing for it but to go home on foot,' said Gautier. 'We shall get muddy to the thighs. But after all it's been worth it.'

Arm in arm to avoid slipping, they made their way by the wall of the Hôtel-de-Nesle. As they went, they continued to search the darkness. There was no sign of the ferryman.

'I wonder who can have given them to them,' Philippe said suddenly.

'What are you talking about?'

'The purses.'

'Oh, you're still thinking of that, are you?' said Gautier. 'For my part, I must admit I don't care a damn. Of all the presents they've made us, we've never had finer ones than these.'

As he talked he stroked the purse at his belt, feeling the precious stones in relief beneath his fingers.

'It can't be anyone connected with the Court,' Philippe went on. 'Marguerite and Blanche would never have risked their being recognised on us. So, who can it be? A present from their family in Burgundy perhaps? It's so odd that they didn't want to tell us.'

'Which do you prefer,' asked Gautier, 'to know or to have?'

Philippe was about to reply when they heard a low whistle in front of them. They started, and at once put their hands to their daggers. They had no other weapons with them, having decided to leave their swords behind as they would be in the way.

An encounter at this hour and in this place had every prospect of being a dangerous one.

'Who goes there?' said Gautier.

They heard a second whistle, and had barely time to draw their daggers.

Six men surged out of the night and hurled themselves upon them. Three attacked Philippe and, holding him back to the wall with arms outstretched, prevented his using his dagger. The other three were not so fortunate with Gautier. The latter had managed to knock one of his attackers down or, more exactly, the man had slipped in trying to avoid a dagger-thrust. But the other two caught Gautier d'Aunay from behind and twisted his wrist till he dropped his weapon. Philippe could feel that they were trying to take his purse from him.

It was impossible to shout for help. If the guard from the Hôtel-de-Nesle came to their aid, they might be questioned about their presence there. They both had the same instinct not to shout. They must get out of it by themselves, or not get out of it at all.

Philippe, spread-eagled against the wall, fought with all the violence of despair, and, since he could not use his dagger, kicked out with his feet. He did not want to lose his purse. It had suddenly become his most precious possession in the world, and he intended to save it at all costs. Gautier was more inclined to come to terms. Let them take their money but leave them their lives. The point was, would they leave them their lives, or would they rob them first and throw their bodies into the Seine afterwards?

It was at this moment that another shadow appeared out

of the night. Gautier, who had not at first seen it, had no time to make up his mind whether it was friend or foe.

Everything happened very quickly.

One of the assailants cried, 'Watch out! Watch out!'

The new arrival rushed into the middle of the fight like a lion, the light shining on his drawn sword.

'Thieves! Scoundrels! Knaves!' he cried in a powerful voice as he distributed a shower of blows about him.

The thieves disappeared like flies before his attack. As one of the cut-throats passed within reach of his hand, he took him by the collar and hurled him against the wall. The whole gang decamped along the river bank without asking for more. They could be heard running towards the Petit-Pré-aux-Clercs, and then there was silence.

Gasping and stumbling, his hands clasped to his chest, Philippe went over to his brother.

'Are you hurt?' he asked.

'No,' said Gautier breathlessly, rubbing his shoulder. 'And you?'

'Nor am I. But it's a miracle to have got away with it.'

Together they turned towards the stranger who, for the last few seconds, had been chasing the thieves and was now returning, putting up his sword. He looked very tall, broad and strong; his breath came deep and fierce.

'Well, Messire,' said Gautier, 'we're very grateful to you. Without your help we should soon have been floating down the river. To whom have we the honour to be beholden?'

The man laughed, a great, fat, rather forced laugh. One could imagine his strong, pointed teeth in the darkness. For an instant the two brothers thought that they recognised the laugh, then the moon came out from behind the clouds and they knew their defender.

'By heaven, Monseigneur, it's you, is it!' cried Philippe.

'And by heaven, young sirs,' replied the man, 'I know you too!'

They had been saved by Robert of Artois.

'The brothers Aunay!' he cried. 'The handsomest young fellows at Court. Devil take it, I didn't expect that. I was just passing along the bank when I heard the row down here, and said to myself, "There's some peaceable townsman getting done in!" I must say, Paris is infested with these rogues, and that fool of a Provost is too busy licking Marigny's boots to attend to cleaning up the town.'

'Monseigneur,' said Philippe, 'we don't know how to thank you.'

'It's nothing,' said Robert of Artois, patting Philippe on the shoulder with a hand that made him reel. 'It's a pleasure! It's every gentleman's natural instinct to go to the assistance of someone in danger. But it's a double pleasure if that someone is of one's acquaintance, and I am delighted to have preserved for my cousins of Valois and Poitiers their best equerries. It's only a pity it was so dark. By heaven, if the moon had only come out sooner I should have taken great pleasure in ripping up some of those rascals. I didn't really dare thrust properly for fear of wounding you. But, tell me young gentlemen, what the devil are you doing in this dirty hole?'

'We ... we were taking a walk,' said Philippe d'Aunay, embarrassed.

The giant roared with laughter.

'Oh, so you were taking a walk, were you? A fine place and a fine hour for a walk! You were taking a walk in mud up to your knees! That's a likely story! Ah, youth! This is a little matter of some love affair, isn't it? A question of women,' he said jovially, crushing Philippe's shoulder once more. 'Always on heat, eh! What it is to be your age!'

He suddenly saw their purses shining in the moonlight.

'Christ!' he cried. 'On heat and to good purpose! Fine ornaments, young gentlemen, fine ornaments!'

He tried the weight of Gautier's purse.

'Gold thread, and fine work. Italian or English maybe. Equerries' salaries don't run to this sort of splendour. The cut-throats would have had a good haul.'

He grew excited, gesticulated, banged the young men about with friendly blows of his fist, enormous, noisy, red-headed and obscene in the half-light. He was beginning to get seriously on the brothers' nerves. But how do you tell a man who has just saved your life to mind his own business?

'Love obviously pays, my fine young sirs,' he said walking beside them. 'Your mistresses must be very great ladies and very generous ones. Good God, you young Aunays, who would have thought it, eh!'

'Monseigneur is in error,' said Gautier rather coldly. 'These purses came to us through the family.'

'Of course they do, I knew it,' said Artois, 'from a family you've visited at midnight under the walls of the Tower of Nesle! Quite, quite, I shan't say anything, honour comes first. I approve of you, young sirs. One must respect the reputation of the women one sleeps with! All right. Good-bye. And don't venture out at night wearing all your jewellery again.'

He went off into another great gale of laughter. With a huge gesture of embracing them, he banged the two brothers one against the other, and then went off, leaving them there, anxious and disquieted, without even giving them time to repeat their thanks.

They were at the Porte de Bucy and went on their way

to the right, while Artois went off through the fields in the direction of Saint-Germain-des-Prés.

'I hope to God he doesn't go telling all the Court where he found us,' said Gautier. 'Do you think he's capable of keeping his great mouth shut?'

'Yes,' said Philippe. 'He's not a bad sort of chap. And the proof is that without his great mouth, as you call it, and his great arms for that matter, we shouldn't be here now. Don't let's be ungrateful, not yet anyway.'

'That's true. Besides, we might have asked him what the hell he was doing there anyway.'

'I'd swear he was looking for a whore! And now he's gone off to a brothel,' said Philippe.

He was wrong. Robert of Artois had not gone off to a brothel. He had made a detour through the Pré-aux-Clercs and, returning to the river bank, had come back to the neighbourhood of the Tower of Nesle.

The moon was obscured once more. He whistled with the same low whistle that had preceded the fight.

The same six shadowy figures detached themselves from the wall, and a seventh stood up in a boat. The shadowy figures stood in respectful attitudes.

'Good, you've done your work well,' said Artois. 'Everything went off as I wished. Here, Carl-Hans!' he called to the chief blackguard, 'share this between you.'

He threw him a purse.

'You gave me a terrible blow on the shoulder, Monseigneur,' said one of the cut-throats.

'Bah! That's all in the day's work,' Artois answered laughing. 'Now, get off with you. If I should need you again, I'll let you know.'

Then he got into the boat. It sank low in the water under

his weight. The man who took the oars was the same ferry-man who had brought the Aunays over.

'So Monseigneur is satisfied with the night's work?' he asked.

He had lost his whining tone, seemed to have become younger by ten years, and gave way with a will.

'Splendid, my dear Lormet! You played your little trick on them wonderfully well,' said the giant. 'Now I know what I wanted to know.'

He leant back in the stern of the boat, stretched out his monumental legs, and let his huge hand trail in the dark water.

PART TWO
THE ADULTEROUS PRINCESSES

I

The Tolomei Bank

MESSER SPINELLO TOLOMEI's expression took on a reflective seriousness, then, lowering his voice as if he feared someone might be listening at the door, he said, 'Two thousand pounds in advance? Would that suit you, Monseigneur?'

His left eye was closed; his right eye shone with calm innocence.

Though he had lived in France for many years, he had never been able to get rid of his Italian accent. He was fat and dark and had a double chin. His greying hair, carefully cut, fell upon the collar of his robe which was of fine cloth and edged with fur. At the belt the robe was stretched taut over his pot-belly. When he spoke, he raised fat, pointed hands and rubbed them together. His enemies asserted that his open eye was the lying one and that he kept the truthful one shut.

He was one of the most powerful bankers in Paris and had the manners of a bishop. At all events he assumed them on this occasion because he was speaking to a prelate.

The prelate was Jean de Marigny, a slender, elegant, almost

graceful young man who, the day before, at the episcopal
tribunal in front of Notre-Dame, had been remarked for his
languid air until the moment came when he lost his temper
with the Grand Master. He was the brother of Enguerrand de
Marigny and had been appointed to the archbishopric of Sens,
from which depended the diocese of Paris, in order to bring
the proceedings against the Templars to a happy conclusion.
He was therefore in the closest touch with the great affairs
of state.

'Two thousand pounds?' he said.

He seemed a little on edge and turned his head away to
hide his gratified surprise at the banker's figure. He had not
expected so much.

'Yes, certainly, that figure will suit me pretty well,' he
said with an assumed air of detachment. 'I'd like to settle the
business as quickly as possible.'

The banker watched him as a cat watches a fat bird.

'We can deal with the matter at once,' he replied.

'Excellent,' said the young Archbishop. 'And when shall
I send you the . . .'

He interrupted himself, thinking he heard a noise beyond
the door. But no, all was quiet. There was nothing to be
heard but the usual morning sounds from the street of the
Lombards, the cries of the knife-grinders, the water-sellers,
the hawkers of herbs, onions, watercress, white cheese and
charcoal. 'Milk, ladies, milk . . . Fine cheeses from Champagne!
. . . Charcoal, a sackful for a penny!' From the triple, mul-
lioned window, built in the Siennese fashion, the light fell
softly upon the rich tapestries on the walls with their warrior
themes, upon tables of polished oak, and upon the great
coffer bound with iron.

'The objects?' said Tolomei, finishing the Archbishop's

sentence. 'At your convenience, Monseigneur, at your convenience.'

He had gone over to a long work-table which was covered
with goose-quills, rolls of parchment, tablets and styles. He
took two bags from a drawer.

'A thousand in each,' he said. 'Take them now if you
wish. They were prepared for you. Will you sign this receipt,
Monseigneur?'

And he handed Jean de Marigny a document which had
also been prepared in advance.

'Certainly,' said the Archbishop, taking up a quill pen.

But as he was about to sign, he hesitated. On the receipt
were listed the 'objects' which he was to send to Tolomei
that the latter might sell them: church plate, gold chalices,
jewelled crucifixes, valuable weapons, all that had been
sequestered from the Templars in the diocese of Sens. Yet all
these valuables should have been handed over either to the
royal treasury or to the Order of Hospitalers. The young
Archbishop was committing, and without losing any time
over it, malversation and embezzlement. To append one's
signature to that list, when the Grand Master had been
roasted only the night before . . .

'I would prefer . . .' he said.

'That the objects should not be sold in France?' said the
Siennese. 'That goes without saying, Monseigneur. *Non sonno
pazzo*, I'm not mad.'

'I meant to say that this receipt . . .'

'It will never be seen by any eyes but mine. It's as much
to my interest as to yours,' said the banker. 'It's merely in
case something should happen to one or other of us . . . may
God preserve us.'

He crossed himself, and then quickly, behind the table,

made the sign for warding off the evil eye with two fingers of
his right hand.

'They won't be too heavy?' he went on, indicating the
bags, as if the matter as far as he was concerned required
no further discussion. 'Would you like me to send someone
with you?'

'Thank you, my servant is below,' said the Archbishop.

'Then, just here, if you please,' said Tolomei, indicating the
place on the document where the Archbishop was to sign.

The latter could no longer refuse. When one is compelled
to have accomplices, one is also compelled to trust them.

'Besides, you must very well realise, Monseigneur,' the
banker went on, 'that in giving you a sum such as this I am
making no profit. I shall have all the trouble and none of the
reward. But I want to help you because you are a powerful
man, and the friendship of powerful men is more precious
than gold.'

He had said all this in an easy good-natured way but his
left eye was still closed.

'After all, the man's telling the truth,' thought Jean de
Marigny. 'He's thought to be cunning; but his cunning is
merely frankness.'

He signed the receipt.

'By the way, Monseigneur,' said Tolomei, 'do you know
how the King received those English hounds I sent him
yesterday?'

'Oh, so that big greyhound that never leaves him and which
he calls Lombard came from you, did it?'

'He calls it Lombard? I am happy to know it. The King is
a man of wit,' said Tolomei, laughing. 'Do you know that
yesterday morning, Monseigneur . . .'

He was going to tell the story when there was a knock on

the door. A clerk appeared and announced that Count Robert of Artois asked to be received.

'Very well. I'll see him,' said Tolomei, dismissing the clerk with a wave of his hand.

Jean de Marigny looked glum.

'I would rather not meet him,' he said.

'Of course, of course,' the banker replied soothingly. 'Monseigneur of Artois is a great talker. He'd tell everyone that he had seen you here.'

He rang a bell. The hangings immediately parted and a young man in a tight-fitting tunic came into the room. It was the same boy who had very nearly knocked over the King of France the day before.

'Nephew,' said the banker, 'take Monseigneur out without passing through the gallery and take care that he should meet no one. And carry these for him down to the street,' he added, placing the two bags of gold in the boy's arms. 'Good-bye, Monseigneur!'

Messer Spinello Tolomei bowed low to kiss the amethyst on the prelate's finger. Then he pulled the hangings aside.

When Jean de Marigny had gone out, the Siennese came back to the table and took up the receipt, rolling it carefully.

'*Coglione!*' he murmured. '*Vanesio, ladro, ma pure coglione.*' (Vain, thieving and a fool to boot.)

And now his left eye was open. He put the document in the drawer and went out to greet his other visitor.

He crossed the great gallery, lit by ten windows, and containing his trade counters; for Tolomei was not only a banker but an importer and merchant of rare goods of every kind, from spices and Cordova leather to Flanders cloth, gold-embroidered Cyprian carpets and the essential oils of Arabia.

A multitude of clerks dealt with the ceaseless coming and

going of clients; the accountants made their calculations on a special kind of abacus, moving the brass counters in the frames; and the whole gallery was filled with a low hum of business.

Passing rapidly through the gallery, the fat Siennese bowed to a client here, corrected a figure there, reprimanded an employee or refused, with a '*niente*' lisped between the teeth, a demand for credit.

Robert of Artois was leaning over a counter of Oriental weapons, weighing a heavy damascened dagger in his hand.

The giant turned quickly when the banker placed his hand on his arm, assuming that boorish, jovial manner which he generally affected.

'Well,' said Tolomei, 'you want to see me?'

'Yes,' said the giant. 'I've got two things to ask of you.'

'And the first is money, I suppose.'

'Quiet!' groaned Artois. 'Must all Paris know, you damned money-lender, that I owe you a fortune? Let's go and talk privately.'

They left the gallery. Once in his private room with the door closed, Tolomei said, 'Monseigneur, if it's a question of a new loan, I very much fear that it is not possible.'

'Why?'

'My dear Monseigneur Robert,' Tolomei went on calmly, 'when you brought a law-suit against your aunt Mahaut for the inheritance of the County of Artois, I paid the costs. Well, you lost the case.'

'But you know very well that I lost it through dishonesty,' cried Artois. 'I lost it through the intrigues of that bitch Mahaut. May she die of it! A thieves' market! She was given Artois so that Franche-Comté should revert to the Crown through her daughter. But if there were any justice in the world, I should be a peer of the realm and the richest baron in France! And I shall be, do you hear me Tolomei, I shall be!'

And he banged the table with his enormous fist.

'My dear fellow, I sincerely hope so,' said Tolomei, still perfectly calm. 'But in the meantime you've lost your case.'

He had discarded his episcopal manners and was a great deal more familiar with Artois than he had been with the Archbishop.

'Nevertheless, I've received the County of Beaumont-le-Roger, and an income of five thousand pounds, as well as the castle of Conches in which I live,' replied the giant.

'Certainly,' said the banker. 'But that has not paid me back. Rather the contrary.'

'I haven't yet succeeded in getting paid. The Treasury owes me for several years in arrears.'

'Of which you've borrowed the greater part from me. You needed money to repair the roof of Conches and the stables.'

'They had been burnt down,' said Robert.

'Very well. And then you needed money to maintain your partisans in Artois.'

'What should I do without them? It's through them, Fiennes and others, that one day I shall win my case, arms in hand if necessary. And then, Messer Banker, tell me . . .'

And the giant changed his tone, as if he had had enough of playing the part of a rebuked schoolboy. He took the banker's robe between his thumb and forefinger, and began slowly pulling him to his feet.

'Tell me this. You paid for my costs, my stables and all the rest of it, of course you did, but haven't you been able to do a very satisfactory deal or two because of me? Who told you that the Templars were about to be arrested, and advised you to borrow money from them which you never had to pay back? Who told you about the debasing of the currency, which permitted you to lay out all your gold in merchandise and re-sell it for twice the amount? Well, who did that for you?'

For Tolomei, obeying a tradition which still exists in high banking circles, had informers who were close to the councils of state, and his principal informer was Robert of Artois who was the friend and close companion of Charles of Valois, who told him everything.

Tolomei disengaged himself, smoothed out the crease in his robe, smiled and, his left eye closed, replied, 'I grant it, Monseigneur, I grant it. You have sometimes given me useful information. But, alas!'

'Alas, what?'

'Alas! The profits I have been able to make through you are very far from covering the advances I have made you.'

'Is that true?'

'It is,' said Tolomei with the most innocent air in the world.

He was lying, and was sure of being able to do so with impunity, for Robert of Artois, though clever in intrigue, understood very little about accountancy.

'Oh!' said the latter, vexed.

He scratched the stubble on his chin and meditatively shook his head.

'All the same, when I think of the Templars . . . You ought to be pretty pleased this morning, eh?' he asked.

'Yes and no, Monseigneur; yes and no. For a long time they have done our business no harm. Who is going to be attacked next? Is it to be us, us Lombards, as we're called. Dealing in gold is not an easy business. And without us nothing could be done. But by the way,' Tolomei went on, 'has Monsieur de

Valois said anything to you about another change in the value of the Paris pound, as I hear is proposed?'

'No,' said Artois who was following his own line of thought. 'But this time I've got Mahaut. I've got Mahaut because I hold her daughters and her niece in the hollow of my hand. And I'm going to strangle them . . . crack! . . . like that!'

Hatred hardened his features and made him almost good-looking. He had moved nearer to Tolomei once more. The latter was thinking, 'This man, due to his obsession, is capable of almost anything. Anyway, I've made up my mind to lend him another five hundred pounds – though he does smell of game.' Then he said, 'How have you done this?'

Robert of Artois lowered his voice. His eyes were bright.

'The little sluts have got lovers,' he said, 'and last night I found out who they are. But, not a word, eh! I don't want anybody to know – yet.'

The Siennese grew thoughtful. He had already heard the story, but had not believed it.

'What good can it do you?' he asked.

'Good?' cried Artois. 'Listen, banker, can't you imagine the scandal? The future Queen of France caught like a whore with her coxcombs. There'll be a row, they'll be repudiated! The whole family of Burgundy will be plunged up to the neck in the midden, Mahaut will lose all credit at Court, their inheritance will no longer be within reach of the Crown; I shall reopen my case and win it!'

He was walking to and fro and the boards and furnishings vibrated.

'And are you proposing to explode the scandal?' asked Tolomei. 'You'll find the King . . .'

'No, Messer, not I. I should not be listened to. But there's someone else, much better placed to do it, who is not in France. And this is the second thing I came to ask you for. I need a sure man who can take a message secretly to England.'

'To whom?'

'To Queen Isabella.'

'Ah! so that's it,' murmured the banker.

There followed a silence in which could be heard the noises from the street, the hawkers offering their wares.

'It is indeed true that Madame Isabella is said not to like her sisters-in-law of France overmuch,' said Tolomei at last. He had no need to hear more to understand how Artois had set about his plot. 'You're very much her friend, I believe, and you were over there a few days ago?'

'I came back last Friday, and got to work at once.'

'Why don't you send a man of your own to Madame Isabella, or perhaps a courier of Monseigneur of Valois's?'

'In this country, where everyone watches everyone else, all my men are known, as are Monseigneur's. The whole business might easily be compromised. I thought a merchant, and particularly a merchant whom one can trust, would be more suitable. You have many agents travelling for you. Moreover, the message will have nothing in it that need cause the bearer any anxiety.'

Tolomei looked the giant in the eyes, meditated a moment, and then rang the bronze bell.

'I shall endeavour to render you service once again,' he said.

The hangings parted and the young man, who had shown the Archbishop out, reappeared. The banker presented him, 'Guccio Baglioni, my nephew, who has but recently come from Sienna. I don't think that the Provosts and sergeants-at-arms of our friend Marigny know him well as yet, although yesterday morning,' Tolomei added in a low voice, looking at the young man with feigned severity, 'he distinguished himself in a pretty exploit at the expense of the King of France. What do you think of him?' Robert of Artois looked Guccio up and down.

'A good-looking boy,' he said, laughing; 'well set-up, a well-turned leg, slim waist, eyes of a troubadour and a certain cunning in the glance – a fine boy. Is it he you propose sending, Messer Tolomei?'

'He is another self,' said the banker, 'only less fat and younger. Do you know, I was like him once, but I alone remember it.'

'If King Edward sees him, we run the risk of his never coming back.'

And thereupon the giant went off into a great gale of laughter in which the uncle and nephew joined.

'Guccio,' said Tolomei when he had stopped laughing, 'you're going to get to know England. You will leave tomorrow at dawn and go to our cousin Albizzi in London. Once there, and with his help, you'll go to Westminster and deliver to the Queen, and to her alone, a message written by Monseigneur. I will tell you later on and in more detail what you have to do.'

'I should prefer to dictate,' said Artois. 'I manage a boar-spear better than your damned goose-quills.'

Tolomei thought, 'And careful into the bargain, my fine gentleman, you don't want to leave any evidence about.'

'As you will, Monseigneur.'

He took down the following letter himself.

The things we guessed are true and more shameful even than we could have believed possible. I know who the people concerned

*are and have so surely uncovered them that they cannot escape
if we make haste. But you alone have sufficient power to
accomplish what we desire, and by your coming to put a term
to this villainy which so blackens the honour of your nearest
relatives. I have no other wish than to be utterly your servant,
body and soul.*

'And the signature, Monseigneur?' asked Guccio.

'Here it is,' replied Artois, handing the young man an iron
ring. 'You will give this to Madame Isabella. She will know.
But are you certain of being able to see her immediately upon
your arrival?' he asked as if in doubt.

'Really! Monseigneur,' said Tolomei, 'we are not entirely
unknown to the sovereigns of England. When King Edward
came over last year with Madame Isabella to attend the great
ceremonies at which you were knighted with the King's sons,
well, he borrowed from our group of Lombard merchants
twenty thousand pounds, which we formed a syndicate to
lend him and which he has not yet paid back.'

'He, too?' cried Artois. 'And by the way, what about that
first matter I came to ask you about?'

'Oh, I can never resist you, Monseigneur,' said Tolomei,
sighing.

And he went and fetched a bag of five hundred pounds and
gave it to him, saying, 'We'll put it down to your account,
together with your messenger's travelling expenses.'

'Oh, my dear banker,' cried Artois, his face lighting up in a
huge smile, 'you really are a friend. When I've regained my
paternal county, you shall be my treasurer.'

'I shall count upon it, Monseigneur,' said the other, bowing.

'Well, if I don't, I shall take you to hell with me instead.
Otherwise I should miss you too much.'

And the giant went out, too big for the doorway, tossing the bag of gold in the air like a tennis ball.

'Do you mean to say you've given him money *again*, Uncle?' said Guccio, shaking his head in reprobation. 'Because you did say . . .'

'*Guccio mio, Guccio mio,*' the banker replied softly (and now both his eyes were wide open), 'always remember this: the secrets of the great world are the interest on the money we lend them. On this one morning, Monseigneur Jean de Marigny and Monseigneur of Artois have given me mortgages upon them which are worth more than gold and which we shall know how to negotiate when the time comes. As for gold, we shall set about getting a little back.'

He thought for a moment and then went on, 'On your way back from England you will make a detour. You will go by Neauphle-le-Vieux.'

'Very well, Uncle,' replied Guccio unenthusiastically.

'Our agent in those parts has not succeeded in getting repayment of a sum due to us by the squires of Cressay. The father has recently died. The heirs refuse to pay. It appears they have nothing left.'

'What's to be done about it, if they've got nothing?'

'Bah! They've got walls, a property, relatives perhaps. They've only got to borrow the money from somewhere else to pay us back. If not, you'll go and see the Provost, have their possessions seized and sold. It's hard and sad, I know. But a banker has got to accustom himself to being hard. There must be no pity for the smaller clients or we should not have the wherewithal to serve the greater. It's not only our money that is involved. What are you thinking about, *figlio mio*?'

'About England, Uncle,' replied Guccio.

The return by Neauphle seemed to him a bore, but he

accepted it with a good grace; all his curiosity, all his adolescent dreams were already centred upon London. He was about to cross the sea for the first time. A Lombard merchant's life was decidedly a pleasant one and full of delightful surprises. To depart, to travel the long roads, to carry secret messages to princesses. . . .

The old man gazed at his nephew with profound tenderness. Guccio was that tired and guileful heart's only affection.

'You're going to make a fine journey and I envy you,' he said. 'Few young men of your age have the opportunity of seeing so many countries. Learn, get about, ferret things out, see everything, make people talk but talk little yourself. Take care who offers you drink; don't give the girls more money than they're worth, and be careful to take your hat off to religious processions. And should you meet a king in your path, manage things this time so that it doesn't cost me a horse or an elephant.'

'Is Madame Isabella as beautiful as they say she is, Uncle?' asked Guccio smiling.

2

The Road to London

SOME PEOPLE ARE ALWAYS dreaming of travel and adventure in order to give themselves airs and an aura of heroism in other people's eyes. Then, when they find themselves in the middle of an adventure and in peril, they begin to think, 'What a fool I was. Why on earth did I put myself in this position?' These were precisely the circumstances in which young Guccio Baglioni found himself. There was nothing he had desired more than to see the sea. But now that he was upon it, he would have given anything in the world to be somewhere else.

It was the period of the equinoctial gales, and very few ships had raised their anchors that day. Having played a somewhat hectoring role on the quay at Calais, his sword at his side and his cape flung over his shoulder, Guccio had at length found a ship's captain who agreed to give him a passage. They had left in the evening, and the storm had risen almost as soon as they had left harbour. Having found a corner below decks, next to the mainmast – 'This is where you will feel the least movement', the captain had said – and where a wooden shelf served as a bunk, Guccio was spending the most disagreeable night of his life.

The waves beat against the ship like battering-rams, and Guccio felt that the world around him was being turned topsy-turvy. He rolled off the shelf on to the floor and for a long time struggled in total darkness, colliding now against the ship's side, now against coils of rope hardened by sea-water or, again, against ill-stowed packing-cases which were noisily sliding from side to side. He kept on trying to clutch invisible objects that escaped his grasp. The hull seemed to be on the point of disintegrating. Between two gusts of the storm, Guccio heard the sails flapping and great masses of water breaking over the deck above him. He wondered whether the whole ship had not been swept clear, and whether he was not the only survivor in an empty ship that was thrown upwards to the sky by the waves and then dropped once more into the depths with a descent so rapid that it seemed to have no end to it.

'I shall most certainly die,' Guccio said to himself. 'How stupid to die in this way at my age, engulfed in the sea. I shall never see my uncle again, or the sun. If only I had waited another day or two at Calais! How stupid I am! But if I come out of this *per la Madonna,* I shall stay in London; I shall become a water-carrier or anything else, but never again shall I set foot in a ship.'

In the end he grasped the foot of the mainmast in his arms and, falling upon his knees in the darkness, clutching, trembling, seasick, his clothes soaked, he waited for death and promised prayers to Santa Maria delle Nevi, to Santa Maria della Scala, to Santa Maria del Servi, to Santa Maria del Carmine – indeed to all the churches of Sienna whose names he could remember.

At dawn the storm suddenly lessened. Guccio, exhausted, looked about him: packing-cases, sails, tarpaulins, anchors and ropes were heaped in terrifying disorder and, in the bilges, beneath the open joints of the planking, water was sloshing.

The hatch which gave access to the bridge opened and a coarse voice cried, 'Hi, there, Signor! Did you manage to have a good sleep?'

'Sleep?' answered Guccio rather angrily. 'I might be dead for all you'd care.'

They let down a rope ladder to him and helped him up on deck. He felt a strong, cold breeze that made him shiver in his wet clothes.

'Couldn't you have told me that there was going to be a storm?' said Guccio to the captain of the ship.

'Good God, my fine young gentleman, we have had something of a bad night! But you seemed in a hurry. For us, you know, it's nothing much out of the ordinary,' replied the captain. 'Anyway, we are now close to land.'

He was an elderly, fine-looking man with little dark eyes. He looked at Guccio rather mockingly.

Pointing to a white line that was taking shape in the mist, the old sailor added, 'That's Dover over there.'

Guccio sighed, wrapping his cloak about him.

'How long before we get there?'

The other shrugged his shoulders and replied, 'Four or five hours, not more. The wind's in the east.'

Three sailors were lying on deck, obviously exhausted. Another, clasping the helm, was eating a piece of salt beef, without ever taking his eyes from the ship's bows and the English coast.

Guccio sat down next to the old sailor, in the shelter of a

little wooden deckhouse which protected them from the wind and, in spite of the day, the cold and the swell, fell asleep.

When he awoke, the harbour of Dover was spread before him with its rectangular basin and its rows of low houses with thick walls and slate roofs. To the right of the channel the Sheriff's house was to be seen, guarded by a number of armed men. The quay, littered with merchandise, sheltered beneath pent roofs, swarmed with an English crowd. The breeze was charged with the smell of fish, tar and rotting wood. Fishermen were going to and fro, dragging their nets and carrying heavy oars upon their shoulders. Children were handling sacks larger than themselves across the cobbles.

The ship, its sails furled, entered the harbour under oars.

Youth quickly regains both its strength and its illusions. Danger overcome but serves to increase its confidence in itself and to encourage it to further enterprise. A few hours' sleep had sufficed to obliterate Guccio's fears of the night. He was not far from attributing to himself the merit of having outridden the storm; he saw in it a sign that his star was in the ascendant, and a proof of his cleverness in choosing competent sailors. Standing upon the bridge, his attitude that of a victor, his hand clasping a stay, he watched the approach of Isabella's kingdom with passionate curiosity.

Robert of Artois's message, sewn into his coat, and the iron ring upon his forefinger, seemed to him to be gauges of a great future. He was about to enter the intimate circles of power, meet kings and queens, learn the contents of the most secret treaties. His mind was excitedly running ahead and he saw himself already a subtle ambassador, an adviser with the ear of the rulers of the world, someone to whom the most distinguished personages would bow respectfully. He would take part in the councils of princes. Had he not the example of Biccio and Musciato Guardi, his compatriots, the two famous Tuscan financiers whom the French called Biche and Mouche, who had been for more than ten years the treasurers, ambassadors and confidential advisers of Philip the Fair, the austere? He would do better than they had, and one day the history of the illustrious Guccio Baglioni would be told, how he had made his start in life by nearly knocking over the King of France at the corner of a street.

The noises of the harbour seemed already to reach him as the acclamation of a crowd. The old sailor threw down a plank, joining the ship to the quay. Guccio paid the cost of his passage and left the sea for dry land; but his legs had become accustomed to the movement of the swell and, reeling, he very nearly fell down on the slippery road.

Since he had no merchandise he did not have to pass through the customs. He asked the first guttersnipe, who offered to carry his luggage, to lead him to the Lombard of the town.

The Italian bankers and merchants of the period had their own postal and transport system. Organised in huge companies, bearing the name of their founders, they had places of business in all the principal towns and ports; these houses of business were like the modern branches of a bank, but to each were also joined a private post office and a travel agency.

The agent of the branch in Dover belonged to the Albizzi company. He was happy to receive the nephew of the head of the Tolomei company, and entertained him as well as he could. In his house Guccio washed, had his clothes dried and ironed, changed his French gold into English gold, and ate a good meal while a horse was made ready for him.

While he was eating, Guccio told the story of the storm, and gave himself a somewhat distinguished role.

There was a man there who had arrived the day before; his name was Boccaccio, and he was travelling for the Bardi company. Four days earlier he had been present at the execution of Jacques de Molay; had heard the curse and recounted the tragedy with a precise, macabre irony which delighted the Italians present. He was a man of about thirty years of age – to Guccio he seemed elderly – had an intelligent, witty face, thin lips and eyes that seemed to be amused by all he saw. As he was also going to London, Guccio and he decided to travel together.

They left in the middle of the day accompanied by a servant.

Remembering his uncle's advice, Guccio made his companion talk, who indeed desired nothing better. Signor Boccaccio appeared to have seen a good deal in his time. He had been everywhere, to Sicily, Venice, Spain, Flanders, Germany, even the Orient, and had survived many adventures with extraordinary presence of mind; knew the customs of all these countries, had his own opinion about the comparative values of their religions, held monks in some contempt and loathed the Inquisition. He was, too, extremely interested in women; he let it be understood that he had loved a great deal in his time, and recounted curious anecdotes about a great many of these affairs, both illustrious and obscure. He appeared to have no regard for women's virtue, and his language, when he talked of them, was redolent with anecdotes that made Guccio pensive. Moreover, he seemed to possess as much audacity as cunning. A free spirit was Signor Boccaccio and out of the common run.

'I should like to have written it all down if I had had the time,' he said to Guccio, 'the harvest of stories and ideas I have garnered upon my travels.'

'Why don't you do it, Signor?' asked Guccio.

The other sighed as if he were admitted to some unattainable dream.

'*Troppo tardi*, one does not start writing at my age,' he said. 'When one's profession is making money, one can do nothing else after thirty. Besides, if I wrote everything I know, I should run the risk of being burned at the stake.'

The journey, in intimate companionship with an interesting fellow-traveller, across a beautiful green countryside, delighted Guccio. He breathed delightedly the air of early spring; the sound of horses' hooves seemed to lend an accompaniment of joyous song to their journey; and he began to have as exalted an opinion of himself as if he had shared every one of his companion's adventures.

In the evening they stopped at an inn. The halts upon a journey tend to the making of confidences. As they sat before the fire, drinking cans of mulled ale, strong beer laced with Geneva rum, spices and cloves, while a meal and a bed were being prepared for them, Signor Boccaccio told Guccio that he had a French mistress by whom he had had, the previous year, a boy who had been baptized Giovanni.[13]

'They say that bastard children are more intelligent and have more vitality than others,' remarked Guccio sententiously. He had several admirable clichés at his disposal to make conversation with.

'Undoubtedly God gives them gifts of mind and body to compensate them for the advantages of inheritance and position that He withholds. Or perhaps, more simply, they have a harder row to hoe in life than others, and do not expect to become famous but by their own efforts,' replied Signor Boccaccio.

'This one, however, will have a father who can teach him much.'

'Unless he comes to owe his father a grudge for having brought him into the world in such unfortunate circumstances,' said the commercial traveller with a slight shrug of the shoulders.

They slept in the same room, sharing the same pallet. At five o'clock in the morning they set out once more. Wisps of mist still clothed the ground. Signor Boccaccio was silent; he was not at his best at dawn.

The weather was cool and the sky soon cleared. Guccio saw about him a countryside whose beauty delighted him. The trees were still bare, but the air smelt of sap working and the earth was already green with young and tender grass. Ivy clothed the walls of cottage and turreted manor house. Fields and hillsides were criss-crossed with innumerable hedges. Guccio was delighted by the undulating wooded countryside, by the green and blue reflection of the Thames seen from a hilltop, by a group of huntsmen and their pack of hounds met at the entrance to a village. 'Queen Isabella has a beautiful kingdom,' he kept repeating to himself.

As they passed on through the land, the Queen who was to give him audience took a more and more important place in his thoughts. Why should he not, he thought, try to please as well as to accomplish his mission? It might well be that through Isabella's interest Guccio would reach that high destiny for which he felt himself designed. The history of princes and empires had many examples of stranger things than that. 'She is no less a woman because she is a queen,' Guccio told himself. 'She is twenty-two and her husband does not love her. The English lords dare not court her for fear of displeasing the King. Whereas I am arriving as a secret messenger; to get to her I have braved a storm. I go down on my knee, I salute her, uncovered, with a deep obeisance, I kiss the hem of her robe . . .'

He was already composing the phrases with which he would place his heart, his intelligence and his right arm at the service of the fair young Queen. 'Madam, I am not of noble birth, but I am a free citizen of Sienna, and I am worthy of my condition of gentleman. I am eighteen and have no greater desire than to gaze upon your beauty and offer you my heart and soul.'

'We are nearly arrived,' said Signor Boccaccio. They had come to the suburbs of London without Guccio being aware of it. The houses had drawn closer together and formed long lines each side of the road; the fresh smell of the woods had disappeared; the air smelt of burning peat.

Guccio looked about him in surprise. His uncle Tolomei had told him how extraordinary the city was, and he saw nothing but an interminable succession of villages, consisting of black-walled hovels and filthy alleys in which thin women, carrying heavy loads, passed to and fro with ragged children and ill-conditioned soldiers.

Suddenly, amid a great crowd of people, horses and carts, the travellers found themselves at London Bridge. Two square towers marked the entrance, between which, in the evening, chains were fastened and huge doors closed. The first thing Guccio noticed was a bloody human head fixed upon one of the pikes which surmounted the gateway. Crows fluttered about the eyeless face.

'The King of England's justice has been enforced this morning,' said Signor Boccaccio. 'This is how criminals, or those who are named criminals in order to get rid of them, finish here.'

'A curious sight to welcome strangers with,' said Guccio.

'It is a warning that they are not entering a town of light-hearted gaiety.'

At that time, this was the only bridge across the Thames; it was built as a street over the river and its houses were of wood, one pressed close against another. Within them every sort of business was carried on. Twenty arches, each sixty feet high, supported the extraordinary structure. It had taken nearly a hundred years to build and Londoners were very proud of it. A strong current boiled about the arches; washing was hung to dry from the windows; and women emptied slops into the river.

Beside London Bridge, the Ponte Vecchio at Florence seemed but a mere trifle in Guccio's memory, and the Arno a brook compared with the Thames. He said so to his companion.

'All the same we teach them everything,' the latter replied.

It took them about twenty minutes to cross the bridge because of the crowd and the stubbornness of beggars who seized them by their boots.

Arrived at the farther bank, Guccio saw the Tower on his right hand, its huge, tragic mass standing out against the grey sky. Following Signor Boccaccio, he went on into the city. The noise, the coming and going in the streets, the strange rumbling of the city under a leaden sky, the heavy smell of burning peat lying over the town, the cries from the taverns, the impertinences of the women of the streets, the brutal, brawling soldiery, all seemed to Guccio at once curious and intimidating. Paris, in his memory, seemed suddenly to possess clarity and light, while London at midday appeared darker than night.

Having progressed some three hundred yards, the travellers turned to the left into Lombard Street, where the houses of the Italian banks were marked by painted iron signs. These houses, of one, two or more storeys, had little exterior splendour, but were exquisitely maintained, with their doors polished and their windows barred. Signor Boccaccio left Guccio in front of the Albizzi Bank. The two travellers separated with affectionate farewells, mutually congratulating each other upon the pleasure of their dawning friendship and promising to meet again soon in Paris. These are things often said by travellers but never fulfilled.

3

At Westminster

MASTER ALBIZZI WAS A TALL, dry-looking man with a long
brown face, thick eyebrows and tufts of black hair appearing
beneath his hat. He received Guccio with serene graciousness
and the condescension of a great lord. He talked of his 'house'
with a casual gesture of the hand, as if he attached no importance to the fortune of which his home was, nevertheless, a
fairly remarkable manifestation. Standing behind his desk, his
thin body clad in a blue velvet robe, ornamented with silver
buttons, Albizzi had the manner of a Tuscan prince.

While the usual greetings were being exchanged, Guccio
looked from the high oaken chairs to the Damascus hangings,
from the stools of precious woods encrusted with ivory to the
rich carpets that covered the whole floor, from the monumental chimney-piece to the massive silver torch-holders.
And the young man could not help making a rapid valuation
in his mind. 'The carpets, sixty pounds apiece, certainly; the
torch-holders, twice as much. The house, if every room in it
is on the same scale as this one, must be worth three times
my uncle's.' For, though he might dream of himself as a

secret ambassador, a knight-errant of the Queen's, Guccio was none the less a merchant, the son, grandson and great-grandson of merchants.

'You should have taken passage in one of my ships, for we are ship-owners too, and sailed from Boulogne,' said Master Albizzi. 'You would have had a more comfortable crossing, Cousin.'

He had Hypocras served, an aromatic wine that one drank with comfits.

'You want to have an audience with the Queen, do you?' said Albizzi, playing with the great ruby that he wore on his right hand. 'Your uncle Tolomei, whom I hold in great esteem, was wise to send you to me. I will not conceal from you that this particular business, impossible perhaps for others, will be easy for me. One of my principle clients, who owes me much, is called Hugh the Despenser.'

'The particular friend of Edward?' asked Guccio.

'No, Hugh the father. His influence is less evident but all the greater for that. He cleverly uses the favour shown his son, and if things go on as they are, he is likely to rule the kingdom. He is, therefore, not precisely of the King's party.'

'In that case,' asked Guccio, 'is he the right person from whom I should ask assistance?'

'Cousin,' interrupted Albizzi with a smile, 'you seem still very young. Here, as elsewhere, are people who, while belonging to neither one party nor the other, profit from both by playing one off against the other. You need only measure out your smiles and words, know how to profit by the weaknesses of the great, indeed, get to know them better than they know themselves. I know what I can do.'

He summoned his secretary and rapidly wrote a few lines which he then sealed.

'You will be at Westminster this very day after dinner, Cousin,' he said, sending the secretary on his way, 'and the Queen will give you audience. You will seem to everyone but a merchant of precious stones and goldsmith's work, come especially from Italy and recommended to her by me. Like all women, Isabella likes pretty things. While showing her jewels, you will be able to give her your message.'

He went to a great coffer, opened it, and took out a casket covered in red velvet and ornamented with a gold lock.

'Here are your credentials,' he added.

Guccio raised the cover; there were rings with shining stones, heavy necklaces of pearls; at the bottom of the box lay a mirror framed in emeralds and diamonds.

'Should the Queen wish to buy one of these jewels, what do I do?'

Albizzi smiled.

'The Queen will buy nothing from you direct, because she has no money in her own right and her expenditure is supervised. If she should wish to purchase something, she will let me know. Last month, I had made for her three purses for which I have not yet been paid.'

When they had eaten, and Albizzi had made excuses for the poorness of the meal, which, nevertheless, was worthy of the most aristocratic table, Guccio mounted his horse again to go to Westminster. He was accompanied by a servant from the bank, a sort of bodyguard, who wore a short black leather coat and carried the casket fastened to his belt by a chain.

Guccio's heart beat with pride as he went along, his chin held high with a great air of assurance, looking out upon the town as if he were to become its proprietor the next day.

The Palace, though imposing from immense proportions, was floridly Gothic in decoration and seemed to him in somewhat bad taste as compared with the buildings of Tuscany, and particularly to those built in Sienna in those years. 'These people already lack sun and it would seem that they do everything they can to prevent the little they have entering their buildings,' he thought.

He entered by the gate of honour and dismounted under a vault where the soldiers of the bodyguard were warming their hands at a fire of huge logs. An equerry came forward.

'Signor Baglioni? You are expected. Will you follow me?' he said in French.

Still escorted by the servant carrying the casket of jewels, Guccio followed the equerry. They crossed a courtyard surrounded by a cloister, then another, then mounted a huge stone staircase and arrived at the private apartments. The ceilings were enormously high and echoed curiously; the light was dim. As they crossed a succession of dark, freezing halls and galleries, Guccio tried vainly to preserve his air of fine assurance, but they made him feel small. In a place like this one could easily die without trace. At the end of a corridor some forty yards long, Guccio saw a group of men dressed in rich clothes, their robes edged with fur; each bore on his left side the bright gleam of a sword-hilt. This was the Queen's guard.

The equerry told Guccio to wait for him and left him there, amid gentlemen who looked at him with a certain mockery in their expression and exchanged among themselves remarks in English which he could not understand. Suddenly Guccio felt a vague, but overwhelming, foreboding. Supposing something unforeseen occurred? Supposing, at this Court, which he knew to be torn by rival factions, divided by intrigue, he should become a suspect? Supposing, before he ever saw the Queen, he was seized, searched, and the message were discovered? All the fears that a panic-struck imagination can conjure up attacked him, combining with his anxiety not to show his disquiet or let it betray him.

When the equerry, returning to fetch him, touched his sleeve, he started. He took the casket from Albizzi's servant's hand but, in his haste, he forgot that it was attached by a chain to the man's belt, who was suddenly dragged forward. The chain became entangled; the padlock fell. There was laughter, and Guccio felt that he was making a fool of himself. As a result, he entered the Queen's presence in a state of embarrassment, humiliation and confusion, and found himself face to face with her before he even realised it.

Isabella was sitting very straight on a chair, which looked to Guccio like a throne, in the same room where, a little while before, she had received Robert of Artois. A young woman with a narrow face and rigid deportment sat beside her on a stool. Guccio went down on one knee and searched his mind for the elusive compliment. He had imagined – from what absurd illusion? – that the Queen would be alone. The presence of a third person damped all his splendid expectations. The Queen spoke first.

'Lady le Despenser,' she said, 'let us look at the jewels this young Italian has brought. I am told they are marvellous.'

The name Despenser disquieted Guccio, made him anxious.

What possible role could a Despenser have about the Queen?

Having risen at a sign from Isabella, he opened the casket and showed it to her. Lady le Despenser, glancing at it, said in a dry, curt voice, 'The jewels are certainly quite beautiful, but they are not for us. We cannot buy them, Madam.'

The Queen looked put out but, containing her anger,

replied, 'I know, Madam, that you, your husband and indeed all your family take such great care of the finances of the kingdom that one might think they were your very own. But here you will permit me to spend my own money as I please. I notice too, Madam, that when some stranger or merchant comes to the Palace, my French ladies are always absent, as if by some accident, so that you or your mother-in-law are in attendance upon me as if you were on guard. I suspect that, if these same jewels were shown to my husband or to yours, they would find a use for them in loading each other with them as women dare not do.'

However much she might try to control herself, Isabella could not help showing her resentment against this abominable family who, while bringing the crown into contempt, pillaged the treasury. For not only did the Despensers, father and mother, profit in an abject way from the love the King bore their son, but even the wife of the latter consented happily to the scandal, even forwarded it. This Lady le Despenser the younger, born Eleanor de Clare, was moreover the sister-in-law of the late Gaveston, that is to say that King Edward II had married the nearest relative of his former lover, who had been beheaded, to his present favourite.

Vexed at the affront, Eleanor le Despenser rose and busied herself in a far corner of the enormous room, though she never took her eyes from the Queen and the young Siennese.

Guccio, recovering some of the self-possession that was ordinarily natural to him, but which today had been so strangely lacking, at last dared look Isabella in the face. Now or never, he must make the young Queen understand that he was on her side, that he pitied her misfortunes and wished for nothing but to serve her. But she was so cold in manner, showed such indifference to his person, that his heart froze.

Undoubtedly she was beautiful, but her beauty seemed to Guccio to repel all thought of desire, tenderness or even understanding. She seemed to him more like a religious statue than a living woman. Her beautiful blue eyes had the same cold, fixed stare as those of Philip the Fair. How could one say to such a woman, 'Madam, we are of similar age, we are both young and I am in love with you'? It seemed that inheritance, royal function and consecration, had created a being who differed from the rest of the human race and for whom time and flesh and blood had other rules.

All Guccio could do was to take Robert of Artois's iron ring from his finger, taking care to hide the gesture from the Despenser, and say, 'Madam, you will do me the favour of looking at this ring and examining its design?'

The Queen nodded her head and, her expression unaltered, looked at the ring.

'It pleases me,' she said. 'I imagine you have other things worked by the same hand?'

Guccio pretended to search the casket, played with some pearls and, taking the message from his pocket, said, 'The prices are all marked.'

'Let us go to the light that I may better see these pearls,' replied Isabella.

She rose and, accompanied by Guccio, went to a window embrasure where she read the message at her ease.

'Are you going back to France?' she said in a low voice.

'As soon as it pleases you to order me to do so, Madam,' replied Guccio softly.

'Then tell Monseigneur of Artois that I shall shortly be in France, and that everything will be done as we agreed.'

Her face showed some animation, but her attention was entirely centred upon the message and not upon the messenger. Nevertheless, a royal desire to recompense those who served her made her add, 'I will tell Monseigneur of Artois that he must reward your trouble better than I know how to do at this moment.'

'The honour of seeing and obeying you, Madam, is the finest reward that I could wish.'

Isabella thanked him with a movement of her head, merely as she would have greeted the simple compliment of a servant, and Guccio realised that between the great-granddaughter of Monsieur Saint Louis and the nephew of a Tuscan banker there was a distance that could never be crossed.

In a loud voice, so that the Despenser might hear, Isabella said, 'I will let you know through Albizzi what I may decide about these pearls. Good-bye, Messire.'

She dismissed him with a gesture.

He went down on one knee again and then retired, relieved at having accomplished his mission, but very disappointed of his dreams.

4

The Debt

DESPITE ALBIZZI'S COURTESY in offering to keep him several days, Guccio left London next morning at dawn, extremely annoyed with himself. He could not forgive himself, that he, a free citizen of Sienna, who on that score alone considered himself the equal of any gentleman on earth, should have allowed himself to be disconcerted by the presence of a queen. Do what he would, he could never forget that he had been tongue-tied, that his heart had beat too quickly, and that his legs had felt weak, when he found himself in the presence of the Queen of England. And she had not even honoured him with a smile. 'After all, she is but a woman like another! What had I to be nervous about?' he kept on repeating to himself with annoyance. Even when he was already far from Westminster he was still muttering to himself in this strain.

Having found no companion, as on his previous journey, he was travelling alone, chewing over his discontent both of others and himself. This state of mind continued during the whole of his journey home, becoming even worse as the miles passed.

Since he had not received the reception he had expected at the English Court nor, on his appearance alone, been given the honours due to a prince, he came to the conclusion, as he stepped on to the soil of France once more, that the English were barbarians. As for Queen Isabella, however unhappy she might be, however contemptibly she might be treated by her husband, it was no more than she deserved. 'Was one to cross the sea at the risk of one's life, only to be given the thanks due to a servant? Those people had a great air, but their manners were not from the heart. They rebuffed the most loyal devotion. They need feel no astonishment if they were so little liked and so often betrayed.'

Upon these very same roads a week ago, he had thought of himself as an ambassador and a royal lover. Now Guccio began to understand that fortune does not smile upon young men as it does in fairy tales. But he would have his revenge. How, or upon whom, he did not yet know, but revenge was what he intended to have.

In the first place, since destiny and the contempt of kings had destined him to be but a Lombard banker, he would be such a banker as had never before been seen. His uncle Tolomei had charged him to return by the branch at Neauphle-le-Vieux to recover a debt. Very well, the debtors would soon discover the sort of lightning that had struck them!

Journeying by Pontoise, in order to turn off across the Île de France, Guccio, who always had to be playing a part to himself, had become the implacable creditor. Beside him the Jew of Venice, who in the legend demanded a pound of flesh for a pound of gold, would have seemed positively tender-hearted.

Thus he arrived at Neauphle on the morning of the feast

of Saint Hugh. The branch of the Tolomei bank occupied a building near the church, on the town square built on the side of a hill.

Guccio hustled the employees of the bank, demanded to see the account-books and rated everyone. What on earth was the chief clerk thinking about? Had he, Guccio Baglioni, the nephew of the head of the company, to go out of his way each time a sum of three hundred pounds was due? *Primo*, who were these squires of Cressay who owed three hundred pounds? He was informed. The father was dead, which Guccio already knew. What more? There were two sons, aged twenty and twenty-two. What did they do? They spent their time hunting. Evidently idlers. There was also a daughter aged sixteen. Certainly ugly, Guccio decided. And what of the mother who ran the house since the Squire of Cressay's death? They were people of good family, but utterly ruined. How much was their house and land worth? Fifteen hundred pounds more or less. They had a mill and a hundred serfs on their property.

'And owning all that, do you mean to say you haven't been able to make them pay up?' Guccio cried. 'You'll see that they'll soon do so for me.' Where did the Provost live? At Montfort-l'Amaury? Very well. What was his name? Portefruit? Good. If they hadn't paid up by tonight, he would go and see the Provost and have their property seized. That was all there was to it!

He mounted his horse again and left for Cressay as if he were going to take a fortress single-handed. 'My gold or distraint, my gold or distraint,' he kept repeating to himself. 'And they can pray to God and his Saints.'

The trouble was that someone had had the same idea before him, and that someone was Provost Portefruit.

Cressay, which is a mile and a half from Neauphle, is a village built on the side of a valley by the bank of the Mauldre, a stream which is not too wide for a horse to jump.

The castle Guccio came in sight of was in fact no more than a large manor house in somewhat poor repair. It had no moat, since the river served it for defence together with low towers and a marshy approach. The whole place was redolent of poverty and decay. The roofs were collapsing in several places; the pigeon-loft appeared ill-stocked; there were cracks in the mossy walls, while wide gaps in the neighbouring woods revealed hundreds of stumps sawn off close to the ground. There was a considerable bustling in the courtyard as the Siennese entered it. Three royal sergeants-at-arms, their be-lilied staves in their hands, were harrying some ragged-looking serfs to gather the livestock, fasten the oxen in pairs and bring sacks of grain from the mill to load on to the Provost's wagon. The shouting of the sergeants, the running to and fro of terrified peasants, the bleating of some twenty sheep and the screeching of chickens together produced an astonishing hubbub.

No one paid any attention to Guccio; no one came to take his horse, so he tied the bridle to a ring. An old peasant passing by merely said, 'Bad luck has fallen upon this house. If the master were alive, he'd die a second death. It's unjust!'

The door of the building was open and from it came the sound of a violent argument.

'It would seem that I have not come on a very propitious day,' thought Guccio, whose bad temper was increasing all the time.

He mounted the steps to the threshold and, guided by the sound of the voices, entered a long, dark chamber, with stone walls and a beamed roof.

A young girl, whom he scarcely bothered to look at, came to meet him.

'I have come on business and wish to speak to someone belonging to the family,' he said.

'I am Marie de Cressay. My brothers are here and so is my mother,' replied the girl in a hesitant voice, pointing to the far end of the room. 'But they are very busy at the moment.'

'No matter, I'll wait,' said Guccio.

And to show that he intended doing so, he went over to the fireplace and extended his boot to the flames, though he did not feel cold.

At the far end of the room, the argument was still going on. With her two sons, one bearded, the other beardless, but both tall and ruddy, Madame de Cressay was stubbornly holding her own with a fourth personage whom Guccio soon realised was Provost Portefruit.

Madame de Cressay – known as Dame Eliabel in all the surrounding district – had a bright eye, a fine bust, and bore her forty years buxomly in her widow's weeds.

'Messire Provost,' she cried, 'my husband got into debt in order to equip himself for the King's war in which he gained more wounds than profit, while the domain, without a man to look after it, got on as best it could. We have always paid our tithes, our State benevolences and given charity to God. Who has done more in the Province, may I ask? And is it to enrich people of your sort, Messire Portefruit, whose grandfather went barefoot in the gutters hereabouts, that we are to be robbed?'

Guccio looked about him. A number of rustic stools, two chairs with backs to them, benches fastened to the wall, some chests and a great pallet bed with curtains which, nevertheless, revealed the palliasse, made up the furniture of the room. Above the hearth hung an old shield with faded colours. The war-shield, doubtless, of the late Squire of Cressay.

'I shall complain to the Count of Dreux,' went on Dame Eliabel.

'The Count of Dreux is not the King, and I am acting upon the King's orders,' replied the Provost.

'I don't believe you, Messire Provost. I will not believe that the King orders people who have formed part of chivalry for two hundred years to be treated like malefactors. Indeed, if that were the case, the kingdom would cease to function.'

'At least give us time!' said the bearded son. 'We will pay by instalments. You cannot strangle people like this.'

'Let us put an end to this argument. I have already given you time,' interrupted the Provost, 'and you have paid nothing.'

He had short arms, a round face and spoke in a sharp voice.

'My job is not to listen to your complaints, but to collect debts,' he went on. 'You still owe the Treasury three hundred and twenty pounds and eight pence: if you haven't got them, that's too bad. I shall seize your belongings and sell them.'

Guccio thought, 'That fellow is using exactly the tone I intended to use myself and, by the time he's finished, there'll be nothing left to seize. This is a peculiarly useless journey. I wonder if I should join them straight away?'

He felt angry with the Provost who had appeared so inopportunely and was taking the wind out of his sails, stealing the very part he had intended to play himself.

The girl who had received him remained standing not far away. He looked at her more closely. She was fair and had beautiful waves of hair showing beneath her coif, a luminous complexion, great dark eyes and a slender, straight and well-turned figure. She seemed very embarrassed that a stranger should be present at the scene. It was no everyday occurrence to see a young cavalier of agreeable appearance, whose clothes testified to a certain wealth, pass through those parts; it was most unfortunate that this should occur upon the family's most disastrous day.

Guccio's eyes remained fixed on Marie de Cressay. However ill-disposed he felt, he realised that he had thought badly of her without knowing her. He had not expected to find so attractive a girl in such a place. Guccio's eyes slid from her breast to her hands; they were white, well-formed and slender, altogether in keeping with her face.

At the far end of the room the argument was still going on.

'Isn't it bad enough to have lost a husband without having to pay six hundred pounds to keep a roof over one's head? I shall complain to the Count of Dreux,' repeated Dame Eliabel.

'We have already paid three hundred,' said the bearded son.

'To seize our possessions is to reduce us to hunger, to sell them is to condemn us to death,' said the second son.

'The law is the law,' replied the Provost. 'I know the law and I shall sell you up as surely as I am levying distraint.'[14]

Once more these were the very words that Guccio had prepared.

'This Provost seems an odious man. What grudge does he owe you?' Guccio asked in a low voice.

'I don't know, and my brothers know little more: we understand very little about these things,' replied Marie de Cressay. 'It is something to do with inheritance tax.'

'And is that what the six hundred pounds are due for?' said Guccio.

'Disaster has overtaken us,' she murmured.

Their eyes met, held for a moment, and Guccio thought the girl was going to burst into tears. But on the contrary, she was brave in the face of adversity, and it was only from modesty that she turned her beautiful dark blue eyes away.

Guccio thought for a moment. His anger against the Provost was beginning to mount, precisely because the man was showing him the disagreeable part that he had been prepared to play himself.

Suddenly, leaping across the room, Guccio flung himself before the agent of authority and cried, 'Wait a moment, Messire Provost! Are you quite sure that you are not in process of committing theft?' In his stupefaction, the Provost turned upon him and asked him who he was.

'That does not matter,' replied Guccio, 'and you'll be much happier in ignorance, if by any chance your accounts are not correct. I, too, have reason to be interested in the inheritance of the Squires of Cressay. Would you be so good as to tell me your estimate of the value of the estate?'

As the other tried to take a high tone with him, threatening him with the sergeants-at-arms, Guccio went on, 'Take care! You are speaking to a man who but the other day was the guest of the Queen of England, and who tomorrow has the power to make known to Messire Enguerrand de Marigny how his Provosts behave. So you'd better answer, Messire: how much is the estate worth?'

These words had considerable effect. At the name of Marigny, the Provost was troubled; the family fell silent, listening astonished; and Guccio felt that he had grown in stature by a couple of inches.

'According to the estimates of the bailiwick, Cressay is worth three thousand pounds,' the Provost at length replied.

'Really, three thousand?' cried Guccio. 'Three thousand
pounds a country manor, while the Hôtel-de-Nesle, one of
the most beautiful houses in Paris, the residence of Monseigneur the King of Navarre, is scheduled on the registers of
the tithe at five thousand pounds? Estimates in your bailiwick
are very high.'

'There is the land too.'

'The whole estate is worth no more than fifteen hundred
and I know this from a sure source.'

Upon part of his forehead, above his left eye, the Provost
had a birthmark, a huge strawberry-mark which turned violet
in emotion. While talking to him Guccio never took his eyes
off it, and this put the Provost somewhat out of countenance.

'Would you mind telling me now,' went on Guccio, 'what
the inheritance tax is?'

'Fourpence in the pound in this bailiwick.'

'You're lying disgracefully, Messire Portefruit. The tax is
two-pence in the pound for nobles in every bailiwick. You are
not the only one who knows the law. I know it too. This
man is taking advantage of your ignorance to cheat you like
the thief he is,' said Guccio, turning to the Cressay family.
'He comes here to cheat you by using the King's name, but he
has failed to tell you that he farms tithes and taxes, and that
he will send to the King's Treasury only what is prescribed
by law while the rest goes into his own pocket. And if he
sells you up, who will then buy the Castle of Cressay, not for
three thousand but for fifteen hundred or less, or merely for
the debt? This is a fine plan, Messire Provost!'

All Guccio's irritation, all his anger and annoyance, accu-
mulated upon the journey, had now found its outlet. He
grew heated as he talked. He had found at last an opportunity
of seeming important, of being respected and of playing the

part of a strong man. Without being altogether aware of it, he had gone over to the camp he had come to attack, he was defending the weak and assuming the role of a righter of wrongs.

As for the Provost, his fat round face had grown pale and the violet strawberry-mark above his eye made a dark patch upon his forehead. He waved his over-short arms up and down like a duck. He protested his honesty. It was not he who had calculated the accounts. A mistake might have been made by his clerks or perhaps by those of the bailiwick.

Very well! We will calculate these accounts over again,' said Guccio.

In a few minutes he was able to show that the Cressays owed no more than a hundred and fifty pounds.

'So you had better order your sergeants to release the oxen, take the corn back to the mill and leave honest people in peace!'

Taking the Provost by the sleeve, he led him to the door. The Provost did as he was bidden and called to his sergeants that a mistake had been made, that the whole matter must be checked, that they would return upon some future occasion, but that for the moment all must be restored to its accustomed place. He thought that he had finished with the affair, but Guccio led him back to the centre of the hall saying, 'Now return us a hundred and fifty pounds.'

Guccio had taken the part of the Cressays to such an extent that he was beginning to say 'us' in defending their cause.

At this point the Provost was wild with anger, but Guccio quickly deflated him.

'Didn't I hear you say a moment ago,' he asked, 'that you had already collected three hundred pounds in the past?'

The two brothers agreed that this was so.

'Well, Messire Provost, a hundred and fifty pounds,' said Guccio holding out his hand.

The fat Portefruit tried to argue. What had been paid had been paid. The accounts of the Provostship must be looked into. Besides, he hadn't so much gold on him. He would come back.

'It would be better for you if you could find the gold about you. Are you sure that you have received no other sums today? Messire de Marigny's agents work very quickly,' said Guccio, 'and it would be healthier for you to have done with this business on the spot.'

The Provost hesitated for a moment. Should he call his sergeants? But the young man looked so peculiarly active and carried such a good small-sword at his side. Besides, the two brothers Cressay were there, and they were solid fellows who had hunting-spears at hand upon a chest. The peasants would undoubtedly take their masters' part. It seemed a bad business in which he should try to avoid complications, particularly since Marigny's name was suspended over his head. He surrendered: taking a heavy purse from beneath his coat, he counted out the amount of the overcharge upon the lid of a chest. Then only did Guccio let him go.

'We shall remember your name, Messire Portefruit,' he shouted to him from the door.

He returned, a broad smile upon his face, revealing fine teeth, white and regular.

The family immediately surrounded him, plying him with thanks, treating him as their saviour. In the general excitement the beautiful Marie de Cressay seized Guccio's hand and raised it to her lips; then seemed suddenly afraid of what she had dared to do.

Guccio, very pleased with himself, found that his new role

suited him admirably. He had conducted himself in precise accordance with his ideals of chivalry; he was a knight-errant who had arrived at an unknown castle to rescue a young lady in distress, to protect a widow and orphans from the machinations of wicked men.

'But who are you, Messire, to whom do we owe all this?' asked Jean de Cressay, the son with the beard.

'My name is Guccio Baglioni; I am the nephew of the banker Tolomei and I have come to collect our debt.'

There was an immediate silence in the room, the faces of the family glazed over. They looked at each other in fear and consternation. And Guccio felt that he had lost his advantage.

Dame Eliabel was the first to recover herself. She quickly swept up the gold the Provost had left and, with a fixed smile, said in a rather sprightly way that they would discuss all that later, but for the present she insisted that their benefactor should do them the honour of dining with them.

She at once began busying herself, sent her children on a variety of errands and, gathering them together in the kitchen, said to them, 'Take care, whatever he may have done, he remains a Lombard. One should always distrust those people, particularly when they have done one a good turn. It is very unfortunate that your poor father should have had to have recourse to them. Let us show this one, who indeed has a sympathetic air, that we have no money, but let us do it in such a way that he is unable to forget that we are nobles.'

For Madame de Cressay was much concerned with nobility, as small provincial gentlemen have always been, and she thought it a great honour for one who was not noble to have the privilege of sitting at her table.

Luckily, the two sons had brought back a sufficiency of game from hunting the day before; several chickens had their necks wrung; and so it was possible to have the two courses of four dishes each which were essential to the keeping-up of seignioral appearances. The first course consisted of a clear German soup with fried eggs in it, a goose, a stewed rabbit and a roasted hare; the second, of a rump of wild boar served with a sauce, a fat capon, bacon stewed in milk, and blancmange.

Only a small menu, but one, nevertheless, that exceeded the usual porridge and fried lentils with which, like peasants, the family had generally to be content.

All this had to be prepared. The wine was brought up from the cellar; the table was laid on trestles in the Great Hall before one of the benches. A white tablecloth reached to the floor and the diners raised it to their knees in order to wipe their hands upon it. There were pewter bowls for two, but a single one for Dame Eliabel, which was consonant to her rank. The platters were placed in the middle of the table and everyone helped themselves with their fingers.

Three peasants, who were normally busy in the farmyard, had been called in to wait. They smelt a little of the pigsty and the kennel.

'Our carver,' said Dame Eliabel with mingled irony and excuse, indicating the lame man who was cutting slices of bread as thick as logs, upon which they were to eat their meat. 'I must admit, Messire Baglioni, that he is more accustomed to chopping wood. That explains . . .'

Guccio ate and drank a lot. The cupbearer was so gener-ous-handed that one might have thought he was watering horses.

The family encouraged Guccio to talk, which was far from difficult. He told the story of the storm in the Channel so well that his hosts let their slices of wild boar fall back into

the sauce. He talked of many things, of his experiences, of
the state of the roads, of the Templars, of London Bridge,
of Italy, of Marigny's administration. To listen to him, one
might have thought that he was an intimate of the Queen
of England's, and he harped so insistently upon the secrecy of
his mission that one might well have concluded that war
was about to be declared between the two countries. 'I can
say no more than this, because it is a State secret and I am
not at liberty to do so.' When showing-off to other people,
it is never difficult to persuade oneself of success, and Guccio
now saw things somewhat differently from the morning. He
began to think of his journey as wholly successful.

The two Cressay brothers, sound young men but not over-
endowed with brains, who had never been more than thirty
miles from home, gazed with envy and admiration upon this
young man, their junior, who had already done and seen so
much.

Dame Eliabel, who was tending to burst out of her dress,
and in whom good food awakened appetites unsatisfied in
widowhood, allowed herself to look upon the young Tuscan
with a certain tenderness; her massive bosom heaved with
sensations that surprised even herself and, despite her dislike
of Lombards, she could not but be aware of Guccio's charm,
of his curly hair, his brilliantly white teeth, his dark, liquid
eyes and even of his foreign accent.

She was assiduous in complimenting him.

'Beware of flattery,' Tolomei had often advised his nephew.
'Flattery is the direst danger that a banker runs. It is very
difficult to resist someone who speaks well of one, yet, as far
as I am concerned, a thief is better than a flatterer.'

That night Guccio was far from thinking anything of the
kind. He drank in every word of praise as if it were hydromel.

Indeed, he was talking particularly at Marie de Cressay. The young girl never took her eyes off him, watching him from beneath beautiful golden eyelashes. She had a way of listening, her lips parted like a ripe pomegranate, which made Guccio want to talk, to talk yet more, and then put his lips for a long moment to that pomegranate.

Distance lends enchantment. For Marie, Guccio was the stranger-prince upon his travels. He was the unexpected, the unhoped-for, the well-known yet impossible being, who knocks suddenly upon the door and is found to have after all a real face, a body and a name.

So much wonderment in Marie de Cressay's eyes and expression soon caused Guccio to think that she was the most beautiful and attractive girl he had ever seen in the world. Beside her, the Queen of England seemed as cold as a tombstone. 'If she appeared suitably dressed at court,' he told himself, 'she would be the most admired of every woman within a week.'

The meal lasted so long that, when the moment came to rinse their hands, everyone was a little drunk and night had fallen.

Dame Eliabel decided that the young man could not leave at that late hour and invited him to stay the night, however modest the accommodation might be.

'You will sleep there,' she said, indicating the large pallet with the curtains upon which six people could have lain with ease. 'In happier times this was where the guard slept. Nowadays, my sons sleep here. You may share their bed.'

She assured him that his horse had been taken to the stables and well cared for. The life of a knight-errant seemed to Guccio to be continuing. He found it most exhilarating.

Soon Dame Eliabel and her daughter retired into the

women's chamber, and Guccio lay down upon the vast palliasse in the Great Hall with the Cressay brothers. He fell asleep at once, thinking of a mouth like a ripe pomegranate to which he pressed his lips, drinking in all the love in the world.

5

The Road to Neauphle

HE WAS AWAKENED BY a hand pressing gently upon his shoulder. He very nearly took the hand and pressed it to his face. Opening his eyes, he saw above him the smiling face and abundant bosom of Dame Eliabel.

'I hope you have slept well, Messire.'

It was broad daylight. Guccio, somewhat embarrassed, assured her that he had passed an admirable night and said that he felt in need of an immediate wash.

'I am ashamed to be seen by you in this state,' he said.

Dame Eliabel clapped her hands and the lame peasant who, the night before, had served at dinner, appeared, an axe in his hand. Madame de Cressay told him to bring a basin of warm water and towels.

'In the old days we had a proper bathroom to wash in,' she said. 'But it has fallen into ruins. It dates from the time of my late husband's grandfather, and we have never had sufficient money to repair it. Today we store wood in it. Life, you know, is not easy for us who live in the country.'

'She is tentatively asking for further credit,' thought Guccio.

His head felt rather heavy from the wine of the night before, and Dame Eliabel was not precisely the person he would have wished to see upon awakening. He asked where Pierre and Jean de Cressay were: they had gone hunting at dawn. More hesitatingly, he asked after Marie. Dame Eliabel explained that her daughter had had to go to Neauphle, where she had shopping to do.

'I shall have to go there myself later on,' Guccio said. 'Had I known, I could have taken her upon my horse and spared her the fatigue of the road.'

That this suggestion was unrealisable did not appear to cause Dame Eliabel much regret; and Guccio wondered if the Lady of the Manor had not sent the whole of her family away in order to be alone with him. More particularly since Dame Eliabel, when the lame man had brought the basin, spilling in the process at least a quarter of its contents upon the floor, remained in the room, warming towels before the fire. Guccio waited till she should retire.

'Why don't you start washing, young Messire?' she said. 'Our servants are such dolts that, if left to dry you, they would be certain to scratch you. The least I can do is to look after you. Go on! Don't mind me: I'm old enough to be your mother.'

Mumbling a thanks he did not feel, Guccio decided to strip to the waist and, taking care not to catch the lady's eye, sprinkled his head and body with warm water. He was rather thin, as young men are at his age, but was well-built and had a slender waist. 'It's just as well that she did not have a tub brought, as I should have had to strip completely under her eyes. These country people have very odd manners.'

When he had finished washing, she came over to him with the warm towels and began drying him. Guccio thought that, if he could leave at once and push on his way at a gallop, he might have a chance of overtaking Marie on the road to Neauphle, or at least of finding her in the town.

'What a pretty skin you have, Messire,' said Dame Eliabel in a lively but, nevertheless, somewhat uncertain voice. 'A woman might well be jealous of such a smooth skin. I suspect there are many who find it attractive. I have no doubt that your lovely olive colouring pleases them.'

While she said this, she was stroking his back, all the length of his vertebrae, with the tips of her fingers. It tickled Guccio, who turned round laughing.

Dame Eliabel looked disturbed, breathless, and there was a peculiar smile upon her face. Guccio quickly put on his shirt.

'Ah, how wonderful youth is!' said Dame Eliabel. 'Only to look at you, I wager you enjoy every moment of it and profit by every opportunity it offers.'

Guccio dressed himself as decently as he could. Madame de Cressay fell silent for a moment and he could hear her breath coming in gasps. Then she said in the same tone of voice, 'Well, my dear Messire, what are you going to do about our debt?'

'Here it comes,' thought Guccio.

'You can ask us for what you please,' she went on. 'You are our benefactor and we bless you. If you want the gold that you made that thief of a Provost give us back, it's yours, take it away: a hundred pounds if you like. But you have seen our circumstances and you have already shown that you have a heart.'

As she said this, she was watching Guccio buckling his breeches, and it did not seem to him a suitable moment to discuss business.

'The man who saved us cannot destroy us now,' she went

on. 'You people who live in towns cannot understand how difficult our life is. If we haven't yet repaid our debt to the bank, it is because we cannot do so. The government officials thieve from us: you have shown this to be the case. Serfs no longer work as they did in the past. Since the Orders in Council,[15] the idea of freedom has gone to their heads: one can get nothing out of them these days, and really the clodhoppers are almost on the point of thinking themselves of the same species as you or I. For though you are not noble,' she said to underline the honour she was doing him by placing him on her side of the divide, 'you certainly very much deserve to be. If you add the fact that whatever we may harvest one year, bad weather deducts it the next, and that our menfolk spend the little one is able to save at the wars, if they don't go and get killed into the bargain.'

Guccio, who had but one idea in his head, and that to find Marie, tried to evade the implication.

'It is not I but my uncle who decides these things,' he said. But he already knew he was beaten.

'You can show your uncle that this is no bad investment; I can only wish for his sake that he never has less honest debtors. Give us another year; we will pay you interest. Do this for me! I shall be most grateful to you,' said Dame Eliabel, seizing his hand.

Then, with a certain modest confusion, which nevertheless did not prevent her gazing into his eyes, she added, 'Do you know, sweet Messire, that since your arrival yesterday – a woman doubtless should not say these things, but there it is – I have felt a peculiar friendship for you; and there is nothing I would not do to give you pleasure?'

Guccio had not the presence of mind to reply, 'Well then, pay your debt and I shall be happy.'

From all the evidence it appeared that the widow was prepared to pay in her own person, and one might well have asked if she were submitting to sacrifice to evade the debt, or whether she was merely using the debt as an opportunity of personal sacrifice.

As a good Italian, Guccio thought that it would be extremely pleasing to have both mother and daughter at the same time. Dame Eliabel still had many charms, particularly for those who did not mind a certain fullness of figure, her hands were soft and her bosom, abundant as it might be, seemed nevertheless to preserve a certain firmness; but this could be no more than an additional amusement. To risk missing the younger in order to linger with the older would destroy the enjoyment of the game.

Guccio managed to get away by pretending that he was touched by Dame Eliabel's advances and by assuring her that he would most certainly arrange the matter; but that, in order to do this, he must go at once to Neauphle and confer there with his clerks.

He went out into the courtyard, found the lame man, persuaded him to saddle his horse, leapt into the saddle and went on his way towards the town. There was no Marie upon the road. While he galloped along, he asked himself if the girl were really as beautiful as he had thought her to be the day before, if he had not counted too much upon the promise he had thought to see in her eyes, and whether indeed the whole business, which was perhaps but an after-dinner illusion, were worth his haste. For there are women who, when they look at you, seem to surrender to you in the first instant; but that is merely their natural expression; they look at a piece of furniture, at a tree, in exactly the same way and, in the end, give nothing at all.

Guccio saw no sign of Marie in the town square. He looked down many of the side-streets, went into the church, but only stayed there long enough to cross himself and fail to find her. Then he went to the bank. There he accused the three clerks of having misinformed him. The Cressays were people of quality, both honourable and solvent. Their credit must be prolonged. As for the Provost, he was frankly a scoundrel. As he shouted all this out, Guccio never stopped looking out of the window. The employees wagged their heads as they gazed at the young fool who changed his mind from one day to the next. They thought it would be a great pity if the bank should ever fall completely under his control.

'It may well be that I shall come back here fairly frequently: this branch obviously requires close supervision,' he said to them by way of good-bye.

He leapt into the saddle and the gravel flew under his horse's hooves. 'Perhaps she has taken a short cut,' he told himself. 'In that case I shall see her at the castle, but it may be difficult to see her alone.'

Shortly after he left the town, he saw a figure hurrying towards Cressay and recognised Marie. Suddenly he heard the birds singing, realised that the sun shone, that it was April and that the tender young leaves were burgeoning on the trees. Because of a girl, walking between green fields, the spring, of which for three days Guccio had been unaware, suddenly burst upon him.

He slowed his pace and caught Marie up. She looked at him, not particularly surprised that he should be there, but rather as if she had just received the most wonderful present in the world. Walking had put some colour in her cheeks, and Guccio thought that she was even prettier than he had imagined her to be the day before.

He offered to take her up on the crupper. She smiled acquiescence, and once again her lips parted like a fruit. He drew his horse into the bank, and leant down to give Marie the support of his arm and shoulder. The girl was very light; she hoisted herself up with agile grace, and they hurried on. At first they rode in silence. Guccio was tongue-tied. For once the boastful fellow could find nothing to say.

He realised that Marie hardly dared put her hands on him to retain her balance. He asked her if she were accustomed to riding thus.

'Only,' she said, 'with my father or my brothers.' She had never travelled like this before, her body to a stranger's back. Little by little she gained courage and grasped the young man more firmly by the shoulders.

'Are you in a hurry to get home?' he asked.

She didn't answer, and he turned his horse into a side road in order to stay upon the high ground.

'Yours is a beautiful part of the country,' he went on after another silence, 'as beautiful as Tuscany.'

This was a lover's compliment he was making her and, indeed, he had never before felt so strongly the charm of the Île-de-France. Guccio's gaze wandered to the far blue distances, to the horizon of hills and forests whose outline was lost in a faint mist, then returned to the lush grass of the surrounding fields, to the great patches of the paler, more fragile green of the young cultivated rye, and to the hawthorn hedges whose sticky buds were opening.

Guccio asked what the towers were that could be seen to the south, appearing upon the far edge of the horizon out of the great green sea of the plain. Marie found some difficulty in replying; they were the towers of Montfort-l'Amaury.

She was suffering from that mingled anguish of pain and

happiness which prevents speech and even thought. Where did this path lead? She no longer knew. Where was this cavalier taking her? She did not know that either. She was under the thrall of something to which, as yet, she could give no name, something which was stronger than her fear of the unknown, stronger than the morality she had been taught, the precepts instilled by her family, the warnings of her confessors. She was entirely subject to a stranger's will. Her hands clutched his coat more firmly, grasped at the back of this man who, at this instant in time, seemed to be, when all else was chaos, the only certainty in the universe. And through the double thickness of the cloth, Guccio felt Marie's heart-beats echoing in his breast.

The horse, ridden on a loose rein, stopped of its own accord to eat a young shoot.

Guccio dismounted and, giving Marie his arm, lowered her to the ground. But he did not let her go. He stood there with his arm about her waist, and he was astonished to find it so small and slim and firm. The girl stood there motionless, a prisoner, anxious but consenting, of his encircling arm. Guccio felt he must say something, but the trite words of seduction would not come to him: only Italian words came to his lips.

'*Ti voglio bene, ti voglio tanto bene.*'[16]

The sense was so implicit in his voice that she appeared to understand.

Looking at Marie's face close-to in sunlight, Guccio saw that her eyelashes were not gold as he had thought the night before; Marie's colouring was auburn with red lights, her complexion that of a blonde, her eyes large and dark blue, their outline firmly chiselled beneath the arch of the eyebrows. What caused the golden light that seemed to emanate from her? From instant to instant, as Guccio gazed at her, Marie's presence became more precise, more real, and that reality seemed to him the perfection of beauty. He drew her closely to him, moving his hand slowly and gently the length of her thigh and then across her breast, learning the reality of her body.

'No,' she murmured, setting his hand aside.

But as if she were afraid of disappointing him, she raised her face a little way towards his. Her lips were parted and her eyes closed. Guccio leaned down towards her mouth, towards that exquisite fruit he so much desired. And thus they remained for a long moment clasped to each other, as birds sang to them, dogs barked in the distance, and the deep panting breath of nature seemed to raise the earth beneath their feet.

When they parted, Guccio became aware of the black twisted trunk of a huge apple-tree that grew near by, and this tree seemed to him astonishingly beautiful and alive; more so than any he had seen until that day. A magpie was hopping about in the young rye, and this boy, brought up in towns, was amazed by the love that had come to him in the depths of the countryside.

Happy at the joy which shone upon his face, Marie could not take her eyes from Guccio.

'You have come, you have come at last,' she murmured.

She might have been waiting for him through the ages, through the long night of eternity, and known his face for all time.

He wanted her mouth again, but this time she pushed him aside.

'No,' she said, 'we must go home.'

She knew for certain now that love had come into her life,

and for the moment she was overwhelmed by it. She had nothing more to wish for.

When she was again seated upon the horse, behind Guccio, she put her arms round the young man's chest, placed her head against his shoulder, and thus rode to the rhythm of the horse's gait, linked to the man God had sent her.

She had a taste for miracles and a sense of the absolute, but lacked the gift of imagination. Not for an instant could she imagine that Guccio's spiritual state might be different from her own, and that their love might have for him a significance other than it had for her.

She neither sat straight nor resumed the deportment proper to her rank till the roofs of Cressay appeared in the valley.

The two brothers had come back from hunting. Dame Eliabel was not altogether pleased to see Marie return in Guccio's company. She felt towards her daughter a certain resentment, which was less inspired by her regard for the conventions than by unconscious jealousy. Though they did their best to conceal it, the young people had an air of happiness about them which displeased the Lady of the Manor. But she dared say nothing in the presence of the young banker.

'I met Demoiselle Marie and asked her to show me round the estate,' said Guccio. 'Your land seems rich.'

Then he added, 'I have given orders that your credit shall be extended till next year: I hope my uncle will approve. It is impossible to refuse anything to so noble a lady!'

He said these last words smiling at Dame Eliabel. She bridled a little, and became less anxious.

They were very grateful to Guccio; nevertheless, when he said that he must leave, they did not try very hard to keep him. They had got from him what they wanted; undoubtedly he was a charming young man, this Lombard, and had done them a great service, but they scarcely knew him. And Dame Eliabel, when she thought of the advances she had made him that morning, and how he had left her with a certain abruptness, could not feel altogether pleased with herself. The essential was that their credit had been extended. Dame Eliabel had little difficulty in persuading herself that her charms had materially helped towards this end.

The only person who really wished that Guccio should stay could neither do nor say anything.

Suddenly the atmosphere became a little embarrassed. Nevertheless, they forced upon Guccio a haunch of roe-deer, which the brothers had killed, to take with him, and made him promise to return. He promised, but it was to Marie he gave a secret glance.

'You may be certain I shall come back to collect the debt,' he said lightly, though it was intended to put them on the wrong scent.

His luggage having been fastened to his saddle, he mounted his horse.

Watching him go off along the bank of the Mauldre, Madame de Cressay sighed and said to her sons, more for her own sake than for theirs, 'Children, your mother still knows how to talk to young men. I was singularly tactful with this one, and you would have found him harder if I had not spoken to him alone.'

For fear of betraying herself, Marie had already gone into the house.

As he made his way along the road to Paris, Guccio, galloping along, thought of himself as an irresistible seducer, who had only to appear in a country-house to harvest every heart. The vision of Marie beside the field of rye was constant in his mind. And he promised himself that he would return to Neauphle very soon, perhaps even in a few days' time.

But these are thoughts one has travelling but which are never put into effect.

He arrived that night at the street of the Lombards and talked to his uncle Tolomei till a late hour. The latter accepted without difficulty the explanations Guccio made about the debt; he had other worries on his mind. But he seemed to take a particular interest in the activities of Provost Portefruit.

All night long, as he slept, Guccio imagined that he was thinking of no one but Marie. But the following day he was already thinking of her rather less.

In Paris he knew two merchants' wives, handsome towns-women of about twenty years of age, who were far from being cruel to him. After some days he had quite forgotten his conquest at Neauphle.

But destiny moves slowly and no one knows which of our actions, sown at hazard, will burgeon like trees. No one could have foretold that an embrace beside a field of rye on a certain day would alter the history of the kingdom of France, and would lead the beautiful Marie to the cradle of a king.

At Cressay Marie began to wait.

6

The Road to Clermont

THREE WEEKS LATER, the little town of Clermont-de-l'Oise was the scene of extraordinary excitement. From the castle to the gates, from the church to the town hall, the streets were crowded. There was joyful animation as people jostled each other in the alleys and taverns. Since morning, hangings had hung from the windows; the town-criers had announced that Monseigneur Philippe, Count of Poitiers, the King's second son, and his uncle, Monseigneur of Valois, had come in the King's name to meet their sister and niece, Queen Isabella of England.

The Queen, having disembarked upon the soil of France two days before, was making her way across Picardy. She had left Amiens that morning and, if all went well, she would arrive at Clermont in the late afternoon. She would sleep there and, next day, her English escort reinforced by that of France, would proceed to Pontoise where her father, Philip the Fair, was awaiting her at the Castle of Maubuisson.

Shortly after vespers, the arrival of the Princes having been announced, the Provost, the Captain of the Guard and the

Aldermen went out of the Porte de Paris to present the keys. Philippe of Poitiers, riding in the lead, received their welcome and was the first to enter Clermont.

Behind him, amid a great cloud of dust raised by the horses, followed more than a hundred gentlemen, equerries, valets and men-at-arms, who formed his and Charles of Valois's suite.

One head overtopped all others, that of the huge Robert of Artois, whose progress attracted every eye. It is true that this lord, mounted upon a huge dappled percheron – a gigantic horse for a gigantic horseman – wearing red boots and cloak and a surcoat of red velvet, was most impressive in appearance. Though many of the horsemen appeared tired, he remained as upright in the saddle as if he had only just mounted.

Indeed, since leaving Pontoise, Robert of Artois had had a feeling of acute triumph to sustain and refresh him. He alone knew the real object of the young Queen of England's journey; he alone knew how events, put in train by himself to appease his longing for revenge, were about to shake the Court of France. Already he felt a secret, bitter joy.

During the whole journey he had unceasingly watched Gautier and Philippe d'Aunay, who formed part of the retinue, the first as equerry to the Count of Poitiers, the second as equerry to Charles of Valois. The two young men were delighted with the journey and the whole royal train. In their innocence and vanity, the better to shine, they had fastened the handsome purses given them by their mistresses upon their smartest clothes. Seeing the purses at their belts, Robert of Artois had felt a cruel and passionate joy in his heart. He had scarcely been able to prevent himself laughing aloud. 'Well my young bucks, my young cocks, fools that you are,' he said to himself, 'you may well smile in thinking of your mistresses' beautiful breasts. Think of them well, for you will never touch them again; and breathe deep of the air of day, for I think that you will have but few more. Your handsome, brainless heads will be cracked open like nuts.'

Meanwhile, like a huge tiger playing with its prey, claws retracted, he spoke with the utmost cordiality to the brothers Aunay, from time to time tossing them a loud-mouthed pleasantry. Since he had saved them from the pretended cut-throats at the Tower of Nesle, the two young men had been most friendly and thought themselves much obliged to him.

When the cavalcade halted in the Grande Place, they invited Artois to a cup of cool light wine. They joked together, toasting each other. 'Drink, my little friends, drink,' said Artois to himself, 'and remember well the taste of this light wine.'

All about them the tavern rang with gaiety, shouts and cries under the sun.

In the rejoicing town business was as good as on a fair-day, and from the Royal Castle[17] to the church a dense crowd slowed down the horses' pace.

The great swathes of multi-coloured hangings ornament-ing the windows floated in the breeze. A horseman arrived at a gallop and announced the Queen's approach. There was immediate commotion.

'Hurry our people along,' said Philippe of Poitiers to Gautier d'Aunay, who had just rejoined them.

Then the King's second son turned to Charles of Valois.

'We are very punctual, Uncle; the Queen will not have to wait.'

Charles of Valois, dressed entirely in blue, a little the worse for fatigue, contented himself with a nod of the head. He

could well have done without the ride and was in a bad
temper.

The church bells began ringing and their hubbub re-echoed
from the town walls. The cavalcade went forward along the
Amiens road.

Robert of Artois joined the Princes and went forward
stirrup to stirrup with Poitiers. Though he had been dispos-
sessed of his inheritance of Artois, Robert was nevertheless
the King's cousin and his place was in the front rank of the
royalty of France. Watching Philippe of Poitiers's hand clasping the reins of his chestnut horse, Robert thought, 'It was
for your sake, my skinny cousin, it was in order to give you
Franche-Comté that I was deprived of Artois which belonged
to me. But before tomorrow is out, you will receive a wound
from which a man's honour does not easily recover.'

Philippe, Count of Poitiers and the husband of Jeanne
of Burgundy, was twenty-one years old. Not only physically,
but in personality too, he was different from all the rest of the
Royal family. He was neither handsome and dominating
like his father, nor fat and impetuous like his uncle. Thin in
face and body, tall of stature, with curiously long limbs, his
gestures were always measured, his voice precise and curt;
everything about him, his physical characteristics, the simplicity of his pleasures, the restrained courtesy of his speech,
expressed a decisive and reflective nature, in which his head
dominated his heart. He was already a power to take account
of in the kingdom.

Three miles from Clermont, the two cavalcades, that of
the Queen of England and that of the Princes, met. Eight
servants of the house of France, grouped by the side of
the road, blew a long and monotonous fanfare upon their
trumpets. The English trumpeters replied upon instruments

similar but with a sharper pitch. Then the Princes walked forward and Isabella, slim and upright upon her white palfrey, listened to a short speech of welcome made by her brother, Philippe of Poitiers. Then Charles of Valois went forward to kiss his niece's hand; then, when it was the Count of Artois's turn, he was able to give her to understand, by the manner of his low bow and the glance he gave her, that all had turned out as he had foreseen.

While compliments, questions and news were being exchanged, the two escorts waited and watched each other. The French horsemen were impressed by the English uniforms. Sitting still and upright upon their horses, the sun in their eyes, the English bore proudly upon their breastplates the three lions of England; they seemed self-assured and were obviously out to make a good impression upon a strange land.

From the great blue-and-gold litter which followed behind the Queen came a loud cry.

'So, Sister,' said Philippe, 'you have brought our little nephew upon the journey, have you? It's a hard road for so young a child.'

'I would never leave him in London without me. You know enough about the people by whom I am surrounded,' Isabella replied.

Philippe of Poitiers and Charles of Valois asked her the object of her journey; she told them merely that she wished to see her father, and they realised that for the moment, at least, they would be told no more.

She said that she was somewhat tired with the journey, and, dismounting from her white mare, took her place in the great litter carried by two mules harnessed in velvet trappings, one placed between the forward shafts and the other between the rear. Both cavalcades moved off again towards Clermont.

Taking advantage of the fact that Poitiers and Valois had taken their places at the head of the cavalcade, Artois drew his horse near the litter.

'You become more beautiful every time I see you, Cousin,' he said.

'Don't talk nonsense; I am certainly not beautiful after twelve hours of dust upon the roads,' the Queen replied.

'Having loved you in memory for many long weeks, the dust is invisible; I can only see your eyes.'

Isabella leaned back a little among the cushions. Once again she felt a recurrence of that curious weakness which had seized her at Westminster in Robert's company. 'Can he really love me,' she wondered, 'or is he merely making compliments as he does, doubtless, to every woman he meets?' Between the curtains of the litter, she could see the Count of Artois's huge red boot and golden spur upon the dappled horse's flank; she could see the giant thigh with its salient muscles, and she wondered whether each time she found herself in this man's presence she would be conscious of the same disquiet, the same desire to let herself go, the same hope of reaching out to unknown territories. She made an effort to control herself. She was not there on her own behalf.

'Cousin,' she said, 'tell me quickly what there is to tell, and let us make the most of this opportunity to talk.'

Rapidly, pretending to point out the countryside, he told her what he knew and what he had done, the watch he had set over the royal Princesses, the trap set at the Tower of Nesle.

'Who are these men who are dishonouring the Crown of France?' Isabella asked.

'They are riding twenty paces from you. They form part of the escort attending us.'

And he gave her the essential information about the brothers Aunay, their estate, their parentage and their family relationships.

'I want to see them,' Isabella said.

Signalling vigorously, Artois called the two young men over.

'The Queen has noticed you,' he said, winking broadly, 'and I have spoken to her of you.'

The faces of the two Aunays reflected their pleasure and their pride.

The giant motioned them towards the litter as if he were in process of making their fortunes, and, as the young men bowed lower than their horses' withers, he said with feigned joviality, 'Madam, here are Messires Gautier and Philippe d'Aunay, the most loyal equerries of your brother and your uncle. I recommend them to your notice. They are to some extent protégés of mine.'

Isabella gazed for an instant at the two young men, wondering what there was about their faces and their persons that could turn kings' daughters from their duty. They were handsome, certainly, and Isabella was always somewhat embarrassed by beauty in men. Then she noticed the purses at the horsemen's belts and glanced from them to Robert's eyes. The latter smiled briefly. From now on he could fade into the shadows. He need not even assume the role of informer before the Court. This chance encounter should be sufficient to decide the fate of the two equerries. 'Good work, Robert, good work,' he said to himself.

The brothers Aunay, their heads full of dreams, returned to their places in the procession.

From Clermont, in the throes of gaiety, could be heard a great clamour of welcome for the beautiful Queen of twenty-two, who was about to bring the most surprising of disasters upon the Court of France.

7

Like Father, Like Daughter

IT WAS THE EVENING OF Isabella's arrival; the King was alone with his daughter in a room of the Castle of Maubuisson, where he liked to isolate himself.

'It is there I think things over,' he had told his familiars one day when he was being particularly forthcoming.

Upon the table was a three-branched silver candelabra whose light fell upon a file of parchments which the King was reading and signing. Beyond the windows the park rustled in the twilight, and Isabella, looking out into the night, watched the dark absorb the trees one by one.

Since the time of Blanche of Castille, Maubuisson, on the borders of Pontoise, had been a royal residence and Philip had made it one of his regular country retreats. He liked the silence of the place, closed in as it was by high walls; he liked his park, his garden and his abbey in which Benedictine sisters lived out their peaceful lives. The castle itself was not very large, but Philip the Fair liked its quiet and preferred Maubuisson to all his greater houses.

Isabella had met her three sisters-in-law, Marguerite, Jeanne and Blanche, with a serenely smiling face, and had replied conventionally to their words of welcome.

Supper had soon been over. And now Isabella was alone with her father for the purpose of accomplishing the task, atrocious but necessary, upon which she was set. King Philip looked at her with that icy glance with which he regarded every human creature, even his own child. He was waiting for her to speak; and she did not dare.

'I shall hurt him so much,' she thought. And suddenly, because of his presence, because of the park, the trees and the silence, Isabella was a prey to a wave of childish memories and her throat constricted with bitter self-pity.

'Father,' she said, 'Father, I am very unhappy. Oh! how very far away France seems since I have been Queen of England. And how I regret the days that are past!'

She found herself trying to fight an unexpected enemy: tears.

After a brief silence, without going to her, Philip the Fair asked gently but without warmth, 'Was it to tell me this, Isabella, that you have undertaken the journey?'

'And to whom should I admit my unhappiness if not to my father?' she replied.

The King looked at the night beyond the gleaming panes of the window, then at the candles, then at the fire.

'Happiness . . .' he said slowly. 'What is happiness, daughter, if it is not to conform to one's destiny? If it is not learning to say yes, always to God . . . and often to men?'

They were sitting opposite each other on cushionless oak chairs.

'It is true that I am a Queen,' she said in a low voice. 'But am I treated as a Queen over there?'

'Are you done wrong by?'

But there was little surprise in the tone of his voice as he put the question. He knew only too well what she would answer.

'Don't you know to whom you have married me?' she said with some force. 'Can he be called a husband who deserted my bed from the very first day? From whom all my care, all my respect, all my smiles, cannot get a single word of response? Who shuns me as if I were ill and confers, not upon mistresses, but upon men, Father, upon men, the favours he denies me?'

Philip the Fair had known all this for a long time, and his reply had also been ready for a long time.

'I did not marry you to a man,' he said, 'but to a King. I did not sacrifice you by mistake. I don't have to tell you, Isabella, what we owe to our position and that we are not born to succumb to personal sorrows. We do not lead our own lives, but those of our kingdoms, and it is there alone that we can find content . . . if we conform to our destiny.'

He had drawn somewhat nearer to her while speaking and the light of the candle-flames etched the shadows upon his face, bringing his beauty into better relief, emphasising his air of always searching for self-conquest and being proud of it.

More than his words, the King's expression and his beauty delivered Isabella from her weakness.

'I could only have loved a man who was like him,' she thought, 'and I shall never love nor shall I ever be loved, because I shall never find a man in his likeness.'

Then, aloud, she said, 'I am glad that you should have reminded me what I owe to myself. It is not to weep that I have come to France, Father. I am glad too that you have reminded me of the self-respect proper to people of royal birth, and that happiness for us must count for nothing. I only wish that everyone about you should think the same.'

'Why did you come?'

She took a deep breath. 'Because my brothers have married whores, Father, and I have discovered it, and because I am as anxious as you to uphold our honour.'

Philip the Fair sighed.

'I know very well that you do not care for your sisters-in-law, but the difference between you . . .'

'The difference between us is the difference between an honest woman and a whore!' said Isabella coldly. 'Wait a minute, Father! I know things that have been concealed from you. Listen to me, because I am not only bringing you words. Do you know the young Messire Gautier d'Aunay?'

'There are two brothers whom I always confuse with each other. Their father was with me in Flanders. The one you mention married Agnes de Montmorency, didn't he? And he is with my son, the Count of Poitiers, as equerry.'

'He is also with your daughter-in-law, Blanche, but in another capacity. His younger brother Philippe, who is at my uncle of Valois' house.'

'Yes,' said the King, 'yes . . .'

A deep wrinkle, a very rare thing with him, showed upon his forehead.

'Well, he is Marguerite's, whom you have chosen to be one day Queen of France! As for Jeanne, she apparently has no lover, but this may merely be that she conceals the fact better than the others. At least it is known that she is a party to the pleasures of her sister and her cousin, that she covers the visits of the gallants to the Tower of Nesle, and appears to be adept at a profession which has a name all its own. And you may as well know that the whole Court talks of it, except you.'

Philip the Fair raised a hand.

'Your proofs, Isabella?'

Isabella then told him about the purses.

'You will find them at the belts of the brothers Aunay. I saw them myself upon the road. That is all I have to tell you.'

Philip the Fair looked at his daughter. It seemed that under his very eyes she had changed both in face and character. She had brought her accusation without hesitation, without weakening, and there she sat, upright in her chair, tight-lipped, with something stern and icy at the back of her eyes. She had not spoken from wickedness or jealousy, but from justice. She was in truth his daughter.

The King rose without replying. For a long moment he stood before the window, and still the long deep wrinkle showed upon his forehead.

Isabella did not move, awaiting the consequences of what she had unleashed, ready to give further proof.

'Come,' the King said suddenly. 'Let us go to them.'

He opened the door, passed through a long dark corridor and pushed open a second door. Suddenly they were in the grip of the night wind, which made their full clothing flow out behind them.

The three daughters-in-law had apartments in the other wing of the Castle of Maubuisson. From the tower, where the King's study was, their apartments were reached by a covered rampart. A guard dozed by each loophole, short gusts of wind shook the slates. From below the smell of damp earth rose up to them.

Without speaking, the King and his daughter followed the ramparts. Their feet rang out in time upon the stone, and every twenty yards an archer rose to his feet.

When they came to the door of the Princesses' apartments,

Philip the Fair paused for a moment. He listened. Laughter and little cries of pleasure came from beyond the door. He looked at Isabella.

'It is necessary,' he said.

Isabella nodded her head without replying, and Philip the Fair opened the door.

Marguerite, Jeanne and Blanche uttered a cry of surprise and their laughter came to an abrupt end.

They had been playing with marionettes and were amusing themselves by recapitulating a scene they had invented and which, produced by a master juggler, had much diverted them one day at Vincennes, but which had much irritated the King. The marionettes were made to resemble the principal personages of the Court. The little scene represented the King's chamber, where he himself appeared sleeping in a bed covered with cloth of gold. Monseigneur of Valois knocked on the door and asked to speak to his brother. Hugues de Bouville, the Chamberlain, replied that the King could not receive him and had given instructions that no one was to disturb him. Monseigneur of Valois went away in a rage. Then the marionettes representing Louis of Navarre and his brother Charles knocked at the door in their turn. Bouville gave the same answer to the two sons of the King. At last, preceded by three sergeants-at-arms carrying maces, Enguerrand de Marigny presented himself; at once the door was opened wide and the Chamberlain said, 'Monseigneur, you are welcome. The King much desires to speak with you.'

This satire upon the habits of the Court had very much annoyed Philip the Fair, who had forbidden a repetition of the play. But the three young Princesses paid no attention, and secretly amused themselves with it all the more because it was forbidden.

They varied the dialogue and improved upon it with new mockeries, particularly when they manipulated the marionettes which represented their husbands.

When the King and Isabella came in, they felt like schoolgirls caught out.

Marguerite quickly picked up a surcoat that lay on a chair and put it round her to hide her too-naked throat. Blanche smoothed back her hair which had become disarranged in simulating her uncle Valois in a rage.

Jeanne, who remained calmer than the others, said vivaciously, 'We have just finished, Sire; we have just this moment finished, and you might have heard it all without there being anything to wound you. We shall tidy it all away.'

She clapped her hands.

'Hallo, there! Beaumont, Comminges, my good women!'

'There is no need to call your ladies,' the King said curtly.

He had barely noticed their game; it was at them he was looking. Eighteen, nineteen and a half, twenty-three; all three pretty, each in her different way. He had watched them grow taller and more beautiful since they had come, each at the age of about twelve or thirteen, to marry one of his sons. But they did not seem to have grown more intelligent than they had been in those days. They still played with marionettes like disobedient little girls. Was it possible that what Isabella said was true? Was it possible that so much feminine wickedness could exist in these beings who seemed to him still children? 'Perhaps,' he thought, 'I know nothing of women.'

'Where are your husbands?' he asked.

'In the fencing-school, Sire,' said Jeanne.

'Look, I have not come alone,' he went on. 'You often say

that your sister-in-law does not love you. And yet I am told that she has given you each a really handsome present.'

Isabella watched Marguerite's and Blanche's eyes fade, as if their brilliance had been doused.

'Will you,' Philip went on slowly, 'show me the purses you received from England?'

The silence that followed seemed to separate the world into two parts. On one side was Philip the Fair, Isabella, the Court, the barons, the kingdom; and on the other were the Iron King's three daughters-in-law, on the point of entering a realm of appalling nightmare.

'Well?' said the King. 'Why this silence?'

He continued to look fixedly at them with his huge, unblinking eyes.

'I have left mine in Paris,' said Jeanne.

'I too, I too,' the others at once assented.

Slowly Philip the Fair went towards the door that gave upon the corridor, and the wood of the floorboards could be heard creaking beneath his feet. Lividly pale, the three young women watched his every movement.

No one looked at Isabella. She was leaning against the wall, at some distance from the hearth; her breath came quickly.

Without looking round, the King said, 'Since you have left your purses in Paris, we shall ask the young Aunays to fetch them at once.'

He opened the door, called one of the guards and ordered him to fetch the two equerries.

Blanche's resistance gave way. She let herself fall upon a stool, the blood had drained from her face, her heart seemed to have stopped, and her head fell to one side, as if she were about to fall prostrate upon the floor. Jeanne seized her by the small of the arm and shook her to make her regain control of herself. Marguerite was mechanically twisting in her little brown hands the neck of the marionette representing Marigny, with which she had been playing but a few moments before.

Isabella did not move. She saw the glances Marguerite and Jeanne cast upon her, looks of hatred which emphasised the role of informer she was playing, and suddenly she felt an enormous lassitude. 'I shall play this out to the end,' she thought.

The brothers Aunay came in, eager, confused, almost falling over each other in their desire to make themselves useful and to show their worth.

Without leaving the wall against which she was leaning, Isabella stretched out a hand and said only, 'Father, these gentlemen seem to have divined your thought, since they have brought my purses attached to their belts.'

Philip the Fair turned towards his daughters-in-law.

'Can you tell me how these equerries come to be wearing the presents that your sister-in-law gave you?'

None of them answered.

Philippe d'Aunay looked at Isabella in astonishment, like a dog that does not understand why he is being beaten, then turned his eyes towards his elder brother, looking for protection. Gautier's mouth was hanging open.

'Guards!' cried the King.

His voice sent cold shivers down the spine of everyone present and echoed, strange and terrible, through the castle and the night. For more than ten years, since the battle of Mons-en-Pévèle to be exact, where he had rallied his army and forced a victory, the King had never been heard to shout. Indeed, everyone had forgotten that he might still have so powerful a voice. Moreover, it was the only word that he produced in this fashion.

'Archers! Send for your captain,' he said to the men who came running.

There was a sound of heavy feet and Messire Alain de Pareilles appeared, bare-headed, buckling on his belt.

'Messire Alain,' said the King, 'seize these two men. Put them in a dungeon in irons. They will have to answer at the bar of justice for their felony.'

Philippe d'Aunay wished to rush forward.

'Sire,' he stammered, 'Sire . . .'

'Enough,' said Philip the Fair. 'It is to Messire de Nogaret that you must speak now. Messire Alain,' he went on, 'the Princesses will be guarded here by your men till further orders. They are forbidden to go out. No one whatever, neither servants, relations, nor even their husbands, may enter here or speak to them. You will answer to me for any breach of these orders.'

However surprising the orders sounded, Alain heard them without flinching. The man who had arrested the Grand Master of the Templars could no longer be surprised by anything. The King's will was his only law.

'Come on, Messires,' he said to the brothers Aunay, pointing to the door. And he ordered his archers to carry out the instructions he had received.

As they went out, Gautier murmured to his brother, 'Let us pray, brother, because this is the end.'

And then their footsteps, lost amid those of the men-at-arms, sounded upon the stone flags.

Marguerite and Blanche listened to the sound of the footsteps dying away. Their lovers, their honour, their fortune, all their lives were going with them. Jeanne wondered whether she would ever manage to exculpate herself. With a sudden movement, Marguerite threw the marionette she was holding into the fire.

Once more Blanche was on the point of fainting.

'Come, Isabella,' said the King.

They went out. The Queen of England had won; but she felt tired and strangely moved because her father had said, *'Viens, Isabelle.'* It was the first time he had addressed her in the second person since she was a small child.

Following one another, they went back the way they had come. The east wind chased huge dark clouds across the sky. Philip left Isabella at the door of her apartments and, taking up a silver candelabra, went to find his sons.

His tall shadow and the sound of his footsteps awoke the guards in the deserted galleries. His heart felt heavy in his breast. He did not feel the drops of hot wax that fell upon his hand.

8

Mahaut of Burgundy

IN THE MIDDLE OF THE night two horsemen rode away from the Castle of Maubuisson. They were Robert of Artois and his faithful, inseparable Lormet, who was at once servant, squire, travelling companion, confidant and general factotum.

Since the day that Artois had selected him from among his peasants at Conches and attached him to his own person, Lormet had become, so to speak, his perpetual shadow. It was a marvel to see how anxiously this fat little man, already grey-haired but still hale and hearty, attended his young giant of a master on all occasions, closely following him in order to protect him. His cunning was as great and effective as his devotion. It was he who had pretended to be the ferryman for the brothers Aunay on the night of the trap.

Dawn was breaking as the two horsemen reached the gates of Paris. They put their smoking horses into a walk and Lormet yawned a dozen times or so. At over fifty, he was still able to stand long journeys on horseback better than any young equerry, but he was inclined to suffer from lack of sleep.

In the Place de Grève they came upon the usual assembly of workmen in search of jobs. Foremen of the King's workshops and employers of lightermen moved among the various groups and hired assistants, dockers, and porters. Robert of Artois crossed the Place and turned into the rue Mauconseil where lived his aunt, Mahaut of Artois, Countess of Burgundy.

'Listen, Lormet,' said the giant, 'I want this fat bitch to hear from me the extent of her disaster. Here begins one of the greatest and happiest days of my life. No beautiful girl in love with me could give me greater pleasure to see than the hideous phiz of my aunt when she hears what I have to tell her about the happenings at Maubuisson. And I want her to come to Pontoise and accelerate her own ruin by braying to the King; I hope she dies of vexation.'

Lormet yawned hugely.

'She'll die all right, Monseigneur; she'll die, you can be certain of that; you're doing everything you can to bring it about,' he said.

They came to the splendid town-house of the Counts of Artois.

'To think that it was my grandfather who built it; to think that it is I who should be living here!' Robert went on.

'You'll live here, Monseigneur; you'll live here all right.'

'And I'll make you doorkeeper with a hundred pounds a year.'

'Thank you, Monseigneur,' replied Lormet as if he had already acquired that high position and had the money in his pocket.

Artois leapt from his percheron, threw the bridle to Lormet and, seizing the knocker, banged it hard enough to break down the door.

The noise echoed from top to bottom of the house. The wicket-gate opened and a huge guard came out, wide awake and carrying in his hand a cudgel heavy enough to fell an ox.

'Who goes there?' demanded the servant, indignant at the row.

But Robert of Artois pushed past him and entered the house. There were plenty of people in the corridors and upon the staircase; a dozen valets and housemaids doing the morning cleaning. There was anxiety upon every face. Robert, creating disorder in his wake, went up to the first floor, to Mahaut's apartments, and cried 'hullo' loud enough to make a row of horses rear.

A terrified servant ran up, a pail in his hand.

'Where's my aunt, Picard? I must see my aunt at once.'

Picard, his head bald and square, put down his pail and replied, 'She's having breakfast, Monseigneur.'

'Well, I don't care! Tell her I'm here and hurry up about it!'

Having organised his face into an expression of dolour and anguish, Robert of Artois, making the floor tremble beneath the weight of his feet, followed the servant to Mahaut's room.

The Countess Mahaut of Artois, Regent of Burgundy and Peer of France, was a strong woman of fifty, solid, massive, strong-limbed. Under a covering of fat, her face, which had once been beautiful, still preserved an expression of assurance and pride. Her forehead was high, wide and bulging, her hair still largely black. There was too much down on her lip, her mouth was red and her chin heavy.

Everything about the woman was on a large scale, her features, her limbs, her appetite, her anger and her avarice, her ambition and her lust for power. With the energy of a warrior and the tenacity of a lawyer, she moved from Artois to Burgundy, from her Court of Arras to her Court of Dôle,

superintending the administration of her two counties, exact-
ing the obedience of her vassals, setting limits to the power
of others, and pitilessly destroying her known enemies.

Twelve years of fighting with her nephew had taught her
to know him well. Whenever a difficulty arose, whenever the
Lords of Artois proved refractory, whenever a town protested
against her taxes, she could be certain that Robert was behind
them.

'He is a savage wolf, a big cruel false wolf,' she said when
speaking of him. 'But I am more intelligent, and he will end
by destroying himself through going too far.'

They had hardly been on speaking terms for many months
and never saw each other except by necessity at Court.

That morning, sitting at a little table set at the foot of her
bed, she was eating slice after slice of a pâté of hare, the first
course of her breakfast.

As Robert took care to feign distress and emotion, she for
her part assumed a natural and casual manner when she saw
him come in.

'Well, you're bright and early, Nephew,' she said, showing
no surprise. 'You come rushing in like the wind! What's all
the hurry about?'

'Aunt, Aunt,' cried Robert, 'all is lost!'

Without changing position, Mahaut calmly drank off a full
tankard of ruby-coloured Artois wine. It came from her own
lands and she preferred it to all others to start the day with.

'What have you lost, Robert? Another lawsuit?' she asked.

'I swear to you, Aunt, that this is no moment for bickering.
The disaster that has come upon our family is very far from
being a joke.'

'What disaster for one of us could possibly be a disaster for
the other?' said Mahaut with calm cynicism.

'Aunt, the King holds us in the hollow of his hand.'

Some slight anxiety showed in Mahaut's expression. She was wondering what trap had been set for her, what this preamble could mean.

With a gesture he knew well, she turned back her sleeves over her forearms. Then she banged the table with her hand and called, 'Thierry!'

'Aunt, I cannot possibly talk before anyone but you,' cried Robert. 'What I have learnt touches our honour.'

'Nonsense! You can say anything before my Chancellor.'

She was suspicious and wanted to have a witness.

For a short moment they measured each other with their eyes, she all attention, he delighting in the comedy. 'Call in everyone,' he thought. 'Call them all in, and let them all hear.'

It was a singular sight to see these two taking each other's measure, to watch these two people with so many natural characteristics in common, these two cattle of the same blood, resembling each other so much, hating each other so well, come face to face.

The door opened, and Thierry d'Hirson came in. An ex-Canon of Arras Cathedral, Mahaut's Chancellor for the administration of Artois, and perhaps something in love with the Countess, this chubby little man with his round face and white pointed nose gave a surprising impression of assurance and authority. He had curiously thin lips, and great cruelty showed in his eyes. He believed in cunning, intelligence and tenacity.

He bowed to Robert of Artois.

'A visit from you is rare, Monseigneur,' he said.

'It appears that my nephew has a grave disaster to inform me of,' said Mahaut.

'Alas!' said Robert, sinking into a chair.

He took his time; Mahaut began to betray some impatience.

'We have had our differences, Aunt,' he said.

'More than that, nephew; horrible quarrels which have ended ill for you.'

'True, true, and God is my witness that I have wished you all the ill in the world.'

He was using his favourite wile, a sound basic frankness, the avowal of his ill-intentions, in order to dissimulate the weapon he held in his hand.

'But I would never have wished you this,' he went on. 'For you know that I am a good knight, and stand firm upon everything that touches one's honour.'

'What on earth is all this about? Speak, for goodness' sake!' cried Mahaut.

'Your daughters, my cousins are convicted of adultery, and have been arrested on the order of the King, and Marguerite with them.'

Mahaut did not immediately react to the blow. She did not believe it.

'Who told you this story?'

'I know it of my own knowledge, Aunt, and the whole Court knows of it, too. This happened yesterday evening.'

From then on he enjoyed himself, teasing the fat woman, putting her in agony, telling her only as much of the business at a time as he wanted to, scrap by scrap, recounting how all Maubuisson had been startled by the King's anger.

'Have they confessed?' asked Thierry d'Hirson.

'I don't know,' Robert replied. 'But doubtless the young Aunays are at this moment confessing on their behalf at the hands of your friend Nogaret.'

'I don't like Nogaret,' said Mahaut. 'Even if they were innocent they'd come out of the affair blacker than pitch, if he's involved.'

'Aunt,' Robert went on, 'I have ridden the thirty miles from Pontoise to Paris through the night in order to warn you, for no one else had thought of doing so. Do you still think that it's ill-will that brings me here?'

Under the shock and uncertainty Mahaut looked at her giant of a nephew and thought, 'Perhaps he sometimes is capable of a kindly gesture.'

Then she said in a surly voice, 'Do you want anything to eat?'

By this question alone Robert knew that she was really hard hit.

He seized a cold pheasant from the table, tore it apart with his hands and began eating it. Suddenly he noticed his Aunt change colour in the most curious way. First, the top of her throat, above her dress edged with ermine, became scarlet, then her neck, then the lower part of her face. The blood could be seen rising across her face, reaching her forehead and turning it crimson. The Countess Mahaut put her hand to her breast.

'That's done it,' Robert thought. 'It's killing her. It will kill her.'

But not at all. The Countess rose to her feet and there was a sudden clatter. With a wide gesture of her arm she had swept the pâté of hare, the tankard and the silver plates to the floor.

'The sluts!' she howled. 'After all I've done for them, after the marriages I arranged for them – to be caught out like a couple of drabs. Well, let them lose all they possess! Let them be imprisoned, impaled, hanged!'

The Canon remained motionless. He was accustomed to the Countess's tempers.

'Do you know that was just what I was thinking, Aunt,' said Robert with his mouth full. 'It really is no proper return for all the trouble you've taken.'

'I must go to Pontoise at once,' said Mahaut without hearing him. 'I must see them and tell them what to say.'

'I doubt if you will be allowed to see them, Aunt. They're in solitary confinement, and no one can . . .'

'Then I shall speak to the King. Beatrice! Beatrice!' she called, clapping her hands.

A hanging moved to one side and a splendid girl of some twenty years, dark, tall, her breasts round and firm, her waist well marked, her legs long, came in unhurriedly. As soon as he saw her, Robert of Artois felt attracted.

'Beatrice, you've heard everything, haven't you?' Mahaut asked.

'Yes, Madam,' replied the girl. 'I was outside the door, as always.'

There was a curious slowness about her voice, as there was about her gestures, about her manner of moving and about her glance. She gave a peculiar impression of a sort of flowing indolence and of abnormal placidity; one would have said that even lightning entering the window would not have made her move more quickly or taken that calm half-smile from the corners of her lips. But there was irony shining in the eyes beneath the long black lashes. Undoubtedly she rejoiced in the disasters, crises, and tragedies of others.

'This is Thierry's niece,' Mahaut told her nephew; 'I have made her my first lady-in-waiting.'

Beatrice d'Hirson looked Robert of Artois up and down with a sort of candid shamelessness. She was obviously curious to know this giant of whom she had heard nothing but evil.

'Beatrice,' Mahaut continued, 'have my litter harnessed and six horses saddled. We are going to Pontoise.'

Beatrice continued to look straight into Robert's eyes, and one might have thought that she had not heard. There was something at once irritating and disquieting about the beautiful girl. She gave men, from the first moment of meeting, a sense of immediate complicity, as if she would offer no resistance to them. And at the same time one wondered whether she was utterly stupid, or, perhaps, on the other hand, was quietly laughing at people.

'I shall have that girl,' thought Robert, as she went slowly out of the room; 'I don't know when, but I shall.'

There was but little left of the pheasant and he threw it into the fire. He was now thirsty. No more wine had been brought. From a side-table Robert took the decanter from which Mahaut had helped herself – and thus ran no risk of being poisoned – and poured a great bumper down his throat.

The Countess was walking to and fro, folding back her sleeves and biting her lips.

'I shall not leave you alone from today, Aunt,' said Artois. 'I shall come with you. It's a family duty.'

Mahaut raised her eyes towards him, once more somewhat suspicious. Then at last she made up her mind to accept his advice.

'You have done me much harm, Robert, and I dare swear that you will do me more. But, I must admit it, today you have behaved like a good fellow.'

9

The Blood Royal

DAY WAS BEGINNING TO enter the long, low, cellar-like room in the old Castle of Pontoise in which Nogaret had interrogated the Aunay brothers. Through the narrow skylights, which had been opened for purposes of ventilation, came puffs of white mist. A cock crowed, then another, a flock of sparrows flew past at ground level. The torch upon the wall flickered, adding its acrid smell to that of the tortured bodies. It gave but little light, and Guillaume de Nogaret said in his curt, impersonal voice, 'The torch.'

One of the two executioners left the wall against which he was leaning and brought a new torch from a corner of the room; he lit it by placing one end against the embers which had heated the now useless irons. Then he placed it in the socket fixed to the wall.

The man went back to his place, next to his companion. The two executioners – 'tormentors,' as they were called – had the same rough exterior, the same doltish faces, while their eyes were now red-circled with fatigue. Their strong hairy forearms, still showing traces of blood, hung down beside their leather jerkins. They smelt horribly.

Nogaret barely looked at them; he got up from the stool upon which he had been sitting during the interrogation, and his thin figure cast an uncertain shadow upon the grey stone.

From the farther end of the room came the sounds of gasping breath mingled with sobs; the two brothers Aunay seemed to groan with one voice. The executioners, their business over, had left them lying on the ground. But, without asking Nogaret's permission, they had fetched Gautier's and Philippe's cloaks and had thrown them over their bodies as if to hide them from themselves.

Nogaret bent forward; the two faces resembled each other strangely. The skin was the same grey, with traces of perspiration, and the hair, clotted with sweat and blood, revealed the shape of the skulls. A continuous trembling accompanied the groans issuing from torn lips upon which the marks of their teeth were visible.

Gautier and Philippe d'Aunay had been children, and later young men, in happy circumstances. They had lived for their desires and their pleasures, their ambitions and their vanities. As were all boys of their rank, they had been trained to arms; but they had never suffered any but minor hardships or such as the imagination invents for itself. Only yesterday they had been part of the cavalcade of power, and every ambition seemed open to them. But one night had gone by and now they were nothing but broken animals; if they were still capable of wishing for anything, it was for death.

Nogaret straightened up; his expression had not changed. The suffering of others, the blood of others, the insults of his enemies, despair and hate, flowed off him like water from a duck's back. He had to make no great effort to manifest that legendary hardness, that insensibility, which had made him the faithful servant of the King's most secret wishes. He was like he was because he had made himself thus. He had a vocation for what he considered to be the public weal, as others have a vocation for love.

Vocation is a noble name for passion. In that heart of lead and iron, which was Nogaret's, there existed the same egotism, the same fierce necessity which compels the lover to sacrifice everything for the body that obsesses him. Nogaret lived in a world in which everything was ordered by one rule: reasons of State. In his eyes individuals counted for nothing, not even himself.

There is a singular strand running through history, always renewing itself, that of fanatics for the general good and for the written law. Logical to the point of inhumanity, pitiless towards others as towards themselves, these servants of abstract gods and of absolute law accept the role of executioners, because they wish to be the last executioner. They deceive themselves because, once dead, the world no longer obeys them.

In torturing the brothers Aunay, Nogaret thought he was benefiting the life of the kingdom; he had looked upon the almost anonymous faces of Gautier and Philippe without it even occurring to him that they were the faces of men; conscience-free, he had cast his shadow across these haggard lineaments; for him they were no more than signs of disorder; he had conquered.

'The Templars were tougher,' was the only remark he made to himself. And what was more, he had only had local executioners available, not those of the Paris Inquisition.

As he straightened up, he frowned, his back felt stiff and he was aware of a vague pain in his bones. 'It's the cold,' he murmured. He had the skylights closed and went over to the brazier where the fire still glowed. He extended his hands, rubbing them together, then massaged the small of his back, muttering to himself.

The two executioners, still leaning against the wall, seemed to be asleep. A moaning came from the ground where the brothers Aunay lay, but Nogaret no longer heard it.

When he had sufficiently warmed himself, he came back to the table and picked up a parchment. Then, with a sigh, he went across to the door and went out.

The executioners went over to Gautier and Philippe and tried to make them stand up. As they could not, they took in their arms the bodies they had tortured and carried them, as one carries sick children, to their cell.

From the old Castle of Pontoise, which was used only as a garrison and a prison, it was about a mile or so to the royal residence of Maubuisson. Messire de Nogaret traversed the distance on foot, preceded by two of the Provost's sergeants-at-arms and followed by a clerk carrying parchments and inkstand.

Nogaret walked quickly, his cloak floating out behind his tall thin body. He enjoyed the cold morning breeze and the damp smell of the forest.

Without replying to the salute of the archers of the guard, he crossed the courtyard of Maubuisson, entered the door-way, paying no attention to the whisperings, to the air of making vigil for the dead, which lay upon the chamberlains and gentlemen gathered in the hall and the corridors. An equerry leapt forward to open a door, and the Keeper of the Seals found himself face to face with the Royal Family.

Philip the Fair was sitting at a long table covered with a silken cloth. His face appeared more drawn than usual. His unblinking eyes had blue shadows beneath them and his lips were a compressed line. Upon his right was Isabella, upright, rather hieratic, her crimped coif surmounted by a light diadem, the golden coils of her hair, framing her face like the handles of an amphora, accentuated the sternness of her expression. She was the author of the disaster. In other people's eyes she shared the responsibility for it and, by that curious link which joins accuser to accused, she felt that she herself was also upon trial.

On Philip the Fair's left sat Monseigneur of Valois, nervously tapping the table with his fingers and wagging his head as if there was some irritating roughness in his collar. The King's other brother, Monseigneur Louis d'Evreux, his manner calm, his dress quiet, was also present.

The King's three sons were there too, the three husbands of the Princesses; they were shattered and made ridiculous by the catastrophe; Louis of Navarre, with his squint and hollow chest, in continuous nervous movement; Philippe of Poitiers whose face, which always looked rather like a greyhound's, was now still thinner and longer from the effort he was making to keep calm; and lastly Charles, whose adolescent good looks seemed ravaged by the first sorrow of his life.

But Nogaret did not look at them; Nogaret wished to look at no one but the King.

He unrolled his parchment and, upon a sign from the sovereign, read the minutes of the interrogation. The tone of his voice was as calm as when he was putting Gautier and Philippe d'Aunay to the question. But in that cold room, lighted by three ogival windows, his voice echoed fearsomely; the Royal Family were now being put to the test. Since Nogaret liked his work to be precise, there was nothing lacking in his recital. Certainly the two Aunays, as gentlemen should, had begun by denying everything; but the Keeper of the Seals had a technique of interrogation before which scruples and honour soon failed. The month in which their liaison with the Princesses had begun, the days upon which the lovers met, the nights spent at the Tower of Nesle, the names of the servants who were privy to their proceedings, everything indeed which had represented passion, excitement and pleasure for those two, was here established and recorded in detail and become no more than slime. One might well wonder how many of those who knew what was taking place were laughing aloud.

One hardly dared to look at the three Princes, and they themselves hesitated to look at each other. For more than three years they had been betrayed, mocked and deceived. Each word Nogaret uttered added to their shame.

For Louis of Navarre there was a terrible suspicion implicit in the establishing of certain dates: 'During the first six years of our marriage, we had no child. And then we had one precisely when Philippe d'Aunay began to sleep with Marguerite. So perhaps my little daughter Jeanne is not really mine.' And he ceased listening to the recital because he was continuously repeating to himself, 'My daughter is not mine . . . My daughter is not mine.' He felt the blood rushing to his head.

The Count of Poitiers, on the other hand, listened with attention to everything Nogaret said. For all his efforts, Nogaret had been unable to extract from the brothers Aunay any indication that the Countess Jeanne had had a lover, not even a name. Having admitted everything else, they would certainly have revealed this too had they known of it. There was no doubt that she had played a sufficiently infamous part. Philippe of Poitiers reflected thus.

When Nogaret had finished, he placed the minutes on the

table and Philip the Fair said, 'Messire de Nogaret, you have presented these painful matters with clarity. When we have made our judgment, you will destroy this' – he indicated the parchment – 'so that no trace of it will remain except in the secrecy of our private ears. You have done well.'

Nogaret bowed and went out.

There was a long silence, then suddenly someone cried, 'No!'

Charles had risen to his feet. 'No!' he repeated, as if the truth were impossible to admit. His chin trembled; his cheeks had a marble hue and he could not restrain his tears.

'The Templars . . .' he said distractedly.

'What are you talking about?' said Philip the Fair, frowning. He disliked this reference to an all-too-recent memory. Because indeed the same thought was present in everyone's mind. 'Accursed to the thirteenth generation of your lines.'

But Charles was not thinking of the curse.

'That night,' he muttered, 'that night, they were together.'

'Charles,' said the King, 'you have been a very weak husband; at least try to appear a strong Prince.'

And that was the only word of comfort the young man got from his father.

Monseigneur of Valois had as yet said nothing, and to remain so long silent was a considerable hardship to him. He took advantage of the moment to explode.

'By God's blood,' he cried, 'there are strange things happening in the kingdom, even under the King's roof! Chivalry is dying, Sire, my brother, and all honour is dying with it!'

Thereupon he went off into a long diatribe which, beneath an appearance of exaggerated blundering, contained, in fact, a good deal of special pleading. For Valois everything hung together; the King's counsellors (he did not mention Marigny by name, but his attack was meant for him) were destroying the orders of chivalry, and public morals were foundering for that reason. Jumped-up lawyers kept on inventing God knows what new laws drawn from Roman law, to replace the good old feudal laws which had so well served their ancestors. The result could be seen by all. At the time of the Crusades, wives could be left for years; they knew how to protect their honour and no vassal would have dared ravish them. Nowadays, there was nothing but shame and licence. To think that two equerries . . .

'One of those equerries belongs to your household, Brother,' said the King drily.

'As the other belongs to your son's,' replied Valois, pointing to the Count of Poitiers.

The latter spread out his long hands.

'Anyone,' he said, 'may be deceived by someone in whom he has placed his trust.'

'That is precisely what I'm saying,' cried Valois, for whom everything was grist to his mill; 'that is what I am saying: there is no worse crime a vassal can commit than to seduce and betray the honour of his suzerain's wife, particularly if she be the wife or daughter of a member of the Royal Family. These two Aunay equerries have almost . . .'

'You may consider them dead, Brother,' interrupted the King with a little gesture of his hand, at once casual and precise, which indicated the most severe of all sentences and destroyed two lives without appeal. 'They are of no importance. We must decide upon the future of the adulterous Princesses. Permit me, Brother,' he continued, interrupting Valois, who was about to speak again, 'permit me, for this once, to ask my sons a few questions first. Louis, speak.'

As he was about to speak, Louis of Navarre was overcome

with a bout of coughing and two red patches appeared on his cheeks. He was overwhelmed by shock and anger. His choking was taken in good part.

'It will be said that my daughter is a bastard,' he said, when he had regained his breath. 'That is what they'll say! A bastard!'

'If you are the first to say it, Louis,' remarked the King, much displeased, 'other people will most certainly not fail to repeat it.'

'Of course, of course,' said Charles of Valois, who had not thought of it till that moment, his large blue eyes suddenly shining with a strange light.

'And why should it not be said, if it is true?' went on Louis, losing all control.

'Be quiet, Louis,' said the King of France, hitting the table with his fist. 'Will you limit yourself to giving us your advice on the subject of your wife's punishment.'

'Let her die!' replied the King of Navarre. 'She and the two others. All three of them. Death, death, death to them!'

He repeated 'death', his teeth clenched and his hand apparently cutting off heads in the void.

Then Philippe of Poitiers, having asked his father's permission to speak with a glance, said, 'You are distracted with pain, Louis. Jeanne has not such a great sin upon her conscience as either Marguerite or Blanche. She is undoubtedly very culpable for having assisted their follies instead of denouncing them to me, and she has lost much in my estimation. But Messire de Nogaret, who generally obtains all the information there is to be got, has been unable to find any evidence that she has betrayed her marriage.'

'Let her be tortured and you'll see if she doesn't confess!' cried Louis. 'She has helped to sully my honour and that of

Charles, and if you pretend to love us, you will see that she is punished in the same degree as the other two bawds.'

Philippe of Poitiers then made an astonishing reply. It was most revealing of his character. 'Your honour is dear to me, Louis; but Franche-Comté is no less so.'

All those present looked at each other; and Philippe went on, 'You, Louis, own Navarre by direct inheritance, which came to you from our mother, and you will have, God willing a long time hence, France. As far as I am concerned, I have but Poitiers, which our father graciously gave me, and I am not even a Peer of France. But, through Jeanne, I am Count Palatine of Burgundy, Lord of Salins, from whose mines I derive the greater part of my revenues, and at Mahaut's death I shall have the whole county. That's all. May Jeanne be shut up in a convent for as long as is necessary for all this to be forgotten, even for ever, if it is essential to the honour of the Crown, but let her life be spared.'

Monseigneur Louis of Evreux, who had said nothing until now, agreed with Philippe.

'My nephew is right, both before God and before the kingdom,' he said. 'Death is a grave matter, which will be a great distress for each one of us, and we should not decide upon it for others while in anger.'

Louis of Navarre gave him a nasty look.

There were two clans in the family dating from long before. Uncle Valois had the affection of his two nephews, Louis and Charles, who were weak and malleable, lost in admiration of his loquacity, the prestige of his adventurous life, and the thrones he had lost and conquered. Philippe of Poitiers, on the other hand, was on the side of his uncle of Evreux, a calm, honest, reflective man who, if fate had willed it, would have made a good king of whom no one would ever have heard. He was without ambition and remained perfectly contented with the estates he administered so intelligently. The salient characteristic of his nature was that he was easily obsessed with the idea of death.

Those present were not surprised when, in this family matter, they saw him supporting the position his favourite nephew had taken up; their affinity was well known.

More astonishing was Valois's attitude, who, after his wild diatribe, now changed front and, for once leaving his dear Louis of Navarre without support, announced that he too was against the death penalty for the Princesses. A convent, certainly, was too light a punishment, but a prison, a fortress for life (he was very positive about this: for life), that was what he advised.

Forbearance was not part of the titular Emperor of Constantinople's disposition. It was always the result of calculation; and, indeed, this particular calculation had occurred to him when Louis of Navarre mentioned the word bastard. Indeed ... indeed, the three sons of Philip the Fair had no male heirs. Louis and Philippe had each a daughter; but now, already, here was the little Jeanne under the grave suspicion of illegitimacy, which might prove an obstacle to her eventual succession to the throne. Charles had had two still-born daughters. If the guilty wives were executed, the three Princes would quickly marry again and have good chances of achieving sons. Whereas, if the Princesses were shut up for *life*, they would still be married and prevented from contracting new unions, and would remain without much posterity. There was of course such a thing as annulment – but adultery was no ground for an annulment. All this passed very rapidly through the imaginative Prince's head. As certain officers who, going to war, dream of the possibility of all their seniors being killed, and already see themselves promoted to command the army, Uncle Valois, looking at his nephew Louis's hollow chest, the thin body of his nephew Philippe, thought that disease might well make unexpected ravages. There were, too, such things as hunting accidents, lances that broke accidentally in tournaments, and horses that came down; and, indeed, one knew of many uncles who had survived their nephews.

'Charles!' said the man with the unblinking eyes, who for the moment was the one and only true King of France.

Valois started as if he feared that his thoughts had been read.

But Philip the Fair was not speaking to him but to his youngest son. The young Prince took his hands from his face. He had been in tears all the time.

'Blanche, Blanche, how can she have done it, Father, how can she have done this?' he groaned. 'She always said how much she loved me, and showed it so well.'

Isabella felt a wave of impatience and contempt. 'This love men have for the bodies they have possessed,' she thought, 'and the ease with which they swallow lies, provided that they have the physical satisfactions they desire! Is this act, which disgusts me, really so important to them?'

'Charles,' insisted the King, as if he were talking to a halfwit, 'what do you advise should be done with your wife?'

'I don't know, Father, I don't know. I want to hide myself, go away, enter a monastery.'

It seemed as if he was on the point of asking to be punished because his wife had deceived him.

Philip the Fair realised that he would get nothing out of him. He looked at his children as if he had never seen them before, and wondered about the value of primogeniture; he thought that nature often served the law of the throne

extremely ill. What absurdities might not Louis, his unreflect-
ing, impulsive, cruel eldest son commit as head of the
kingdom? And what support to him would be the youngest,
this mere rag of a man, who collapsed at the first crisis? The
most qualified to reign was undoubtedly the second, Philippe.
But it was clear that Louis would never listen to him.

'What do you advise, Isabella?' he asked his daughter in a
low voice, leaning towards her.

'A woman who has sinned,' she replied, 'should be prevented for ever from transmitting the blood of kings. And the
punishment should be known to the people, so that they may
realise that the wife or daughter of a king is punished more
severely than would be the wife of a serf.'

'That is sound,' said the King.

Of all his children, it was undoubtedly she who would have
made the best ruler. It was a great pity that she was not a man
and born the eldest.

'Justice will be done before vespers,' said the King rising.

And he retired to take his final decision, as always, in the
company of Marigny and Nogaret.

10

The Judgment

DURING THE JOURNEY FROM Paris to Pontoise, the Countess
Mahaut, in her litter, had thought of nothing but of how
she was going to attempt to make the King relent, but she
found it difficult to think coherently. She was assailed by too
many thoughts, too many fears, too great an anger at the folly
of her daughters and her cousin, at the stupidity of their
husbands, the imprudence of their lovers, against all those
who, through frivolity, blindness or sensuality, ran such grave
risks of ruining the whole edifice of her power. As the mother
of repudiated Princesses, what would Mahaut be? She decided
to accuse Marguerite in order to save the other two. After
all, Marguerite was not her daughter. Moreover, she was the
eldest and one might be able to place the blame on her easily
enough for having led the younger ones astray.

Robert of Artois had led the cavalcade at a good pace, as if
he wished to demonstrate his zeal. He took pleasure in watching Beatrice d'Hirson's exquisite bosom moving to the rhythm
of their progress; but he enjoyed still more the spectacle of
the ex-Canon shaken up and down in the saddle, and above all

in listening to the groans of his aunt. Whenever he heard a complaint, as her fat body was shaken by the jolting, Robert increased the pace as if by chance. The Countess sighed with relief when at last the towers of Maubuisson appeared above a line of trees.

Soon the Countess's cavalcade entered the courtyard of the Castle. Only the sound of the archers' feet broke the deep silence that reigned over it.

Mahaut got out of her litter and, addressing the Commander of the Guard, asked, 'Where is the King?'

'He is distributing justice in the Chapter Hall.'

Followed by Robert, Thierry d'Hirson and Beatrice, Mahaut went rapidly towards the Abbey. She walked quickly and with a firm tread in spite of her fatigue.

The Chapter Hall that day was an unusual spectacle; between the grey pillars, beneath the huge cold vault, there were no nuns at prayer; the whole Court of France was standing motionless and silent before their King.

As Countess Mahaut entered, a few heads turned, and a low murmuring was heard. A voice which was Nogaret's stopped reading, and the King exchanged a glance with his austere counsellor.

Mahaut found no difficulty in making her way through the crowd; it opened before her. She saw the King, seated upon his throne, his crown upon his head, his sceptre in his hand, his face even colder than usual, his eyes more staring.

He did not appear to be of this world. Was he not, in fulfilling his terrible function, brought up as he had been upon the precepts of his grandfather, Saint Louis, the representative of divine justice?

Isabella, Enguerrand de Marigny, Monseigneur of Valois and Monseigneur of Evreux were seated, as were the three

Princes and some of the greater barons. Before the platform three young monks, their shaven heads bent low, were kneeling upon the flagstones. Alain de Pareilles, the man charged with every execution, was standing somewhat in the background, at the sovereign's feet. 'God be praised,' thought Mahaut, 'I have arrived in time. Some matter of sorcery or sodomy is being tried.'

And she hurried forward to reach the platform, where in the nature of things she should take her place, since she was a Peer of the Realm. Suddenly she felt her legs give way beneath her; one of the kneeling penitents had raised his head; she saw that it was her daughter Blanche. The three young 'monks' were the three Princesses who had been shaven and clothed in rough fustian. With a low cry Mahaut staggered under the shock, as if she had been hit in the stomach. Automatically, she clutched at her nephew's arm, because it was the first arm within her reach.

'Too late, Aunt; alas, we have arrived too late,' Robert of Artois said simply, savouring his vengeance to the full.

The King made a sign to the Keeper of the Seals who continued his reading.

A succession of degrading scenes passed through the shaven heads of the Princesses of Burgundy at the sound of Nogaret's hard voice. Mahaut was also affected by their shame, as were the three Princes, the deceived husbands, who, sitting beside their father, lowered their heads as if they themselves were culprits.

'. . . in consequence of which and by right of the above evidence and confessions of the above-mentioned Gautier and Philippe d'Aunay, having been proved adultresses, the said Ladies Marguerite and Blanche of Burgundy shall be imprisoned in the fortress of Castle Gaillard, and this for the whole of those days which it may please God shall remain to them.'

'For life,' murmured Mahaut; 'they are condemned to prison for life.'

'Lady Jeanne, Countess Palatine of Burgundy and Countess of Poitiers,' continued Nogaret, 'in respect of the fact that she has not been convicted of having offended the state of matrimony and that this crime cannot in justice be imputed to her, but as it is established that she has been guilty of complicity and culpable complacence, she shall be imprisoned in the Castle of Dourdan for as long as shall be necessary to effect her repentance and during the King's pleasure.'

There was a moment's silence during which Mahaut thought, as she looked at Nogaret, 'He has done it, he's the dog who has done it all, with his passion for spying, informing and torturing. He'll pay for this. He'll pay for it with his life.' But the Keeper of the Seals had not yet finished reading.

'The Sieurs Gautier and Philippe d'Aunay, having committed a crime against honour and betrayed their feudal ties upon persons of the Royal Majesty shall be flayed alive, broken upon the wheel, drawn, decapitated and hung from the public gibbet, this upon the morning of the day following today. This is the judgment of our gracious, most powerful and most beloved King.'

The Princesses' shoulders were seen to quiver at the terrible words announcing the tortures which awaited their lovers. Nogaret rolled up his parchment, and the King rose. The Hall began to empty amid a continuous murmuring within walls more accustomed to echo prayers. People shunned Mahaut, and took care not to catch her eye. She felt all about her the cowardice of human nature. She wished to go to her daughters, but Alain de Pareilles barred the way. 'No, Madam,' he said. 'The King will only permit his sons, should they so desire, to receive the farewells and repentance of their wives.'

She then tried to turn to the King, but he had already left, with Louis of Navarre behind him, choking with rage and humiliation, while Philippe of Poitiers, in the same condition, left without even glancing towards his wife.

'Mother!' cried Blanche, seeing Mahaut moving away supported by her Chancellor and Beatrice. Alone of the three deceived husbands, Charles had remained behind. He went up to Blanche, but could do no more than murmur, 'How could you do this, how could you?'

Blanche trembled all over and shook her shaven head upon which the razor had left red patches. She looked like a bird in moult.

'I didn't know . . . I didn't want to . . . Charles,' she said, bursting into tears.

At that moment Isabella said in a hard voice, 'No weakness, Charles. Remember you are a Prince.'

Upright beneath her narrow crown, she too had remained, like a guard, a line of contempt about her lips.

At this moment the long-contained fury of Marguerite of Burgundy was released.

'No weakness, Charles! No pity!' she cried. 'Copy your sister, Isabella, who runs no risk of understanding the weaknesses of love. She has nothing but hatred and gall in her heart. But for her, you would never have known. But she hates me, she hates you, she hates us all.'

Isabella crossed her hands upon her breast and gazed at Marguerite with cold anger.

'May God forgive you your crime,' she said.

'He will forgive me my crime more readily than He will make you a happy woman.'

'I am a Queen,' replied Isabella. 'Even if I lack happiness, I have at least a sceptre and a kingdom.'

'And I, even if I have not had happiness, at least I have known pleasure, which is worth all the crowns of the world, and I regret nothing.'

Face to face with the Queen of England, this woman with her shaven head, her face furrowed with fatigue and tears, had still the strength to insult, wound, and plead for her bodily rights.

'It was springtime,' she said in a hurried, breathless voice, 'there was the love of a man, the warmth and strength of a man, the joy of taking and of being taken, everything of which you know nothing, which you would give your life to know and which you never will. Ah! you can't be very good in bed since your husband prefers boys!'

Ghastly pale, but incapable of reply, Isabella made a sign to Alain de Pareilles.

'No,' cried Marguerite, 'you can have nothing to say to Messire de Pareilles. He has been at my orders in the past, and perhaps one day will be at my orders again. He will not refuse to go at my orders this once more.'

She turned her back upon the Queen and Charles, and made a sign that she was ready. The three prisoners went out, crossed the corridors and the courtyard under escort, and returned to the room which served as their prison.

When Alain de Pareilles had closed the door upon them, Marguerite ran to the bed and threw herself upon it, biting the sheets.

'My hair, my beautiful hair,' sobbed Blanche.

II

The Place du Martrai

Dawn came slowly for those who had spent the night without rest and without hope, without forgetfulness and without illusion.

In a cell in the prison of Pontoise two men, lying side by side on a heap of straw, were awaiting death. Upon the order of Guillaume de Nogaret, the brothers Aunay had been solicitously cared for. Thus, their wounds no longer bled, their hearts beat more strongly, and some particle of strength had returned to their torn muscles and crushed flesh, the better to suffer and experience the horror of the sentence to which they were condemned.

Neither the condemned Princesses, nor Mahaut, nor the King's three sons, nor indeed the King himself, slept that night. Nor was Isabella able to sleep; the words of her sister-in-law Marguerite throbbed in her head. Only two men had fallen asleep without difficulty: Nogaret, because he had accomplished his duty, and Robert of Artois because, in order to satisfy his vengeance, he had ridden sixty miles.

A little before prime,[18] heavy footsteps sounded on the

stones of the corridor; the archers of Messire Alain de
Pareilles were come to fetch the Princesses. In the courtyard,
three carts draped in black awaited them with an escort of
sixty horsemen clothed in leather jerkins, coats of mail and
steel helmets. Alain de Pareilles bade the Princesses get on
to the carts, gave the signal for departure, and the punitive
procession set itself in motion in the clear rose of the
morning.

At a window in the castle, the Countess Mahaut stood with
her forehead pressed against the pane, her wide shoulders
shaking with sobs.

'Are you weeping, Madam?' asked Beatrice d'Hirson.

'It can happen to me too,' answered Mahaut in a hoarse
voice.

Beatrice was dressed to go out.

'Are you going out?' said Mahaut.

'Yes, Madam; I am going to see . . . if you permit me.'

The Place du Martrai at Pontoise, where the execution of
the Aunay brothers was to take place, was already crowded.
Townsmen, peasants and soldiers had been flowing into it
since dawn. The landlords of the houses giving on to the
Place had let their windows at advantageous prices; people
could be seen at every opening. The fact that the condemned
were noble, that they were young and, above all, that they
were lords of that region exacerbated curiosity. And the very
nature of their crime, this huge sexual scandal, excited all
imaginations.

The scaffold had been built during the night. It was raised
six feet above the ground, and the two gibbets rising above it
attracted every eye.

The two executioners arrived, their red caps and jerkins
heralding their approach from afar. Behind them, their

assistants carried the black chests containing their tools. The executioners mounted the scaffold and a sudden silence fell upon the crowd. Then one of the executioners turned one of the wheels with a creak. The crowd laughed as if at a mounte-bank's trick. They made jokes, nudged each other, a jug of wine was passed from hand to hand up to the executioners. The crowd applauded as they drank.

As the tumbril containing the brothers Aunay appeared, a great clamour arose, becoming louder as the crowd distin-guished the two young men. Neither Gautier nor Philippe was able to move. Without the ropes that bound them to the tumbril's rail, they would have been unable to remain upright.

A priest had visited their prison to receive their mumbled confessions and the last words to be sent to their family.[19] Exhausted, gasping, half-insensible, they were incapable of making any stand against their fate, they had but little realisa-tion of what was happening to them, and wished only for a rapid end to their nightmare and annihilation.

The executioners hoisted them on to the scaffold and stripped them naked.

Seeing them thus, like two huge rose-coloured puppets, the crowd shouted as if at a fair. As the two men were being tied to the wheels, their faces turned towards the sky, a flood of gross and obscene remarks spread across the crowd. Everyone waited. The executioners were leaning against the poles of the gibbets, their arms crossed. Several minutes went by. The crowd began to grow impatient, to ask questions, to become turbulent. Suddenly, the reason for the delay became evident. Three carts draped in black arrived at the entrance to the Place. Nogaret, in agreement with the King, and through a superb refinement of punishment, had ordered that the Princesses should be present at the execution.

Blanche fainted when she saw the two naked bodies tied in the form of crosses to the wheels.

Jeanne, in tears, clutching the side of her cart, screamed to the crowd, 'Tell my husband, tell Monseigneur Philippe that I am innocent.'

Until that moment she had been able to control herself, but now her nerves gave way, and the crowd laughed at her despair.

Marguerite of Burgundy, alone, had the courage to look at the scaffold, and those about her wondered for a moment if she did not feel an appalling, an atrocious pleasure at seeing, exposed to every eye, rosy under the sun, the man who was about to die for having possessed her.

As the executioners raised their maces to break the bones of the condemned, she cried, 'Philippe!' in a voice that seemed far removed from anguish.

Then the maces fell; there was a cracking of bones, and for the brothers Aunay the sky above them went out. With iron hooks, the executioners tore the skin from the insensible bodies; blood flowed down from the scaffold.

The crowd was moved to a sort of hysteria when the two master executioners, with long butchers' knives, mutilated the two culprit lovers and, at one and the same time, with the precision of jugglers, threw the offending parts high in the air.

The crowd jostled forward the better to see. Women cried to their husbands, 'This doesn't mean you can do the same thing, you lecherous old man!'

'You see what will happen to you!'

'You deserve as much!'

The bodies were taken down from the wheels and the axes glinted in the sunlight as the heads were cut off. Then, what remained of Gautier and Philippe d'Aunay, those two fair equerries who but a day or two ago were still riding upon the road to Clermont, was hoisted, shapeless bloody masses, on to the forks of the gibbets. And the crows from the neighbouring churches began already to circle about them.

Then the three black-draped carts began to move again; the Provost's sergeants-at-arms began to empty the Place, and everyone went back to his business, his forge, his butcher's shop or his garden, with the strange spiritual calm of people for whom the death of others was no more than a spectacle.

For, in those centuries, when numbers of children died in the cradle and half the women in childbirth, when epidemics ravaged adult life, when wounds were but rarely cured, and sores did not heal, when the Church's teaching was ceaselessly directed towards a consciousness of sin, when the statues in the sanctuaries showed worms gnawing at corpses, when each one carried throughout his life the spectre of his own decomposition before his eyes and the idea of death was habitual, natural and familiar, to be present at a man's last breath was not, as it is for us, a tragic reminder of our common destiny.

While upon the road to Normandy, a woman with a shaven head in a black-draped cart, was screaming, 'Tell Monseigneur Philippe that I am innocent! Tell him that I have not deceived him!' the executioners, upon the Place du Martrai, divided in the presence of some determined loafers the belongings of their victims. Indeed, the custom was that the executioners should keep for themselves everything worn by the condemned 'below the belt'. Thus it was that the handsome purses from the Queen of England fell into their hands. Each of the master executioners took one; it was a rare piece of good luck, something that might happen only once during the whole of their lives as executioners.

They were engaged in this division when a handsome dark woman, clothed more as a daughter of the nobility than as a townswoman, approached them and, in a low, somewhat languorous voice, asked for the tongue of one of the executed men. This beautiful girl was Beatrice d'Hirson.

'They say that it is good for the stomach-ache,' she said. 'The tongue of whichever one you like; it's all the same to me.'

The executioners looked at her somewhat suspiciously, wondering whether this had not something to do with sorcery. For it was well known that the tongue of a man who had been hanged, particularly one who had been hanged upon a Friday, was useful for raising the Devil. But could the tongue of a man who had been decapitated serve the same purpose?

However, since Beatrice had a handsome shining piece of gold in the palm of her hand, they acceded to her request and discreetly gave her what she desired.

12

The Horseman in the Dusk

WHILE THE BLOOD OF the brothers Aunay dried upon the yellow earth of the Place du Martrai, where the dogs, for many days, came to sniff and yelp, Maubuisson was slowly recovering from its nightmare.

The King's three sons remained invisible till evening. No one visited them, except for the gentlemen attached to their persons; everyone kept clear of the doors of their apartments, behind which the three men were in the profound grip of anger, humiliation or sorrow.

Mahaut, with her small escort, had returned to Paris at midday. Distracted with hate and sorrow, she had tried to force herself into the King's presence. Nogaret had come to inform her that the King was working and did not wish to be disturbed. 'It is he; it is this watchdog who bars the way and prevents my reaching his master.' Everything confirmed the Countess Mahaut's impression that the Keeper of the Seals was the sole artisan of the disaster which had overtaken her daughters and of her own personal disgrace. Everything tended to make her believe this: Nogaret was capable of anything.

'I leave you to God's mercy, Messire de Nogaret, God's mercy,' she said in a threatening voice as she left him.

Other passions and interests were already in question at Maubuisson. The familiars of the exiled Princesses tried to renew the invisible threads of power and intrigue, even by denying the friendships of which they had been so proud but a short time before. The loom of fear, vanity and ambition set itself going once more to weave again, upon a new design, the cloth so brutally torn.

Robert of Artois, always prudent, had the cunning not to boast of his triumph; he waited merely to harvest its fruits. But already the respect that normally was given to the Burgundy clan was turning towards himself.

In the evening, at supper, the King had about him not only his two brothers and his daughter, Marigny, Nogaret and Bouville, but also Robert of Artois; from which fact it became evident that he was already regaining favour.

It was a small supper; almost a mourning supper. In the long narrow room, next to the King's chamber, where the repast was served, there reigned a heavy silence. Even Monseigneur of Valois was silent, and the greyhound Lombard, as if he felt the diners' embarrassment, had left his master's feet to go and lie before the fireplace.

When the equerries, between two courses, were changing the slices of bread, Lady Mortimer came in, carrying in her arms the little Prince Edward, so that he might kiss his mother good night.

'Madame de Joinville,' said the King, calling Lady Mortimer by her glorious maiden name, 'bring my grandson to me.'

'My *only* grandson,' he added to himself.

He took up the child and for a long moment held him before his eyes, studying the little innocent face, round and rosy, the dimples marked by shadows. 'Whose child will you show yourself to be?' Philip the Fair wished to ask. 'Your weak, unstable and debauched father's, or my daughter Isabella's? For the honour of my blood, I should like you to take after your mother; but for the welfare of France, I pray heaven that you should only be your weak father's son.'

'Edward! Give a smile for Monsieur your grandfather,' said Isabella.

The child appeared to have no fear of the unblinking stare fixed upon him. Suddenly, putting out his little hand, he buried it in the sovereign's golden hair, and pulled out a curly lock.

Philip the Fair smiled. At once there was a sigh of relief among the diners, everyone laughed, and dared at length to speak.

When the child had gone and the meal was over, the King dismissed everyone but Marigny and Nogaret whom he signalled to remain. For a long moment he said nothing and his counsellors respected his silence.

'Are dogs creatures of God?' he asked suddenly, though his audience had no idea from what train of thought the question arose.

He had risen to his feet and placed his hand on the warm neck of the greyhound who had got up at his approach and was stretching himself before the fire.

'Sire,' replied Nogaret, 'we know a great deal about men because we are men ourselves, but we know very little about the rest of the phenomena of nature.'

Philip the Fair went to the window and remained there looking out, though he saw nothing but the confused shapes

of stone and vegetation. As often happens to men in positions of great power on the evenings of days when they have
assumed tragic responsibilities, his mind was engaged with
a vague and mysterious problem, seeking some certainty in
the order of the universe which might justify his life, his
position and his acts.

At last he turned round and said, 'Enguerrand, what is
done is done, and the marks of fire and steel cannot be effaced.
The culprits are at this moment face to face with God. But
where tends the kingdom? My sons have no heirs.'

Marigny said without raising his head, 'They will have,
Sire, if they take new wives.'

'They have wives before God.'

'God can efface,' said Marigny.

'God does not obey the laws of the earth. God does not
consider my kingdom but only His own. It is not by prayer
that I shall free my sons from their ties!'

'The Pope can free them,' said Marigny.

The King then turned to look at Nogaret.

'Adultery is no motive for annulling a marriage,' said the
Keeper of the Seals drily.

'We have no other recourse today but Clement,' said Philip
the Fair. 'And my first consideration must not be the common
law, even if it is in the hands of the Pope. A King must foresee
the fact that he may die at any time. To whom, Nogaret, and
you Enguerrand, would you first go to announce my death, if
it occurred at this moment? To Louis. He is the eldest; so he
must be the first to be freed.'

Nogaret raised his long thin hand which caught the light
from the hearth.

'Indeed, I cannot see how Monseigneur of Navarre can
ever wish to take back his wife, nor can I see that it would

in any circumstances be a desirable thing for the kingdom.'

'I feel sure,' said Philip the Fair, 'that you will know how to convince the Curia and Pope Clement that a King's reasons are not those of an ordinary man, but that they are, in short, reasons.'

'I will devote myself to it with the utmost zeal, Sire,' replied Nogaret.

There was a sound of galloping hooves. Marigny rose and went to the window, while Nogaret said to the King, 'The Duchess of Burgundy[20] will most certainly do the best she can to put obstacles in our way with the Holy See. Monseigneur Louis must be warned not to destroy his chances by his temperamental peculiarities.'

'Yes,' said Philip the Fair. 'I will speak to him tomorrow and you will go as soon as possible to see the Pope.'

The noise of galloping hooves, which had drawn Marigny to the window, ceased upon the flagstones of the courtyard.

'A horseman, Sire,' said Marigny. 'He seems to have come a long way; his clothes are covered with dust and his horse is exhausted.'

'From whence does he come?' asked the King.

'I do not know; I cannot see his livery.'[21]

Indeed, night had fallen and the precincts of the castle were lost in shadow. Marigny turned from the window and came back to the fire.

A moment later there was a hasty step in the corridor and Bouville, the first chamberlain, entered.

'Sire, a courier has arrived from Carpentras and demands an audience of you.'

'Show him in.'

A young man of about twenty-five years of age came in. He was tall and broad in the shoulder. His yellow-and-black

tunic was covered with dust; the embroidered cross of the
Papal Couriers gleamed on his chest. He held his hat, covered
with dust and mud, in his left hand and the carved staff which
was the insignia of his function. He advanced towards the
King, knelt on his right knee, and took from his belt the silver-
and-ebony box which contained the message.

'Sire,' he said, 'Pope Clement is dead.'

The King and Nogaret started and their faces turned pale.
An appalling silence followed upon the announcement. The
King opened the ebony box, took out the parchment and
broke the seals. He read it with concentration as if to make
sure of the truth of the news.

'The Pope we created is now dead,' he murmured, handing
the parchment to Marigny.

'When did he die?' asked Nogaret.

'Six whole days ago. On the night of the nineteenth-
twentieth,' replied the courier.

'Forty days,' said the King.

He had no need to say more, for his three ministers were
in process of making the same calculation. Forty days had
passed, and no more, since upon the Island of Jews the voice
of the Grand Master of the Templars had cried from among
the flames, 'Pope Clement, Chevalier Guillaume de Nogaret,
King Philip, I summon you to the Tribunal of Heaven before
the year is out!' No more than six weeks had elapsed and the
curse had already fallen upon the first of them.

'Tell me,' said the King, speaking to the courier and making
him a sign to rise, 'how did the Holy Father die, and what was
he doing at Carpentras?'

'Sire, he was journeying to Cahors and was forced to stop
on the way. He was suffering from fever and pain for several
days. He said that he wished to return to die in his birthplace.

The doctors tried everything to cure him, even to the point of making him take a powder of powdered emeralds which, so it appears, is the best remedy for the illness from which he suffered. But nothing was any good. He choked to death. The cardinals were at his bedside. I know no more.'

He fell silent.

'Leave us,' said the King.

The courier went out. There was no sound in the room but the breathing of the four men, rooted to the place where they had heard the news, and the snoring of a greyhound, torpid with heat.

The King and Nogaret looked at each other. 'Which of us two next?' they thought. Philip the Fair's eyes appeared even larger and more unblinking than usual. His face was astonishingly pale, and within the long royal robe that covered his body he felt stiff with the icy rigor of death.

PART THREE
THE HAND OF GOD

I

The Rue des Bourdonnais

EIGHT DAYS AFTER THE execution of the Aunay brothers and the sentence pronounced upon the Princesses, the people of Paris had already adopted a story in which cruelty, shame and love each played their part. By an unconscious simplification, the whole story centred upon Marguerite of Navarre. No longer was a single lover attributed to her, but ten, fifty. People looked at the Tower of Nesle with terror. And there, when night had fallen, guards watched at the foot of the walls, pike in hand, ready to drive off anyone so rashly curious as to be attracted to the accursed spot. For the affair was not over yet. There was murmuring of strange things in the streets. Too many corpses had been recovered from the river in that locality during the last few days, and it was said that Monseigneur Louis le Hutin, shut up in his Palace, was torturing those of his servants who might have been privy to his wife's adultery, and that he threw their bodies into the Seine.

That morning, beautiful Beatrice d'Hirson left the Countess Mahaut's house at an early hour. It was the beginning of May and the sun played upon the windows of the houses.

Beatrice went on her way unhurriedly, delighted to feel the warm breeze upon her face. Her body loved warmth; she savoured the scent of early spring and took pleasure in attracting the glances of men, particularly those of lowly condition. 'If they but knew what I was doing! If they but knew what I carry in my purse!' she thought amusedly.

She reached the Saint-Eustache quarter and soon came to the rue des Bourdonnais. It was a strange place with a secret life of its own. The public scribes had their shops there, as had the wax-merchants, for these manufactured the writing-tablets, as well as tapers, candles and polishes. But a strange traffic was carried on in many of the back rooms of the rue des Bourdonnais. With infinite precautions the mysterious ingredients needed by those who practised sorcery could be bought here for gold: powdered snakes, ground toads, cats' brains, tongues of the hanged, bawds' hairs, and all kinds of plants from which love-philtres were made or the poisons with which enemies could be destroyed. This all gave excellent reason to those who called this narrow street, where the Devil bought and sold wax, the prime material for casting spells, the 'street of the sorcerers'.

Casually, unhurriedly, looking about her, Beatrice d'Hirson entered a shop whose painted sign bore the following inscription:

ENGELBERT
FURNISHES TAPERS AND CANDLES
TO THE ROYAL COURT
AND MANY CHURCHES AND CHAPELS

The shop, wedged between two houses, was long, low and dark. From the ceiling hung every size of taper and, upon large shelves fixed to the wall, lay bundles of candles tied in dozens as well as cakes of the brown, red and green wax used for seals. The air was heavy with the smell of wax and everything felt rather greasy to the touch.

The shopkeeper, a little old man wearing a large bonnet of brown holland, was poking the embers of a furnace and attending to his moulds. As soon as he saw Beatrice, his face crumpled into a wide toothless smile.

'Master Engelbert,' said Beatrice, 'I have come at once to pay you the bill from the Hôtel d'Artois.'

'That is very kind of you, my beautiful young lady, because business is very bad. Purchase tax,[22] that invention of the Devil, is killing us. Indeed, I really don't know whether I shall be able to keep my shop open much longer!' said Master Engelbert, wiping his dirty hands on his apron.

He went to a corner of the room and came back with a tablet which he consulted with a frown. 'Let us see if we agree the figure!'

'I am sure that we shall agree upon it,' said Beatrice softly, placing several pieces of silver in the shopkeeper's hand.

'Well, well, that's the way to go about things; I only wish more people would do likewise!' said the fellow, laughing as he counted the money.

Then he added, with an air of complicity, 'I shall call your protégé. I am well pleased with him, because he works willingly and talks little. Master Everard!'

The man who came in from the back of the shop was about thirty years old, thin but solidly built. His face was bony, his eyes dark and sunken, his lips thin. He limped and his limping made him grimace nervously from time to time.

He was an ex-Knight Templar of the Commandery of Artois. Having been tortured for twelve hours, he had escaped from his executioners, but that one night of inhuman suffering, of which his crushed foot was a constant reminder, had left him slightly crazy. He had lost his faith; and had learnt to hate. He lived only for the vision of revenge. Without the tic which from time to time suddenly twisted his face, and without the disquieting wildness of his eyes, he would not have been lacking in a certain rough charm. He had come one day to take refuge, like a hunted animal, in the stables of the Hôtel d'Artois. Beatrice had placed him with Engelbert, who fed him, gave him a bed to lie upon and, above all, provided him with an alibi for the agents of the Provost; in exchange for this, the ex-Knight, besides doing the rough work, kept the accounts and sent out the bills.

As he did each time Beatrice came to the shop, Master Engelbert pretended that he had an urgent appointment and went out. He went without anxiety. Other clients might come; Everard would never hand over goods without payment. As for the traffic in wax for casting spells, Engelbert preferred that it should take place out of his sight and that somebody else should be responsible for it. He wished to know nothing of it, and was content merely to put the money in his pocket.

As soon as they were alone, the ex-Templar seized Beatrice by the hands and said, 'Come.'

The young woman followed him, passed through a curtain which he raised for her, and found herself in the store where Master Engelbert kept the cakes of raw wax, casks of tallow, and parcels of wicks. This was where Everard slept, lying on a narrow pallet squeezed between an old chest and the leprous wall.

'My castle, my domain, the Commandery of the Chevalier Everard,' he said with bitter irony, indicating with a wild gesture of his hand the dark and sordid habitation. 'All the same it is better than death,' he added.

Then, taking Beatrice by her shoulders, he pulled her to him.

'And you,' he murmured, 'are better than eternity.'

The more Beatrice's voice grew slow and calm, so Everard's became excited.

Beatrice smiled with that air she always wore and which seemed vaguely to mock both men and things; she gazed at the ex-Templar's forehead. She felt a perverse joy in knowing that people were in her power. Indeed, this man was doubly at her mercy, in the first place because he was a secret fugitive and she could give him up at any moment; and also because he had an erotic obsession for her. While he feverishly passed his hands over her body, which she suffered with her usual placidity, she said, 'You must be pleased. The Pope is dead.'

'Yes ... yes ...' said Everard, a savage joy lighting up his eyes. 'His doctors made him eat powdered emeralds. An excellent remedy which pierces the bowels. Whoever they are, those doctors are friends of mine. The curse begins to work out, Beatrice. One of them is dead already. The hand of God strikes swiftly, particularly when assisted by the hand of man.'

'And the Devil's too,' she said smiling.

She did not appear to notice that he had raised her skirt. The ex-Templar's wax-covered fingers caressed her fine, smooth, warm thigh.

'Do you want to help the curse to work again?' she went on.

'Upon whom?'

'The man to whom you owe your crushed foot.'

'Nogaret,' murmured Everard.

He stepped back a pace, and three times his face twitched with the tic.

She went close to him.

'You can avenge yourself if you will,' she said. 'Doesn't he buy his lights here?'

Everard looked at her without understanding what she meant.

'Don't you make his candles?' she went on.

'Yes,' he said, 'they are the same as those we deliver for the King's apartment.'

'What sort of candles are they?'

'Long candles of white wax with specially treated wicks which give very little smoke. He also uses long yellow tapers in his house. But he only uses these particular candles when he sits up to work late and he needs no more than two dozen a week.'

'Are you sure?'

'I know it from his concierge who comes to fetch them by the gross. For we do not deliver them ourselves; it is not so easy to gain admittance to his house. The dog is suspicious and guards himself well.'

He pointed to some parcels on a shelf.

'Look, his next consignment is already prepared and also the King's which is beside it . . . and to think that it is I,' he added in sudden anger, beating his breast, 'that it is I who have to prepare the candles with which he lights all the crimes his mind conceives. Whenever I see those parcels going to him, I long to spit upon them with the devil's poison.'

Beatrice still smiled.

'I can tell you a better one than that,' she said. 'There is no need to come face to face with Nogaret if you wish to strike him down. I know how to poison a candle.'

'Is it possible?' asked Everard.

'He who breathes its flame for an hour never sees another unless it be the flames of Hell. It is a method which leaves no trace and has no remedy.'

'How do you know of it?'

'Oh . . . well!' said Beatrice shrugging her shoulders and lowering her eyes, as if it were a matter of coquetry. 'It is only a question of mixing a powder with the wax.'

'And why should you wish . . . ?' said Everard.

She pulled him by the shoulder, placing her mouth close to his ear as if about to kiss him.

'Because there are other people besides yourself,' she whispered, 'who wish to avenge themselves. Believe me, you risk nothing.'

Everard thought for a moment. He was breathing quickly and harshly. His eyes grew brighter, more intelligent.

'Then we must hurry,' he said, the words falling over each other. 'I may have to leave here soon. Don't tell anyone of this, but the nephew of the Grand Master, Messire Jean de Longwy, has begun to take account of us. He has also sworn to avenge Messire de Molay. We are not all dead, in spite of that dog's hounding us. The other day, I saw one of my old brothers, Jean Dupré, who brought me a message, telling me to prepare to go to Langres. It would be a fine thing to be able to take to Messire de Longwy the soul of Nogaret as a present. When can you give me the powder?'

'Here it is,' said Beatrice, opening her purse.

She handed Everard a little bag which he opened cautiously. The bag contained two ill-mixed materials, one grey, the other white and crystalline.

'That is ash,' said Everard, pointing to the grey powder.

'Yes,' she replied, 'the ash of the tongue of a man who was

killed by Nogaret – to bring the Devil upon him and make no mistake about it.' She pointed to the white powder, 'That is Pharaoh's Serpent.[23] Don't be afraid. It can kill only when burning. When will you make the candle?'

'At once,' said Everard.

'Have you time? Won't Engelbert come back?'

'Not before a good hour is out. You will keep watch in case a customer should come.'

He went and fetched the brazier, bringing it into the storeroom, and poked the embers. Then he took a candle which had been prepared for the Keeper of the Seals, placed it in a mould and set it to melt. Then he slit it down its length with a knife and tipped the contents of the bag into it.

Beatrice, in the shop, looked like a customer who was waiting to be attended to, but through a chink in the curtain she watched Everard, his face lit up by the embers, limping busily about the brazier. In the meantime she muttered the words of a spell in which the Christian name of Guillaume was repeated three times. Everard went and cooled the candle in a vat of water.

'There,' he said, 'it is done. You can come back.'

The candle had been remade and showed no trace whatever of the operation.

'For a man who is more accustomed to handle a sword, it is a pretty good piece of work,' said Everard with a cruel, self-satisfied air.

And he went to replace the candle where he had taken it from.

'Let us hope that it is a good harbinger of eternity.'

The poisoned candle, in the middle of the packet and indistinguishable from the others, was like the winning prize in a lottery. Upon which day would the servant whose duty it was to furnish the candelabras of the Keeper of the Seals pull that particular one out? Seeing the King's candles next to them, Beatrice laughed lightly, but already Everard had come back to her and taken her in his arms.

'It is perhaps the last time I shall see you.'

'It may be . . . or it may not,' she said, screwing up her eyes.

He carried her, utterly unresisting, to the pallet.

'How did you manage to remain chaste when you were a Templar?' she asked.

'I never could remain so,' he replied in a low voice.

Then beautiful Beatrice closed her eyes; her upper lip curled curiously, uncovering little white teeth; and she gave herself up to the illusion that she was in the Devil's grasp.

Besides, did not Everard limp?

2

The Tribunal of the Shadows

NOGARET WORKED EVERY NIGHT as he had done all his life. And every morning the Countess Mahaut hoped for the arrival of news which would re-open to her the King's door. In vain. Messire de Nogaret seemed to be in peculiarly good health, and Beatrice had to bear the fury of the terrible Countess. She went back to Master Engelbert. As she expected, Everard had suddenly disappeared. She began to have doubts about him, and also doubted the power of Pharaoh's Serpent; she feared that out of spite or because of the calcined tongue of one of the Aunays the Devil had directed his blows elsewhere.

One morning in the third week of May, Nogaret, unusually, arrived rather late for a meeting of the Privy Council and entered the hall upon the heels of the King, brushing against Lombard as he passed.

All the usual counsellors were present and, for once, the two brothers and the three sons of the King were all gathered together.

The most urgent matter in hand was the election of the

Pope. Marigny had just received a report from Carpentras, where the cardinals, who had been holding a conclave since the death of Clement V, were in process of disputing to such an extent that an early issue seemed unlikely.

The pontiff's throne had now been vacant for four weeks, and the situation required that the King of France should make known his intentions without delay.

All present knew the King's desire; he wished the Papacy to remain at Avignon, under his hand; he wished to choose himself, if not apparently at least in fact, the future head of the Christian Church, and to put him under an obligation by the mere fact of selecting him; he wished that the huge political organisation which was the Church should not be able to act, as it had so often done in the past, contrary to the policy of the Kingdom of France.

But, indeed, the twenty-three cardinals who were present at Carpentras, cardinals who came from all over the Christian world, from Italy, from France, from Spain, from Sicily and from Germany, and who had acquired their dignity for peculiarly unequal services, were divided into almost as many rival camps as there were birettas.

Theological argument, political opposition, rivalry of interest, and family jealousies exacerbated their disagreement. With the Italian cardinals in particular, there existed irremediable hatreds between the Caetani, the Colonna and the Orsini.

'These eight Italian cardinals,' said Marigny, 'are agreed upon one point only, that of removing the Papacy back to Rome. Fortunately, they are not in agreement as to who should be elected Pope.'

'That agreement may well come with time,' remarked Monseigneur of Valois.

'That is why they must not be allowed to have the time,' replied Marigny.

There was a brief silence, and at that moment Nogaret felt a sensation of nausea in his stomach and a difficulty in breathing. He found it hard to sit upright in his chair and to control the trembling of his body. Then suddenly his fatigue disappeared; he breathed deeply and wiped his forehead.

'For many Christians,' said Charles of Valois, 'Rome is the seat of the Papacy, in their eyes Rome is the centre of the world.'

'That, undoubtedly, would be convenient for the Emperor of Constantinople, but not for the King of France,' said Marigny.

'All the same, Messire Enguerrand, you cannot undo the labour of centuries and prevent the throne of Saint Peter being situated where it was founded.'

'But whenever the Pope wishes to rule from Rome, he is never able to remain there,' cried Marigny. 'He is invariably compelled to fly before the different factions that divide the City and to take refuge in some castle or other under the protection of this town or that, with troops to guard him who do not even belong to him. He is in fact much happier under the protection of our garrison of Villeneuve installed upon the farther bank of the Rhône.'

'The Pope will remain in his establishment at Avignon,' said the King.

'I know Francesco Caetani well,' went on Charles of Valois; 'he is a man of great learning and merit upon whom I may be able to bring some influence to bear.'

'I don't want to have this Caetani at all,' said the King. 'He belongs to the family of Boniface, and he will renew the errors of the bull Unam Sanctam.'[24]

Philippe of Poitiers, who had said nothing until that moment, now interrupted with a forward movement of his long body.

'There are,' he said, 'so many intrigues in this business that one intrigue should cancel out another. If we don't bring pressure to bear, we shall be involved in a conclave which may well last a year. In more difficult circumstances than these, Messire de Nogaret has shown what he is capable of doing. It is up to us to be the most tenacious and stubborn party.'

After a moment's silence, Philip the Fair turned to Nogaret.

The latter was pale in the face and seemed to be breathing with difficulty.

'What do you advise, Nogaret?'

'Yes, Sire,' said the Keeper of the Seals with an effort.

He put a shaking hand to his forehead.

'May I be excused. This appalling heat . . .'

'It is not hot at all,' said Hugues de Bouville.

Nogaret, with a great effort, said in a distant voice, 'The interests of the kingdom and of the Faith demand that we should act in this way.'

He fell silent, and no one could understand why he had said so little.

'And your advice, Marigny?'

'I propose that we should find some pretext for removing the remains of the late Pope, as was his desire, to Cahors, in order to show the conclave that this is a matter for haste. Bertrand de Got, Clement's nephew, might well be charged with this pious mission. Messire de Nogaret would set out upon his journey, with all necessary powers, accompanied by a sufficient armed escort. His escort would guarantee his powers.'

Charles of Valois turned his head away; he disapproved of this show of force.

'And how does my annulment come into all this business?' asked Louis of Navarre.

'Be quiet, Louis,' said the King. 'That is exactly what we are endeavouring to determine.'

'Yes, Sire,' said Nogaret without even realising that he had spoken.

His voice was low and hoarse. He felt troubled in mind and appeared to see things out of focus. The beams of the hall suddenly seemed to him as high as those of the Sainte-Chapelle. Then, suddenly, they seemed as near as those of the subterranean chambers in which he was accustomed to interrogate his prisoners.

'What is going on?' he asked, trying to loosen the buttons of his coat. He appeared to have suffered a sudden cramp, his knees were raised against his stomach, his head was lowered, and his hands clutched at his chest. The King rose, followed by all those present. Nogaret cried aloud as if strangled and fell vomiting upon the floor.

It was Hugues de Bouville, the Grand Chamberlain, who took him back to his house where he was immediately visited by the King's doctors.

These consulted lengthily among themselves before coming to give the Sovereign their diagnosis. Their report meant nothing whatever. But very soon, both at the Court and in the town, there was talk of some unknown malady. Poison? It was said that the most powerful antidotes had been tried. Affairs of state, that day, were to all intents and purposes suspended.

When the Countess Mahaut learnt the news from Beatrice, she merely said, 'He is paying,' and sat down to eat.

Nogaret was paying. For some hours now he had not recognised those about him. He was at death's door upon his bed and, lying on his side, his body shaken with spasms, was spitting blood.

At first he had endeavoured to remain sufficiently upright to lean over a basin, but now he no longer had the strength to do so and his blood, flowing from his mouth, fell upon a thick sheet that a servant changed from time to time.

The room was full of people; couriers in relays, taking the latest news to the King, servants, major-domos, secretaries and, in a corner, forming a small, sly, talkative group, were Nogaret's relations, thinking of the possible spoils and putting a value upon the furniture.

As far as Nogaret was concerned, these were all un-recognisable spectres, moving upon a far, illogical, pointless plain, amid what seemed to him but a confused noise. But there were other more visible presences that appeared to him alone.

For, at this hour, when the anguish of sin had come upon him for the first time, he thought of the death of others, and felt at the last that he was the brother of all those whom he had persecuted, hounded, made martyrs of, and exe-cuted. Those who had died under interrogation, in prison, at the stake, on the wheel, now arose from his overwrought imagination and appeared to close in upon him, almost near enough to touch him.

'Go back, go back!' he screamed in terror.

The doctors ran to him. Nogaret, haggard, twisting upon his bed, his eyes rolling in terror, was endeavouring to repulse the shades.

And the smell of his own vomited blood seemed to him to be the smell of the blood of his, victims.

He suddenly sat up and then fell back again. Those present had retreated to a distance and were watching him, he who was one of the masters of the kingdom, fade into the shadows. With his hands to his throat, he struggled to ward off the red-hot irons which had so often burnt naked breasts in his presence. His legs were at the mercy of appalling cramps and he was heard to cry, 'The pincers, the pincers! Take them away for mercy's sake!'

It was the same cry that the brothers Aunay had uttered in their prison of Pontoise.

The nightmare in which Nogaret fought was no other than the reflection of his own life, in so far as it had affected others.

'I did nothing in my own name! I served the King, the King alone.'

Before the bar of agony the lawyer was making a last pleading.

The room emptied towards eleven o'clock at night. Only one doctor, a barber-surgeon and one old retainer remained with Nogaret. The King's couriers, wrapped in their cloaks, slept side by side upon the floor of the ante-chamber. His family had gone, not without certain regrets. One of them had slipped a purse into a servant's hand, saying, 'Let me know when it is all over.'

Bouville, who had come to get news, questioned the doctor on duty.

'Nothing we can do has been any use,' the latter said in a low voice. 'He is vomiting less, but he is still in delirium. We can but await the end! Unless some miracle . . .'

With the death rattle in his throat, Nogaret, lying upon his bed, alone knew that the dead Templars awaited him in the shades.

They passed before him, some on horseback, clothed in their surcoats of war, others raising their bodies shattered by torture; there they stood, lining an empty road, bordered by precipices and lit by the light of pyres.

'Aymon de Barbonne . . . Jean de Furne . . . Pierre Suffet . . . Brintinhiac . . . Guillaume Bocelli . . . Ponsard de Gizy . . .'

Was it the shades who uttered their names, or was it merely the dying man no longer aware of his own words?

'The sons of Cathare!'[25] cried a voice which suddenly drowned all others.

And, surging suddenly out of darkest night, the tall figure of Boniface VIII became manifest in that immense distance of space that was Nogaret's consciousness, that space which contained mountains and valleys, and in which huge crowds marched onwards towards the Last Judgment.

'Sons of Cathare!'

At the sound of Boniface's voice, the whole drama of Nogaret's life revived. He saw himself, upon a September day, beneath the bright Italian sun, riding at the head of six hundred horsemen and a thousand artillerymen towards the rock of Anagni; beside him rode Sciarra Colonna, the mortal enemy of Boniface, the man who had preferred to serve three years chained to an oar in a Berber galley rather than be recognised and risk being handed over to the Pope. Thierry d'Hirson was a member of that expedition. The little town had opened its gates of its own accord; the Caetani Palace was taken and, passing through the interior of the Cathedral, the attackers had invaded the Pope's apartments. And there the old Pope, who was then eighty-six, his tiara upon his head, crucifix in hand, alone in a huge deserted hall, had watched the armed horde burst in upon him. Summoned to abdicate, he had replied, 'This is my neck, this is my head; if

I die, I shall die as Pope.' Sciarra Colonna struck him in the face with his steel gauntlet.

From the profound depths of his agony, Nogaret cried, 'At least I prevented his killing him.'

The City had been given over to pillage. Two days later, the inhabitants had changed sides, had fallen upon the French troops, and had wounded Nogaret who had been compelled to fly for his life. Nevertheless he had achieved his object. The old man's mind had not been able to resist fear, anger and outrage. When he had been released, Boniface had wept like a child. When he had been brought back to Rome he had become subject to wild dementia, insulting everyone who approached him, refusing all food and dragging himself upon all fours about the room in which he was held prisoner. A month later, the King of France had triumphed, the Pope was dead, blaspheming and refusing, in an access of rage, even the last sacraments.

Bending over Nogaret, a doctor looked down upon this body which was still imperceptibly struggling against an excommunication from which he had long ago been relieved.

'Pope Clement . . . the Chevalier Guillaume de Nogaret . . . King Philip.'

As Nogaret's lips feebly articulated the words, the echo of the Grand Master's voice suddenly burst upon his mind.

'I am burning,' he said again.

At four o'clock in the morning, the Bishop of Paris came to administer the last sacraments to the Keeper of the Seals. It was a simple ceremony. A prayer was said above the prostrate body, those present knelt, trembling with fatigue and un-reasoning fear.

The Bishop remained a moment in prayer at the foot of the bed. Nogaret was motionless, sunk among his sheets as

MAURICE DRUON

if already a heavy stone were resting upon him. The Bishop departed, and it seemed that all was over; the doctor went up to the bed; Nogaret was still alive.

The windows grew grey in the faint light of dawn, and an insistent bell rang out across the Seine from beyond the end of the world. The old servant opened a window, greedily breathing in the fresh air. Paris smelled of springtime and new leaves. The city was awakening to a subdued clamour.

The patient was heard to murmur, 'Have pity!'

When they looked round, Nogaret was dead and a trickle of blood was already drying at his nostrils. The doctor said, 'God has taken him!'

Then the old servant went and took from Master Engelbert's last delivery two long white candles which he placed in a candelabra and moved near the bed to light the last vigil of the Keeper of the Seals of France.

3

The Documents of a Reign

Hardly had the Keeper of the Seals given up the ghost, when Messire Alain de Pareilles, in the name of the King, entered Nogaret's house to seize all the documents, papers and dossiers. He had every chest and drawer opened. The few drawers of which Nogaret had kept the key in some secret place were forced.

In an hour's time, Alain de Pareilles had returned to the palace with a mass of archives, papers, parchments and tablets which, upon the order of Hugues de Bouville, were placed in the middle of the great oak table filling one whole side of the royal study.

Then the King himself came to pay a last visit to Nogaret. He remained but a short time before the body. He prayed silently. His eyes never for a moment left the face of the dead man, as if he still had one last question to ask him who had shared all his secrets and had served him so well.

Returning to the palace, Philip the Fair, followed by three sergeants-at-arms, appeared somewhat bowed as he walked. In the clear morning, servants were calling the citizens to the public baths. Life in Paris was beginning again and care-free children were already chasing each other through the streets.

Philip the Fair crossed the Mercers' Hall and re-entered the palace. He at once set himself, with the assistance of Maillard, his private secretary, to examine the documents which had been brought from Nogaret's house. The sudden disappear-ance of the Keeper of the Seals left many important matters pending.

At seven o'clock Enguerrand de Marigny came to see the King. The two men looked at each other in silence while the secretary retired.

'The Pope,' the King said curtly, 'and now Nogaret . . .'

There was concern, even distress in his voice as he said the words. Marigny went to the table and took the chair the sovereign indicated. For a moment he remained silent, then he said, 'Well, these are but strange coincidences, Sire, that is all! Similar things happen every day, but we are not concerned about them because they do not come to our notice.'

'We are getting older, Marigny.'

He was forty-six years of age, and Marigny was forty-nine. Comparatively few men, at that period, reached their fiftieth year.

'We shall have to look into all this,' the King went on, indicating the papers.

And, without saying anything more, they both devoted themselves to the business of selecting what should be destroyed, classifying what Marigny should preserve, or what should be handed to the various legal advisers.

There was silence in the King's study, hardly disturbed by the distant cries of the street-sellers, the rumour of workaday Paris. The King's pale forehead was bent over the open files of which the most important were bound in leather bindings bearing Nogaret's cipher. Philip saw the whole of his reign pass before his eyes, twenty-nine years in which he had held the fate of millions of men in his hands, and imposed his influence upon the whole of Europe.

And suddenly this whole series of events seemed remote from his true life, his real destiny. Everything suddenly appeared to him in a new light with strange shadows.

He was discovering what others thought and wrote about him, he saw himself from outside. Nogaret had kept reports from agents, the minutes of interrogations, letters, even police records. From all these lines of written words arose a picture of the King which he himself could not recognise, the picture of someone distant, hard, a stranger to the hardships of mankind, inaccessible to pity. Astonished, he read a couple of sentences written by Bernard de Saisset, the Bishop whose revolt had unleashed the quarrel with Boniface VIII. There were two cold and terrible phrases: 'He may well be the most handsome man in the world, but he knows only how to look at people in silence. He is not a man, nor a beast; he is a statue.'

And there were also these words written by another witness of his reign: 'Nothing will make him bend, he is an Iron King.'

'An Iron King,' murmured Philip the Fair. 'Have I so successfully concealed my weaknesses? How little others know us, and how wrongly judged I shall be!'

Suddenly, seeing a written name, he remembered an extraordinary embassy which he had received at the very beginning of his reign. Rabban Kaumas, a Chinese Nestorian Bishop, had come to France, sent by the Great Khan of Persia, the descendant of Gengis Khan, in order to suggest an alliance to the King of France, and war against the Turks with an army of a hundred thousand men.

At that time Philip the Fair was twenty years old. How wonderfully seductive to a young man had seemed this dream of a crusade, a crusade in which Europe and Asia would participate; what an enterprise worthy of Alexander! Nevertheless, on that day, he had chosen a different road. No more crusades, no more warlike adventures; it was to France and to peace that he wished to devote all his efforts. Had he been right? How strong would France be, had he accepted the Khan of Persia's alliance? For one moment he dreamed of a gigantic reconquest of the Christian territories which would have carried his glory far down the centuries. . . . Then he returned to reality and selected a new pile of dusty parchments.

Suddenly his shoulders appeared to become bowed. It was simply the matter of a date – 1305! It was the year of the death of his wife Jeanne, who had brought Navarre to the kingdom, and to him the only love of his life. He had never wanted any other woman; and since she had died nine years ago he had looked at none other and would never do so. He had recovered from the sorrow of his widowhood only to enter upon the uprising of 1306 in which, in the face of Paris rioting because of his Orders in Council about currency, he had had to take refuge in the Temple. The following year he had arrested those who had taken him in and defended him. The depositions of the Templars were preserved here, in huge rolls of parchment whose fastenings had been sealed by Nogaret. The King did not open them.

And now? Like so many others, Nogaret's face had lost the light and warmth which gave it life. His indefatigable mind, his strength of will, his tough and exalted spirit, were

all effaced. Only his work remained. For Nogaret's life had
not been that of a man who, behind his official position,
bequeaths those small, sorrowfully intimate memorials that
people leave behind them and which are so often ignored
by the heedlessness of others. Nogaret was indeed exactly as
he appeared. He had identified his life with the life of the
kingdom. His secrets were all here, written into the evidence
of his labour.

'How many forgotten things are here,' thought the King.
'So many prosecutions, so much torture, so many tears.
A river of blood ... and all for what? What earth has been
nourished by it all?'

His eyes unblinking, he was lost in thought.

'And all for what?' the King asked himself once more. 'To
what end? Where are my victories? Never a thing that is
sure to live after me.'

He felt the great need to act which men feel when assailed
by the idea of their own death, and the total negation which
lies in wait for them, as if the world had never existed.

Marigny remained still, disquieted by the King's gravity.
Most things in his continually increasing work, in his responsibilities and honours came easily to him, except the understanding of his Sovereign's silences. He was never certain of
judging them aright.

'We made Boniface canonise King Louis,' Philip the Fair
said suddenly in a low voice, 'but was he really a saint?'

'It was useful to the kingdom, Sire,' replied Marigny.

'But was it necessary, afterwards, to use force against
Boniface?'

'He was on the point of excommunicating you, Sire,
because you were not putting the policies he desired into
practice in your kingdom. You have not failed in the duty of

kings. You have remained in the place God designed for you, and you have publicly proclaimed that you hold your kingdom from no one but God himself.'

Philip the Fair indicated one of the rolls of parchment. 'And the Jews? Have we not burnt rather too many of them? They are human beings, mortal and capable of suffering as we are. God did not order that.'

'Messire Saint Louis, Sire, hated them, and the kingdom had need of their wealth.'

The kingdom, the kingdom, every action was justified by the kingdom. 'We had to do this or that because of the kingdom . . . We must do this because of the kingdom . . .'

'Messire Saint Louis loved the Faith and the greatness of God! But what have I loved?' said Philip the Fair in a low voice.

'Justice,' said Marigny. 'The justice which is necessary for the common good and overtakes all those who diverge from the tendency of the world.'

'Those who have diverged from the tendency of the world have been very numerous throughout my reign, and they will continue to be numerous if one century resembles another.'

He picked up Nogaret's dossiers and let them fall back on the table, one after another.

'Power is a bitter thing,' he said.

'Nothing is great that has not its bitter side,' replied Marigny, 'and Christ knew it. You have reigned in the grand manner. Think merely that you have united under the crown Chartres, Beaugency, Champagne, Bigorre, Angoulême, Marche, Douai, Montpellier, Franche-Comté, Lyons, and part of Guyenne. You have fortified your cities, as your father, Monsieur Philippe III wished, so that they should no longer be at the mercy of foreigners. You have remade the laws in accordance with the law of ancient Rome. You have remodelled Parliament so that

it may be in a position to make sounder laws. You have con-
ferred upon many of your subjects the *bourgeoisie du roi*.[26] You
have enfranchised the serfs of many bailiwicks and seneschalships. No, Sire, you are in error if you fear having done wrong.
From a kingdom torn by dissension you have built a country
which begins to beat with a single heart.'

Philip the Fair rose. The impregnable conviction of his
Coadjutor reassured him, and he leant upon it in order to
fight a weakness which was not truly natural to him.

'You may be right, Enguerrand. But if you are satisfied
with the past, what do you say of the present? Yesterday a
crowd had to be dispersed in the rue Saint-Merri by the
archers. Read what the Governors of Champagne, Lyons and
Orleans write to me. There are outcries and complaints all
over the country about the rising cost of wheat and the low-
ness of wages. And those who complain, Enguerrand, will
never know that what they demand and what I should like
to give them depend upon time and not upon my will. They
will forget my victories in order to remember my taxes,
and I shall be accused of not having fed them throughout
their lives.'

Marigny listened, more disquieted now by the King's words
than by his silences. He had never heard him talk so much,
nor admit to such uncertainty, nor show such discourage-
ment.

'Sire,' he said, 'we must decide several matters.'

Philip the Fair gazed once more upon the documents of
his reign spread over the table. Then he straightened up, as
if he had given himself an order to forget the pain and blood
of human beings, and to become a king once more.

'Yes, Enguerrand,' he said, 'we must.'

4

The King's Summer

WITH NOGARET'S DEATH, PHILIP the Fair seemed to be inhabiting a country in which no one could join him. Spring reigned over the earth and upon the houses of men; Paris was alive in the sunshine; but the King appeared to be exiled in some interior winter of his own. And the Grand Master's prophecy was constantly present to his mind.

He often went to spend a few days in one of his residences, or would distract himself for a moment from his obsession by hunting. But he was quickly recalled to Paris by alarming reports. The situation in town and country was bad. The cost of food was rising; the more prosperous regions did not export their surplus wealth to the poorer ones. 'Too many police and not enough wheat,' was the phrase upon everyone's lips. Taxes remained unpaid and people were in open revolt before the Provosts and tax-gatherers. Taking advantage of this bad period, the leagues of the barons, in Burgundy and Champagne, re-formed themselves and made unreasonable demands. In Artois, Robert, turning the scandal of the Princesses and the general discontent to his own advantage, was beginning once more to agitate.

'A bad springtime for the kingdom,' Philip the Fair allowed himself to remark to Monseigneur of Valois.

'We are in the fourteenth year of the century,' replied Valois, 'a year that fate has marked out for disaster.'

In saying this he was evoking the unhappy precedents of the past; 714, the invasion of the Spanish Moors; 814, the death of Charlemagne; 914, the Hungarian Invasion and the Great Famine; 1114, the loss of Brittany; 1214, Bouvines – a victory that was nearly a catastrophe, a victory dearly paid for. Only the year 1014 was without disaster or crisis.

Philip the Fair looked at his brother as if he did not see him. He let his hand fall upon Lombard's neck, stroking his hair the wrong way.

'All the difficulties of your reign, Brother, derive from your advisers,' said Charles of Valois. 'Marigny now knows no bounds. He uses the confidence you repose in him to deceive you and constantly engages you in the policies that suit him. If you had listened to me over the Flanders business . . .'

Philip the Fair shrugged his shoulders in a gesture which meant, 'As for that, there is nothing I can do about it.'

The question of Flanders recurred that year, as it often recurred, like a mounting flood. Bruges, which he was unable to reduce, stood in the way of the King's efforts; the County of Flanders continually escaped from the hands that wished to encircle it. From the field of battle to secret treaties the Flemish question remained an open wound in the kingdom's flank. What remained of the sacrifices of Furnes and of Courtrai, what remained of the victory of Mons-en-Pévèle? Once more it was becoming necessary to use force.

But the raising of an army required more gold, and if a

campaign were to be initiated, the budget would undoubtedly overtop that of 1299, which remained in everyone's memory as the highest the kingdom had ever known: 1,642,649 pounds, with a deficit of 70,000 pounds.[27] When for several years the ordinary receipts of the Treasury had amounted to approximately 500,000 pounds, where was the balance to be found?

Marigny, against the advice of Charles of Valois, ordered a Popular Assembly for the first of August 1314. Twice already resort had been made to this means, but each time it had been upon the occasion of conflict with the Papacy, the first over the affair of Boniface and the second over the affair of the Templars. It was in helping the civil power to free itself from obedience to the power of the Church that the bourgeoisie had acquired the right of speech. Now, and this was something new, the people were to be consulted over a matter of finance.

Marigny made the preparations for the Assembly with the greatest possible care, sending messengers and agents into the towns, multiplying interviews and promises. His genius was that of a superb diplomat, he spoke to everyone in their own language.

The Assembly was held in the Mercers' Hall, where the stalls on that particular day were closed down. The forty statues of Kings, and that of Marigny, seemed to watch from their pillars. A platform had been erected upon which the King, the members of his Council, and the great barons of the kingdom, took their places.

Marigny spoke first. He stood up to speak at the foot of his own marble effigy, and his voice seemed even more assured than usual, more certain of expressing the truth on behalf of the kingdom. He was superbly dressed; he had all the presence and all the gestures of an orator. Above him, in the huge double-aisled nave, several hundred people listened.

Marigny explained that if food was short – and therefore more expensive – it was a fact which was far from surprising. Peace, which King Philip had maintained, favoured an increase in the population. 'We grow the same amount of wheat, but we are a greater number to share it,' he said. More must therefore be sown. Then he turned to the charge; the towns of Flanders threatened the peace. But, without peace, there could be no increase in the harvest, there would be no hands to till the uncultivated lands. And without the revenues and riches which came from Flanders, taxes would fall more heavily upon the other provinces. Flanders must yield; it must be forced to yield. For this, money was necessary, not for the King but for the kingdom. And everyone present must understand that their own personal security and prosperity were threatened.

'We shall now see,' he concluded, 'who will give help to an expedition against the Flemish.'

There was a murmuring in the crowd, immediately silenced by the piercing voice of Pierre Barbette.

Barbette, a citizen of Paris, recognised by his equals as the most capable in argument with the royal authority upon questions of law and tax, rich from a cloth-business and also from horse-dealing, was Marigny's creature and ally. The two men had prepared this interruption. In the name of the first city of the kingdom, Barbette promised the required aid. He carried the gathering with him, and the deputies from forty-three 'good towns' acclaimed the King and Marigny unanimously and Barbette, their loyal servant.

If the Assembly had been a victory, the financial results that were expected from it soon appeared insufficient. The Army was placed upon a war footing before the subscription had been fully raised.

The royal troops made a demonstration in Flanders, and Marigny, wishing to gain a victory at the earliest possible moment, hastened to negotiate and conclude, in the first days of September, the Convention of Marquette. As soon as the Army had left, Louis of Nevers, Count of Flanders, denounced the Convention and the trouble started all over again. Monseigneur of Valois and his supporters among the great barons accused Marigny of allowing himself to be bought by the Flemish. The bill for the campaign still remained to be paid, and the royal officers continued to demand, to the great discontent of the provinces, the special contribution which was from now on without an object. The Treasury was empty and Marigny, once more, had to consider exceptional means of raising money.

The Jews had already twice been attacked. To shear them once again would produce but little wool. The Templars no longer existed and their gold had long since melted away. There remained only the Lombards.

Already, in 1311, they had had to buy off a threat of expulsion from the kingdom. This time there could be no question of buying off; it was the seizure of all their goods, and their expulsion from France, which Marigny was preparing. Their trade with Flanders could serve as a pretext, as could also the financial support they gave to the leagues of discontented nobles.

It was a considerable organisation that he was proposing to attack. The Lombards, *bourgeois du roi*, all worked together; they were well organised and had a Captain-General at their head. They were everywhere, dominating trade and controlling finance. They lent money to the barons, to the towns, and to the King. They even gave money in charity when it was necessary.

Marigny spent several weeks in perfecting his scheme and in convincing the King.

Necessity found in Marigny a tenacious advocate, and towards the middle of October all was ready for an immense campaign, whose unfolding would very much resemble that which, seven years before, had been the prelude to the destruction of the Templars.

But the Lombards of Paris were very well-informed. Having learnt from experience, they paid dearly for the secrets of the King's Council.

Tolomei watched with his single open eye.

5

Power and Money

CHARLES OF VALOIS HAD conceived such a hatred for Marigny that he could even wish for some disaster to overtake the kingdom if that disaster would destroy the Coadjutor. He also felt bound to place obstacles in the way of all his plans. Robert of Artois seconded him in his own way; asking larger and larger sums from Tolomei, he mollified the banker by reporting Marigny's intentions.

One evening in mid-October there was a meeting at Tolomei's of some thirty men who represented one of the most extraordinary organisations of power of the period.

The youngest, Guccio Baglioni, was eighteen years old; the oldest was sixty-five: this was Boccanegra, Captain-General of the Lombard companies. However different these men were in age and appearance, there was nevertheless a singular resemblance between them: the same richness of clothing, the same assurance in speech, the same mobility of expression and gesture, the same attentive attitude when leaning forward to miss nothing of Tolomei's discourse.

Lit by huge candles placed in sconces along the walls, these dark-skinned men, with their mobile faces, formed a single family with a common language. They were, too, a tribe at war, and their strength, in spite of their small numbers, was equal to that of all the leagues of nobles and all the assemblies of bourgeois.

There were present the Peruzzi, the Albizzi, the Guardi, the Bardi, the Pucci, the Casinelli, all from Florence, as was old Boccanegra and Signor Boccaccio, the head traveller for the Bardi; there were, too, the Salimbene, the Buonsignori, the Allerani, and the Zaccaria, from Genoa; there were the Scotti, from Piazenca, and the Siennese clan led by Tolomei. There existed between all these men rivalries of prestige, commercial competition, and long-inherited family quarrels or those created by matters moral or marital. In danger, however, they acted together like brothers.

Tolomei explained the situation without in any way brightening the colours that the picture presented.

When all the Lombards were prepared to make the great decision – that was to leave France, put their banking houses into liquidation, enter claims for money owed them by un-grateful lords, and provoke, by a great expense of gold, serious uprisings in the capital – when everyone had been roused to the boiling point, and was thinking with anger of what he would be compelled to abandon, this one his luxurious house, that one the marriage he had arranged for himself, that other his three mistresses, Tolomei said, 'I possess a means of binding the Coadjutor's hands and possibly of destroying him.'

'Don't hesitate then. Destroy him!' said Buonsignori, the chief of the Genoese clan. 'We have had enough of making a fortune for these pigs who grow fat upon our labour.'

'We shall no longer bare our backs to the whip!' cried one of the Albizzi.

'What are your means?' Scotti asked.

Tolomei shook his head. 'I cannot tell you.'

'Debts I suppose?' said Zaccaria. 'And what good will that do us? Have they ever embarrassed these upstarts? On the contrary! If we leave, they'll merely take the opportunity to forget what they owe us.'

Zaccaria was bitter: he represented a small company and was jealous of those who had important clients. Tolomei turned towards him and, in a tone of voice that at once expressed prudence and determination, said, 'Much more than debts, Zaccaria! A poisoned weapon of which he knows nothing and which, forgive me, I must keep secret. But, in order to be able to use it, I need your help. Because in dealing with the Coadjutor we must match power with power. I hold a threat to him in my hand; I want to be able to confront him with a dilemma. Marigny must choose between agreement or war to the death.'

He developed his idea. If the Lombards were to be despoiled, it was because the King lacked the money to pay for his war in Flanders. At all costs Marigny must fill the Treasury; his personal destiny was at stake. The Lombards would show themselves good subjects, and spontaneously propose a huge loan at very low interest. If Marigny refused, Tolomei would draw his sword from its scabbard.

'Tolomei, you must tell us more,' said Bardi.

'What is this sword of which you speak?'

After a moment's hesitation, Tolomei said, 'If you wish, I will reveal it to Boccanegra alone.'

They whispered together for a moment and consulted each other with their eyes.

'Si . . . va bene . . . faciamo cosi' was heard.

Tolomei led the Captain-General into a corner of the room

and spoke to him in a low voice. The others watched the old Florentine's face with its narrow nose, thin lips and tired old eyes.

Tolomei told him of Jean de Marigny's embezzling of the Templars' wealth, and of the existence of the receipt signed by the young Archbishop.

'Two thousand pounds well laid out,' murmured Tolomei. 'I knew that they would serve me well one of these days.'

Boccanegra gave a little laugh with a sound of gargling at the bottom of his old throat; then he resumed his seat and said briefly that they might have confidence in Tolomei. The latter then began, with style and tablet, to record the figures that each one would subscribe to the eventual royal loan.

Boccanegra was the first to have his considerable figure recorded; ten thousand and thirteen pounds.

'Why the thirteen pounds?' he was asked.

'To bring him bad luck.'

'Peruzzi, how much are you good for?' asked Tolomei.

Peruzzi made a calculation, scratching rapidly upon his tablet.

'I'll tell you in one moment,' he replied.

'And you, Guardi?'

They all had the look of men from whom a pound of flesh was being torn. The Genoese, gathered round Salimbene and Zaccaria, were holding council together. They were known to be the hardest in matters of business. It was said of them, 'If a Genoese merely looks at your purse, it is already empty.' Nevertheless, they were prepared to act and some among them murmured, 'If he succeeds in getting us out of this, he will one day succeed Boccanegra.'

Tolomei went up to the Bardi who were talking softly to Boccaccio, 'How much, Bardi?'

The eldest Bardi smiled, 'As much as you, Tolomei.'

The Siennese's left eye opened.

'Then it will be twice the sum you think.'

'It would nevertheless be much more expensive to lose everything,' said Bardi, shrugging his shoulders. '*Non e vero*, Boccaccio?'

The latter nodded his head, then rose to take Guccio aside. Their meeting on the road to London had given rise to a sort of intimacy between them.

'Has your uncle really the means of twisting Enguerrand's neck?'

Guccio put on his most serious expression and replied, '*Caro* Boccaccio, I have never heard my uncle announce what he was unable to perform.'

When the meeting came to an end, Benediction was over in all the churches and night had fallen upon Paris. The thirty bankers left Tolomei's house by the little door which gave on to the Cloister of Saint-Merri. Escorted by their servants carrying torches, they formed, in the shadowy darkness lit by the red flames, a strange procession of menaced wealth, a procession of the penitents of gold.

Tolomei, alone with Guccio, was in his study adding up the total of the promised sum, as one counts the soldiers of an army. When he had finished, he smiled. His eyes half-closed, his hands clasped behind his back, he murmured, as he gazed into the fire where the logs were turning into ash, 'Messire de Marigny, you have not won yet.'

Then to Guccio he said, 'If we succeed, we shall demand new privileges in Flanders.'

For, even though he was so near to disaster, Tolomei, in spite of himself, still thought of drawing a profit from his fear and the risks he ran. Carrying his immense stomach before him, he went over to a chest, opened it, and took out a leather box.

'The receipt signed by the Archbishop,' he said. 'With the hatred Monseigneur of Valois bears them, and with what is already being said of the two Marignys, and with what Enguerrand has made the Flemish pay him, there is enough here to hang both of them. You will mount the best horse and leave at once for Neauphle, where you will put this document in safety.'

He looked Guccio straight in the eyes and added gravely, 'If anything were to happen to me, Guccio, you will give this parchment to Monseigneur of Artois. He will certainly know how to use it well. But take care, for our branch at Neauphle will not be safe from archers either.'

Suddenly Guccio, in spite of the danger he was about to run, remembered Cressay, the beautiful Marie and the embrace by the field of rye.

'Uncle, Uncle,' he said excitedly, 'I have an idea. I will do as you wish. I will go not to Neauphle but to Cressay, where the squires are under an obligation to us. I was once of considerable assistance to them and the debt they owe us is a sufficiently good excuse. Besides I think the daughter, if things have not much changed, will not refuse me her help.'

'That is a good idea,' said Tolomei warmly. 'You are growing up, my boy! Kindness of heart in a banker must always serve some purpose. Go ahead then! But since you need these people's help, you must go to them with presents. Take some ells of embroidered cloth and the lace that I received yesterday from Bruges for the women, didn't you tell me that there are also two boys?'

'Yes,' said Guccio. 'They care for hunting and nothing else.'

'Splendid! Take the two falcons that I got for Artois. He can wait . . . *A proposito* . . .'

He broke off suddenly in the middle of a laugh; an idea had suddenly occured to him.

He leant over the chest once more and took out of it another parchment.

'Here are Monseigneur of Artois' accounts,' he went on. 'He won't refuse to help you, if there were to be some difficulty in the matter. But I am more certain of his support if you present your petition with one hand and his accounts with the other. And here also is the loan to King Edward. I do not know, nephew, if you will be rich with all this, but you will be in a position to do plenty of harm! Go along then! Don't waste time now. Go and have your horse saddled.'

He put one hand on the young man's shoulder and concluded, 'The fate of our companies is in your hands, Guccio, and don't forget that. Arm yourself and take two men with you. Take also this bag of a thousand pounds; it is a weapon worth many swords.'

Guccio embraced his uncle with an emotion he had never felt before. There was no need this time to create an imaginary part for himself or to imagine that he was a conspirator in flight; the part had come to him; a man is formed by the risks he runs, and Guccio was in process of growing up.

Less than an hour later, with two escorting servants trotting at his side, he took the road to the Porte Saint-Honoré.

Then Messire Spinello Tolomei put on his fur-lined cloak because the month of October was chilly, called two servants with torches and daggers and, thus protected, went to Enguerrand de Marigny's house to give battle.

'Tell Monseigneur Enguerrand that the banker Tolomei wishes to see him urgently,' he said to the porter.

Tolomei waited for some time in a sumptuous ante-chamber; royal state was kept in the Coadjutor's house.

'Come in, Messire,' said a secretary, opening a door.

Tolomei crossed three large rooms and found himself face to face with Enguerrand de Marigny who was working in his study and finishing supper at the same time.

'This is an unexpected visit,' said Marigny coldly, making a sign to the banker to sit down. 'What is it about?'

Tolomei gave a slight bow, sat down and replied equally coldly, 'An affair of state, Messire. For some days now there have been rumours that the King's Council are preparing certain measures which relate to my business and which, I must tell you, we find highly embarrassing. Confidence is being destroyed, buyers are rare, our creditors are demanding satisfaction, and as for those who have other business with us, debtors for instance, they are trying to put off the due date. We are having considerable difficulty.'

'This has nothing to do with the affairs of the kingdom,' replied Marigny.

'We shall see,' said Tolomei. 'We shall see. If this were only a personal matter, I should sleep easy. But the business affects a great many people, here and elsewhere. There is anxiety everywhere, in my various branches.'

Marigny rubbed his rough chin.

'You are a reasonable man, Messire Tolomei, and you should not give credence to these rumours, I give you my word for it,' he said, looking calmly at one of the men he was about to destroy.

'Of course, of course, your word ... but the war has cost the kingdom dear,' replied Tolomei. 'The revenue is perhaps not coming in as well as might be hoped, and the Treasury may well be finding itself in need of new gold. What is more, we have prepared, Messire, a plan of our own.'

'What is it? Your business, I repeat, is no affair of mine.'

Tolomei raised a hand as if to say, 'Patience, Messire Coadjutor, you do not yet know all.' And went on, 'We desire to make some great effort to come to the assistance of our much beloved King. We are in process of organising ourselves to offer the Treasury, a considerable loan in which all the Lombard companies will participate, and for which we will ask but the lowest possible interest. I have come here to tell you this.'

Then Tolomei leant forward towards the fire and muttered a figure so important that Marigny was taken aback. But the Coadjutor immediately thought, 'if they are prepared to deprive themselves of this sum, it can only mean that there is twenty times the amount to be seized.'

Reading as much as he did and sitting up late as so frequently happened, his eyes were liable to fatigue and his eyelids were red.

'This is a splendid scheme and a worthy thought for which I am grateful,' he said after a moment of brief silence. 'Nevertheless I must tell you that I am surprised. I have heard that certain companies have been dispatching important sums of gold to Italy. This gold cannot be both there and here at the same time.'

Tolomei completely shut his left eye.

'You are a reasonable man, Monseigneur, and you must not give credence to rumours such as that, I give you my word,' he said, ironically emphasising his last words. 'Is not the offer I am making you a proof of our good faith?'

'Fortunately,' the Coadjutor coldly replied, 'I do believe in your assurances. If that were not the case, the King would not have permitted these attacks upon the French monetary reserves, and we should have had to put a stop to them.'

Tolomei did not flinch. The export of Lombard capital had begun owing to the threat of expropriation, and it was indeed this export itself which Marigny was endeavouring to use to justify his actions. It was a vicious circle.

'I think that we have said to each other all that is necessary, Messire Tolomei,' Marigny went on.

'Certainly, Monseigneur,' replied the banker, rising. 'But don't forget our offer, if events should make it useful.'

Then, going towards the door, he suddenly said, as if he had just remembered something,

'I am told that Monseigneur your brother the Archbishop is in Paris at the moment.'

'He is indeed.'

Tolomei nodded his head, as if in thought.

'I hardly dare,' he said, 'to take up the time of so important a prelate, even if he is under some obligation to me. But I would be happy that he should know that I am always at his service, from today onwards if he should so wish, and at any hour. What I have to say will be of some importance to him.'

'What have you to say to him?'

'Monseigneur,' said Tolomei smiling, 'the prime virtue of a banker is to know how to hold his tongue.'

Then, as he was about to leave, he repeated drily, 'From today onwards, if he should so wish.'

6

Tolomei Wins

THAT NIGHT TOLOMEI SLEPT hardly at all. He wondered whether he would have time to employ the means of bringing pressure upon Marigny.

Philip the Fair's signature at the bottom of a parchment put before him by Enguerrand de Marigny would suffice to ensure the destruction of the Lombards. Would not Enguerrand hurry things forward? 'Had he warned his brother?' Tolomei asked himself. 'And has the Archbishop told him the nature of the weapon that I have in my possession? Will he not perhaps obtain the King's signature this very night and so forestall me? Or will these two brothers come to an arrangement to have me assassinated?'

Tolomei, restless in his insomnia, thought bitterly of this, his second country, which he had hoped to serve so well by his work and his money. Because he had become rich there, he was more devoted to France than to his native Tuscany. Indeed, he really loved France in his own way. Never to feel beneath his feet the cobbles of the street of the Lombards, never to hear the bourdon of Notre-Dame, never to attend another meeting at the City Centre,[28] never to smell the Seine again in the spring, all these renunciations tore at his heart. Without realising it, he had become a true Parisian, one of those Parisians who are born far from the frontiers of France and yet have no other city. 'To begin trying to make a fortune again elsewhere at my age, even if I am allowed to live to begin again!'

He went to sleep only with the dawn and was almost immediately awakened by the trampling of feet in his courtyard and the sound of knocking at his door. Tolomei thought that he was about to be arrested, and dressed as quickly as he could. A distracted servant appeared. 'Monseigneur the Archbishop asks to speak to you urgently,' he said.

From the ground floor could be heard a confused sound of heavy boots and pikes banging against the flagstones.

'What is all the noise about?' asked Tolomei. 'Is not the Archbishop alone?'

'He has six guards with him, Signor,' the servant replied.

Tolomei frowned; his expression changed to a certain hardness.

'Open the shutters in my study,' he said.

Monseigneur Jean de Marigny was already climbing the stairs. Tolomei waited for him, standing upon the landing. The Archbishop, slim and with a golden crucifix jiggling at his breast, immediately came to the point.

'What, Messire, does this mean, this strange message that my brother has sent me during the night?'

Tolomei raised his plump, pointed hands in a pacific gesture.

'Nothing, Monseigneur, that can in any way worry you, or was worth disturbing yourself for. I would have come to the Bishop's Palace at your convenience. Will you come into my study? I think it will be more convenient to speak of our business there.'

The two men went into the room in which Tolomei normally worked. The servant was just finished removing the inner shutters which were ornamented with paintings. Then he put an armful of thin wood upon the embers still red in the fireplace and soon flames were crackling upwards. Tolomei made a sign to his servant to leave them.

'You come accompanied, Monseigneur,' he said. 'Was that necessary? Do you not trust me? Do you think that you are in danger here? I had become accustomed, I must say, to a different kind of behaviour.'

He tried to make his voice sound formal, but his Tuscan accent was more noticeable than usual, which was a sign of anxiety.

Jean de Marigny sat down before the fire to which he extended his ringed hands.

'This man is uncertain of himself and does not know quite how to take me,' thought Tolomei. 'He arrives here with a great to-do of armed men as if he were going to pillage the house, and now he sits there looking at his nails.'

'Your haste to warn me has given me some disquiet,' said the Archbishop at last. 'I intended to come to see you, but I would have preferred to choose the time of my visit.'

'But you have chosen it, Messire, you have chosen it. What I have said to Messire Enguerrand is no more than a matter of politeness, believe me.'

The Archbishop glanced quickly at Tolomei. The banker, apparently quite calm, fixed a single eye upon him.

'Indeed, Messire Tolomei, I have a service to ask of you,' he said.

'I am always ready to render your lordship a service,' replied Tolomei quietly.

'Those ... objects ... that I ... confided to you?' said Jean de Marigny.

'Extremely valuable objects indeed, which came from the possessions of the Templars,' said Tolomei, defining them without a change in his tone of voice.

'Have they been sold?'

'I do not know, Monseigneur, I do not know. They have been sent out of France, as we agreed, since they could not be disposed of here. I imagine that some of them will have found a purchaser; I shall receive the advice notes at the end of the year.'

Tolomei, his fat body comfortably settled, his hands clasped upon his stomach, nodded his head good-humouredly.

'And the receipt I signed? Do you still need it?' said Jean de Marigny.

He was hiding his fear, but he hid it badly.

'Are you sure you are not cold, Monseigneur? You are very white in the face,' said Tolomei, leaning forward to place a log on the fire.

Then, as if he had forgotten the question put by the Archbishop, he went on, 'What do you think of the matter that has been several times under discussion by the King's Council during the last week, Monseigneur? Is it possible that they are intending to steal our goods, to reduce us to penury, to exile and death?'

'I have no information,' said the Archbishop. 'These are affairs of state.'

Tolomei shook his head.

'Yesterday I made Monseigneur your brother a proposition which it seems to me he does not wholly understand. It is most unfortunate. It is said that we are about to be despoiled in the interests of the kingdom. But indeed, we are offering to serve the kingdom by making an enormous loan, Monseigneur, and your brother remains silent. Has he not said a word of it to you? This is most regrettable, very regrettable indeed!'

Jean de Marigny got up.

'I cannot discuss the decision of the King, Messire,' he said drily.

'As yet it is not a decision of the King,' replied Tolomei. 'Can you not tell the Coadjutor that the Lombards, called upon to surrender their lives which are at the King's disposition, believe me, and their gold which is also his, wish, if possible, to preserve their lives? They willingly offer their gold when it is intended to take it from them by force. Why not listen to them?'

There was a silence. Jean de Marigny, completely immobile, seemed to be looking into some distance beyond the wall.

'What are you going to do with that parchment I signed for you?' he asked.

Tolomei ran his tongue across his lips.

'What in my place would you do with it, Monseigneur? Just think for a moment. It is naturally a strange thought for you. But just imagine that there was a threat to ruin you and that you possessed something – a talisman, that's it, a talisman which might serve you to evade ruin.'

He went towards the window, hearing a noise in the courtyard. Porters were arriving, loaded with packing-cases and bales of cloth. Tolomei automatically valued the merchandise entering his premises that day and sighed.

'Yes, a talisman against ruin,' he murmured.

'You are not suggesting that that receipt . . .'

'Yes, Monseigneur, that is exactly what I am suggesting and wish to suggest,' said Tolomei in a hard voice. 'That receipt is evidence that you have embezzled the possessions of the Templars which were forfeit to the Crown. It is evidence that you have stolen, and stolen from the King.'

He looked the Archbishop straight in the face. 'I have done it now,' he thought. 'It is a question of who will flinch first.'

'You will be held to have been my accomplice!' said Jean de Marigny.

'In that case we shall swing together at Montfaucon like a couple of thieves,' replied Tolomei coldly. 'But I shall not swing alone.'

'You are an unmitigated rascal!' cried Jean de Marigny.

Tolomei shrugged his shoulders.

'I am not an archbishop, Monseigneur, and it is not I who have embezzled the gold in which the Templars paraded the body of Christ. I am but a merchant. And at this moment we are making a deal, whether you like it or not. That is the basic meaning of everything we are saying. If there is no robbing the Lombards, there will be no scandal as far as you are concerned. Should I fall, Monseigneur, you will fall too. And from a greater height. And the Coadjutor, who is too rich not to have made enemies, will be brought down with you.'

Jean de Marigny seized Tolomei by the arm.

'Give me back the receipt,' he said.

Tolomei looked at the Archbishop; his lips were white; his chin, hands, indeed the whole of his body was trembling.

Tolomei gently disengaged himself from the gripping fingers.

'No,' he said.

'I will give you back the two thousand pounds you advanced me,' said Jean de Marigny, 'and you may keep all the profits of the sale.'

'No.'

'Five thousand.'

'No.'

'Ten thousand! Ten thousand pounds for that receipt.'

Tolomei smiled.

'And where will you find them? I know better than you do yourself of what your fortune consists. I should have to lend you them, too.'

Jean de Marigny, his hands clenched, said, 'Ten thousand pounds! I shall find them. My brother will help me.'

'Monseigneur, I have offered, as my contribution alone, seventeen thousand pounds to the royal Treasury!'

The Archbishop realised that he must change his tactics.

'And supposing I succeed in obtaining from my brother the assurance that you will be excepted from the Order in Council? You will be allowed to leave with all your fortune and begin again elsewhere.'

Tolomei reflected for a moment. He was being made the offer of escaping by himself. Against this assurance, was it worth while risking a huge throw of the dice?

'No, Monseigneur,' he replied. 'I will suffer the fate of everyone else. I do not want to begin again elsewhere, and indeed have no reason to do so. By now, I have as many roots in France as you. I am a *bourgeois du roi*. I wish to continue living in this house, which I have built, and in Paris. I have lived thirty-two years of my life in it, Monseigneur, and, if God wills, it is here that I shall die.'

His resolution and the tone of voice in which it was expressed were not lacking in grandeur.

'Moreover,' he added, 'even if I desired to give you back the receipt, I could not do so; it is no longer here.'

'You lie!' cried the Archbishop.

'It has gone to Sienna, Monseigneur! To my cousin Tolomei with whom I have many business interests in common.'

Jean de Marigny did not reply. He went quickly to the door and called, 'Souillard! Chauvelot!'

'Now, we must put a brave face on it!' Tolomei thought.

Two great fellows of six foot apiece appeared, pikes in their hands.

'Watch this man; see that he doesn't move an inch from where he stands!' said the Archbishop. 'And close the door. Tolomei, if you cross me, you'll regret it! I'm going to search till I find the document! I shall not leave without it!'

'I shall regret nothing, Monseigneur, and you will find nothing. You will leave here in the same state as you arrived, whether I am alive or dead. But if by chance I am dead, you may as well know that it will do you no good. For my cousin in Sienna has been warned, if I should die before my time, to make the existence of this receipt known to King Philip,' said Tolomei.

His heart was beating too quickly in his fat body, and he felt the cold sweat trickling down the small of his back. Feeling a sort of internal support, as if his back were against an invisible wall, he managed to remain calm.

The Archbishop searched the chests, turned out the drawers full of credit notes upon the floor, scattered the files of papers and the rolls of parchment. From time to time he looked secretly at the banker in order to see whether his effort at intimidation was succeeding. He went into Tolomei's room and the latter heard him turning his cupboards to chaos.

'Luckily Nogaret is dead,' thought Tolomei. 'He would

have gone about this business differently and would certainly have found some way of defeating me.'

The Archbishop reappeared.

'You can go,' he said to the two guards.

He was defeated. Tolomei had not given way to fear.

Some agreement must be reached.

'Well then?' asked Marigny.

'Well, Monseigneur,' said Tolomei calmly, 'I have nothing more to say to you than I said a little while ago. All this disorder is completely useless. Talk to the Coadjutor and press him to accept the offer I have made while there is yet time. Otherwise . . .'

Without finishing his sentence, the banker went to the door and opened it. Jean de Marigny went out without another word.

The scene which took place that very day between the Archbishop and his brother was terrifying. Suddenly face to face, their personalities nakedly revealed, the two Marignys who, until then, had walked in step, were now at odds.

The Coadjutor overwhelmed his younger brother with contemptuous reproaches, and the younger brother defended himself as best he could, but meanly.

'You're a fine one to blame me!' he cried. 'Where does your wealth come from? From what Jews sent to the stake? From what Templars you have burnt? I have only followed your example. I have been useful enough to you in your plots; now it's your turn to be useful to me.'

'Had I known what you were like, I would not have made you an archbishop,' said Enguerrand.

'You would have found no one but me to sentence the Templars, and you very well know it.'

The Coadjutor knew very well that the exercise of power

leads to unworthy relationships. But he felt suddenly oppressed by being brought face to face with the consequences in his own family. A man who would agree to betray his own conscience for the sake of a mitre, might well also steal and betray. This man happened to be his brother, that was all.

Enguerrand de Marigny took up the mass of papers upon which he had prepared the Orders in Council against the Lombards and, with a furious gesture, threw it into the fire.

'A lot of work for nothing,' he said. 'Such a lot of work!'

7

Guccio's Secrets

CRESSAY, IN THE CLEAR LIGHT of spring, with the transparent leaves of the trees and the quivering silver surface of the Mauldre, remained a happy memory for Guccio. But when, on this October morning, the young Siennese, continuously looking over his shoulder to make certain that he was not being followed by archers, arrived upon the heights of Cressay, he wondered for a moment whether he had not made a mistake. The autumn seemed somehow to have shrunk the Manor House, to have made it sink into the earth. 'Were its towers so low?' Guccio said to himself. 'And can one's memory alter so much in a mere six months?' The courtyard had become, under the rain, a muddy bog into which the horses sank above their pasterns. 'At least,' thought Guccio, 'there is little chance that anyone will look for me here.'

To the limping servant who came forward he threw the reins, saying, 'Rub the horses down and feed them!'

The door of the house opened and Marie de Cressay appeared.

'Messire Guccio!' she cried.

Her surprise was so great that she turned pale and had to lean against the door frame.

'How beautiful she is,' thought Guccio; 'and she still loves me.'

The cracks in the walls disappeared and the towers of the Manor House regained their remembered proportions.

But Marie was already shouting towards the inside of the house, 'Mother! Messire Guccio has come back.'

Dame Eliabel received the young man warmly, kissed him on both cheeks and clasped him to her extensive bosom. The thought of Guccio had often been present to her widowed nights. She took his hand, made him sit down, and ordered wine and pasties to be brought him.

Guccio accepted his welcome gratefully and explained the reason for his coming as he had thought it out: he had come to Neauphle to put some order into the branch of the bank which appeared to be suffering from maladministration. The clerks were not keeping proper track of the debtors. At once Dame Eliabel grew anxious. 'You gave us a whole year,' she said. 'Winter has come upon us after a very bad harvest and we have not as yet . . .'

Guccio was indefinite about this, intimating that the squires of Cressay, since they were his friends, would not be allowed to be unduly pressed. Dame Eliabel asked Guccio to stay in the Manor House. He would, she said, find nowhere in the town where he would be more comfortable or have more society. Guccio accepted the invitation and sent for his luggage.

'I have brought,' he said, 'some pieces of cloth and some ornaments which I hope will please you. As for Pierre and Jean, I have a couple of well-trained falcons for them which will help them to be even more successful in hunting, if that is possible.'

The cloth, the ornaments and the falcons astonished the whole household and were received with cries of joy. Pierre and Jean, having returned from their daily hunting expedition, with that odour of earth and blood which adhered to them like a garment, asked Guccio a hundred questions. This companion, miraculously arrived, when they were making up their minds to the long boredom of the bad months, seemed to them more worthy of affection than even upon his first visit. One might have thought that they had known each other all their lives.

'And what has happened to our friend Provost Portefruit?' asked Guccio.

'He continues to steal as much as he can, but thank God no longer from us, thanks to you.'

Marie slipped in and out of the room, bending over the fire as she poked it, placing new straw upon the curtained pallet. She said nothing, but never stopped looking at Guccio. The latter, finding himself alone with her towards evening, took her gently by the elbows and drew her to him.

'Can you see nothing in my eyes which reminds you of felicity?' he said, borrowing the phrase from a romance of chivalry he had recently read.

'Oh yes, Messire!' replied Marie in a shaken voice, her eyes opening wide. 'I have never ceased from imagining you here, distant though you may have been. I have forgotten nothing and go back on nothing.'

He tried to think of some excuse for not having returned for six months, and for having sent no message. To his surprise, Marie, far from reproaching him, thanked him for having returned quicker than she had expected.

'You said that you would come back at the end of the year on business,' she said. 'I didn't expect to see you sooner. But even if you had not come at all, I should have waited for you all my life.'

Guccio had retained from Cressay the memory of a sweet and beautiful girl, and a certain regret for a love affair which had come to nothing, but to be quite frank he had thought of her but seldom during all these months. Now he found her wonderful and fascinating, grown like a plant through spring and summer. 'How lucky I am!' he thought. 'She might have forgotten me or got married.'

As often happens with men of unfaithful nature, this particular young man, infatuated though he was with her, was fundamentally modest about love, because he imagined other people to be like himself. He could not believe, having seen her so little, that he had inspired so strong and rare a feeling.

'Marie,' he said with newly found warmth, 'in order not to lie to you as men usually do, not only have I never ceased thinking of you, but nothing has altered the feelings I had for you.'

They stood face to face, both overcome by their feelings, and both somewhat embarrassed by their words and gestures.

'The field of rye . . .' Guccio murmured.

He bent down and put his lips to Marie's which opened like a ripe fruit.

He thought this was the appropriate moment to ask her for the help he needed.

'Marie,' he said, 'I have not come here on any business to do with the branch of our bank, nor upon any question of your family's debt. But I do not wish to, nor indeed can I, hide anything from you. It would be an offence to the love I bear you. The secret I am going to tell you is a new link which I offer you, and it is a serious one, because it affects the lives of many people, as well as my own. My uncle and powerful friends have charged me with the business of hiding in a sure place a certain document, which has to do both with affairs of state and their own safety. Undoubtedly, at this moment, there are archers searching for me,' went on Guccio who, as usual, was beginning to boast. 'There were twenty places in which I could have looked for a hiding-place, but it was to you, Marie, that I came. My life from now on depends upon your silence.'

'No, it is upon you,' Marie said, 'that my life depends, my lord. I have faith only in God and in the man who first held me in his arms. My life is his.'

Having convinced himself as he talked, Guccio felt for Marie a great surge of gratitude, tenderness and desire. However conceited he might be, he was nevertheless surprised at having inspired so persistent, powerful, and reliable a passion.

'My life is yours,' the girl went on. 'Your secret is mine. I shall conceal what you want concealed. I shall be silent about what you wish me to keep silent and your secret will die with me.'

Tears were forming in her dark blue eyes. 'Like this,' thought Guccio, 'she resembles those spring mornings when the sun shines and rain falls at the same time.'

Then, coming back to what was on his mind, he said, 'What I have to hide is contained in a leaden box hardly bigger than my two hands. Is there anywhere here?'

Marie thought for a moment.

'In the chapel,' she replied. 'We will go there tomorrow at dawn. My brothers leave the house to hunt at first light. Tomorrow my mother will leave but a little later, since she has to shop in the town. I only hope that she will not want to take me with her! But in that case I shall say that I have a sore throat.'

Guccio murmured his thanks, while Dame Eliabel's step could be heard outside.

Upon this occasion, since Guccio was staying for a longer time, he was lodged on the first floor, in a vast, clean but chilly room. He went to bed, his dagger within reach, and the leaden box containing the Archbishop's receipt beneath his head. He had made up his mind not to go to sleep. He did not know that at that precise hour the two brothers Marigny had had their terrible interview and that the Orders in Council directed against the Lombards were already burnt.

Fighting to keep his eyes open, he counted up the number of women he had already had (he was not yet nineteen and the addition took but little time to make), thought of the two young townswomen whom he was currently engaged in assisting to deceive their husbands and, comparing them to Marie, came to the conclusion that they were both immoral and not particularly beautiful.

He did not know that he had fallen asleep. A sound woke him up with a start; for a moment he thought that they were coming to arrest him and ran to the window. However, it was Pierre and Jean de Cressay, accompanied by two peasants, with their new falcons at their wrists, leaving the house. Then doors banged; a grey mare, weary with age, was brought for Dame Eliabel, who departed in her turn, escorted by the limping servant. Guccio put on his boots and waited.

A few moments later Marie called him from the ground floor, and Guccio went down, hiding the leaden box beneath his cloak.

The chapel was a small vaulted room, part of the interior of the Manor House, facing east; its walls were whitewashed.

Marie lit a taper at the oil-lamp burning before a statue of Saint John the Evangelist indifferently carved in wood. In the

Cressay family the Christian name of Jean was always given the eldest son.

'I found the hiding place when I was a child, playing with my brothers,' said Marie. 'Come.'

She took Guccio to one side of the altar.

'There, push this stone,' she said, lowering the taper to light the spot.

Guccio pushed the stone, but nothing moved.

'No, not like that.'

Marie handed the taper to Guccio and leant upon the stone in a particular way that made it swivel back upon itself, opening up a hiding place under the base of the altar. In the light of the flame Guccio saw a skull and some pieces of bone.

'Who is it?' he asked.

He was superstitious and made the sign against the evil eye behind him with his fingers.

'I don't know,' said Marie. 'No one knows.'

Next to the whitened skull Guccio deposited the leaden box which contained the damning evidence against the most powerful prelate in France.

When the stone was pushed back into place it was impossible to tell that anyone had touched it.

'Our secret is locked in the hands of God,' Marie said.

Guccio took her in his arms and tried to kiss her.

'No, not here,' she said in a frightened voice. 'Not here in the chapel.'

They came back into the Great Hall where a servant was laying the table with the bread and milk of the first meal of the day. Guccio stood in front of the fire until the servant had gone and Marie came to him.

Then they linked hands, Marie leaning her head on Guccio's shoulder and thus they remained for a long moment.

As she leaned against him, she was learning to understand his male body, the first that she had ever held in her arms and the only one that she ever would.

'I shall love you for ever, even if you cease to love me,' she said.

Then she went and poured the milk into the bowls, and broke the bread into it. Every movement she made was implicit with happiness. Guccio thought of the chalky skull he had seen under the altar steps.

Four days went by. Guccio accompanied the two brothers hunting and was not unskilful. He made several visits to the branch at Neauphle in order to justify his stay in the district. Once he met Provost Portefruit, who recognised him and saluted him with servility. This salute reassured Guccio. If some persecution of the Lombards had taken place, Messire Portefruit would not have treated him with such politeness. 'And should it be he who comes to arrest me one day soon,' thought Guccio, 'the thousand pounds I've brought will be a help in bribing him.'

Apparently Dame Eliabel had no suspicion of what was going on between her daughter and the young Siennese. Guccio was convinced of this by overhearing a conversation one evening between the good lady and her younger son. Guccio was in his room on the first floor. Dame Eliabel and Pierre de Cressay were talking by the fire in the Great Hall, and their voices came up through the chimney.

'What a pity Guccio is not of noble birth,' Pierre said. 'He would make a good husband for my sister. He is good-looking and well-educated, and in a desirable position in the world. I wonder if this is not something we should think about.'

Dame Eliabel did not receive the suggestion kindly.

'Never!' she cried. 'Money has turned your head, my son.

We are poor at the present moment, but our blood gives us the right to expect the best alliances, and I shall not give my daughter to a young man of plebeian birth who, moreover, is not even a Frenchman. Certainly the young man is pleasing, but let him not be so ill-advised as to make love to Marie. I should stop it at once. A Lombard! My daughter given to a Lombard! Besides, he has not even thought of it, and if my age did not give me a certain modesty, I would admit to you that he has more eyes for me than he has for her, and that is why he is here, as much at home as a graft upon a tree.'

Guccio, even though he smiled at the Lady of the Manor's illusions about him, was hurt by the contempt she felt for his plebeian birth and his profession. 'These people borrow money from you to live, don't pay you back what they owe you, and still consider you less than one of their peasants. And what would you do, my good lady, without the Lombards?' Guccio said to himself in annoyance. 'All right, then! You try to marry your daughter off to some great lord and see how she accepts the idea.'

At the same time he felt a certain pride at having so successfully seduced a daughter of the nobility, and it was that night that he determined to marry her in spite of all the obstacles that could be placed in his path, indeed because of these very obstacles. He succeeded in persuading himself of a vast number of admirable reasons for this course, without admitting the only true one: that he loved her.

During the meal that followed, he looked at Marie, thinking, 'She is mine: she is mine!' And every feature of Marie's face, her lovely upturned eyelashes, her eyes flecked with gold, her parted lips, all seemed to answer him, 'I am yours.' And Guccio kept asking himself, 'Why can't the others see it?'

The following day Guccio found at Neauphle a message

from his uncle which informed him that the danger, for the moment, was over; Guccio was to return at once.

Guccio had, therefore, to make it known that important business called him back to Paris. Dame Eliabel, Pierre and Jean evidenced much regret. Marie said nothing, merely went on with the embroidery at which she was working but, as soon as she was alone with Guccio, she allowed her sorrow to become manifest. Had some disaster occurred? Was Guccio in danger?

He reassured her. On the contrary, thanks to himself, thanks to her, thanks to the document concealed in the chapel, the men who desired the destruction of the Italian financiers were defeated.

Then Marie burst into tears because Guccio was going away.

'You are leaving me,' she said, 'and it is as if I were dying.'

'I shall come back as soon as I can,' said Guccio.

And he covered Marie's face with kisses. He felt suddenly angry with the events which interfered with his personal desires. That all the Lomard banks were saved gave him no pleasure, quite the contrary indeed! He would have liked still to be in danger, and therefore have a motive for remaining at Cressay. He blamed himself for not having known how to take advantage in time of this beautiful proffered body, lying in surrender and abandon in his arms. 'To wait like this is not possible for a man,' he thought.

'I shall come back, beautiful Marie,' he said again; 'I swear it, because there is nothing I want so much in the world as you.'

And this time he was sincere. He had come to find a hiding place; he went away with love in his heart.

Since his uncle in his message had said nothing of the

Archbishop's receipt, Guccio pretended to believe that it was his duty to leave it in the chapel at Cressay, thus arranging a pretext for his early return. But new events were on their way which would change the destinies of them all.

8

The Meet at Pont-Sainte-Maxence

ON THE FOURTH OF November the King was due to hunt in the forest of Pont-Sainte-Maxence. In company with his first chamberlain Hugues de Bouville, his private secretary Maillard, and a few intimate friends, he had slept the night at the Castle of Clermont, six miles from the meet.

The King appeared carefree and in better humour than he had been for a long time. The affairs of the kingdom permitted him to take a holiday. The loan from the Lombards had put the Treasury in funds. Winter would soon put a stop to the rebellious barons of Champagne and the townsfolk of Flanders.

It had been snowing during the night, the first snow of the year, so early as to be almost without precedent; the morning frost, coming on top of it, had frozen the fine snow hard and transformed the whole countryside into an immense white sea. One was aware with surprise, as happens once a year, that the colours of the world were reversed, there was light where normally was shadow, and the sky in full daylight was darker than the earth.

Men, hounds and horses were preceded by great puffs of misty breath which faded in the air like clouds of thistledown.

The hound, Lombard, trotted along by the King's horse. Even though he was intended for coursing hares, he also played his part in the hunting of stag and wild boar; working on his own he often brought the pack back on to the line. For though greyhounds are normally reputed to hunt only by eye and not by scent, this particular one, nevertheless, had a nose like a Poitevin hound.

Distant and difficult as he might be with men, Philip the Fair was easy and understanding with animals. He showed them greater friendship than he did his closest relations. Having all the characteristics of the Capet family, he was a countryman, at home on the land. Among trees, plants and animals, King Philip found peace and satisfaction.

In the middle of the clearing where the meet took place, amid a great hullabaloo of stamping horses and men, of neighing and barking, the King stayed for some time inspecting his magnificent pack, asking news of some bitch, absent because she had recently pupped, and talking to his hounds.

'Well, me beauties! Bike here then, bike here then, me beauties!' he called to them.

The chief huntsman, accompanied by a number of whippers-in, came to make his report to the King. At dawn several stags had been harboured, of which one was a royal and, so said the hunt servants in charge of the tufters, a twelve-pointer – the most noble beast to be found in the forest. Moreover, this was a lone stag of the kind which, unattached to a herd, goes from forest to forest and is the stronger and braver for being on its own.

'Set on,' said the King.

The hounds were uncoupled, led to the covert, and put on

the scent, while the huntsmen spread out, taking positions where the stag might break cover.

'Tallyho! Tallyho!' was soon heard.

The stag had been viewed; hounds were heard giving tongue so that the forest was filled with the noise, the sound of horns, the thundering of hooves and crashing of broken branches.

Generally speaking, stags for some time circle the place where they are found, make cunning diversions within the forest itself, cover their tracks, try to find a younger stag beside which they will run for a short time to make the hounds change line, and then return to their original lair.

This particular stag surprised everyone by running straight to the north. In the face of danger, his instinct was to return to the distant forest of the Ardennes from which, doubtless, he had originally come.

The King, in considerable excitement, cutting through the wood to get well forward, came to its edge and waited for the stag to break into the open.

But nothing can be so easily lost as a hunt. You believe that you are no more than two hundred yards from hounds and huntsmen, who appear to be well within earshot, and a second later you are left in total silence and solitude, amid towering trees without clue as to where the pack, which was giving tongue so loudly, has disappeared, nor what fairy has cast a spell over your companions to make them vanish so suddenly.

Moreover, on that particular day, the frosty air carried sound badly, and hounds could only hunt with difficulty since the frozen snow was not holding scent.

The King was lost, and gazing across the wide white valley, where as far as the eye could see the fields with their low hedges, the stubbles of past harvest, the roofs of a village and the distant undulations of a forest were all covered with the same flawless sparkling bed of snow, he was overcome with a sort of stupor. The sun had broken through and the country-side shone beneath its rays; and the King suddenly felt a curious lassitude, a sensation of complete estrangement from the universe. He did not pay overmuch attention to it, for he was healthy and had never been let down by his physical stamina. He thought that perhaps he had become too heated with galloping.

Concentrating upon whether his stag had broken cover or not, he followed the edge of the wood at a walk, gazing at the ground in order to find the animal's slot. 'Surely his slot should be easy to see in the snow,' he said to himself. He saw a peasant not far off.

'Hullo there, my man!' The peasant turned and came towards him. He was a labourer of some fifty years of age, with broad shoulders and short legs, his weather-tanned face strongly marked with wrinkles; his legs were clothed in thick canvas gaiters and he was holding a cudgel in his right hand. He removed his cap, revealing greying hair.

'Have you seen a big hunted stag?' the King asked him.

The man nodded his head, replying, 'Indeed I have, Sire. A beast like that crossed in front of my nose no longer ago than it would take me to repeat an *Ave*, no more. He had certainly been hunted for at least two hours, he was tired and his tongue was hanging out. He was certainly your stag. You won't have to hunt him much further because, in the state he was in, he was looking for water. And he will only find it at the lake of Fontaine.'

'Were the hounds on his line?'

'There were no hounds, Sire. But you will find his slot, the cleft wide, just about by that big white birch over there. You'll take your stag at the lake, with or without hounds.'

The King was astonished.

'You seem to know the country and hunting,' he said.

The weather-beaten face broke into a smile. Small cunning brown eyes gazed up at the King.

'I know a bit about hunting and the country,' said the man, 'and I hope that so great a King as you are may long take his pleasure in it, as long as God wills.'

'So you recognise me, do you?'

The other nodded his head again and proudly said, 'I am a free man, thanks to you, Sire, and no longer the serf I was born. I know my figures and can hold a style to add with if I have to. I once saw Monseigneur of Valois, when he enfranchised the serfs of the county, and from your look and what I have heard about you, I knew at once that you were his brother.'

'Are you happy to be a free man?'

'Happy? Of course I am. That's to say it makes you feel quite different; you no longer feel like the living dead. And we chaps know very well that we owe to you the Order in Council that Monseigneur of Valois read out to us. And we often repeat to ourselves as our prayer here on earth: "Given that every human being, formed in the image of Our Lord, should in general be free by natural right . . ." It's good to hear that, when you thought that you were once and for all no more nor less than an animal.'

'How much did you have to pay for your freedom?'

'Seventy-five pounds.'

'And you had them?'

'From the work of a lifetime, Sire.'

'What's your name?'

'André – André of the Woods, they call me, because that's where I live.'

The King, who was not ordinarily generous, felt that he wished to give this man something. Not out of charity, but as a present.

'Be a good servant of the kingdom, André of the Woods,' he said, 'and keep this as a remembrance of me.'

He detached his horn and handed it to the peasant. The latter took it, a fine piece of carved ivory with silver mountings, which was worth more than the man had paid for his liberty. The peasant's hands shook with pride and emotion.

'Oh!' he murmured, 'Oh this, this! . . . I shall place it under the statue of the Virgin Mary that it may protect our house. May God preserve you, Sire.'

The King moved away, conscious of a happiness which he had not known for many months past. A man had spoken to him among the solitudes of the forest, a man who, thanks to himself, was both free and happy. The weighty burden of power and of the years was alleviated at a single stroke. 'It is easy enough to know when one is being ruthless,' he said to himself; 'but one can never tell, from the height of a throne, if the good one has wished to do has really been done, nor for whom.'

This approval, which had unexpectedly come to him from among the masses of his subjects, was more precious to him and more delightful than all the praises received from courtiers. 'When my brother needed money, I told him, "Don't demand more taxes from your serfs without giving anything in exchange. Free the serfs of your apanage, as I have done those of Agenais, Rouergue, Gascony, and the seneschalships of Carcassonne and Toulouse." I should have extended the franchise to the whole kingdom. Supposing this man I have just seen had been educated when he was young, he might have made a provost or the captain of a town and been a good deal better than many.'

He thought of all the Andrés of the Woods, of the valleys and of the fields, the Jean-Louis of the pastures, the Jacques of the hamlet or the vineyard, whose children, freed from their servile state, would constitute a great reserve of manpower for the kingdom. 'I shall have the edict for freeing the serfs applied to the other bailiwicks.' He felt the quieter for this meeting. It had dissolved the haunting fear he had suffered since the deaths of the Pope and Nogaret. He felt that God had spoken to him through one of the most humble voices among his subjects to approve his royal work.

At that moment he heard a sharp hoarse barking on his right and recognised Lombard giving tongue.

'Get forrard then, get forrard then!' shouted the King.

Lombard was on the line, running fast, his nose a few inches from the ground. It was not the King who was lost, but all the rest of the hunt, and Philip the Fair felt a youthful pleasure at the thought that he would bring the royal stag to bay and kill it, alone with his favourite hound.

He put his horse into a gallop and, for nearly an hour, across fields and valleys, jumping hedges and fences, he followed Lombard. He felt hot, and the sweat trickled down his back.

Suddenly, as they came out of a copse, he saw a black shape flying away in front of him.

'On, on, on!' shouted the King. 'Forrard on, Lombard, forrard on!'

It was quite certainly the hunted stag, a great black beast with a pale belly. He no longer ran as lightly as he had at the beginning of the hunt; he ran heavily, stopping from time to time, looking back, and then starting again, bounding heavily. He was, indeed, making his way towards the lake of which the peasant had spoken. He was looking for water to refresh himself, the water which is fatal to animals at bay, weighing down their limbs so that they cannot emerge from it again. Lombard bayed now that the stag was in view and he was gaining ground on it. But all of them, the King, his horse, the hound, and the stag, were at the end of their tether.

There seemed to the King to be something peculiar about the stag's antlers; there seemed to be something upon them which glittered from time to time and then went out. There was, however, nothing about it of the fabulous and legendary stags which one never meets in fact, such as the famous stag of Saint Hubert with a golden cross growing upon its forehead. This one was no more than a great, exhausted beast, which had behaved with a curious lack of cunning during the hunt, running straight across country from its fear. It would soon be brought to bay.

With Lombard at its heels, it entered a copse of beech-trees and remained in it. And now the King heard Lombard's baying take on that higher more sonorous note, at once furious and poignant, that hounds give tongue to when the hunted beast is at bay.

The King went into the copse; the rays of the sun filtered through the branches but without heat, turning the crisp, frozen snow to rose.

The King came to a halt and loosened the hilt of his short sword. Lombard was baying continuously. There was the stag, his back to a tree, at bay, his head lowered and his muzzle almost touching the ground, his coat running wet and steaming. Between his enormous horns, there was indeed a cross, as high as the cross upon an altar. It was shining in the light.

For an instant the King was aware of this vision, for in that moment his stupefaction turned to appalling fear; his body had ceased to obey him. He wished to dismount, but his foot would not leave the stirrup; his legs were like two marble boots against the horse's flanks. Then the King, terrified, wished to call for help upon his horn, but where was it? He no longer had it, he could no longer remember where he had lost it, and his hands, loosing the reins, were immovable. He tried to shout, but no sound came from his throat.

The stag had raised its head and, its tongue hanging, looked with huge tragic eyes upon the horseman from whom it expected death, the horseman upon whom sudden petrification had fallen. Among his horns the cross shone out again. Before the King's eyes, the trees, the ground, the whole aspect of the world were taking on a new shape. He felt an appalling bursting sensation in his head, and then he subsided into total darkness.

A few moments later, when the rest of the hunt reached the copse, the body of the King of France was found lying at his horse's feet. Lombard was still baying before the hunted stag, whose tines were seen to be laden with two dead branches, caught up doubtless in the undergrowth. They had assumed the shape of a cross and shone in the sunlight because of their coating of frost. But there was no time to lose with the stag; while the whips stopped the pack, it galloped off again, somewhat rested now and followed only by a few of the keener hounds which would hunt it till nightfall, or drive it into the lake to drown.

It was Hugues de Bouville who arrived first at Philip the Fair's body. He realised that the King was still breathing and cried, 'The King lives!'

With two poles cut with their swords, and belts and cloaks,

they produced a makeshift stretcher upon which the King was laid. He but moved a little to vomit and to void from every orifice like a duck that is being strangled. His eyes were glazed. Where was the athlete who but a short time ago could make two men-at-arms bend low merely by placing his hands on their shoulders?

He was carried thus to Clermont where, that night, some of his power of speech returned. The doctors, sent for hurriedly, had bled him. To Bouville, who was watching by his bedside, his first words, painfully articulated, were, 'The cross . . . the cross.'

And Bouville, thinking the King wished to pray, went and fetched him a crucifix.

Then Philip the Fair said, 'I am thirsty.'

At dawn he stammered out that he wanted to be taken to Fontainebleau where he had been born. The similarity between the King and Pope Clement V who, when dying, had also wished to return to his birthplace and had died upon the journey, was remembered.

It was decided to carry the King by water that he might be less shaken; and the following morning he was taken on board a large flat-bottomed boat which floated down the Oise. The courtiers, the servants and the archers of the escort followed in other boats or on horseback along the banks.

The news travelled quicker than the strange boat, and the dwellers upon the riverside gathered to see the huge, fallen statue pass. The peasants took off their caps, as they did when the Rogation processions passed by their fields. At each village archers went in search of braziers which were placed upon the boat to warm the air. Above the royal eyes the sky was uniformly grey, heavy with snow-clouds.

The lord of Vauréal came down from his manor, which

commanded a loop of the Oise, in order to salute the King; he saw that there was a look of death upon his face. The King answered him only by moving his eyelids; but he was beginning to recover some slight use of his limbs.

Night fell early. Huge torches were lit in the bows of the boats and their red dancing light shone upon the river banks so that the procession looked like a cave of flame moving through the night.

In this way they arrived at the junction with the Seine, and from there went on as far as Poissy. The King was carried to the castle where his grandfather, Saint Louis, had been born. The Dominicans and the two royal convents set themselves to pray for his recovery.

He stayed there for some ten days, at the end of which he seemed somewhat recovered. Speech had returned to him; he could stand, but his movements were numbed and restricted. He insisted on going to Fontainebleau, which appeared to be a fixed determination, and, making a great effort of will, he demanded to be placed on horseback. In this way he went gently as far as Essonnes; but there, for all his courage, he had to give up: the royal body no longer obeyed the royal will. He was placed in a litter, and it was thus that he finished the journey. Snow had begun to fall again and muffled the horses' hooves. Couriers sent in advance had had fires lit on every hearth in the castle and a greater part of the Court had already arrived.

As he went in, the King murmured, 'The sun, Bouville, the sun . . .'

9

A Great Shadow over
the Kingdom

FOR A FORTNIGHT THE King seemed to be wandering in his
mind like a lost traveller. At times, though he was quickly
tired, he seemed to be recovering his former activity, became
anxious about affairs of state, insisted on dealing with financial matters, demanded with authoritative impatience that all
letters and edicts should be presented to him for signature; he
had never shown so great a desire to sign documents before.
Then, suddenly, he fell into a curious sort of idiocy, from
time to time uttering pointless and disconnected remarks. He
would pass his hand across his forehead, a hand grown feeble
with fingers grown stiff.

It was murmured in the Court that the King was out of his
mind. In fact, he was beginning to take his way out of the
world.

Illness, in so short a time, had made of this man of forty-six
a senile figure with sunken features, but half-alive, at the end
of a huge room in the Castle of Fontainebleau.

He suffered from perpetual thirst and ceaselessly asked for
something to drink.

To people from outside who inquired for news, it was answered that the sovereign had fallen from his horse and been charged by a stag. But the truth was beginning to spread and it was whispered that the hand of God had made him mad.[29]

The doctors asserted that he would not recover, and Martin the astrologer, in prudent and ambiguous terms, announced that towards the end of the month a powerful monarch in the Occident would undergo some appalling ordeal, an ordeal which would coincide with an eclipse of the sun. 'Upon that day,' wrote Master Martin, 'a great shadow will fall over the kingdom.'

And then suddenly, one evening, Philip the Fair once again felt in his brain the immense sensation of bursting darkness followed by the appalling fall into the night that had come upon him in the forest of Pont-Sainte-Maxence. This time there was neither stag nor cross. There was but a tall body lying prostrate on a bed, unconscious of the attentions that were being lavished upon it.

When he emerged from this dark realm of the unconscious, he did not know whether it had lasted one hour or two days. The first thing the King saw was a large white figure leaning over him. He heard, too, a voice addressing him.

'Ah, it is you, Father Renaud,' the King said feebly. 'I recognise you very well . . . but you look as if you were surrounded by a mist.'

Then, at once, he added, 'I am thirsty.'

Father Renaud, of the Dominicans of Poissy, Grand Inquisitor of France, moistened the patient's lips with a little Holy water.

'Has Bishop Pierre been sent for? Has he arrived yet?' the King then asked.

By one of those curious whims so frequent in the dying, leading them back to their earliest memories, it had been during the last few days an obsession of the King's to send for Pierre de Latille, Bishop of Châlons, a companion of his childhood, to come to his bedside. Why Pierre de Latille in particular? People wondered about this particular request, looked for hidden motives, whereas they need only have seen in it an accident of memory. And it was precisely this obsession that seized upon the King as he came out of the coma, following his second attack.

'Yes, Sire, he has been sent for,' replied Brother Renaud, 'and I am surprised that he has not already arrived.'

He was lying. A messenger had certainly been sent to the Bishop of Châlons but, in agreement with Monseigneur of Valois, he had been sent so that the Bishop would be warned too late.

Brother Renaud had a part to play and he could not agree that any other ecclesiastic should share it. Necessarily, the King's confessor had to be Grand Inquisitor of France. They had too many secrets in common to risk the danger that, at the moment of the King's death, they would be imparted to other ears. Thus the all-powerful monarch could not obtain the services of the friend he desired to help him upon his great journey.

'Have you been speaking to me long, Brother Renaud?' the King asked.

Brother Renaud, his chin lost in his mountainous flesh, his eyes small and dark, his naked skull surrounded with a thin coronet of straight yellow hair, was charged, under cover of his religious offices, to make known to the King what the living still desired to get from him.

'Sire,' he said, 'if God were to call you to Him, as indeed

He may call any of us at any time, you would be happy to leave the affairs of the kingdom in good order.'

For a moment the King did not answer.

'Have I made my confession, Brother Renaud?' he asked.

'Yes, Sire, the day before yesterday,' the Dominican replied.

'A beautiful confession,' went on Brother Renaud, 'which we have all greatly admired, as your subjects will. You said that you repented having laid too many taxes upon your people and particularly upon the Church, but that you had no need to implore forgiveness for those who have died as a result of your actions, because fate and justice must be given every assistance.'

The Grand Inquisitor had raised his voice so that those present might hear him clearly.

'Did I say that?' asked the King. 'Did I really say that?'

He no longer knew the truth. Had he really said those words, or was Brother Renaud inventing for him that edifying end which all great personages should make? He merely murmured, 'The dead . . .' but he no longer had the strength to argue. He knew that he was going to join them.

'You must make known your last wishes, Sire,' continued Brother Renaud patiently.

He moved a little from in front of the King's eyes, and the latter suddenly realised that the whole room was full of people.

'Ah!' he said, 'I recognise you very well, all of you gathered here.'

And he seemed surprised that the power of recognising faces should still be his. They were all there about his bed, his three sons, his two brothers, and the doctors with their basins and their lancets, and the Grand Chamberlain, and

Enguerrand de Marigny. The end of the room was filled with
the Peers of France, the great lords of the kingdom and other
people of less importance who happened to be there by
hazard of their duties. There was a great whispering among
the crowd.

'Yes, yes,' he whispered, 'I recognise you very well.'

But he saw them through a fog.

Who was that over there, leaning against the wall, whose
head rose above all others? Ah, yes, that was Robert of Artois,
that blunderer who had caused him so much concern. And
that strong-looking woman close by, who turned up her
sleeves with the gesture of a midwife? He recognised her too;
it was his cousin, the terrible Countess Mahaut.

The King thought of all the things he was leaving in a
condition of suspense, of all the opposing interests that make
up the life of a people.

'The Pope has not been elected,' he murmured.

Other problems chased and jostled through his tired mind.
The affair of the Princesses had not been settled: his sons
were without wives, but unable to take others; the business in
Flanders had not been settled . . .

Every man believes to some extent that the world began
when he was born and, at the moment of leaving it, suffers at
having to let the Universe remain unfinished.

The King moved his head to look at Louis of Navarre who,
his hands hanging down beside his body, his chest hollow,
seemed never to take his eyes off his father, but was thinking
only of himself.

'Weigh well, Louis, weigh well,' Philip the Fair murmured,
'what it is to be the King of France! Learn as early as you can
the state of your kingdom.'

The Count of Poitiers forced himself to remain calm,

and Charles, the third son, found it difficult to restrain his tears.

Brother Renaud exchanged a look with Monseigneur of Valois which meant, 'Monseigneur, take a hand, or we shall be too late!'

During these last days the Grand Inquisitor had followed the movement of power with subtlety. Philip the Fair was about to die. Louis of Navarre would succeed him, and Monseigneur of Valois was all-powerful with the heir. And so the Grand Inquisitor, by every gesture he made and every action he took, sought Valois's advice and manifested a growing devotion.

Valois went up to the dying man and said, 'Brother, are you sure there is nothing that should be changed in your will of 1311.'

'Nogaret is dead,' replied the King.

Brother Renaud and Valois exchanged another look, thinking that the King was no longer in his senses and they had waited too long. But Philip the Fair went on, 'He was the executor of my will.'

Valois immediately made a sign to Maillard, the King's private secretary, who came up with his pens and writing materials.

'It would be a good thing, brother, if you would make a codicil newly appointing your executors,' said Valois.

'I am thirsty,' Philip the Fair murmured.

Once again, a little Holy water was put to his lips.

Valois went on, 'I think you would wish me to watch over the execution of your wishes.'

'Certainly,' said the King. 'And you too, Brother Louis,' he added, turning his head towards Monseigneur of Evreux, who asked nothing, said nothing, and was thinking of death.

Maillard had begun to write. The King's eyelids were still. His eyes still had the same fixity, but instead of that brilliance which had so frightened his contemporaries, his immense blue irises seemed to be covered with a dull veil.

After Louis of Evreux's name, other names came to the King's lips, as his glance picked out the faces about him. He thus named a Canon of Notre-Dame, Philippe le Convers, who was there to assist Brother Renaud, and Pierre de Chamely, a friend of his eldest son's, and then again Hugues de Bouville, the Grand Chamberlain.

Then Enguerrand de Marigny approached and managed to mask the others present with his stout body.

Marigny knew that, during the preceding days, Monseigneur of Valois had unceasingly endeavoured to injure him in the King's enfeebled thoughts. The accusations made against him had been reported to the Coadjutor. 'Your illness, Brother,' Valois had said, 'is due to all the anxieties that this bad servant has caused you. It is he who has separated you from all those who love you and, for his own profit, has placed the knigdom in the sad state it is at present. And it is he, Brother, who counselled you to burn the Grand Master of the Templars.'

Was Philip the Fair about to name Marigny among the executors of his will and thus give him an ultimate gauge of his confidence?

Maillard, his pen raised, waited. But Valois said at once, 'I think the list is complete, Brother.'

And he made Maillard a sign which meant that he should close the list. Then Marigny said, 'I have always served you faithfully, Sire. I pray you to recommend me to your son.'

Between these two wills seeking to sway his mind, between Valois and Marigny, between his brother and his First Minister, the King had a moment of irresolution. How everyone, at this moment, was thinking of his own self and how little anyone was thinking of him!

'Louis,' he said tiredly, 'let no harm come to Marigny if it is proved that he has been faithful.'

With that Marigny realised the accusations had borne fruit.

But Marigny knew his power. He held in his hand the administration, the finances and the Army; he even had the Church upon his side – save for Brother Renaud. He was sure that the Government could not be carried on without him. Crossing his arms, gazing at Valois and Louis of Navarre where they stood at the other side of the bed upon which his sovereign lay dying, he seemed to be defying the reign that was to come.

'Sire, have you any other wishes?' asked Brother Renaud.

At that moment, Hugues de Bouville straightened a candle which was threatening to fall from the high candelabra of wrought iron that was already transforming the room into a lying-in-state.

'Why is it growing so dark?' asked the King. 'Is it still night, has day not broken?'

Those present automatically turned towards the windows. Indeed, upon that day, the sun was in eclipse and there was darkness over the whole land of France.

'I return to my daughter Isabella,' the King suddenly said, 'the ring she gave me which carries the great ruby known as the Cherry.'

He fell silent for a moment, then asked, 'Has Pierre de Latille arrived?'

As no one replied, he added, 'I leave him my fine emerald.'

And then he went on bequeathing golden sovereigns, 'To the value of a thousand pounds,' he added each time, to a variety of churches, to Notre-Dame of Boulogne because his daughter had been married in it, to Saint-Martin-de-Tour, and to Saint-Denis. This man who, all his life, had looked so carefully to his expenditure, still measured out the exact size of his gifts, as if he expected some indulgence from them.

Brother Renaud leant down towards him and whispered in his ear, 'Sire, do not forget our Priory of Poissy.'

Upon Philip the Fair's sunken face was visible an expression of annoyance.

'Brother Renaud,' he said, 'I bequeath to your Monastery the fine Bible which I have annotated in my own hand. It will be useful to you, to you and to all the confessors of the Kings of France.'

The Grand Inquisitor who, from having burnt so many heretics and having so often been an accomplice of power, expected more than this, lowered his eyes to hide his vexation.

'And to your sisters of the Dominican Order of Poissy,' the King added, 'I bequeath the great Cross of the Templars. It will be safe in your keeping.'[30]

All those present felt a great chill. Valois made an imperious sign to Maillard to finish and ordered him to read the codicil aloud. When the secretary came to the words 'In the King's name', Valois, drawing his nephew Louis towards him and holding him by the arm, said, 'Add, "And by the consent of the King of Navarre".'

Then Philip the Fair looked at this son who was to succeed him, and knew that his own reign had come to an end at that moment.

His hand had to be guided as he signed at the bottom of the parchment. Then he murmured, 'Is that all?'

But it was not, and the last day of the King of France was not yet over.

'And now, Sire, you must transmit the royal miracle,' said Brother Renaud.

And he ordered the room to be cleared so that the King might transmit to his son, according to the prescribed rites, the mysterious power of curing the King's evil.

With his head fallen back, Philip the Fair groaned, 'Brother Renaud, see what the world is worth. Here lies the King of France!'

Even at the moment of dying, a last effort was demanded of him so that he might teach his successor how to relieve a comparatively mild disease.

It was not Philip the Fair who gave instructions as to the sacramental gestures and words: he had forgotten them. It was Brother Renaud. And Louis of Navarre, kneeling beside his father, his burning hands joined to the King's icy ones, received the secret inheritance.

When this ceremony was over, the Court was once more admitted into the King's room, and Brother Renaud began to recite the prayers, which were taken up in low voices by all those present. They were in the middle of reciting the prayer, '*In manus tuas, Domine*', 'Into thy hands, O Lord, I commend my spirit' when a door opened: Pierre de Latille came in. Everyone looked at the new arrival and, for a moment, while all lips were mechanically reciting, no one paid any attention except to the newcomer.

'*In manus tuas, Domine,*' said the Bishop, taking up the refrain with the others.

Then everyone turned back to the bed. Prayer died upon everyone's lips: the Iron King was dead.

Brother Renaud moved forward to close the King's eyes. But the eyelids, which had never blinked, opened of their own accord. Twice the Grand Inquisitor tried in vain to close them. They had to use a bandage to conceal the stare of this monarch who was entering eternity with open eyes.

THE IRON KING

Historical Notes

1. In 1314, King Saint Louis had been dead 44 years. He had been canonised twenty-seven years after his decease, in 1297, during the reign of his grandson, Philip the Fair, under the Pontificate of Boniface VIII.

2. The succession of Artois is one of the greatest dramas of inheritance in the whole of history.

   In 1237, Saint Louis had given the county of Artois in appanage to his brother Robert. This Robert I of Artois had a son, Robert II, who married Amicie de Courtenay, Dame of Conches. There were two children, Philippe, who died in 1298 as a result of wounds received in the battle of Furnes, and Mahaut, who married Othon, Count Palatine of Burgundy.

   Upon the death of Robert II, killed at the battle of Courtray in 1302, 'pierced by thirty lances', the inheritance of the county was claimed both by his grandson Robert III (son of Philippe), and by his daughter Mahaut.

   Philip the Fair decided in favour of Mahaut in 1309. The latter, having become Regent of the County of Burgundy through the death of her husband, had in the meantime married her two daughters, Jeanne and Blanche, to the second and third sons of Philip the Fair, Philippe and Charles. The decision in her favour was largely influenced by these alliances which brought to the crown notably the County of Burgundy, called the Franche-Comté, which was given to Jeanne as a marriage portion.

Robert refused to submit to this decision and, for twenty years, using every possible means at his disposal, battled determinedly against his aunt.

3. Edward II was the first King of England to bear the title of Prince of Wales before succeeding to the throne. According to some authors, he was three days old when the Welsh barons came to ask his father, Edward I, to give them a prince who might understand them and could speak neither English nor French. Edward I replied that he would accede to their wishes and presented them with his son who as yet could speak no language at all.

4. The Sovereign Order of the Knights Templar of Jerusalem was founded in 1128 to guard the Holy Places in Palestine and to protect the pilgrim routes. Their rule, which they had received from Saint Bernard, was strict. Chastity, poverty, and obedience were imposed upon them. They must not 'look women too much in the face,' nor, 'love any female whatever, neither widow, nor virgin, nor mother, nor sister, nor aunt, nor any other woman.' When engaged in warfare, they must fight at odds of one against three and were not allowed to ransom themselves. They were permitted to hunt only lions.

As the only well-organised military force, these soldier-monks formed disciplined cadres among the rabble hordes which were then the crusading armies. The advance-guard of every attack, the rearguard of every retreat, subject to the incompetence or rivalry of the princes who commanded the adventuring armies, they lost during two centuries more than twenty thousand of their effectives on the field of battle, a considerable number in proportion to the size of the Order. None the less, towards the end, they committed some strategical errors which were fatal to them.

But, during all this time, they had also shown themselves to be good administrators. Both because they were necessary, and out of gratitude for all the services they rendered, the gold of Europe flowed into their coffers. Whole provinces were placed under their protection. For a hundred years they guaranteed the effective government of the Latin Kingdom of Constantinople. They travelled the world as masters, having to pay neither tax, tribute, nor toll. They obeyed no one but the Pope. They had commanderies in the whole of Europe and the whole of the Middle East, but the centre of their administration was in Paris. They had set themselves up as great bankers. The Holy See and the principal sovereigns of Europe kept current accounts with them. They lent money on security and advanced the ransoms of prisoners. The Emperor Baldwin pawned 'the True Cross' to them.

Everything appertaining to the Templars, their military expeditions, their conquests, their treasure, even the manner in which they were suppressed, has a fabulous quality. Even the roll of parchment which contains the report of the interrogations of 1307 measures twenty-five yards in length. Controversy concerning this prodigious law-case has never ceased. Certain historians have taken the part of the accused, others that of Philip the Fair.

There is no doubt that the accusations brought against the Templars were generally exaggerated or false; but it is an undoubted fact, nevertheless, that there were profound deviations of dogma to be found within their ranks. Their long stay in the Orient had placed them in contact with certain surviving rites of primitive Christianity, even with some of the esoteric traditions of ancient Egypt. It was concerning their ceremonies of initiation that, by a process of confusion common to the medieval Inquisition, the accusation of adoring idols, demoniac practices and sorcery arose. This explains why King Philip the Fair, who, like every sovereign of the Middle Ages, showed great respect for the Inquisition and was much attached to the letter of Catholic dogma (whatever may have been, in other circumstances, his conflict with the Papacy), pursued the destruction of the Order with such determination, exactly as if it were the destruction of a heresy. This also explains why the Pope, in spite of all the interest he might have in maintaining the power of the Templars, ended by consenting to their suppression. Besides all this, King Philip was, by suppressing them, conducting a gigantic financial operation.

The suppression of the Templars would not interest us so much if it had not been followed by effects which have lasted into the history of the modern world. It is known that the Order of the Knights Templar, immediately after its official destruction, reconstituted itself in the guise of an international secret society, and the names of the secret Grand Masters are recorded right down to the eighteenth century. The Templars are the origin of the guilds, institutions which still exist today. They had need, in their distant commanderies, of Christian workmen.

They organised them in accordance with their own peculiar philosophy and gave them a rule called 'duty'. These workmen, who did not bear arms, were clothed in white. They went through the Crusades and built in the Middle East the most splendid castles. They acquired there certain methods of construction inherited from antiquity and these served them in building the gothic churches of the West. In Paris, the members of these guilds lived either within the precincts of the Temple or in the neighbouring quarter where they enjoyed certain rights. This district remained for five hundred years the centre for initiated workmen. Finally, the Order, by a natural development of these guilds, is related to the origins of Freemasonry. Here can be found the tests which derive from the ceremonies of initiation, and even the precise emblems which, being not only those of the ancient guilds, are, more astonishingly still, yet to be seen upon the walls of certain tombs of ancient Egyptian architects; these walls are veritable manuals of professional initiation. All the evidence therefore leads one to suppose that these rites, emblems, and professional methods of work, can only have been brought back at this period of the Middle Ages by the Templars and their guilds of workmen.

5. The methods used in the Middle Ages for dividing up the year were not the same as those in use today; moreover, they changed from country to country.

The official year began, in Germany, Switzerland, Spain and Portugal, on Christmas Day; in Venice, upon the 1st March; in England, upon the 25th March; in Rome, at one time upon the 25th January and at another upon the 25th March; in Russia, at the spring equinox.

In France the official year began on Easter Day. This curious custom of taking a movable feast as the beginning of the year (this is what is known as the Easter style, or the French style, or the ancient style), led to the year varying in length from three hundred and thirty to four hundred days. Some years had two springtimes, one at the beginning and one at the end.

This ancient style is the source of infinite confusion and creates great difficulties in establishing exact dates; for, if one is not very careful, one can discover a date of decease earlier by several months than the marriage of the character concerned, or again battles which appear to have been fought after the treaty of peace.

According to the old manner of dating things, the end of the trial of the Templars took place in 1313, since the year 1314 did not begin till the 7th April.

It was only in December 1564, under the reign of Charles IX, the last but one of the Kings of the Valois dynasty, that the beginning of the official year was fixed on the 1st January.

Russia did not adopt this 'new style' till 1725, England in 1752, and Venice after the Napoleonic conquest.

All dates in this book are translated into the 'new style'.

6. The Palace of the Temple, its annexes and gardens and all the neighbouring streets, formed the quarter of the Temple which still bears that name. It was in its Great Tower that Louis XVI was confined during the revolution. He left it only to go to the guillotine. The Tower disappeared in 1811.

7. The Sergeants-at-Arms (*sergents*) were junior functionaries whose duty it was to perform a variety of tasks connected with public order and the execution of justice.

Their functions overlapped those of the doorkeepers (*huissiers*) and the mace-bearers (*massiers*). Part of their duty consisted in escorting or preceding the King, the Ministers, the leaders of Parliament and of the University. Under the reign of Charles IV, the youngest son of Philip the Fair, a certain Jourdain de l'Isle, a seigneur of Gascony, was executed for having, among more important crimes, impaled some of the King's Sergeants-at-Arms upon their belilied staves.

8. This concession, made to certain merchant corporations, of selling in the neighbourhood of, or even within, the sovereign's habitation seems to come from the Orient. At Byzantium, it was the sellers of perfumes who had the right to erect their stalls before the entrance to the Palace, their essences being the most agreeable odour that was likely to reach the Imperial nostrils.

  The Palace of Justice in Paris occupies the site of Philip the Fair's palace; some of its buildings still date from that period.

9. The Hôtel-de-Nesle and its Tower occupied the present site of the French Institute and part of the Mint. Its dimensions were much the same as those of the Louvre of the period.

10. Paper made from cotton, which is thought to be a Chinese invention, and which originally was known as 'Greek parchment' because the Venetians had found it in use in Greece, made its appearance in Europe about the tenth century. Paper made from flax (or rags) was imported from the Orient somewhat later by the Spanish Moors. The first paper factories were established in Europe during the course of the thirteenth century. For reasons of strength and conservation, paper was never

used for official documents to which were to be affixed depending seals.

11. It was from these assemblies, first instituted under Philip the Fair, that the Kings of France derived the habit of resorting to national consultations which, later on, became known as États-Généraux and from which in turn issued, after 1789, the first parliamentary institutions.

12. This little island, off the point of the Island of the Cité, owed its name to the numbers of Jews who were burned upon it. Joined to a second island, it forms today the garden of Vert-Galant.

13. This child was to become the illustrious Boccaccio, author of *The Decameron*.

14. Provosts were royal functionaries who united in themselves the duties which are today spread among Prefects and sub-Prefects, the Commanders of military subdivisions, Superintendents of Police, Collectors of Taxes, and various other agents of the national economy. It is enough to say that they were rarely loved. But already, at this period, in certain provinces, they were beginning to share their duties with 'Receivers' who raised the taxes, and with 'Captains of Towns' who were concerned with military affairs.

15. The Orders in Council of Philip the Fair concerning the freeing of the serfs in certain bailiwicks and seneschalships. There will be more talk of these later on.

16. Literally: 'I wish you well.' A euphemism for 'I love you.'

17. It was in the Castle of Clermont that Prince Charles, third son of Philip the Fair and future Charles IV, was born.

18. The notion of time in the Middle Ages being much less precise than it is today, the ecclesiastical method of

division into prime, tierce, nones and vesper was in general use.

Prime corresponded roughly to 6 o'clock in the morning. Tierce was applied to the later morning hours. Nones to midday and the middle hours. And vesper to all the rest of the day till the sun set.

19. Gautier d'Aunay left two sons, named Philippe and Gautier. One of his grandchildren was Master of the Household to King Charles V and King Charles VI, and one of his great-grandsons became, in 1413, Grand Master of Waters and Forests (Eaux et Forêts) of France.

20. Agnes of France, daughter of Saint Louis, Duchess of Burgundy and mother of Marguerite of Burgundy, wife of Louis le Hutin.

21. At this period, when the postal service had not yet been organised, official messages were carried by couriers. Sovereign princes, the Pope, and the great nobles and principal ecclesiastical dignitaries had each their own organisation of couriers who wore their livery. The royal couriers had a priority right to requisition an exchange of horses upon their road.

22. This purchase tax (*maltote*) was a tax on purchases of a penny in the pound. It was this tax of less than .5 per cent, at a period when there was no tax on profits, which gave rise to riots and left in history the memory of a crushing financial measure.

23. This poison must have been sulphocyanide of mercury. This salt, by combustion, gives off sulphuric acid fumes of mercury and hydrocyanic compounds which can produce an intoxication at once hydrocyanic and mercurial.

Nearly all the poisons of the Middle Ages had mercury, a favourite material of alchemists, as their base. The

name Pharaoh's Serpent (*serpent de Pharaon*) later became
the name of a children's toy, in the composition of which
this salt is used.

24. Philip the Fair may be considered as the first Gallican
King.

Boniface VIII, by the bull 'Unam Sanctam', had declared: 'that every human creature is subject to the
Roman Conclave and this submission is necessary to his
salvation.'

Philip the Fair constantly fought for the independence
of the civil power in temporal affairs. Charles of Valois,
his brother, was on the contrary resolutely ultramontane.

25. The Cathares were the members of a religious sect
which found many adherents, particularly in the South of
France, at the end of the twelfth and the beginning of the
thirteenth century.

The Cathares, divided into Perfectionists (*Parfaits*) and
Believers (*Croyants*), professed indifference to the physical
body and earthly life; they encouraged sterility and
honoured suicide; they refused to look upon marriage as
a sacrament and nursed a solid enmity for the Church
of Rome. They were declared heretics; Pope Innocent III
launched a crusade against them which is known as the
Albigensian Crusade and which was conducted in the
most savage manner by the famous Simon de Montfort.
A true religious civil war, it ended with a treaty signed in
Paris in 1229.

Guillaume de Nogaret's father and mother belonged to
the Cathares.

26. Created towards the middle of the thirteenth century, the
bourgeoisie du roi were a particular category of subjects
who, having the right to the King's justice, were freed,

either from their subjection towards an overlord, or from their obligations to reside in a particular town, and owed allegiance only, wherever they might be in the kingdom, to the central power. Under Philip the Fair this institution increased in scale. One might say that the *bourgeoisie du roi* were the first French citizens to have a legal system similar to that of modern times.

27. The English word 'budget' was adopted in France to designate the state's accounts only in the nineteenth century; but this use of it was but a return to the French language, for the term 'budget' came from the word *bougette* which designated the little purse that the Norman lords, who conquered England, wore at their belts.

28. City Centre. The 'Parloir aux Bourgeois' has become the Hôtel-de-Ville of Paris and was upon the same site.

29. From the documents and reports of ambassadors, which still exist, it is possible to conclude that Philip the Fair died of a haemorrhage which did not affect the motor part of the brain. The aphasia at the start may have been due to a temporary oedema following the haemorrhage. The persistence of thirst, his difficulty in moving and his torpor may have been due to a lesion in the region of the base of the brain. He had a fatal relapse on the 26th or 27th November.

30. This cross was encrusted with pearls, rubies and sapphires. It was attached to a shaft of chased silver gilt. In the centre of the cross a little crystal container allowed a fragment of the 'True Cross' to be seen. It was taken to the Monastery of Poissy, as was the heart of Philip the Fair. This heart was, according to those who saw it, so small 'that it might be compared to that of a newborn child or a bird.'

In the reign of Louis XIV, on the night of July 4th 1695, lightning struck the monastery church and almost completely burnt it down. Philip the Fair's heart and the Templars' Cross were destroyed.